TALES OF THE SCHOOL ZOMBIES

STONE ARCH BOOKS
a capstone imprint

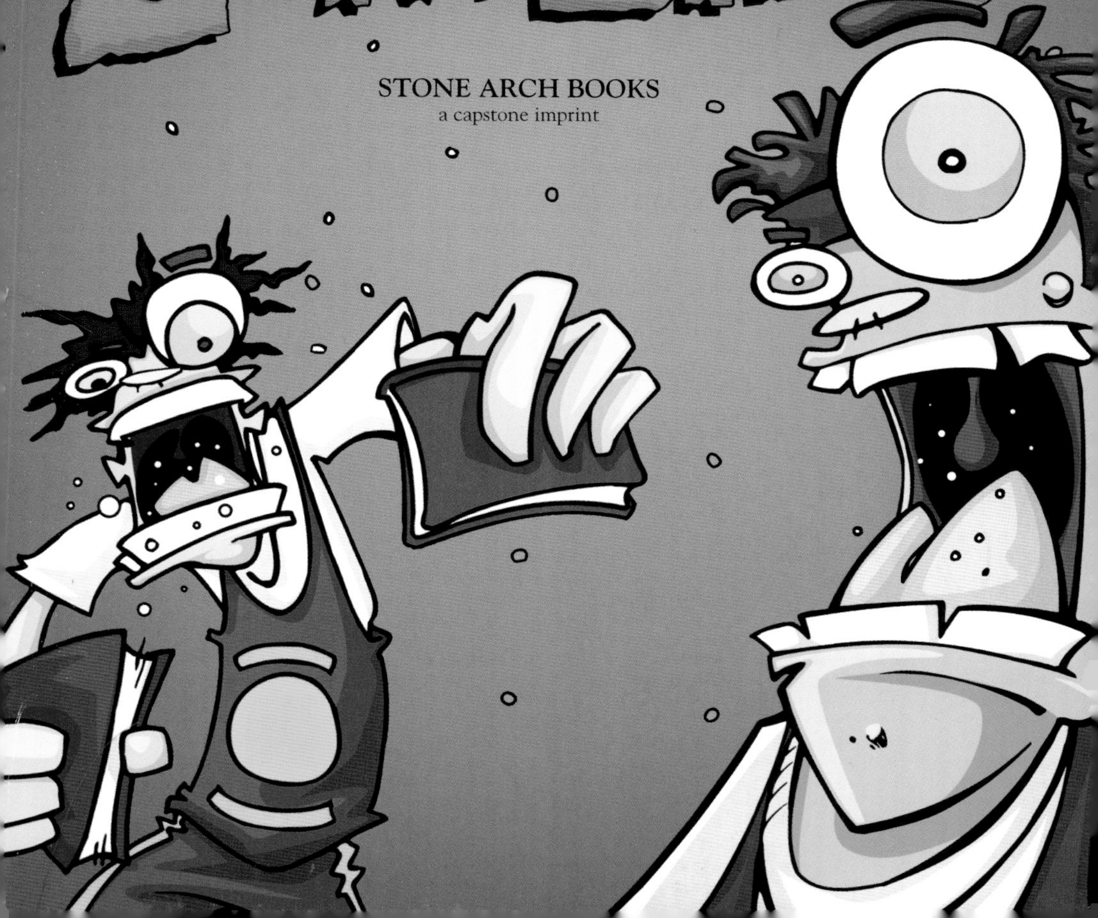

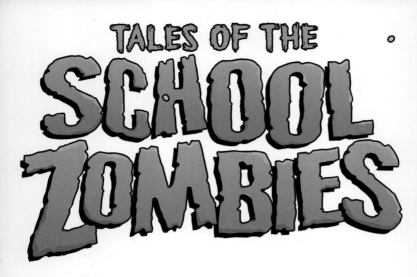

TALES OF THE SCHOOL ZOMBIES

WRITTEN BY
SCOTT NICKEL

ILLUSTRATED BY
MATT LUXICH, STEVE HARPSTER, AND CEDRIC HOHNSTADT

DESIGNER: **HILARY WACHOLZ** AND **BRANN GARVEY**
ART DIRECTOR: **BOB LENTZ**   EDITOR: **CHRISTIANNE JONES**
SERIES EDITOR: **DONALD LEMKE**   EDITORIAL DIRECTOR: **MICHAEL DAHL**
PRODUCTION SPECIALIST: **MICHELLE BIEDSCHEID**

Graphic Sparks are published by Stone Arch Books, a Capstone Imprint
151 Good Counsel Drive, P.O. Box 669
Mankato, Minnesota 56002
www.capstonepub.com

Library of Congress Cataloging-in-Publication Data is available on the Library of Congress website.

Paperback ISBN: 978-1-4342-3457-5

Summary: Homework, field trips, and summer school. Oh yeah, and zombies! Trevor's
boring school days are over when zombies arrive. It looks like Trevor has more than just
summer school and homework to worry about in these four zombie adventures!

Printed in China.
072011
006241

TABLE OF CONTENTS

NIGHT OF THE HOMEWORK ZOMBIES

BY SCOTT NICKEL
ILLUSTRATED BY STEVE HARPSTER

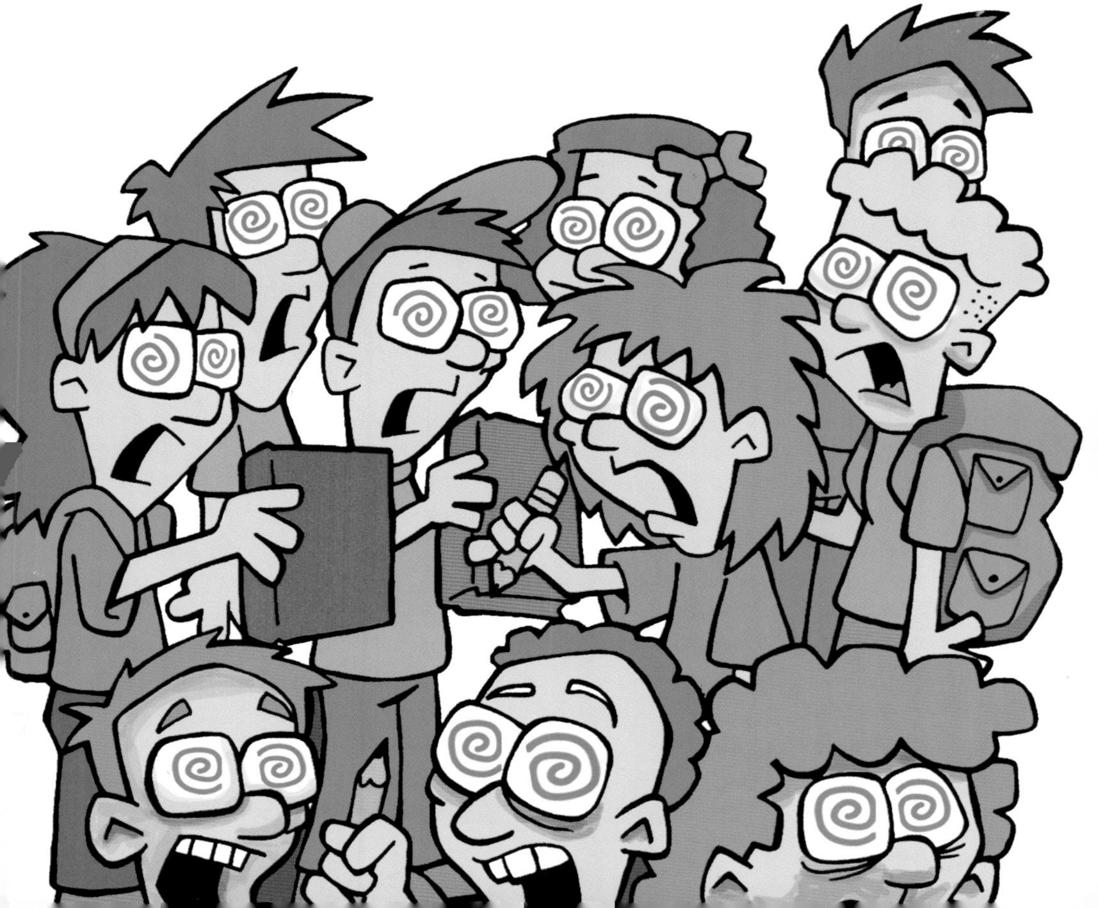

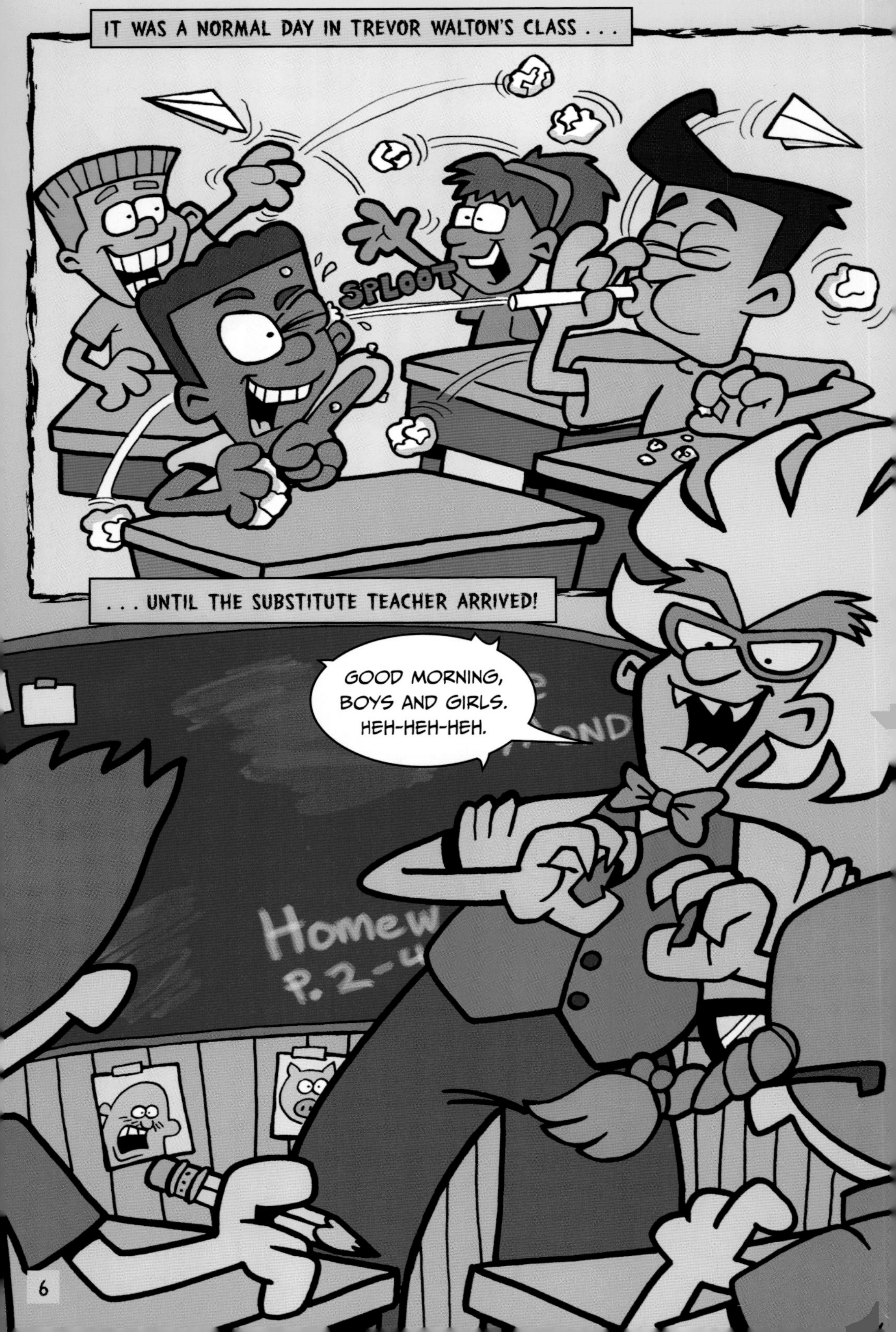
IT WAS A NORMAL DAY IN TREVOR WALTON'S CLASS . . .
SPLOOT
. . . UNTIL THE SUBSTITUTE TEACHER ARRIVED!
GOOD MORNING, BOYS AND GIRLS. HEH-HEH-HEH.

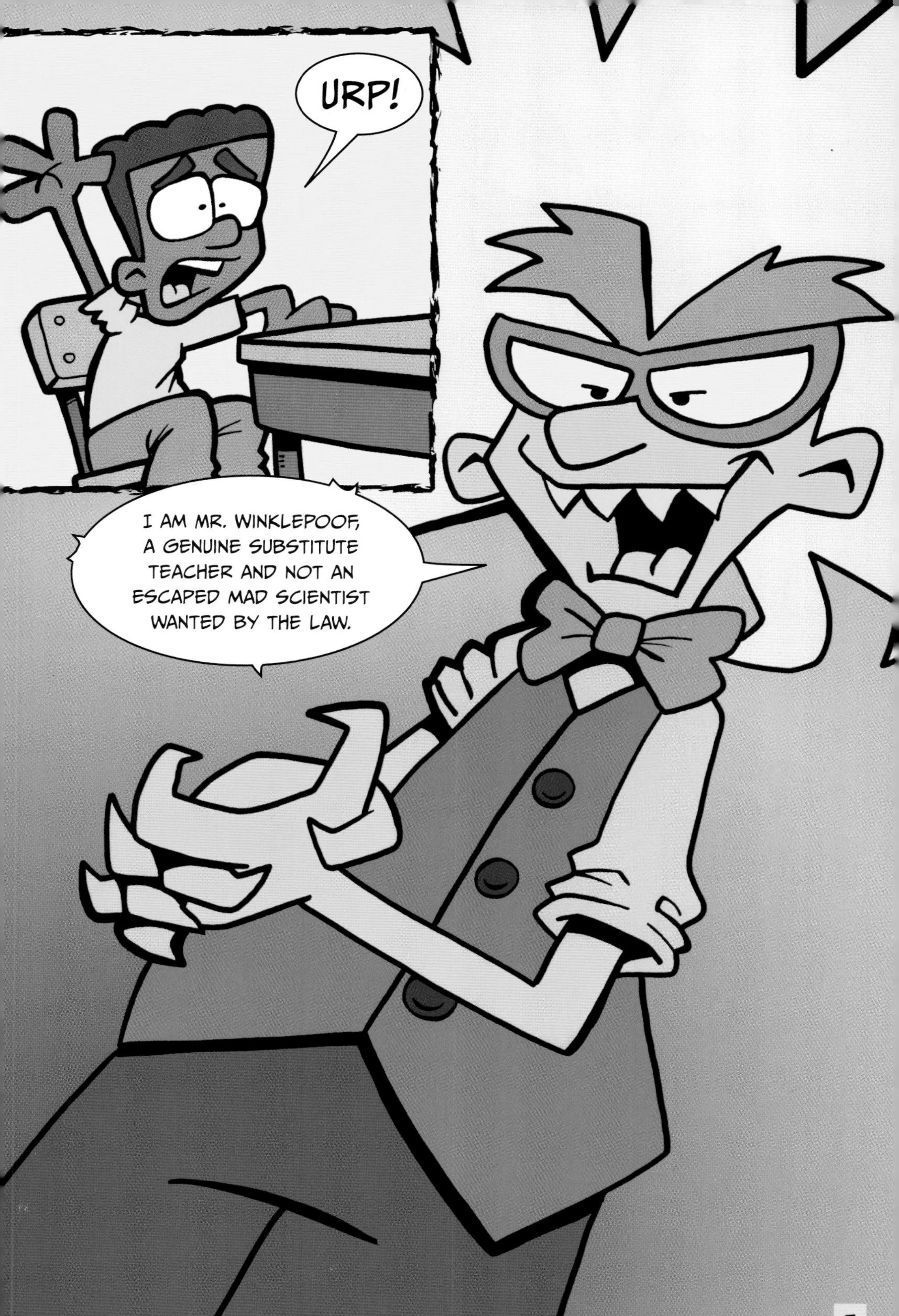
URP!
I AM MR. WINKLEPOOF, A GENUINE SUBSTITUTE TEACHER AND NOT AN ESCAPED MAD SCIENTIST WANTED BY THE LAW.

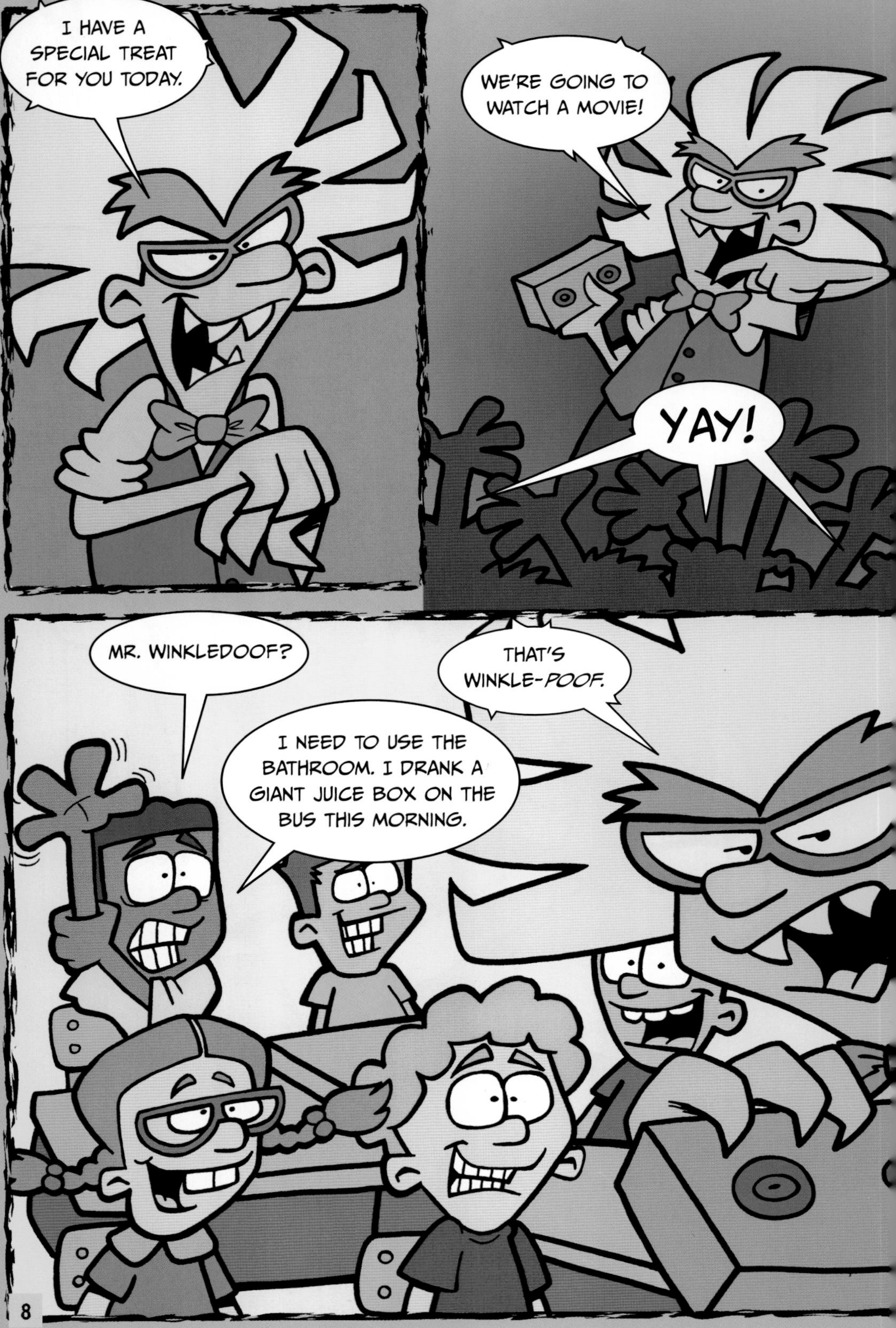

I HAVE A SPECIAL TREAT FOR YOU TODAY.
WE'RE GOING TO WATCH A MOVIE!
YAY!
MR. WINKLEDOOF?
THAT'S WINKLE-*POOF*.
I NEED TO USE THE BATHROOM. I DRANK A GIANT JUICE BOX ON THE BUS THIS MORNING.

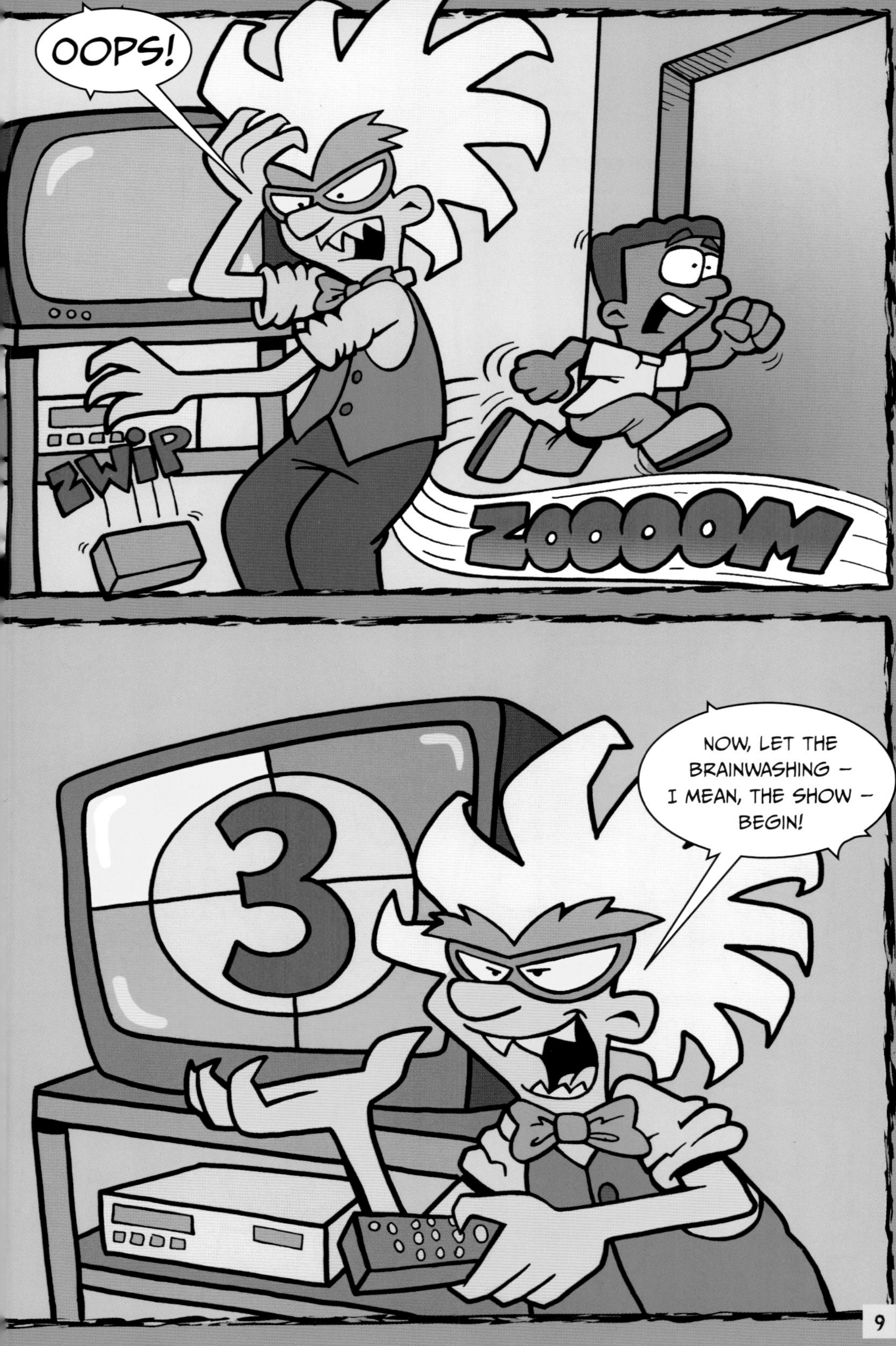
OOPS!
ZWIP
ZOOOOOM
NOW, LET THE BRAINWASHING — I MEAN, THE SHOW — BEGIN!

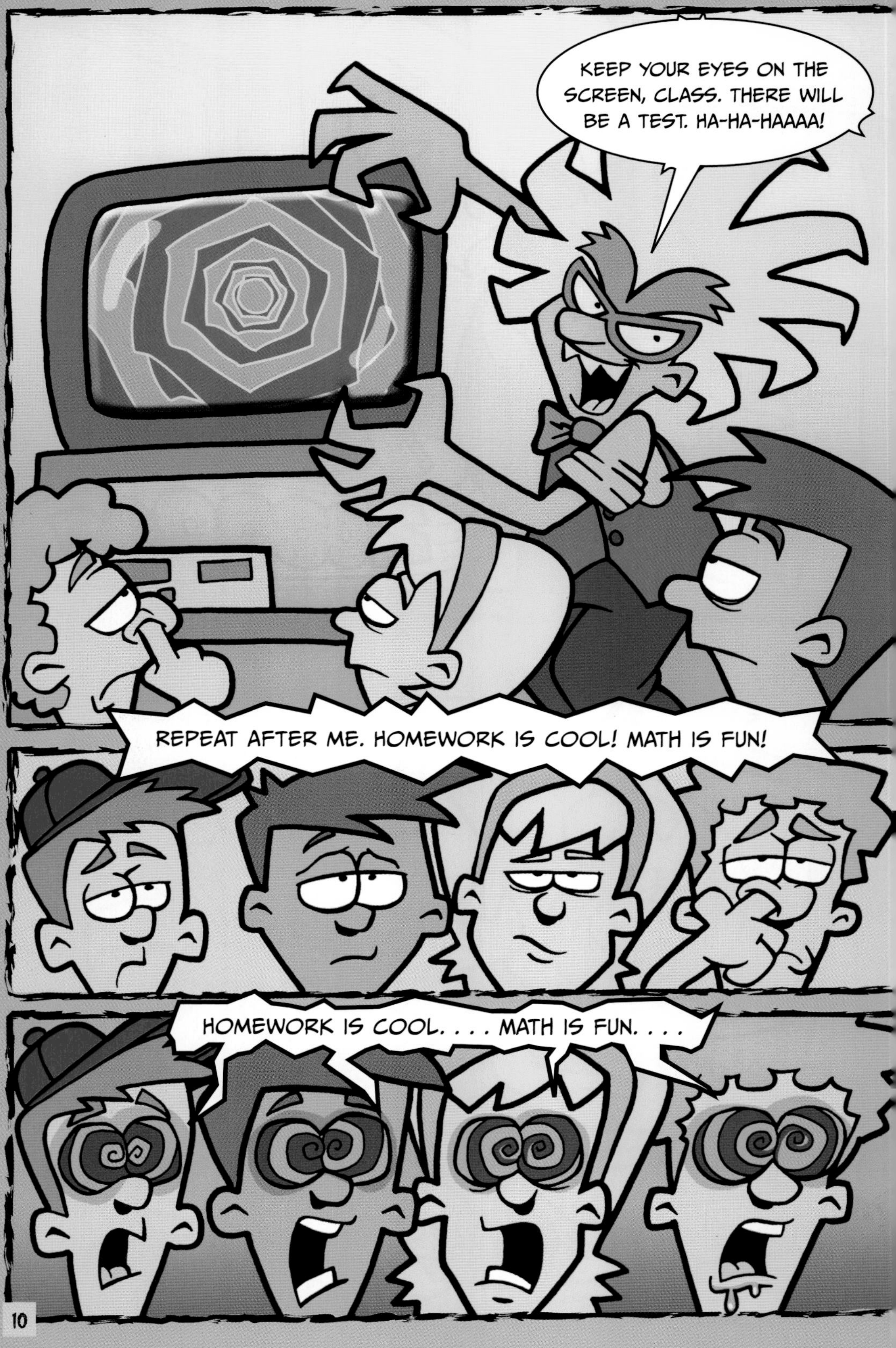
KEEP YOUR EYES ON THE SCREEN, CLASS. THERE WILL BE A TEST. HA-HA-HAAAA!
REPEAT AFTER ME. HOMEWORK IS COOL! MATH IS FUN!
HOMEWORK IS COOL. . . . MATH IS FUN. . . .

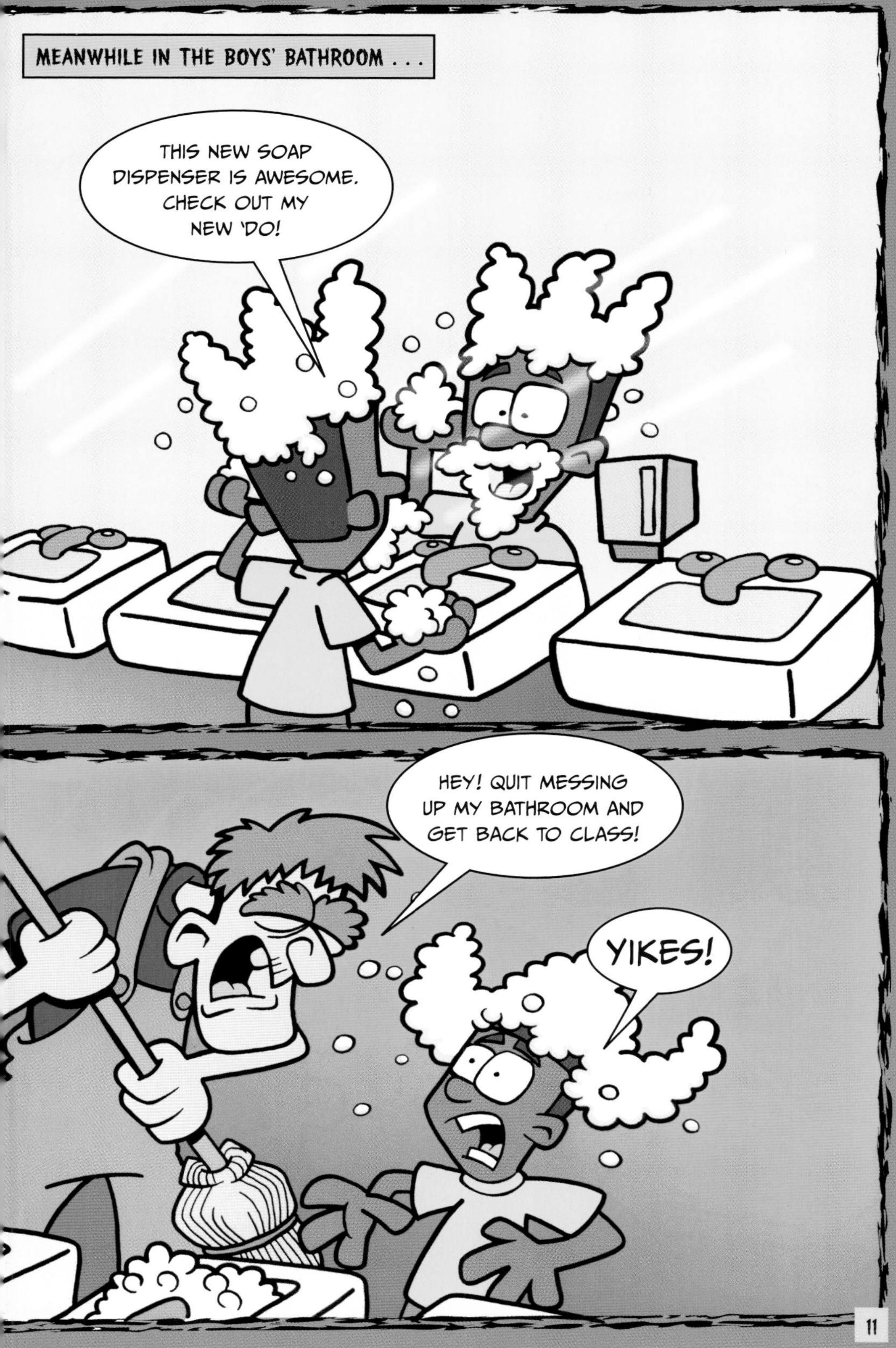
MEANWHILE IN THE BOYS' BATHROOM . . .
THIS NEW SOAP DISPENSER IS AWESOME. CHECK OUT MY NEW 'DO!
HEY! QUIT MESSING UP MY BATHROOM AND GET BACK TO CLASS!
YIKES!

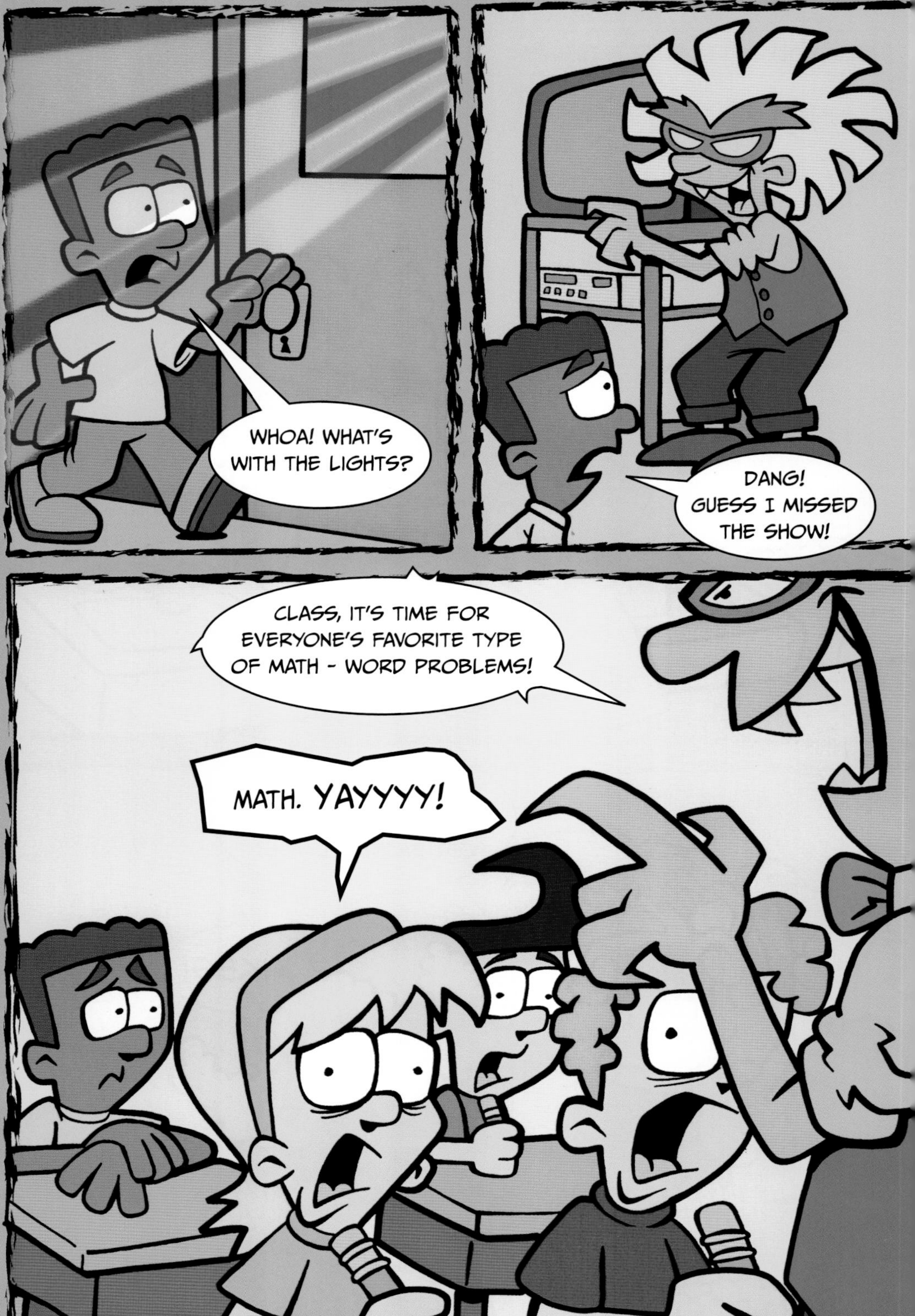
WHOA! WHAT'S WITH THE LIGHTS?
DANG! GUESS I MISSED THE SHOW!
CLASS, IT'S TIME FOR EVERYONE'S FAVORITE TYPE OF MATH - WORD PROBLEMS!
MATH. YAYYYY!

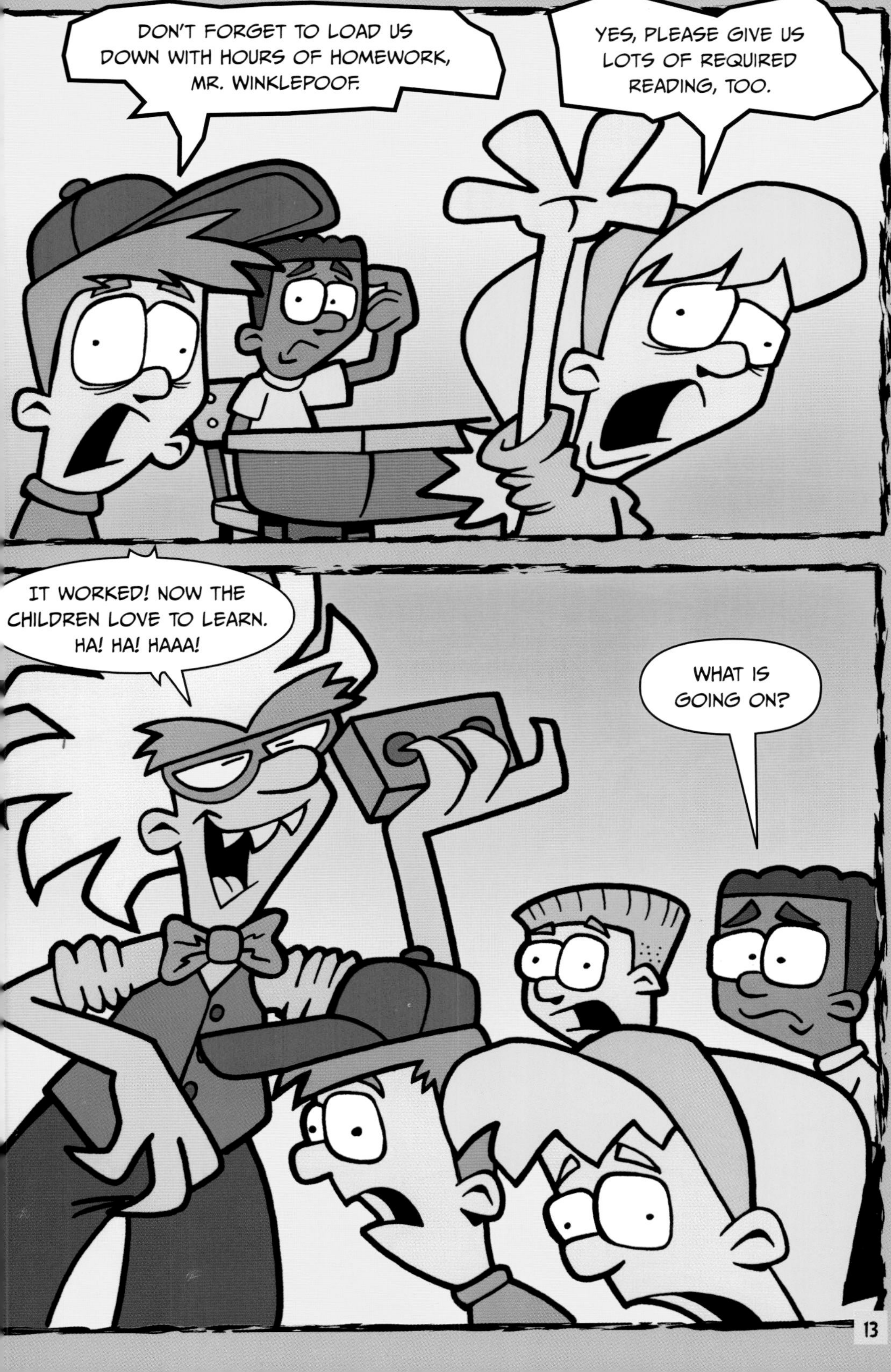
DON'T FORGET TO LOAD US DOWN WITH HOURS OF HOMEWORK, MR. WINKLEPOOF.
YES, PLEASE GIVE US LOTS OF REQUIRED READING, TOO.
IT WORKED! NOW THE CHILDREN LOVE TO LEARN. HA! HA! HAAA!
WHAT IS GOING ON?

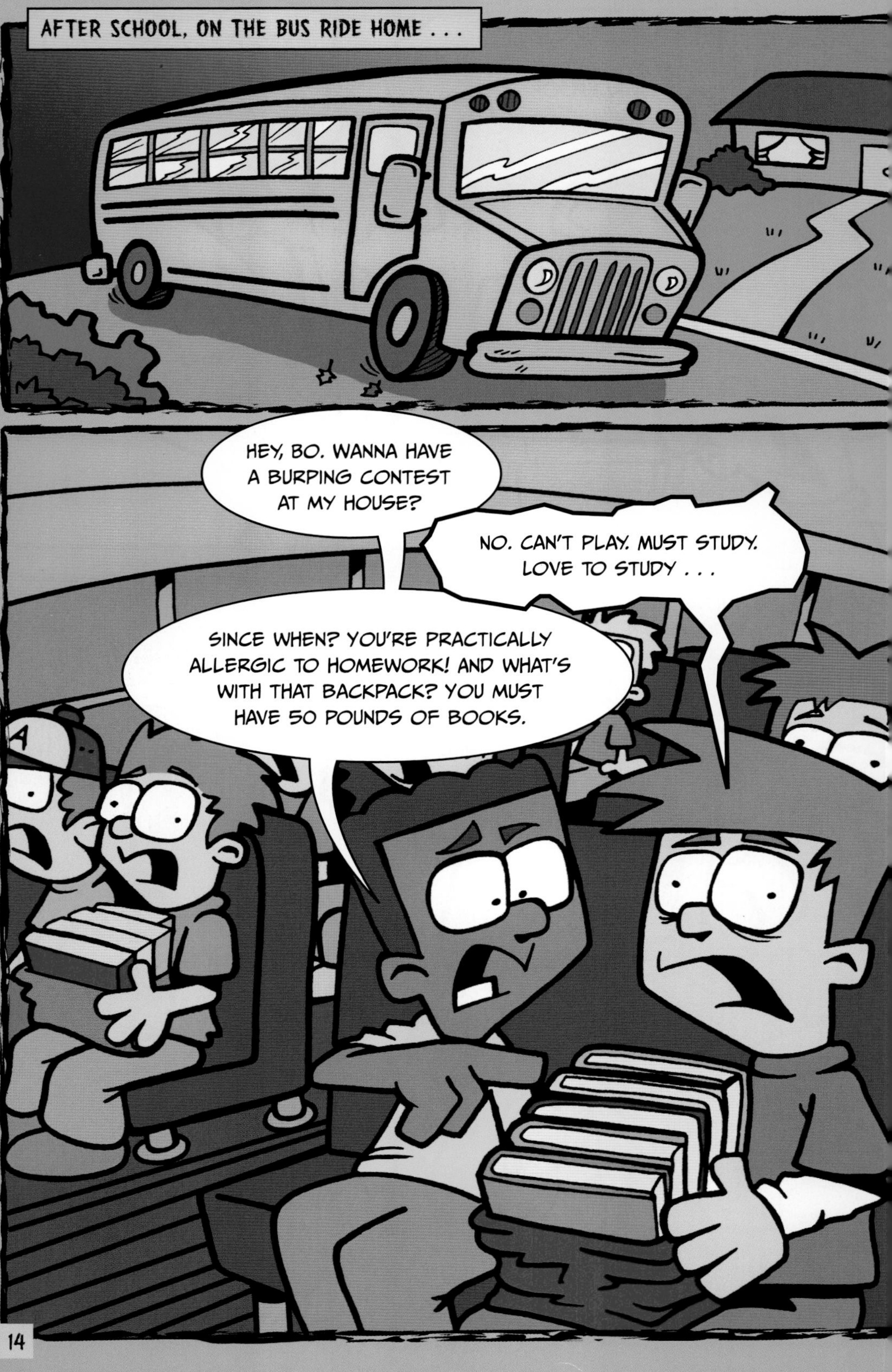
AFTER SCHOOL, ON THE BUS RIDE HOME . . .
HEY, BO. WANNA HAVE A BURPING CONTEST AT MY HOUSE?
NO. CAN'T PLAY. MUST STUDY. LOVE TO STUDY . . .
SINCE WHEN? YOU'RE PRACTICALLY ALLERGIC TO HOMEWORK! AND WHAT'S WITH THAT BACKPACK? YOU MUST HAVE 50 POUNDS OF BOOKS.

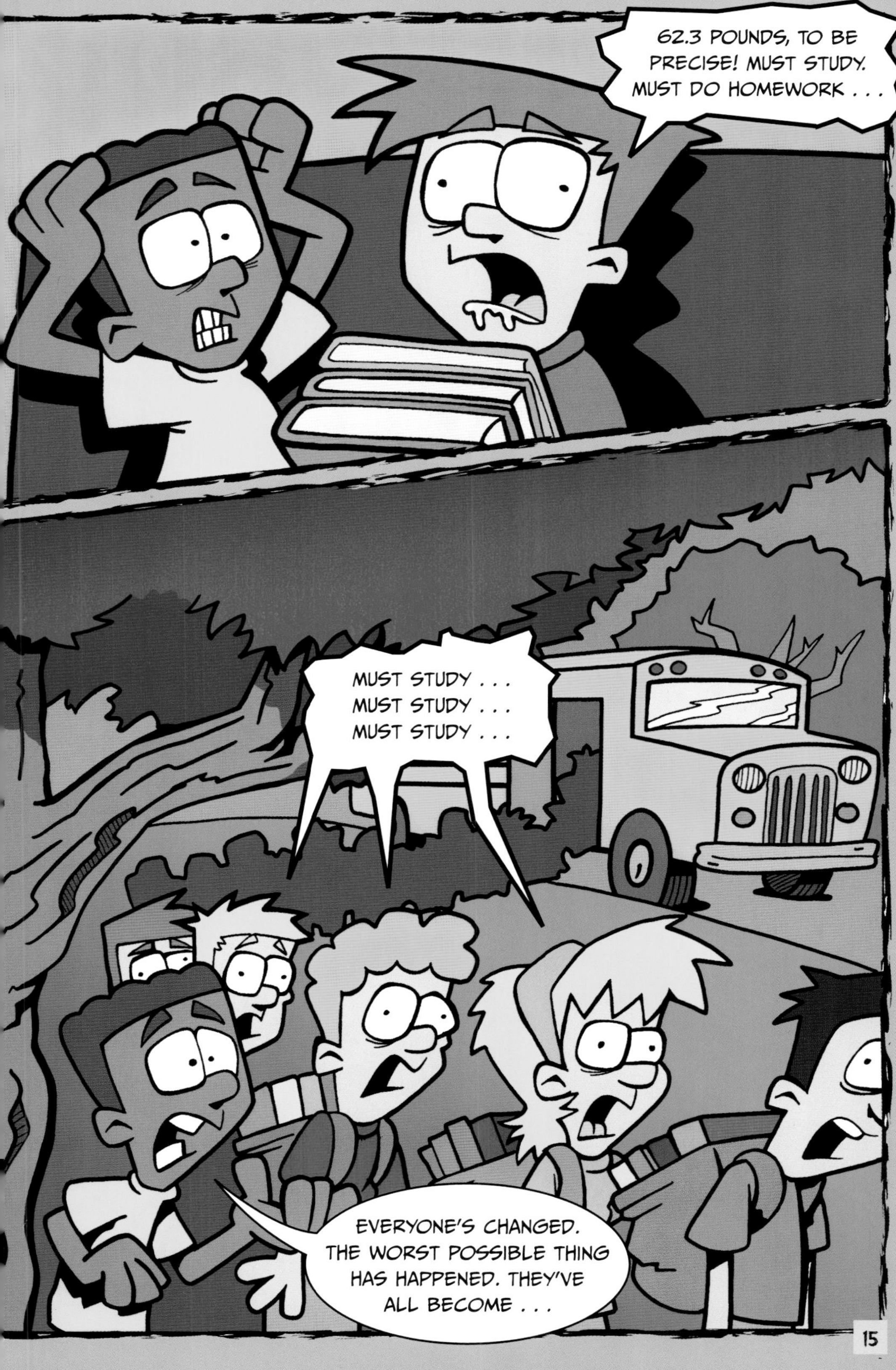
62.3 POUNDS, TO BE PRECISE! MUST STUDY. MUST DO HOMEWORK . . .
MUST STUDY . . . MUST STUDY . . . MUST STUDY . . .
EVERYONE'S CHANGED. THE WORST POSSIBLE THING HAS HAPPENED. THEY'VE ALL BECOME . . .

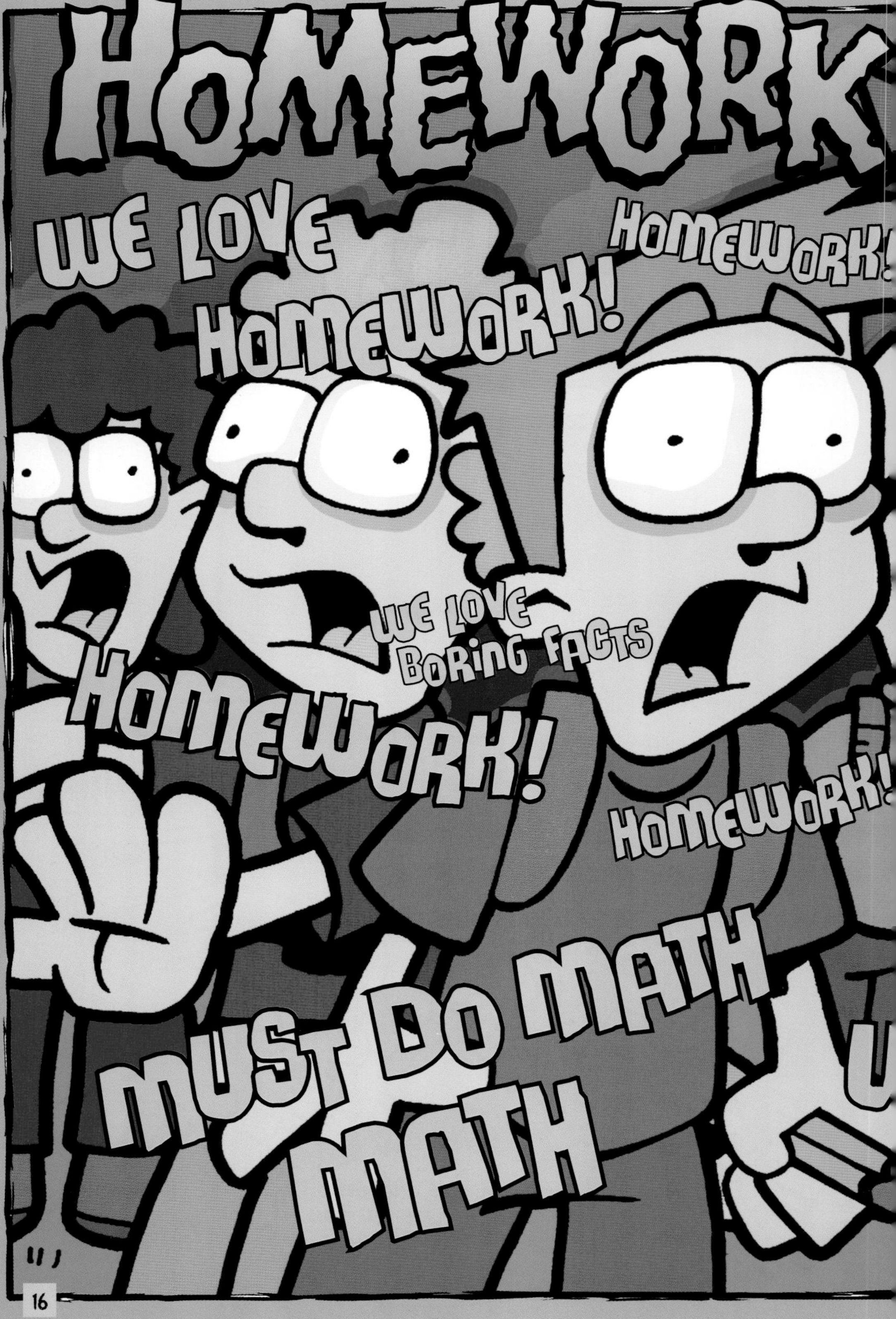
HOMEWORK
WE LOVE HOMEWORK!
HOMEWORK!
WE LOVE BORING FACTS
HOMEWORK!
HOMEWORK!
MUST DO MATH
MATH

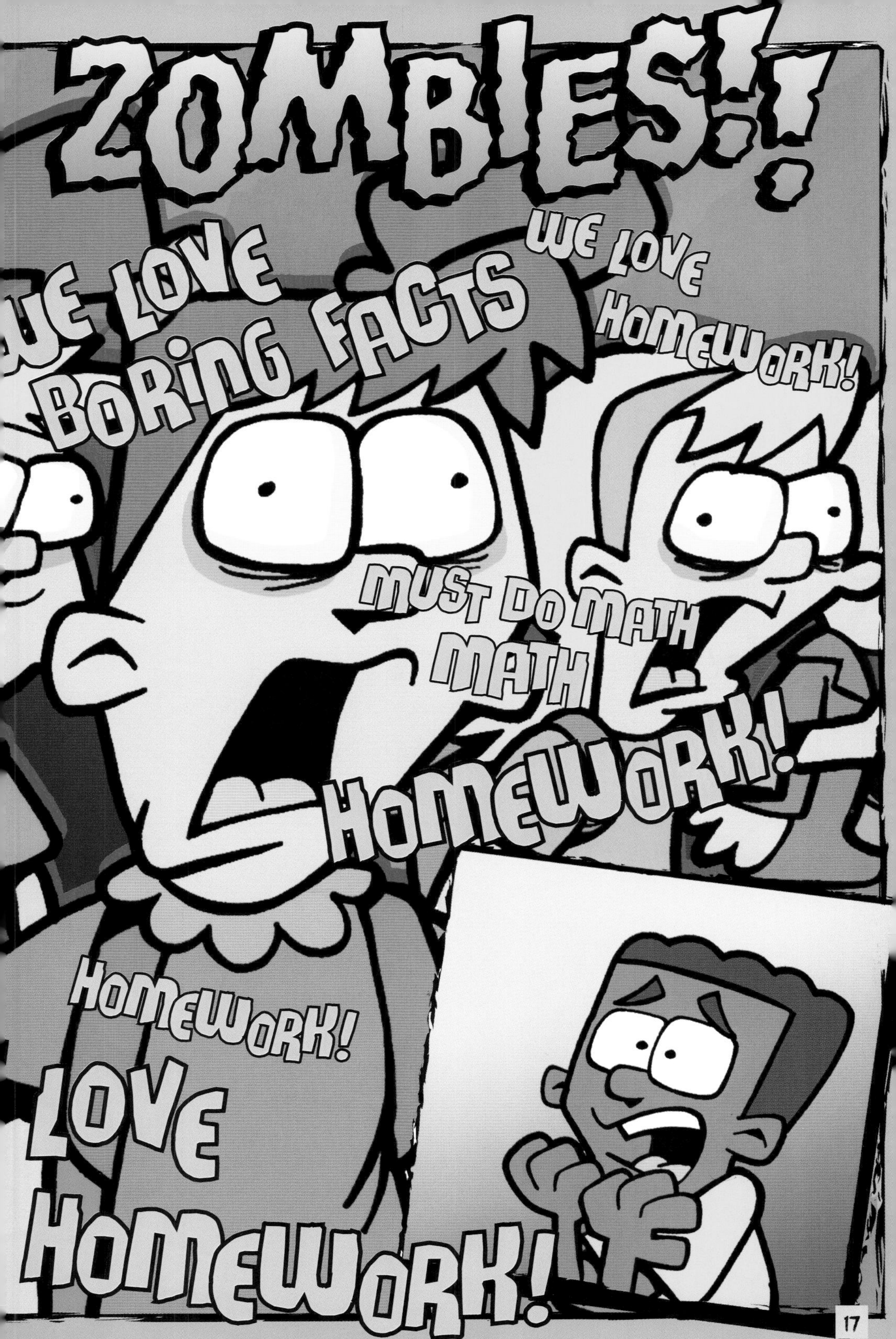
ZOMBIES!!
WE LOVE BORING FACTS
WE LOVE HOMEWORK!
MUST DO MATH MATH
HOMEWORK!
HOMEWORK!
LOVE
LOVE HOMEWORK!

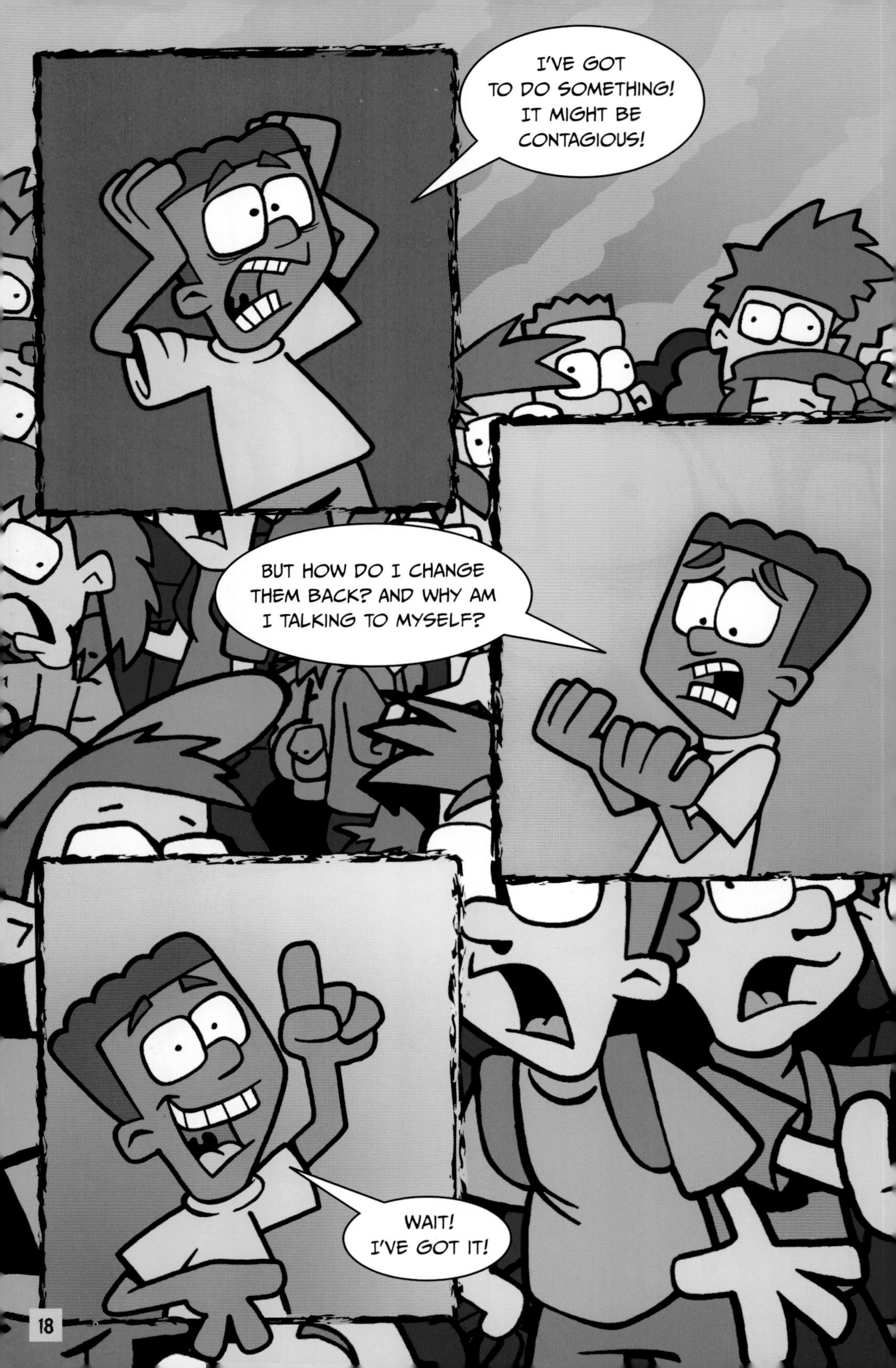
I'VE GOT TO DO SOMETHING! IT MIGHT BE CONTAGIOUS!
BUT HOW DO I CHANGE THEM BACK? AND WHY AM I TALKING TO MYSELF?
WAIT! I'VE GOT IT!

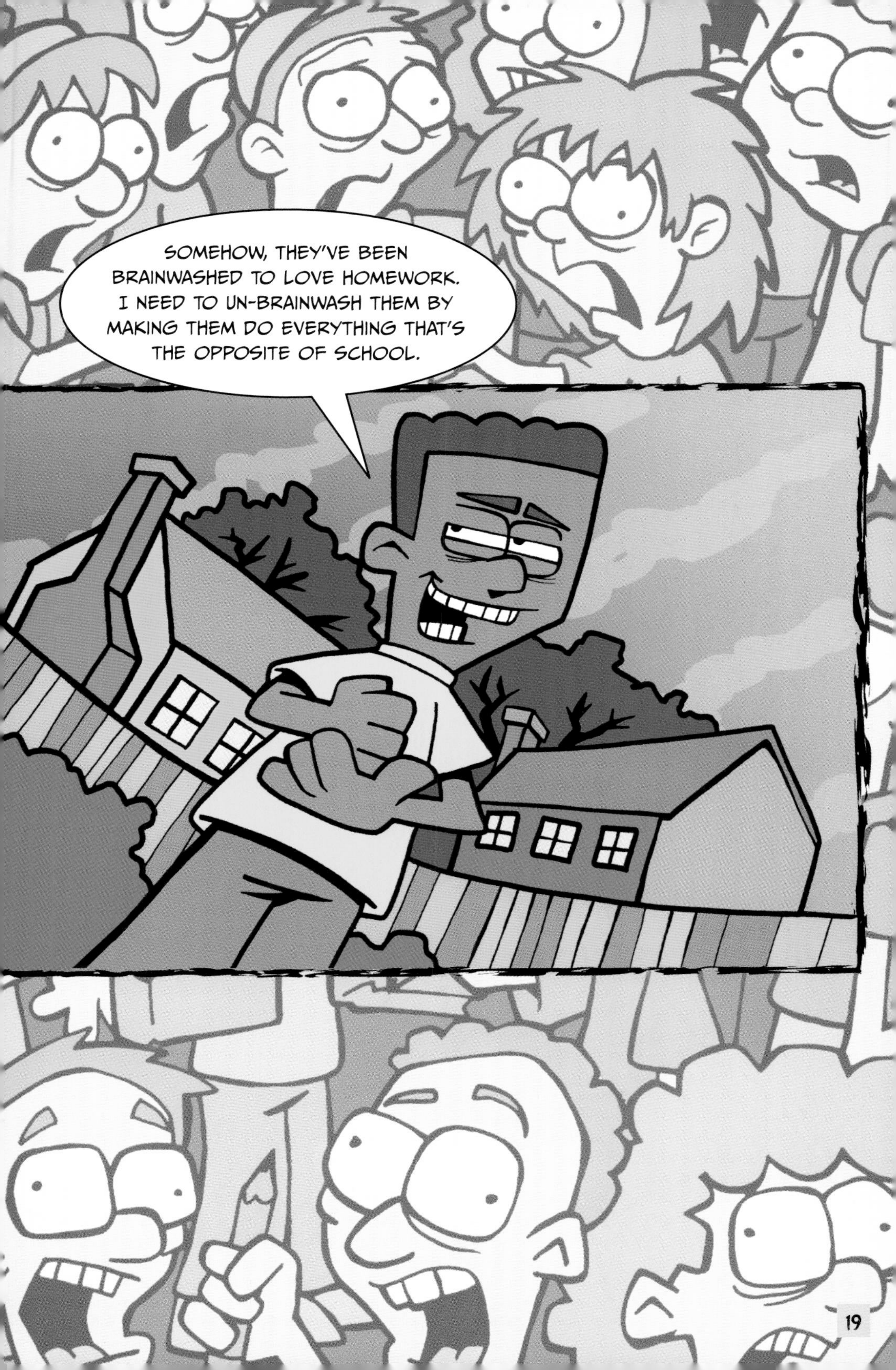
SOMEHOW, THEY'VE BEEN BRAINWASHED TO LOVE HOMEWORK. I NEED TO UN-BRAINWASH THEM BY MAKING THEM DO EVERYTHING THAT'S THE OPPOSITE OF SCHOOL.

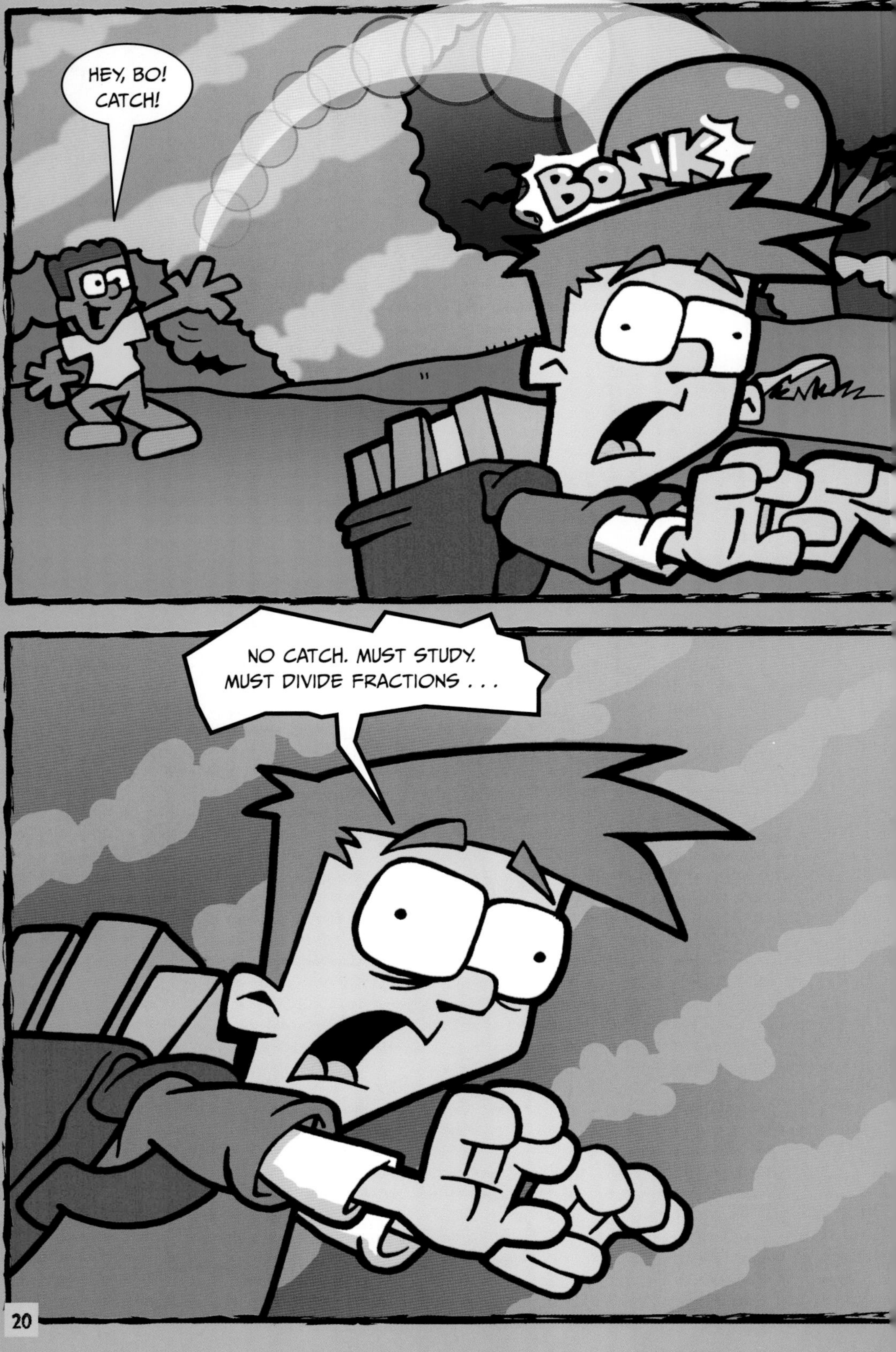
HEY, BO! CATCH!
BONK
NO CATCH. MUST STUDY. MUST DIVIDE FRACTIONS . . .

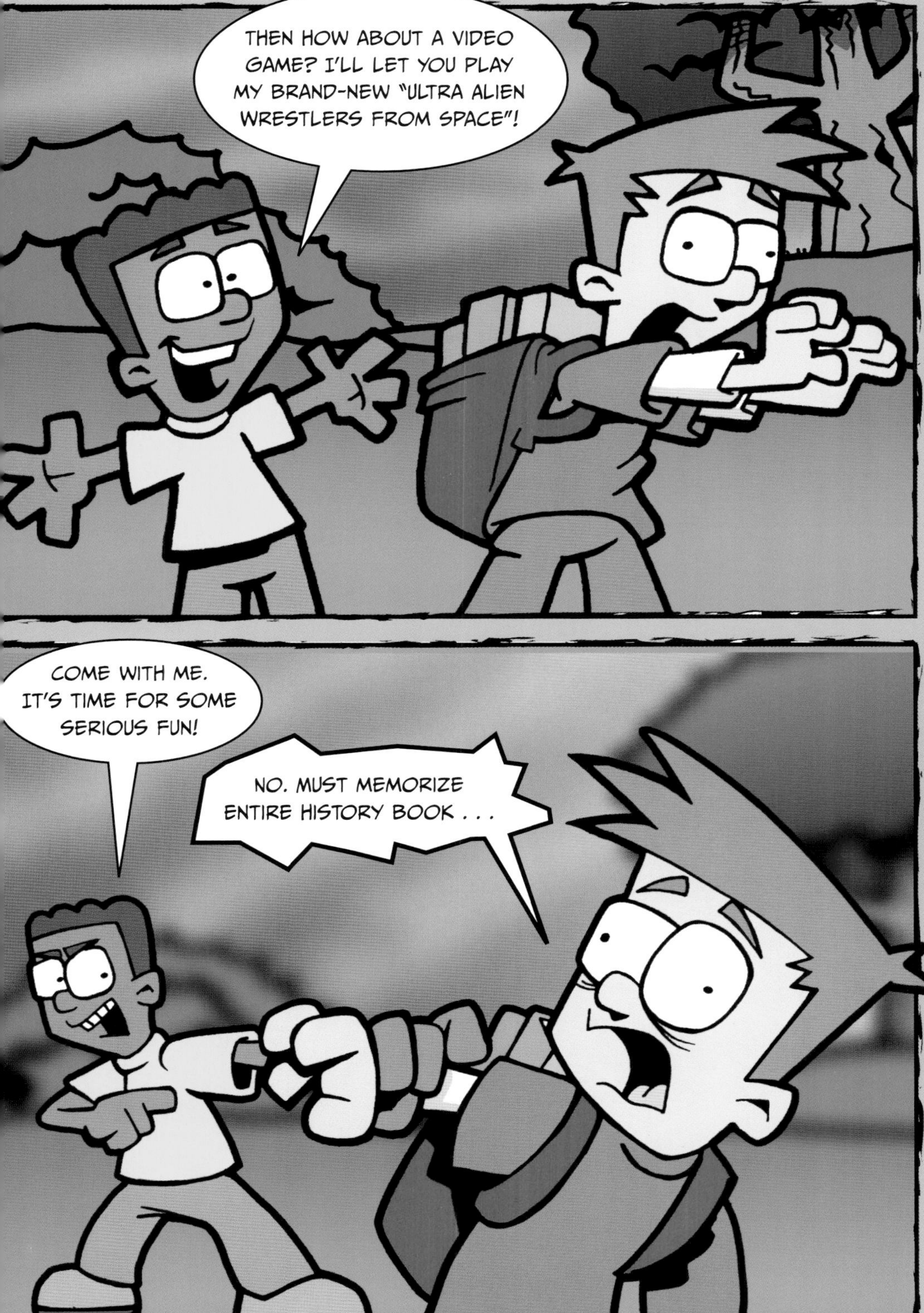
THEN HOW ABOUT A VIDEO GAME? I'LL LET YOU PLAY MY BRAND-NEW "ULTRA ALIEN WRESTLERS FROM SPACE"!
COME WITH ME. IT'S TIME FOR SOME SERIOUS FUN!
NO. MUST MEMORIZE ENTIRE HISTORY BOOK . . .

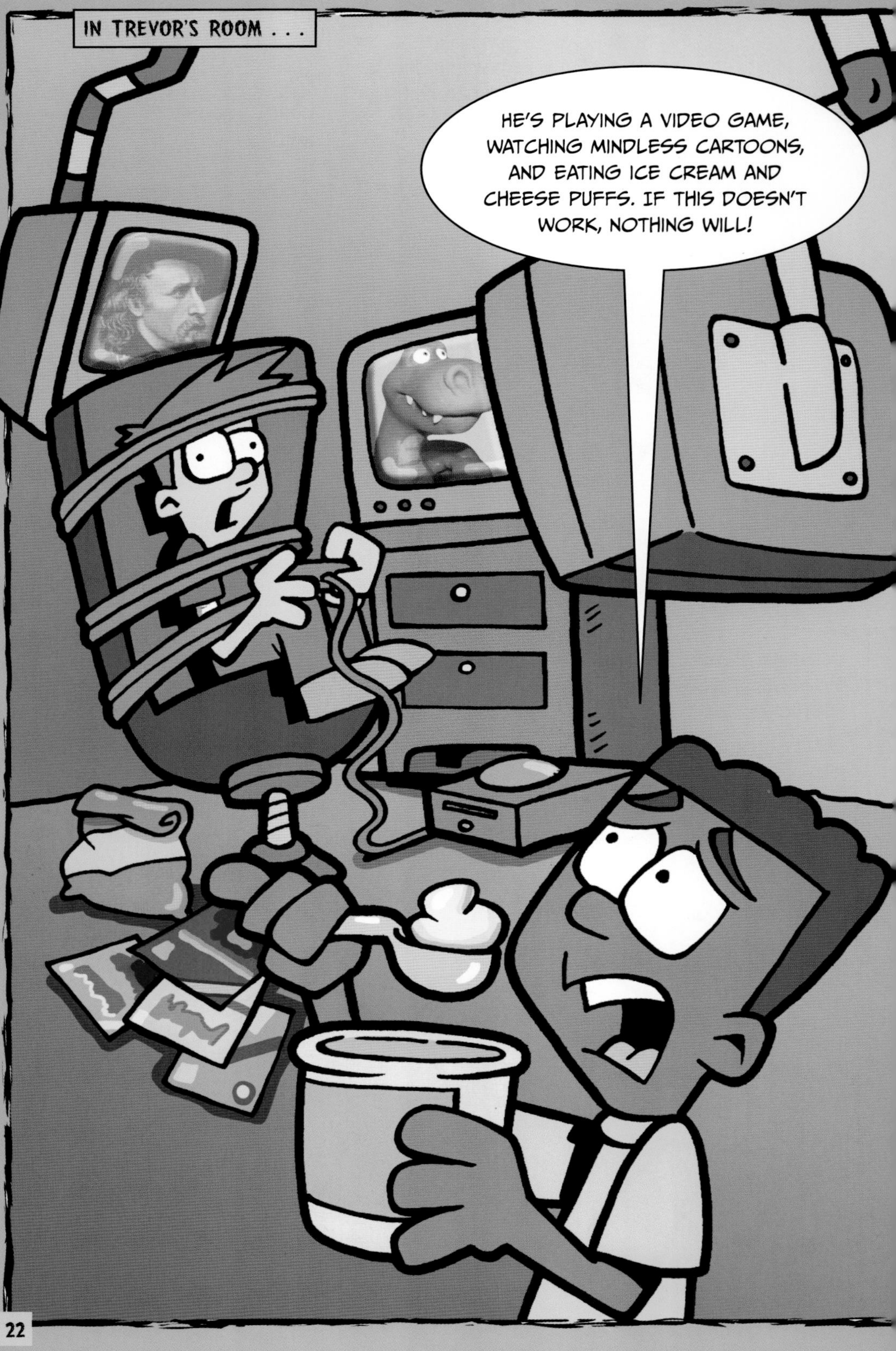
IN TREVOR'S ROOM . . .
HE'S PLAYING A VIDEO GAME, WATCHING MINDLESS CARTOONS, AND EATING ICE CREAM AND CHEESE PUFFS. IF THIS DOESN'T WORK, NOTHING WILL!

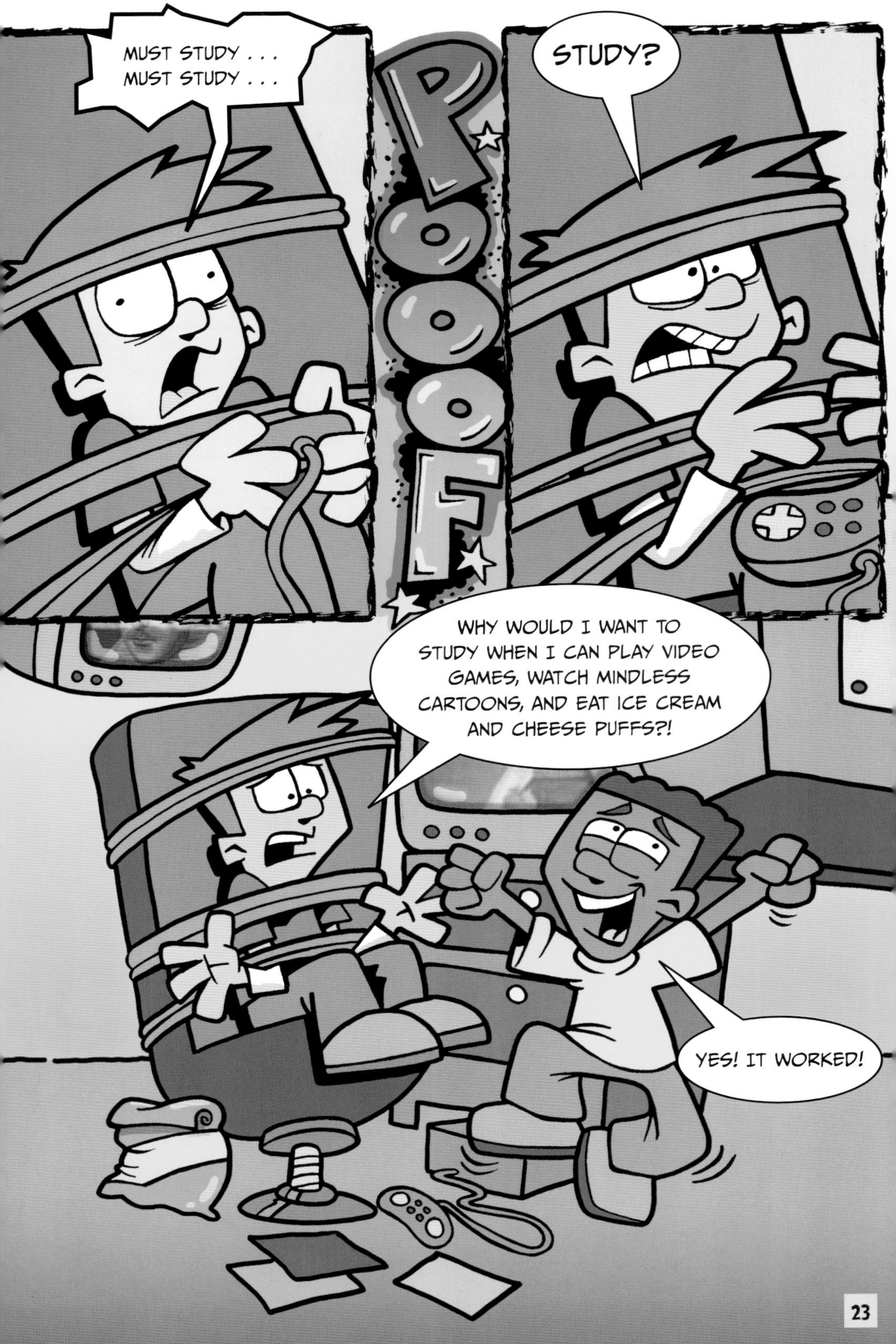
MUST STUDY . . .
MUST STUDY . . .
POOOF
STUDY?
WHY WOULD I WANT TO STUDY WHEN I CAN PLAY VIDEO GAMES, WATCH MINDLESS CARTOONS, AND EAT ICE CREAM AND CHEESE PUFFS?!
YES! IT WORKED!

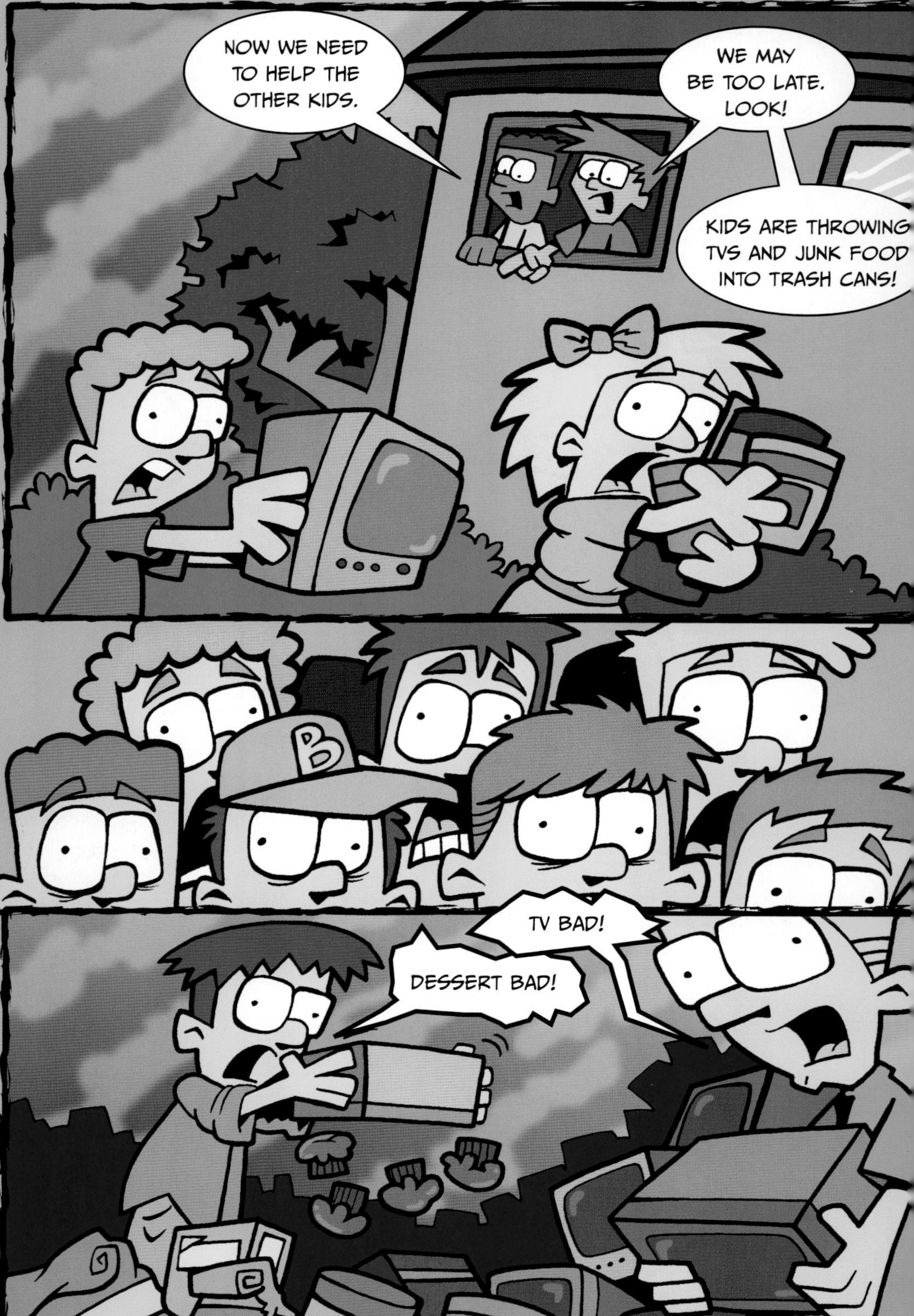
NOW WE NEED TO HELP THE OTHER KIDS.
WE MAY BE TOO LATE. LOOK!
KIDS ARE THROWING TVS AND JUNK FOOD INTO TRASH CANS!
B
DESSERT BAD!
TV BAD!

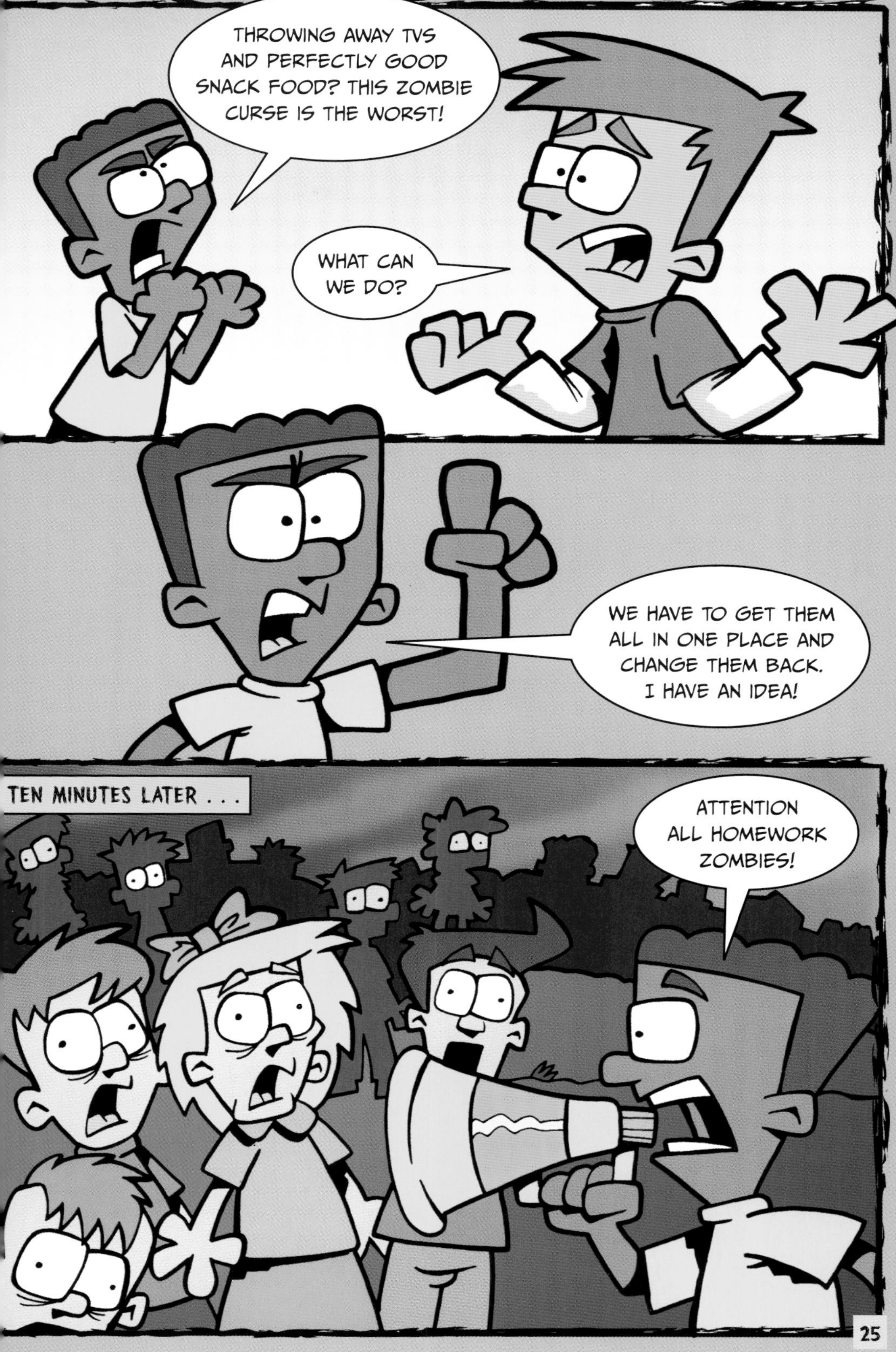

THROWING AWAY TVS AND PERFECTLY GOOD SNACK FOOD? THIS ZOMBIE CURSE IS THE WORST!
WHAT CAN WE DO?
WE HAVE TO GET THEM ALL IN ONE PLACE AND CHANGE THEM BACK. I HAVE AN IDEA!
TEN MINUTES LATER . . .
ATTENTION ALL HOMEWORK ZOMBIES!

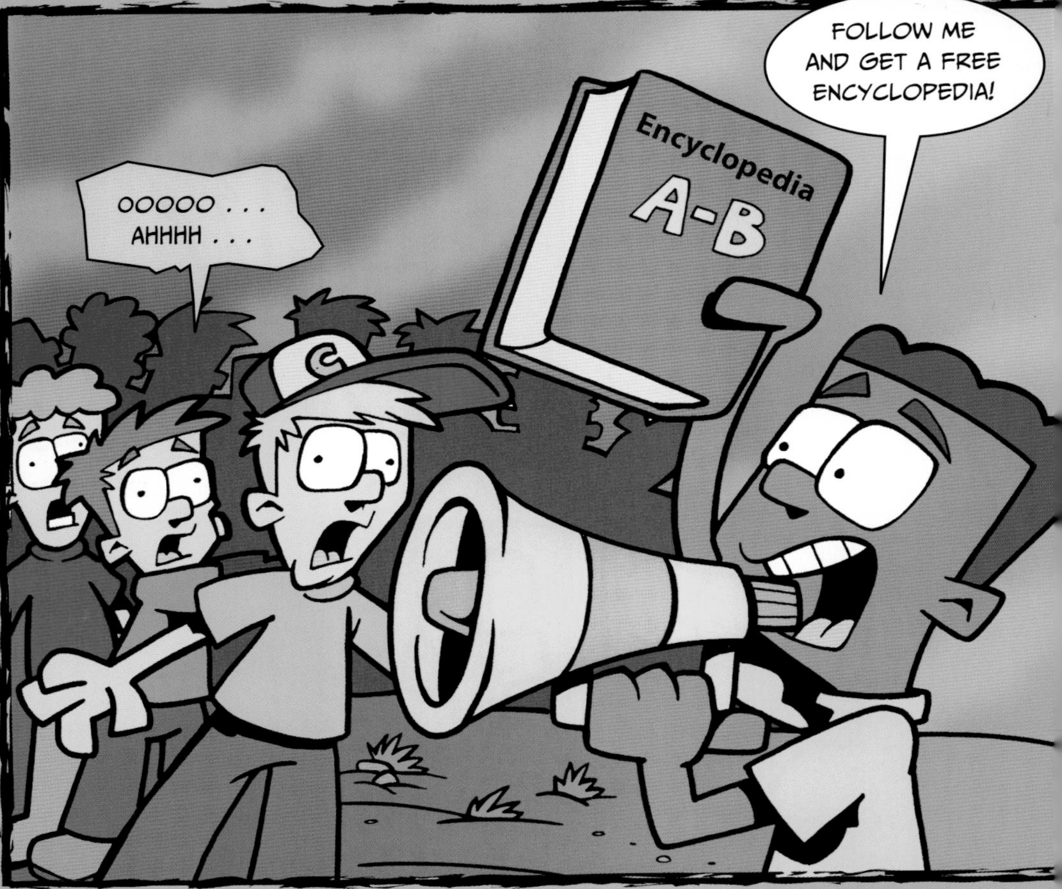
OOOOO . . .
AHHHH . . .
FOLLOW ME AND GET A FREE ENCYCLOPEDIA!
Encyclopedia
A-B

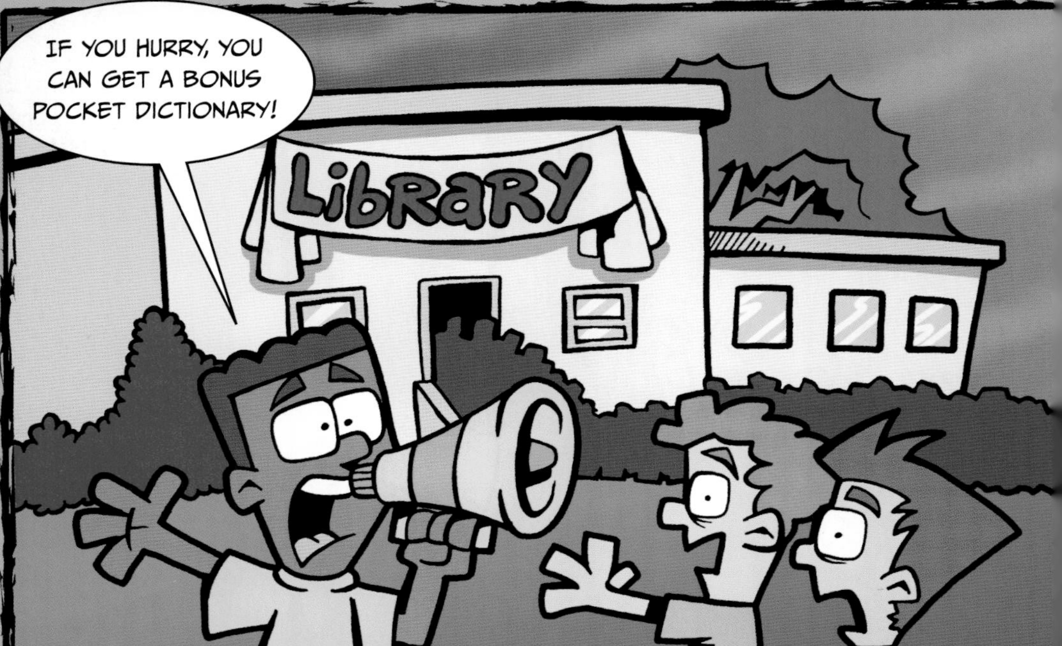
IF YOU HURRY, YOU CAN GET A BONUS POCKET DICTIONARY!
LIBRARY

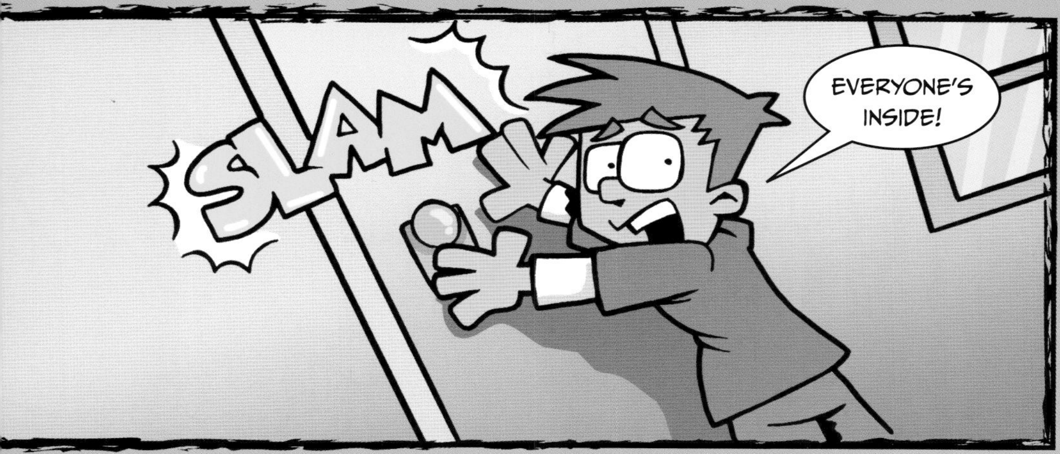
SLAM
EVERYONE'S INSIDE!

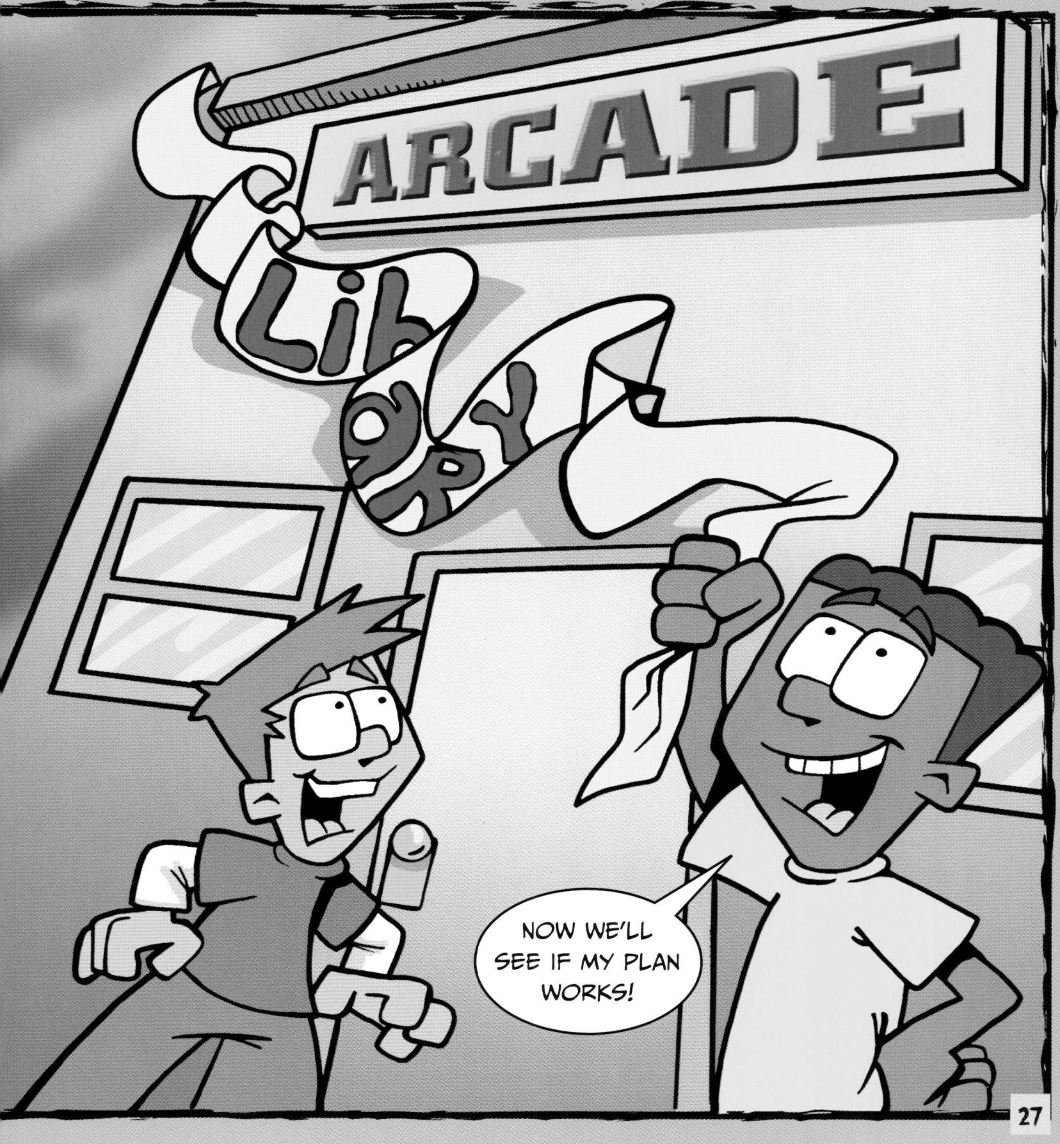
ARCADE
NOW WE'LL SEE IF MY PLAN WORKS!

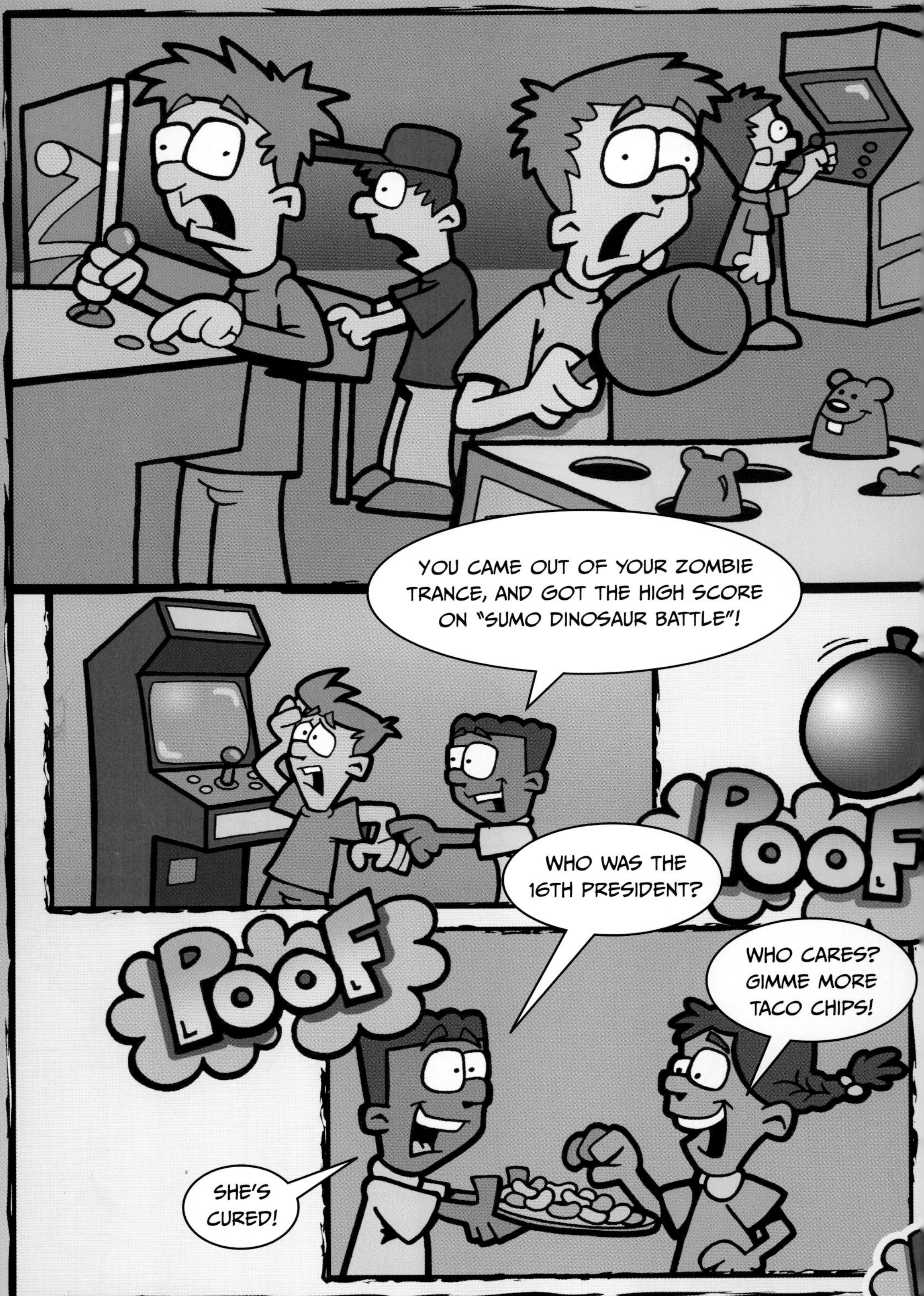
YOU CAME OUT OF YOUR ZOMBIE TRANCE, AND GOT THE HIGH SCORE ON "SUMO DINOSAUR BATTLE"!
POOF
WHO WAS THE 16TH PRESIDENT?
POOF
WHO CARES? GIMME MORE TACO CHIPS!
SHE'S CURED!

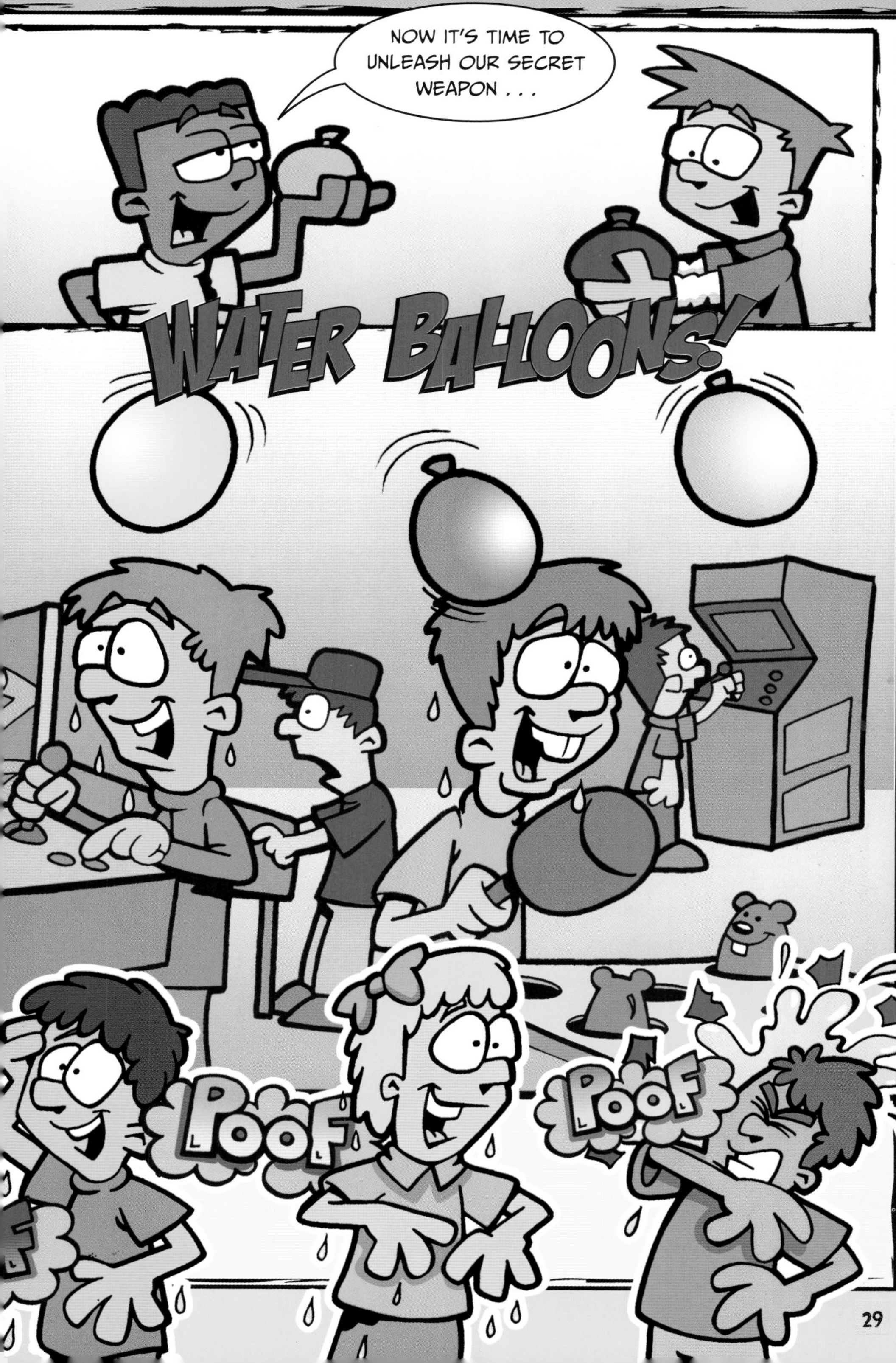
NOW IT'S TIME TO UNLEASH OUR SECRET WEAPON . . .
WATER BALLOONS!
POOF
POOF

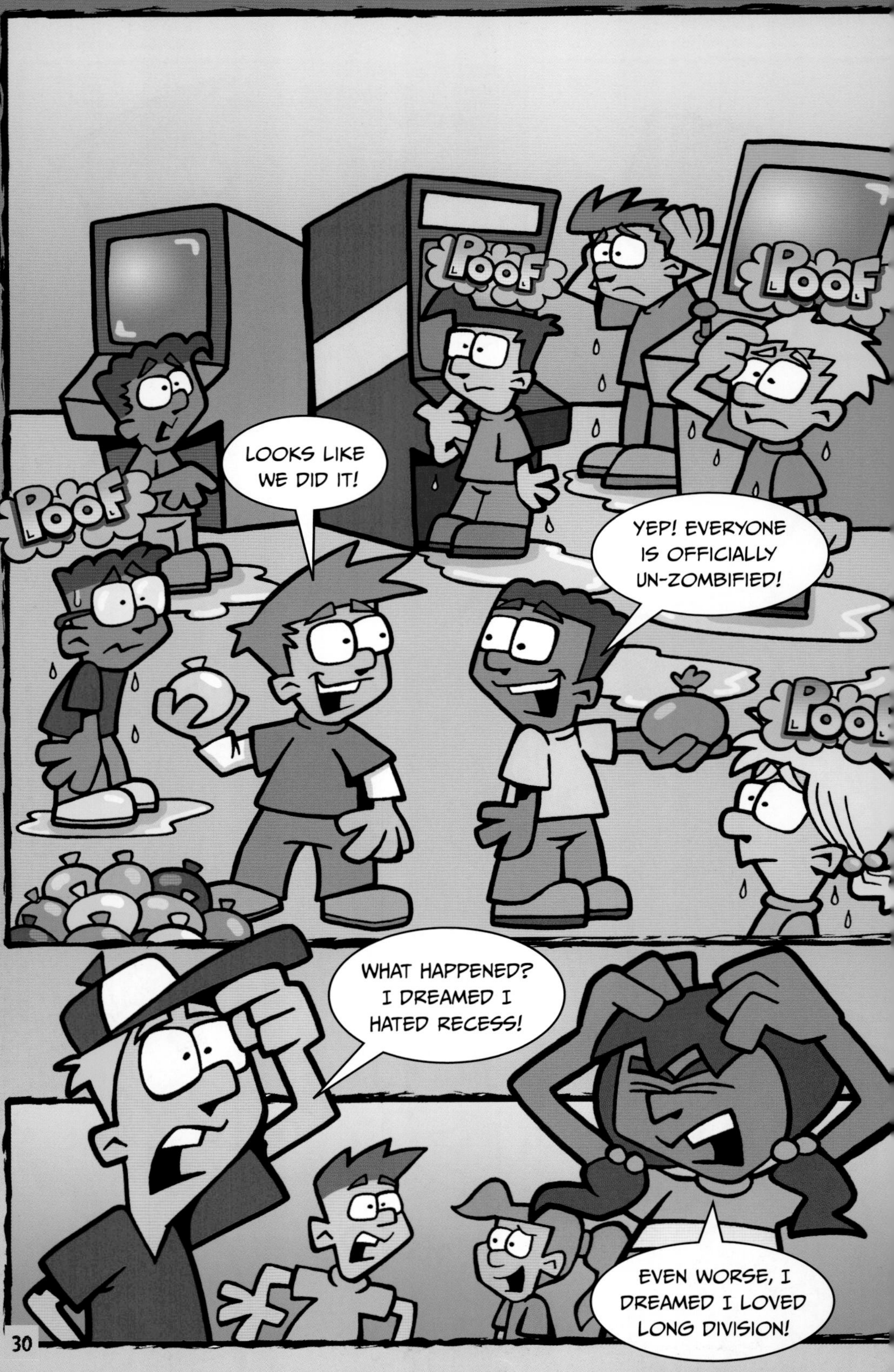
POOF
POOF
POOF
POOF
POOF
LOOKS LIKE WE DID IT!
YEP! EVERYONE IS OFFICIALLY UN-ZOMBIFIED!
WHAT HAPPENED? I DREAMED I HATED RECESS!
EVEN WORSE, I DREAMED I LOVED LONG DIVISION!

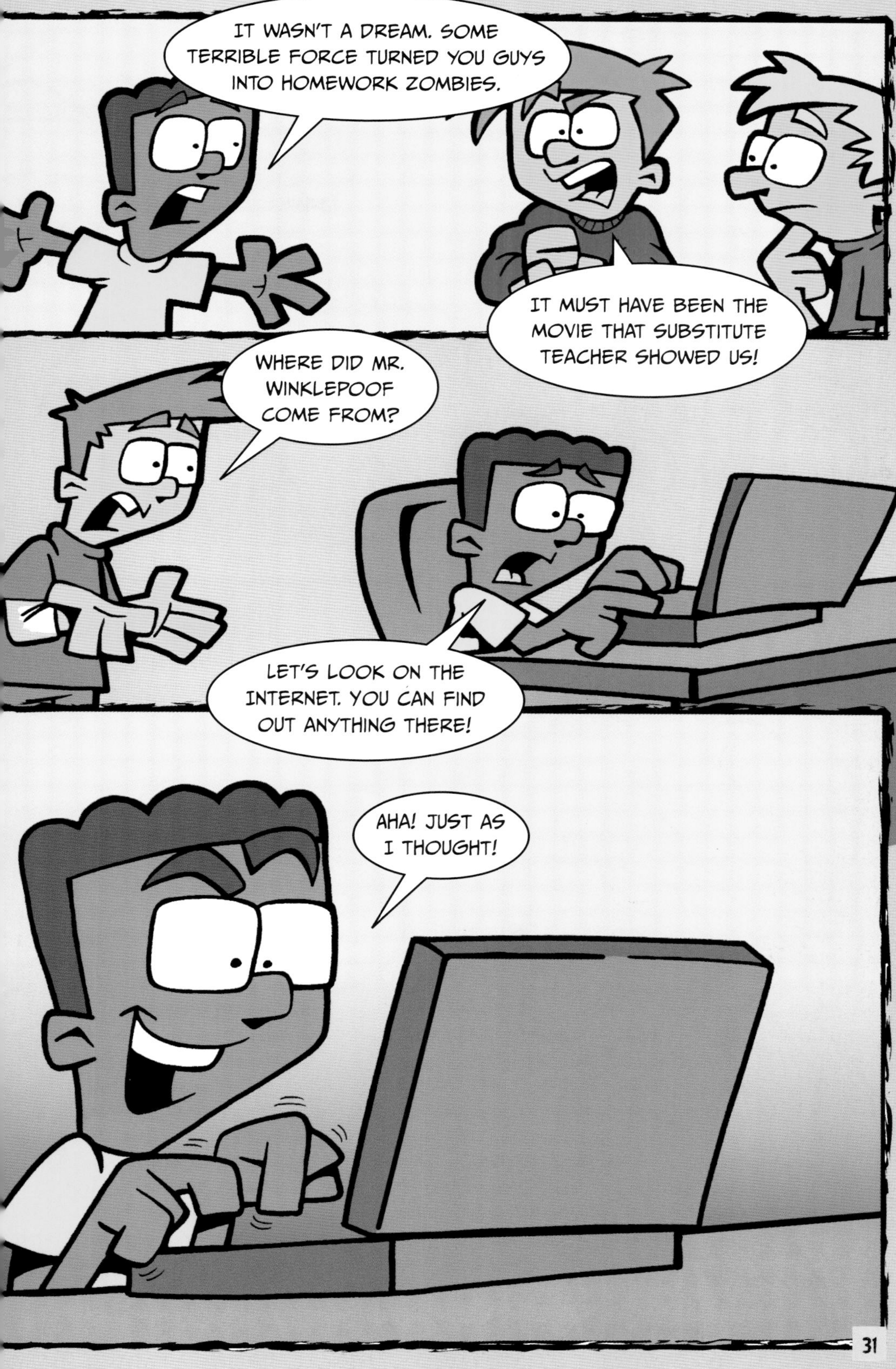
IT WASN'T A DREAM. SOME TERRIBLE FORCE TURNED YOU GUYS INTO HOMEWORK ZOMBIES.
IT MUST HAVE BEEN THE MOVIE THAT SUBSTITUTE TEACHER SHOWED US!
WHERE DID MR. WINKLEPOOF COME FROM?
LET'S LOOK ON THE INTERNET. YOU CAN FIND OUT ANYTHING THERE!
AHA! JUST AS I THOUGHT!

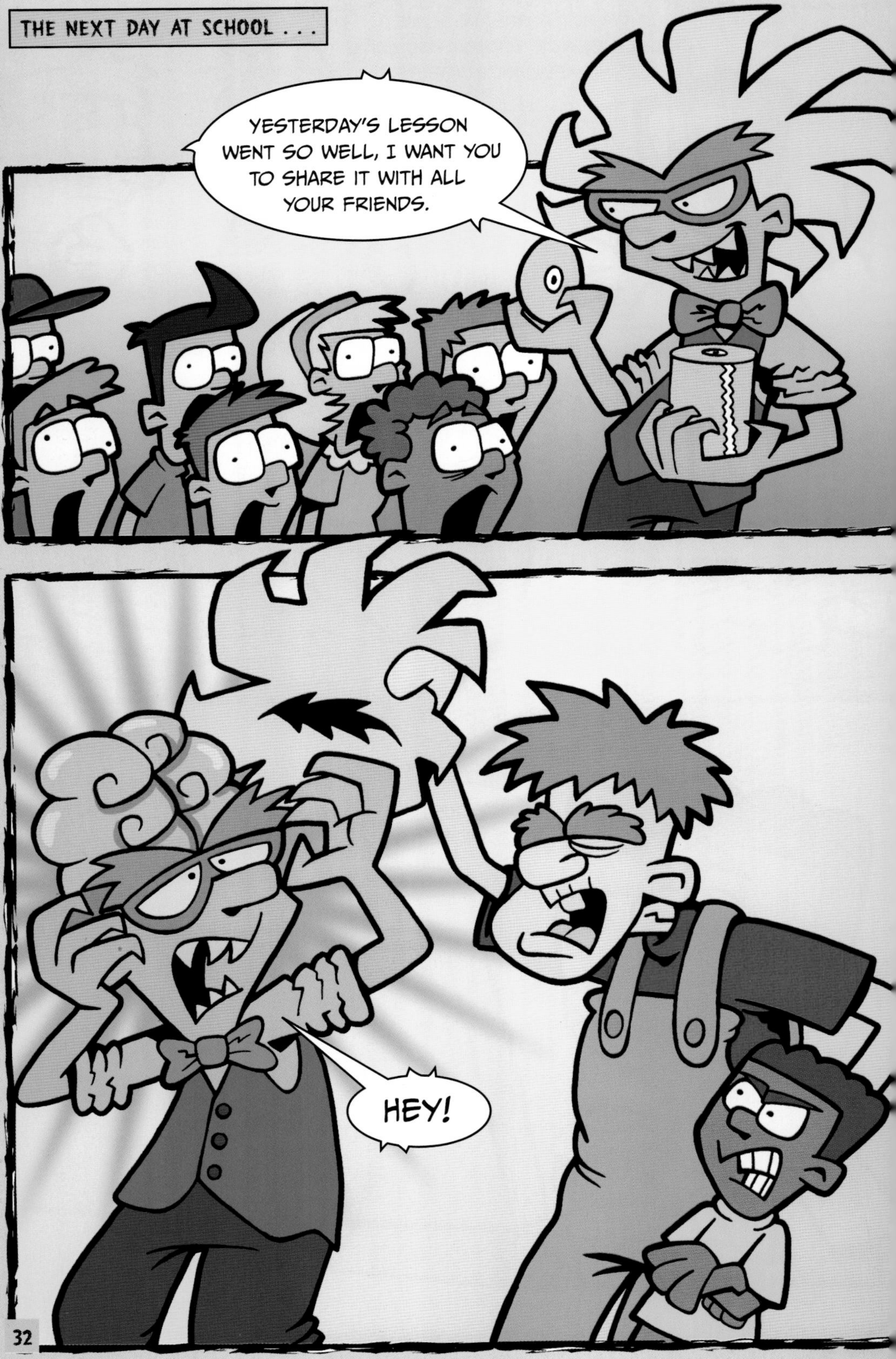
THE NEXT DAY AT SCHOOL . . .
YESTERDAY'S LESSON WENT SO WELL, I WANT YOU TO SHARE IT WITH ALL YOUR FRIENDS.
HEY!

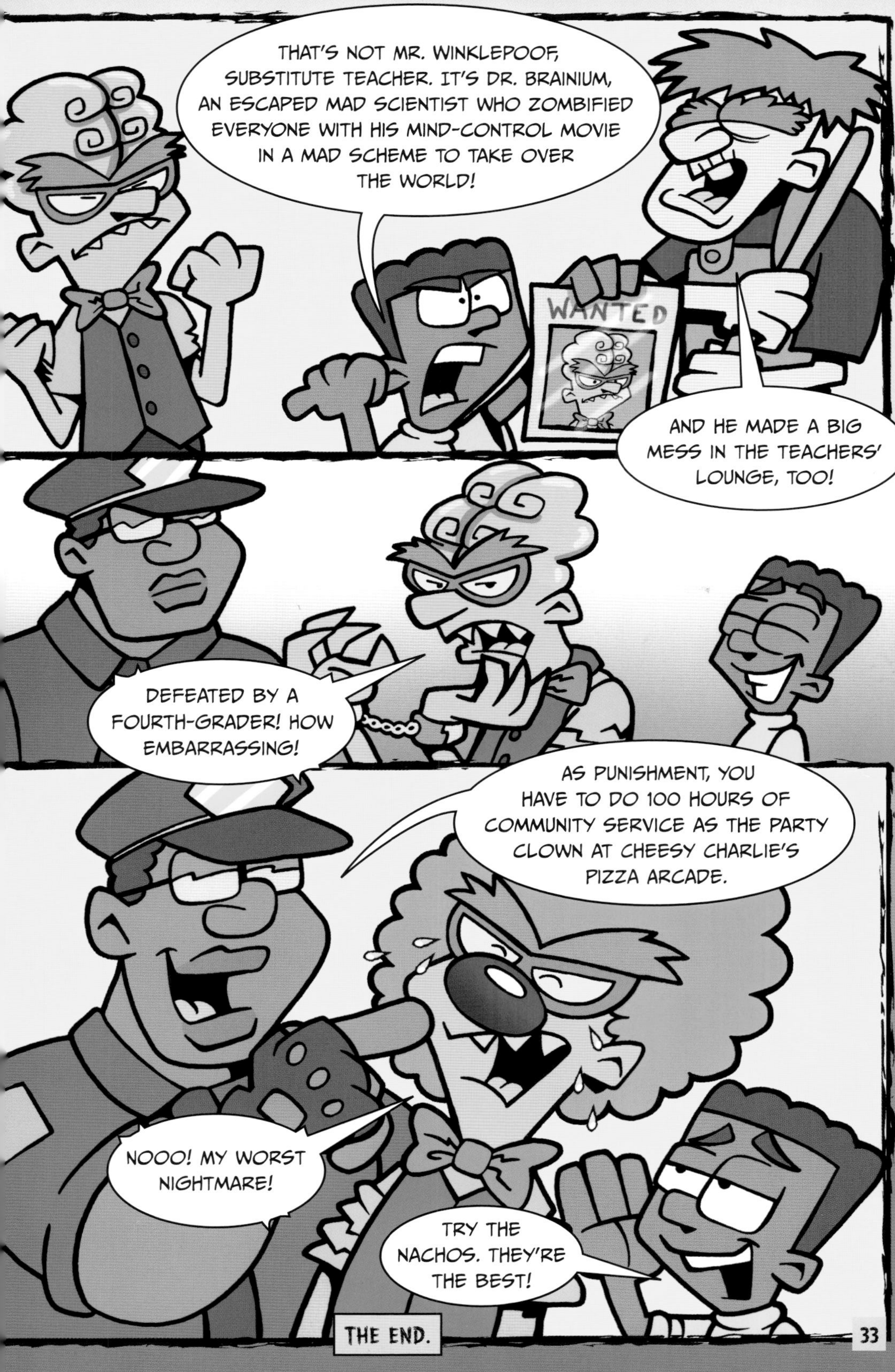
THAT'S NOT MR. WINKLEPOOF, SUBSTITUTE TEACHER. IT'S DR. BRAINIUM, AN ESCAPED MAD SCIENTIST WHO ZOMBIFIED EVERYONE WITH HIS MIND-CONTROL MOVIE IN A MAD SCHEME TO TAKE OVER THE WORLD!
WANTED
AND HE MADE A BIG MESS IN THE TEACHERS' LOUNGE, TOO!
DEFEATED BY A FOURTH-GRADER! HOW EMBARRASSING!
AS PUNISHMENT, YOU HAVE TO DO 100 HOURS OF COMMUNITY SERVICE AS THE PARTY CLOWN AT CHEESY CHARLIE'S PIZZA ARCADE.
NOOO! MY WORST NIGHTMARE!
TRY THE NACHOS. THEY'RE THE BEST!
THE END.

INVASION OF THE GYM CLASS ZOMBIES

BY SCOTT NICKEL

ILLUSTRATED BY MATT LUXICH

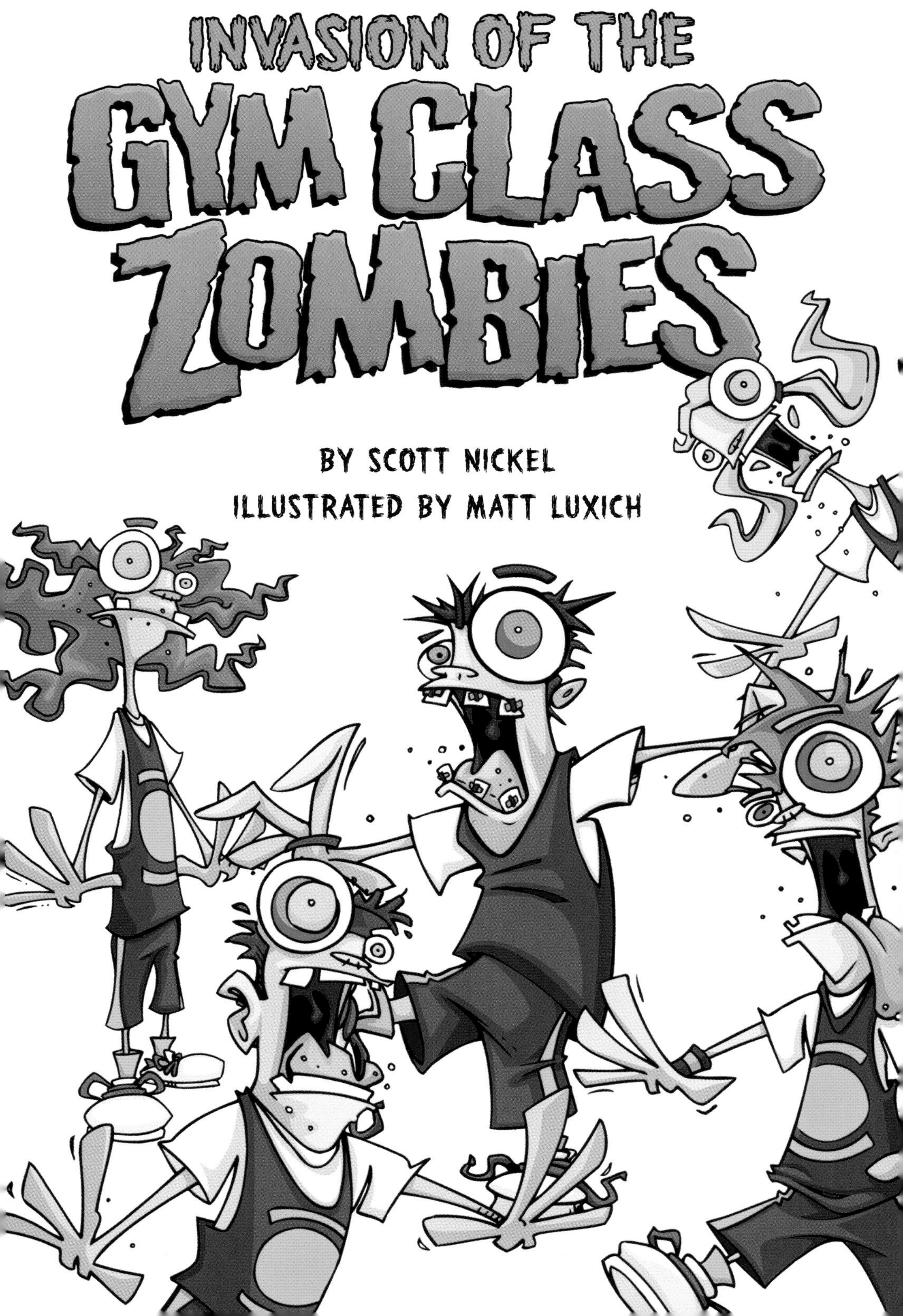

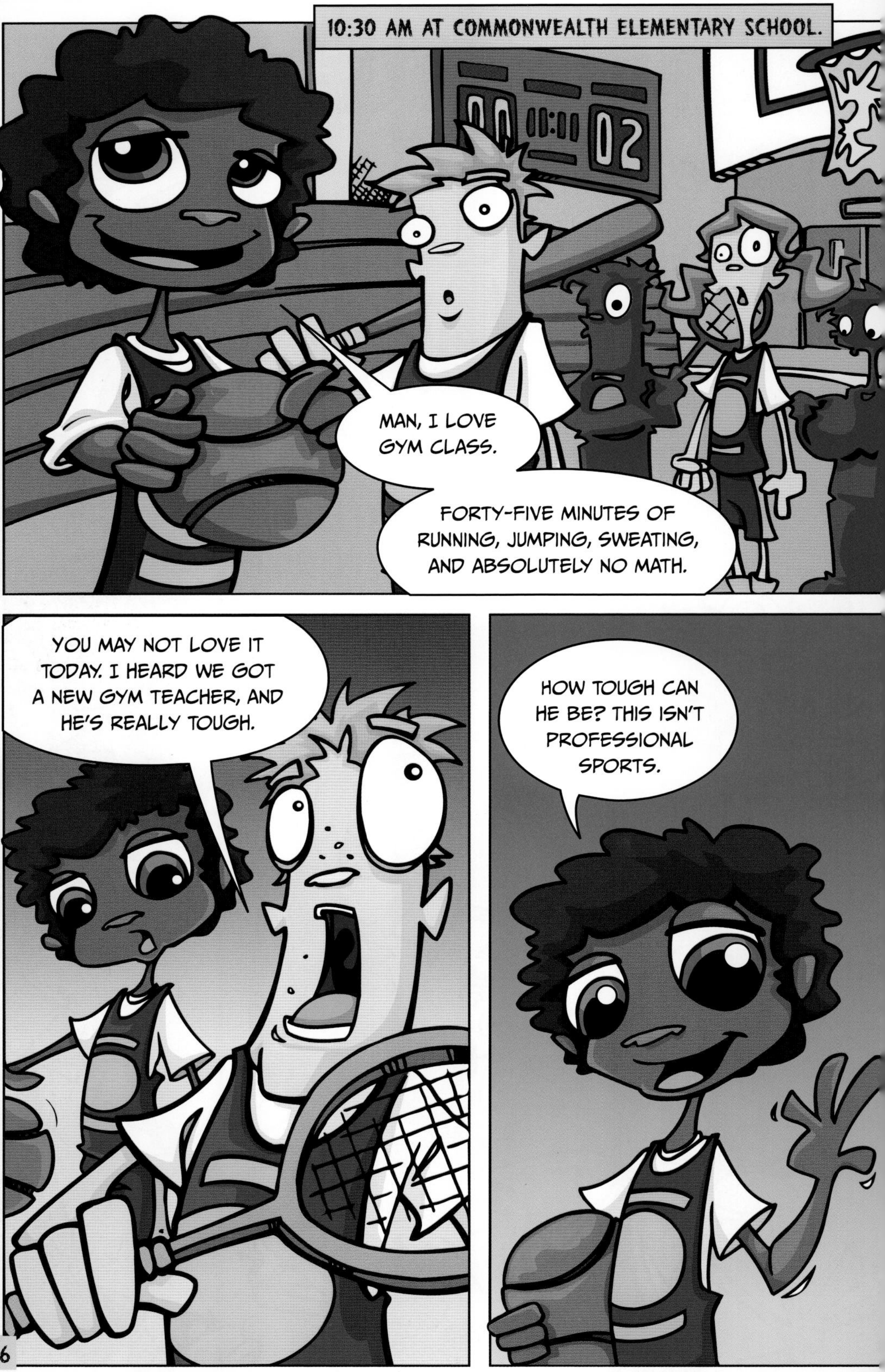
10:30 AM AT COMMONWEALTH ELEMENTARY SCHOOL.
MAN, I LOVE GYM CLASS.
FORTY-FIVE MINUTES OF RUNNING, JUMPING, SWEATING, AND ABSOLUTELY NO MATH.
YOU MAY NOT LOVE IT TODAY. I HEARD WE GOT A NEW GYM TEACHER, AND HE'S REALLY TOUGH.
HOW TOUGH CAN HE BE? THIS ISN'T PROFESSIONAL SPORTS.

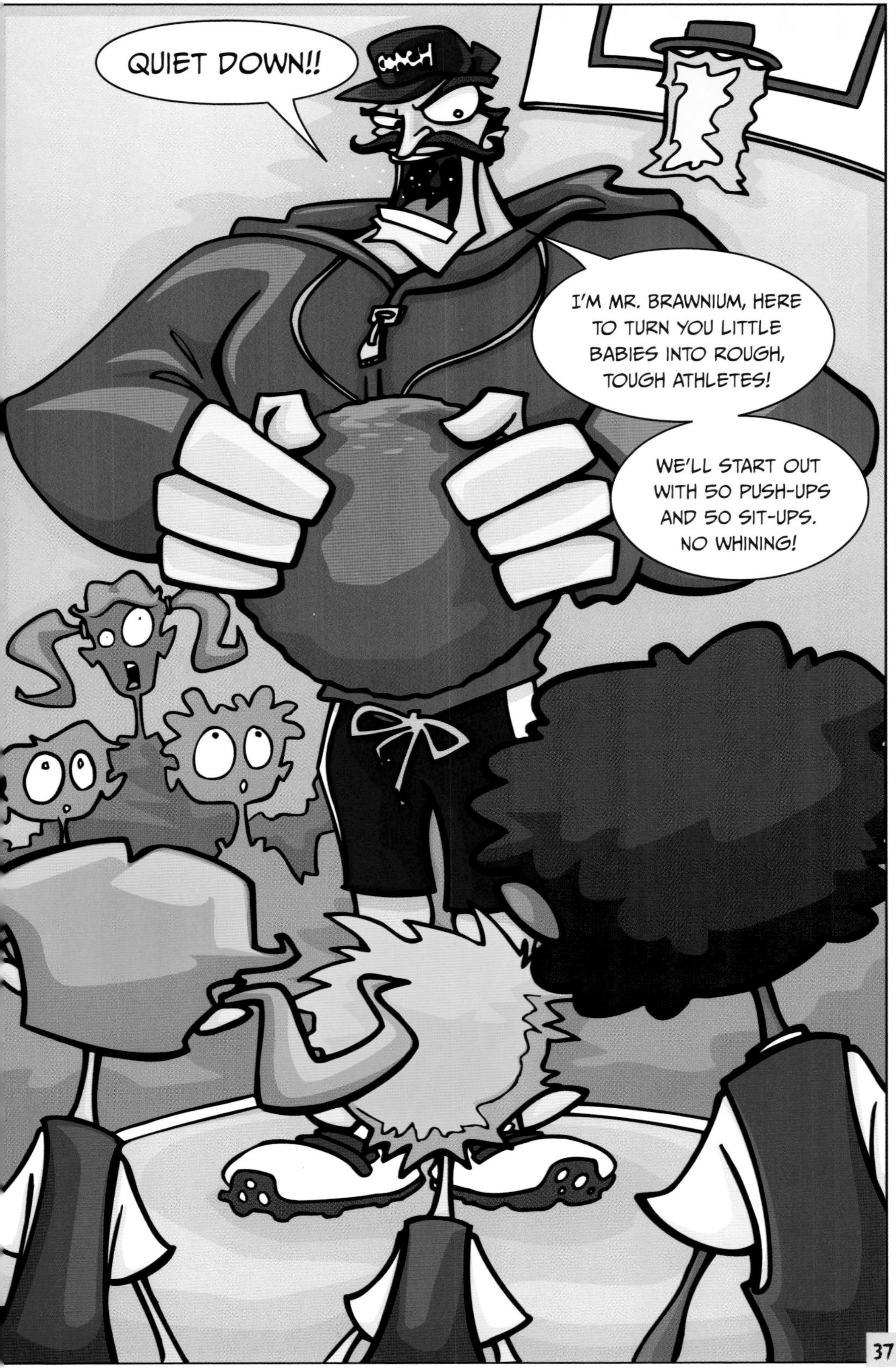
QUIET DOWN!!
COACH
I'M MR. BRAWNIUM, HERE TO TURN YOU LITTLE BABIES INTO ROUGH, TOUGH ATHLETES!
WE'LL START OUT WITH 50 PUSH-UPS AND 50 SIT-UPS. NO WHINING!

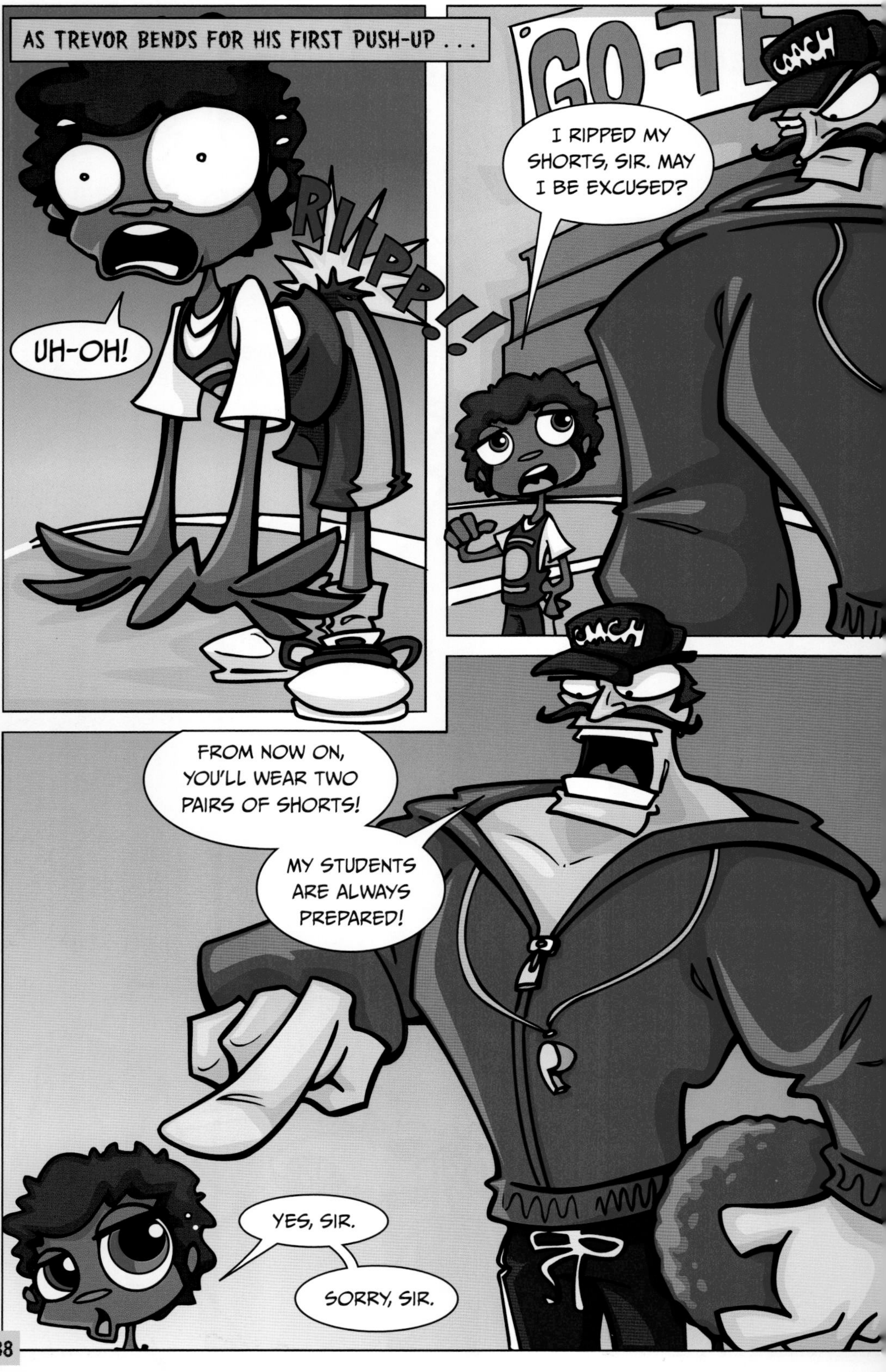
AS TREVOR BENDS FOR HIS FIRST PUSH-UP . . .
UH-OH!
RIIPP!!!
GO-TE
COACH
I RIPPED MY SHORTS, SIR. MAY I BE EXCUSED?
COACH
FROM NOW ON, YOU'LL WEAR TWO PAIRS OF SHORTS!
MY STUDENTS ARE ALWAYS PREPARED!
YES, SIR.
SORRY, SIR.

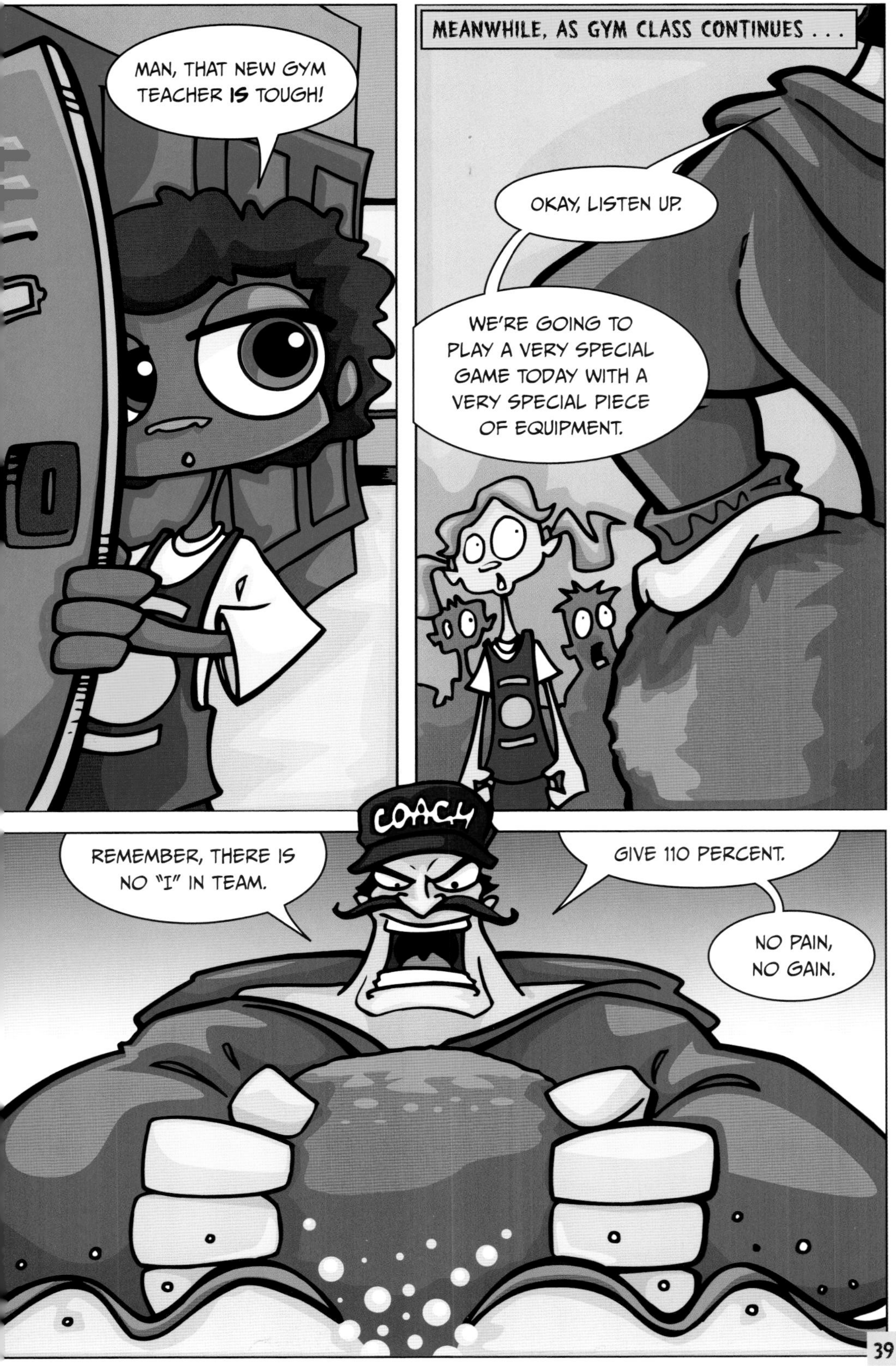
MAN, THAT NEW GYM TEACHER IS TOUGH!
MEANWHILE, AS GYM CLASS CONTINUES . . .
OKAY, LISTEN UP.
WE'RE GOING TO PLAY A VERY SPECIAL GAME TODAY WITH A VERY SPECIAL PIECE OF EQUIPMENT.
COACH
REMEMBER, THERE IS NO "I" IN TEAM.
GIVE 110 PERCENT.
NO PAIN, NO GAIN.

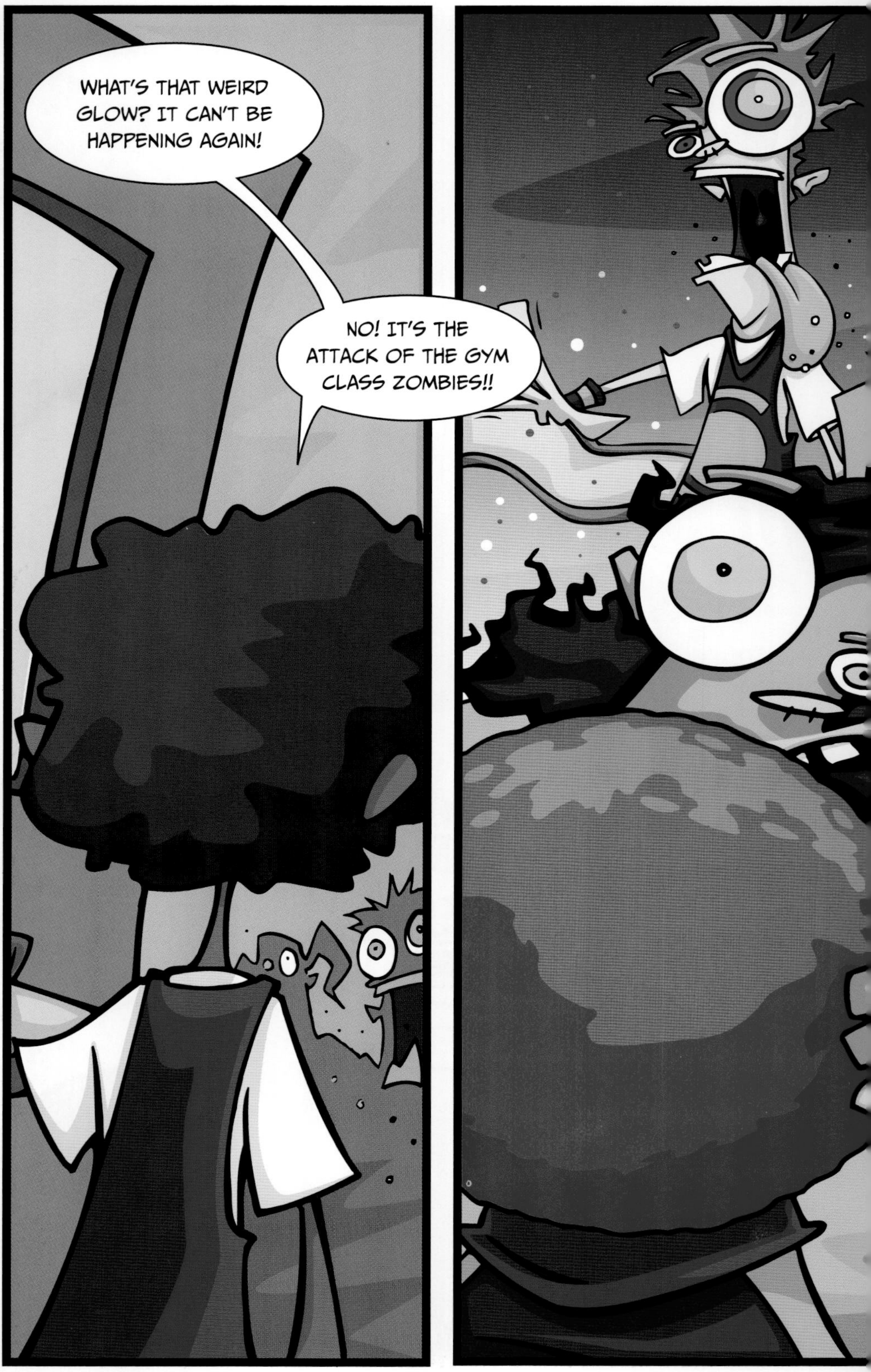
WHAT'S THAT WEIRD GLOW? IT CAN'T BE HAPPENING AGAIN!
NO! IT'S THE ATTACK OF THE GYM CLASS ZOMBIES!!

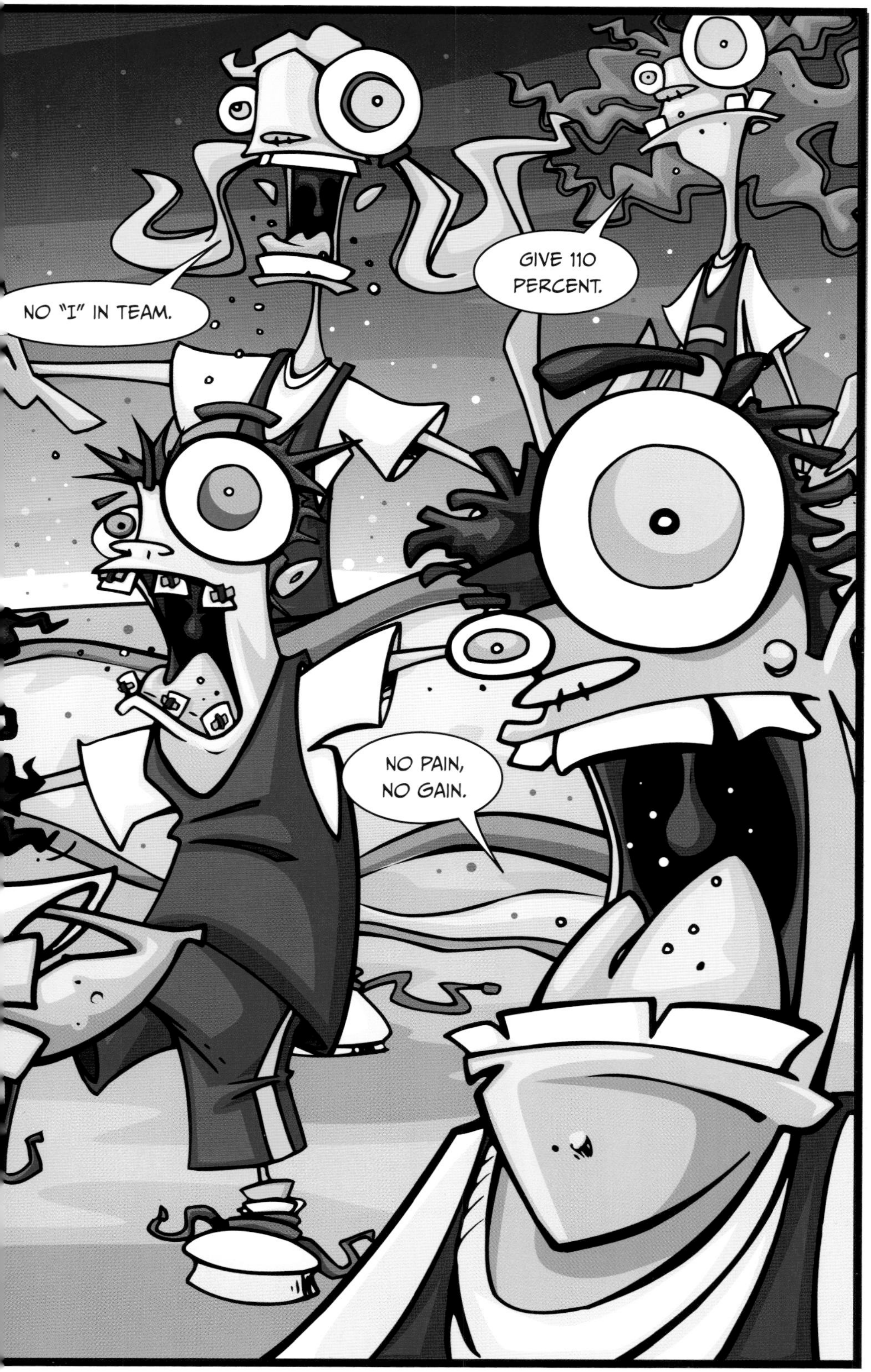
NO "I" IN TEAM.
GIVE 110 PERCENT.
NO PAIN, NO GAIN.

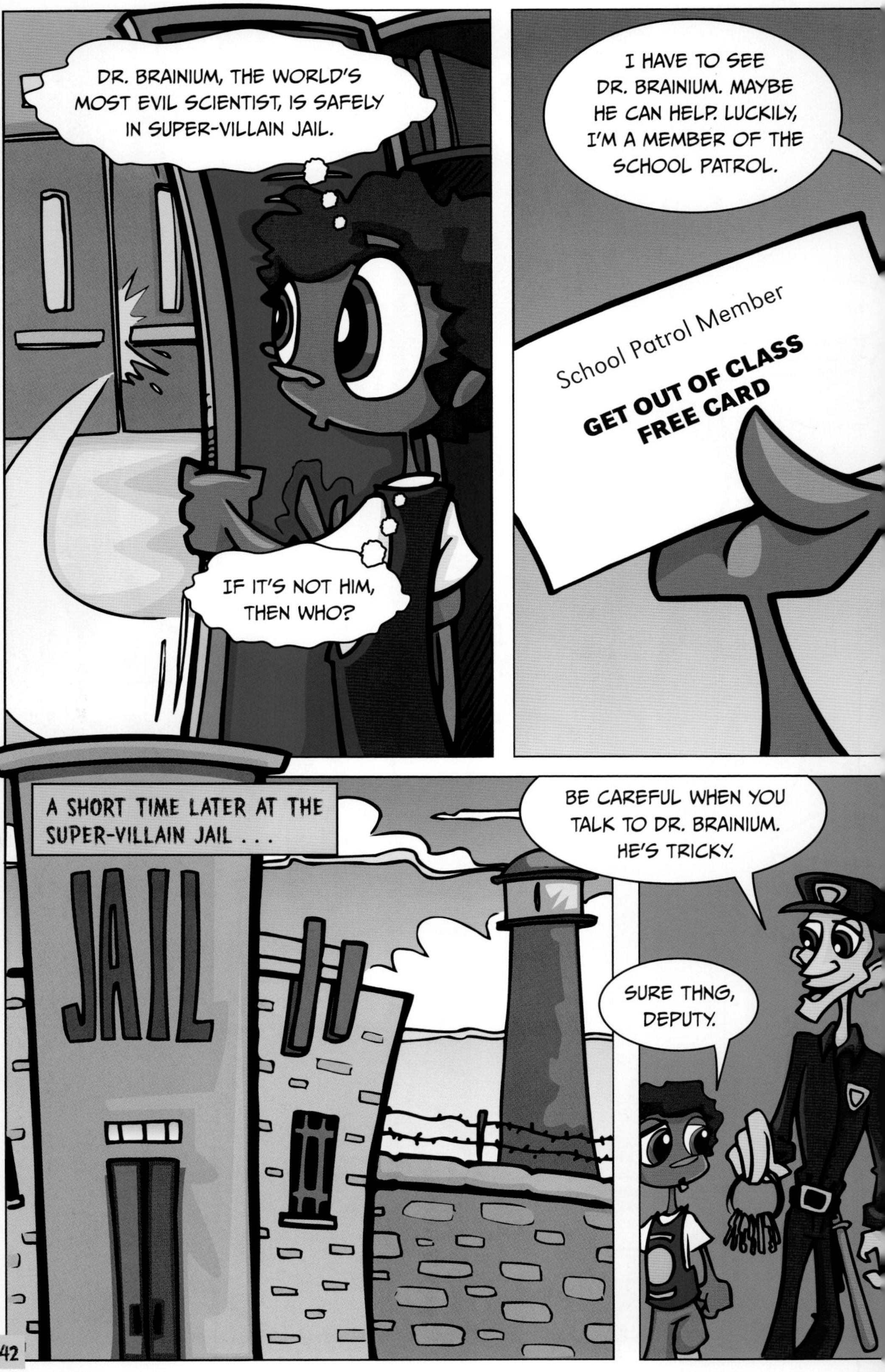
DR. BRAINIUM, THE WORLD'S MOST EVIL SCIENTIST, IS SAFELY IN SUPER-VILLAIN JAIL.
IF IT'S NOT HIM, THEN WHO?
I HAVE TO SEE DR. BRAINIUM. MAYBE HE CAN HELP. LUCKILY, I'M A MEMBER OF THE SCHOOL PATROL.
School Patrol Member
GET OUT OF CLASS FREE CARD
A SHORT TIME LATER AT THE SUPER-VILLAIN JAIL . . .
JAIL
BE CAREFUL WHEN YOU TALK TO DR. BRAINIUM. HE'S TRICKY.
SURE THNG, DEPUTY.

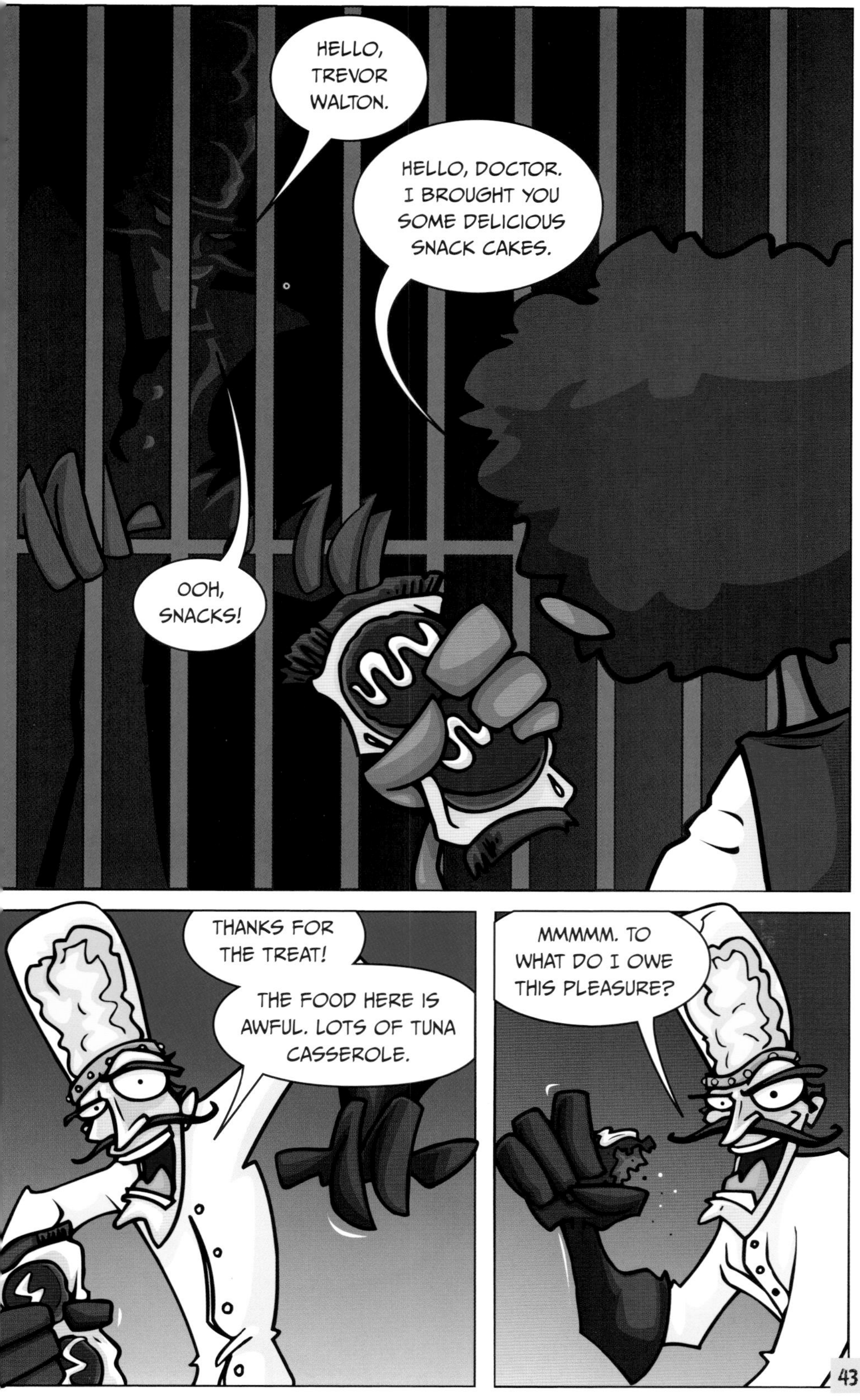
HELLO, TREVOR WALTON.
HELLO, DOCTOR. I BROUGHT YOU SOME DELICIOUS SNACK CAKES.
OOH, SNACKS!
THANKS FOR THE TREAT!
THE FOOD HERE IS AWFUL. LOTS OF TUNA CASSEROLE.
MMMMM. TO WHAT DO I OWE THIS PLEASURE?

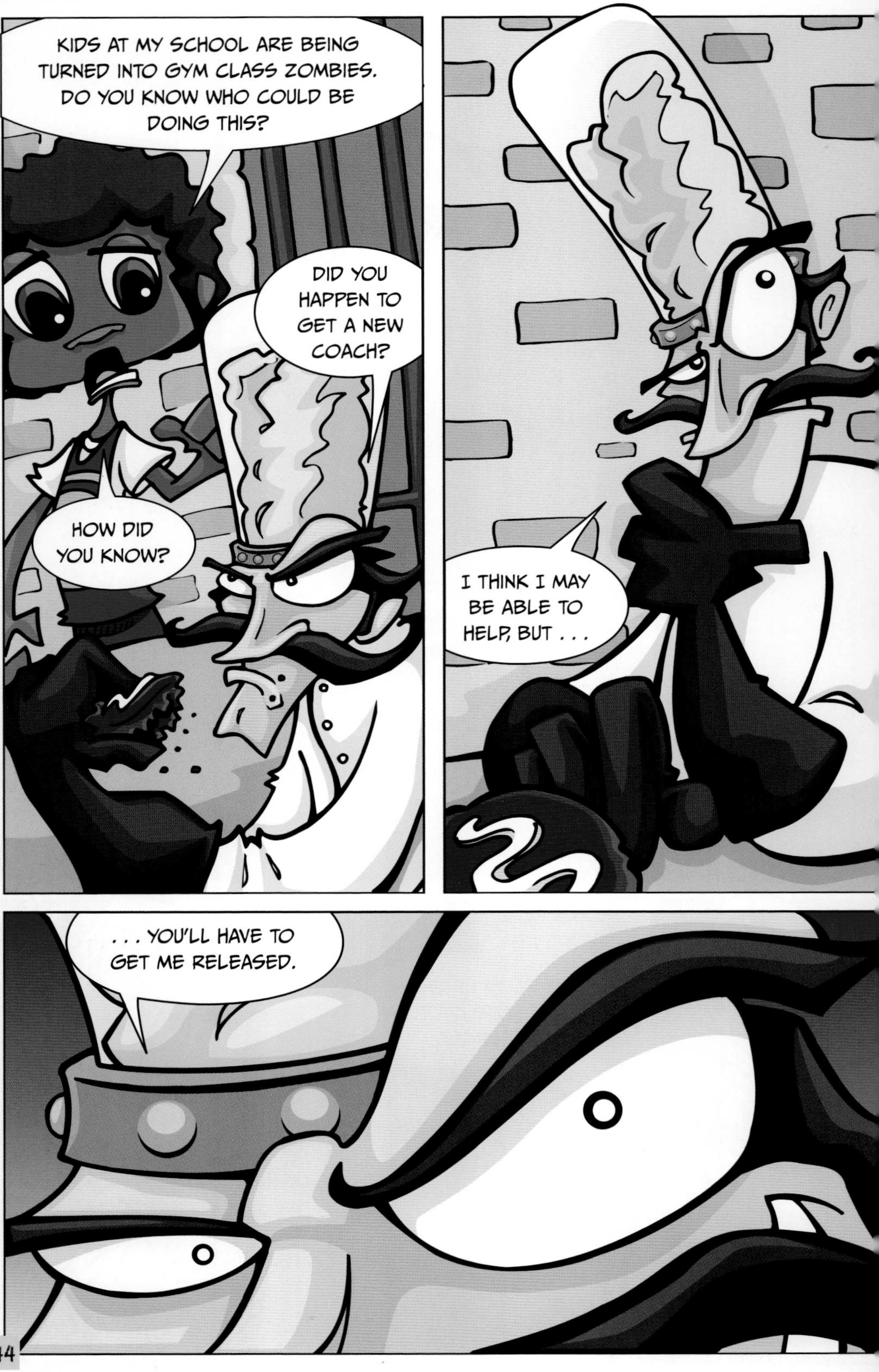
KIDS AT MY SCHOOL ARE BEING TURNED INTO GYM CLASS ZOMBIES. DO YOU KNOW WHO COULD BE DOING THIS?
DID YOU HAPPEN TO GET A NEW COACH?
HOW DID YOU KNOW?
I THINK I MAY BE ABLE TO HELP, BUT . . .
. . . YOU'LL HAVE TO GET ME RELEASED.

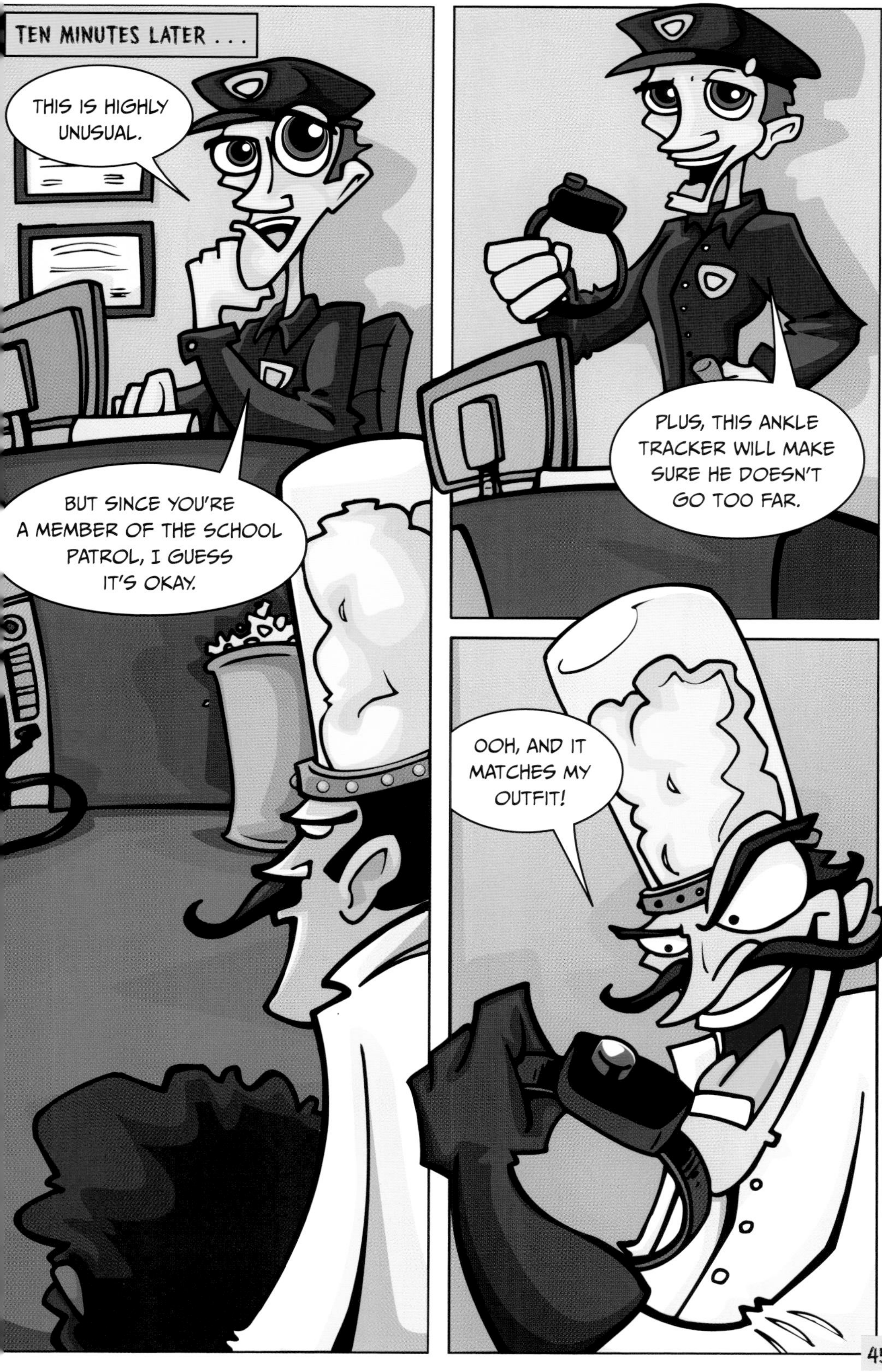
TEN MINUTES LATER . . .
THIS IS HIGHLY UNUSUAL.
BUT SINCE YOU'RE A MEMBER OF THE SCHOOL PATROL, I GUESS IT'S OKAY.
PLUS, THIS ANKLE TRACKER WILL MAKE SURE HE DOESN'T GO TOO FAR.
OOH, AND IT MATCHES MY OUTFIT!

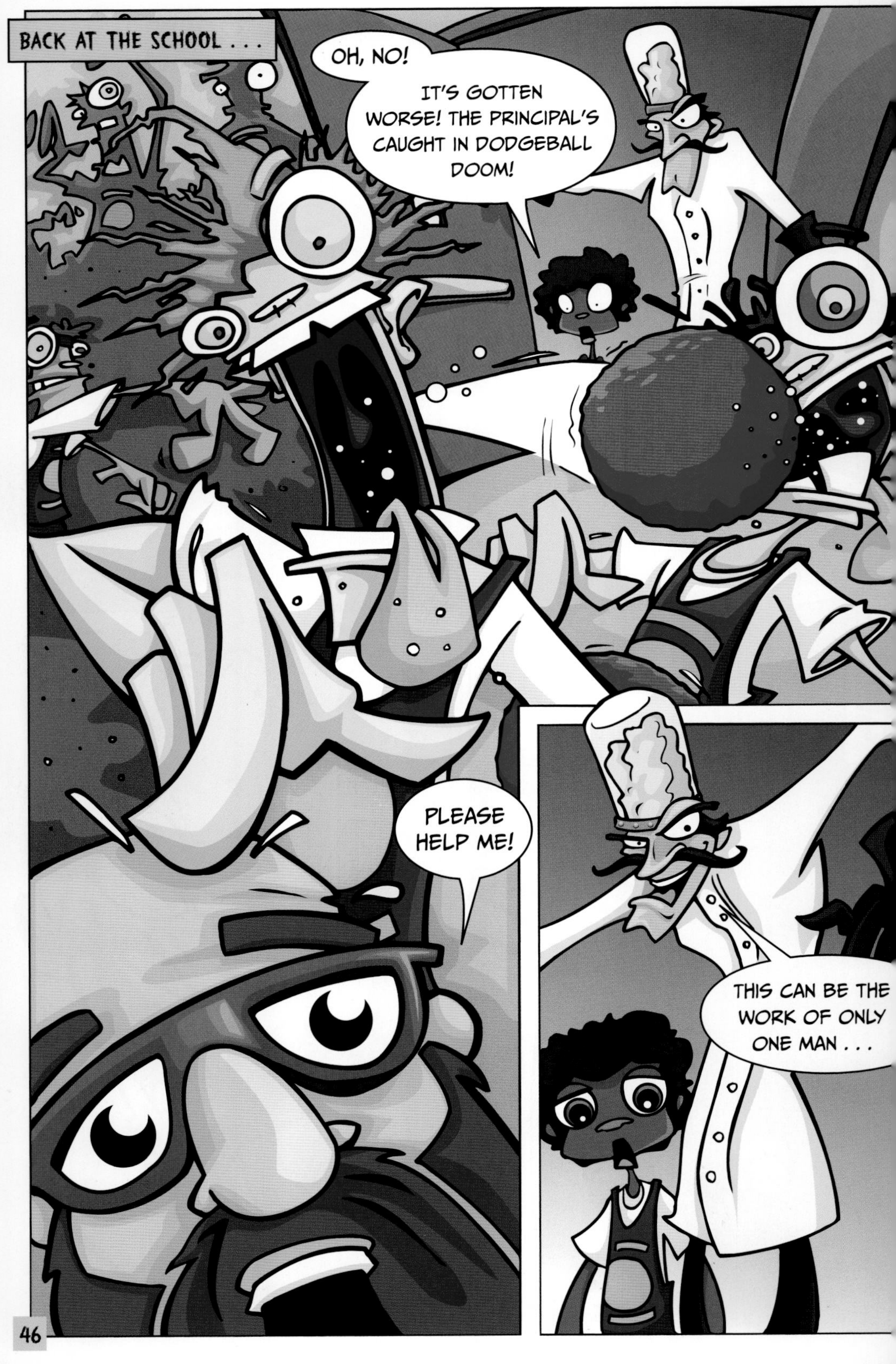
BACK AT THE SCHOOL . . .
OH, NO!
IT'S GOTTEN WORSE! THE PRINCIPAL'S CAUGHT IN DODGEBALL DOOM!
PLEASE HELP ME!
THIS CAN BE THE WORK OF ONLY ONE MAN . . .

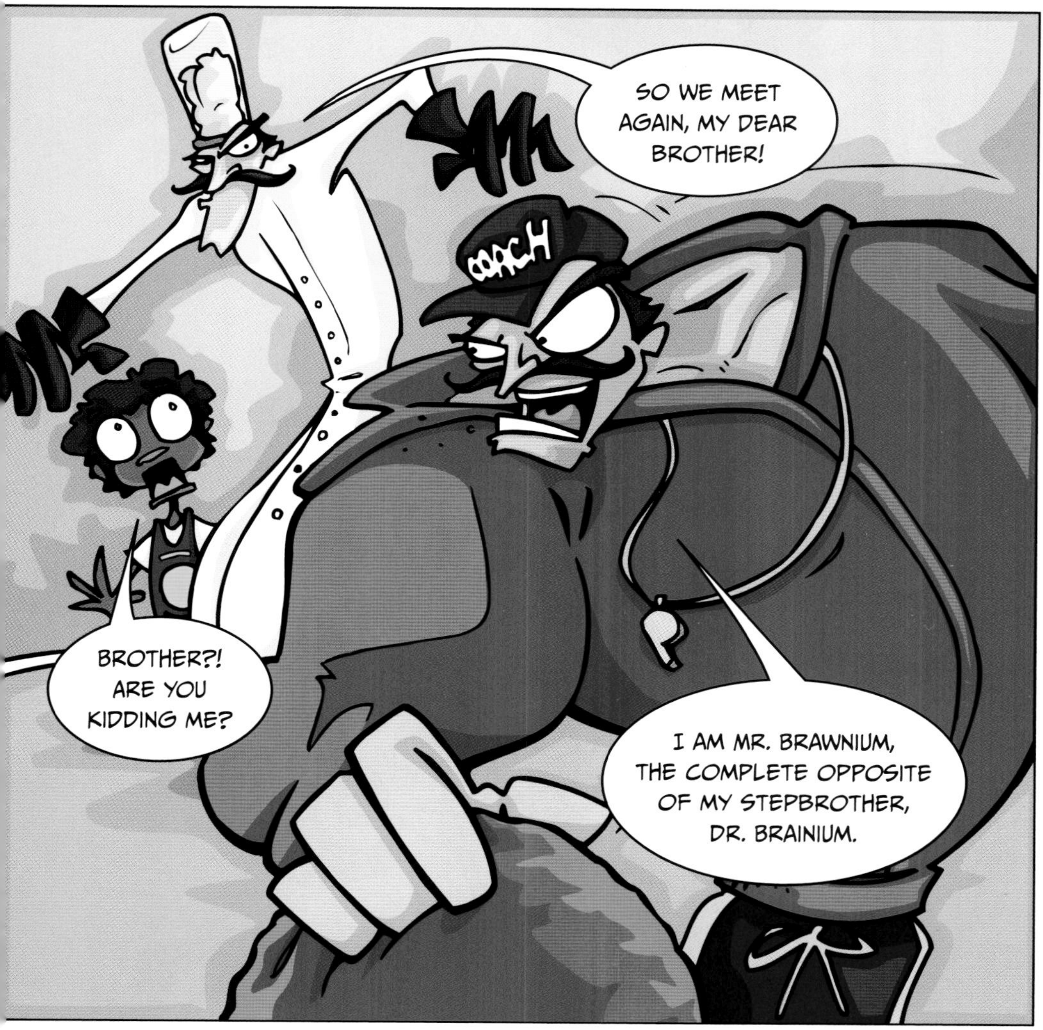
SO WE MEET AGAIN, MY DEAR BROTHER!
COACH
BROTHER?! ARE YOU KIDDING ME?
I AM MR. BRAWNIUM, THE COMPLETE OPPOSITE OF MY STEPBROTHER, DR. BRAINIUM.

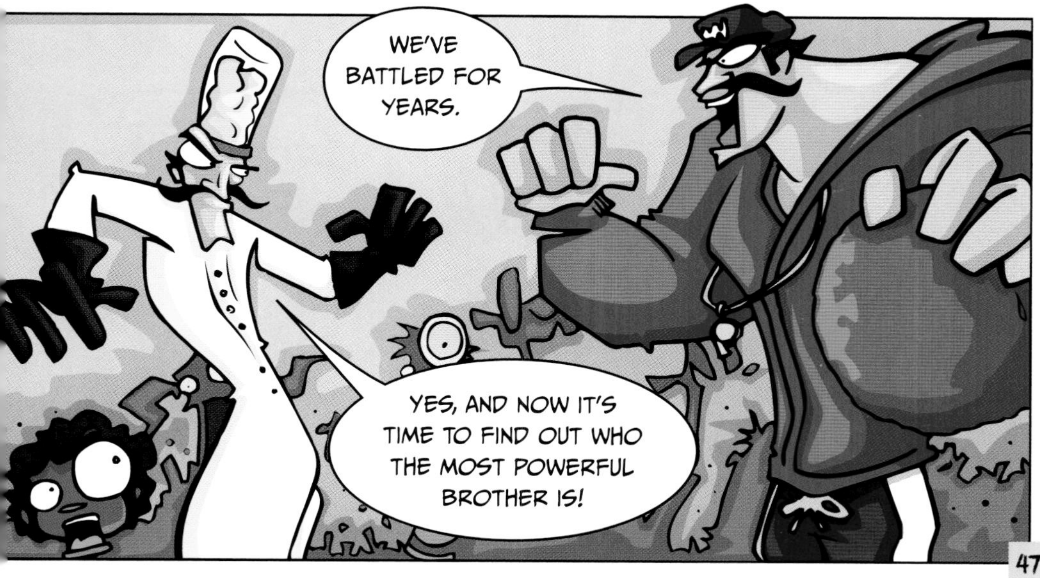
WE'VE BATTLED FOR YEARS.
YES, AND NOW IT'S TIME TO FIND OUT WHO THE MOST POWERFUL BROTHER IS!

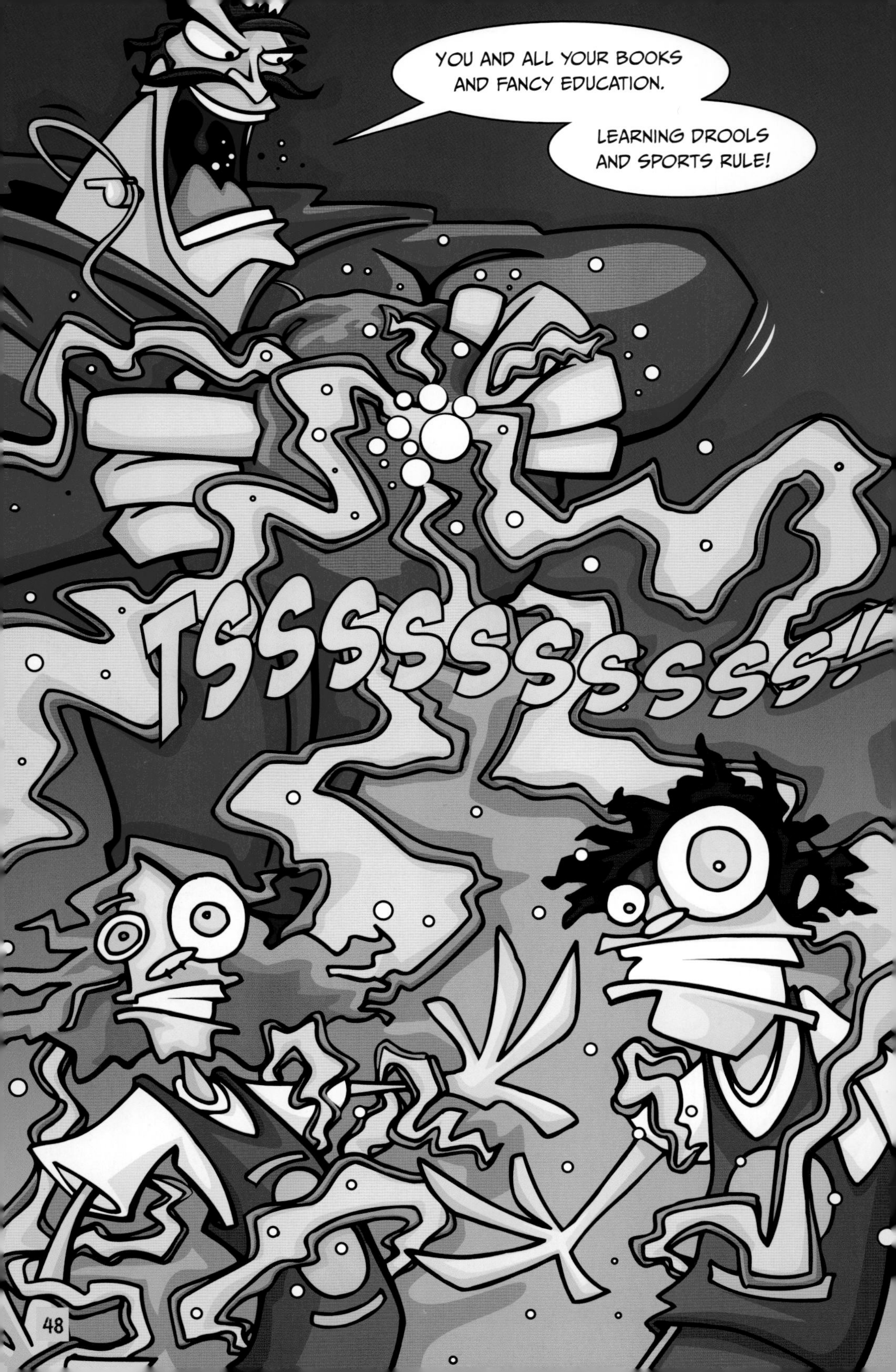
YOU AND ALL YOUR BOOKS AND FANCY EDUCATION.
LEARNING DROOLS AND SPORTS RULE!
TSSSSSSSSSS!

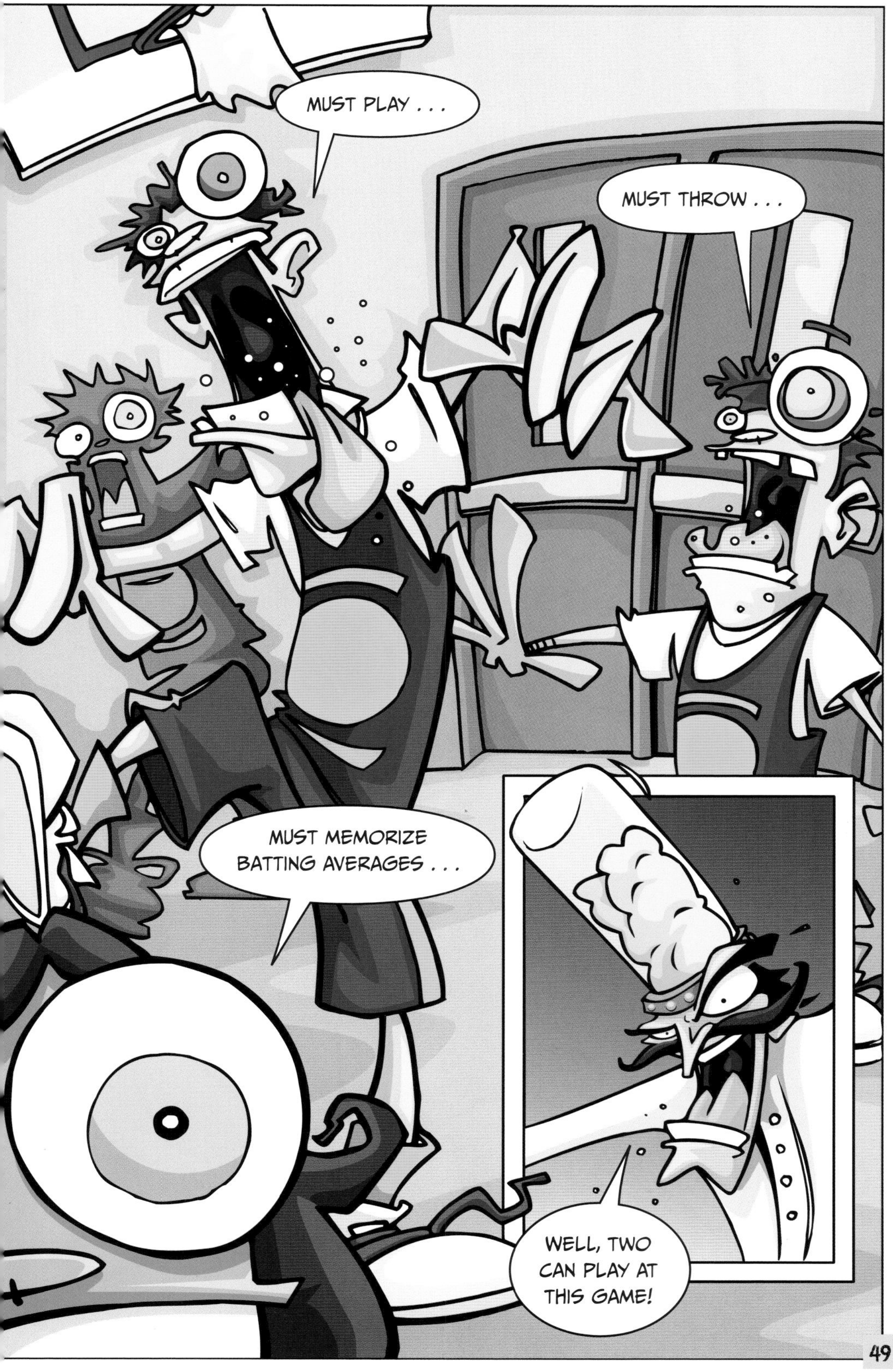
MUST PLAY . . .
MUST THROW . . .
MUST MEMORIZE BATTING AVERAGES . . .
WELL, TWO CAN PLAY AT THIS GAME!

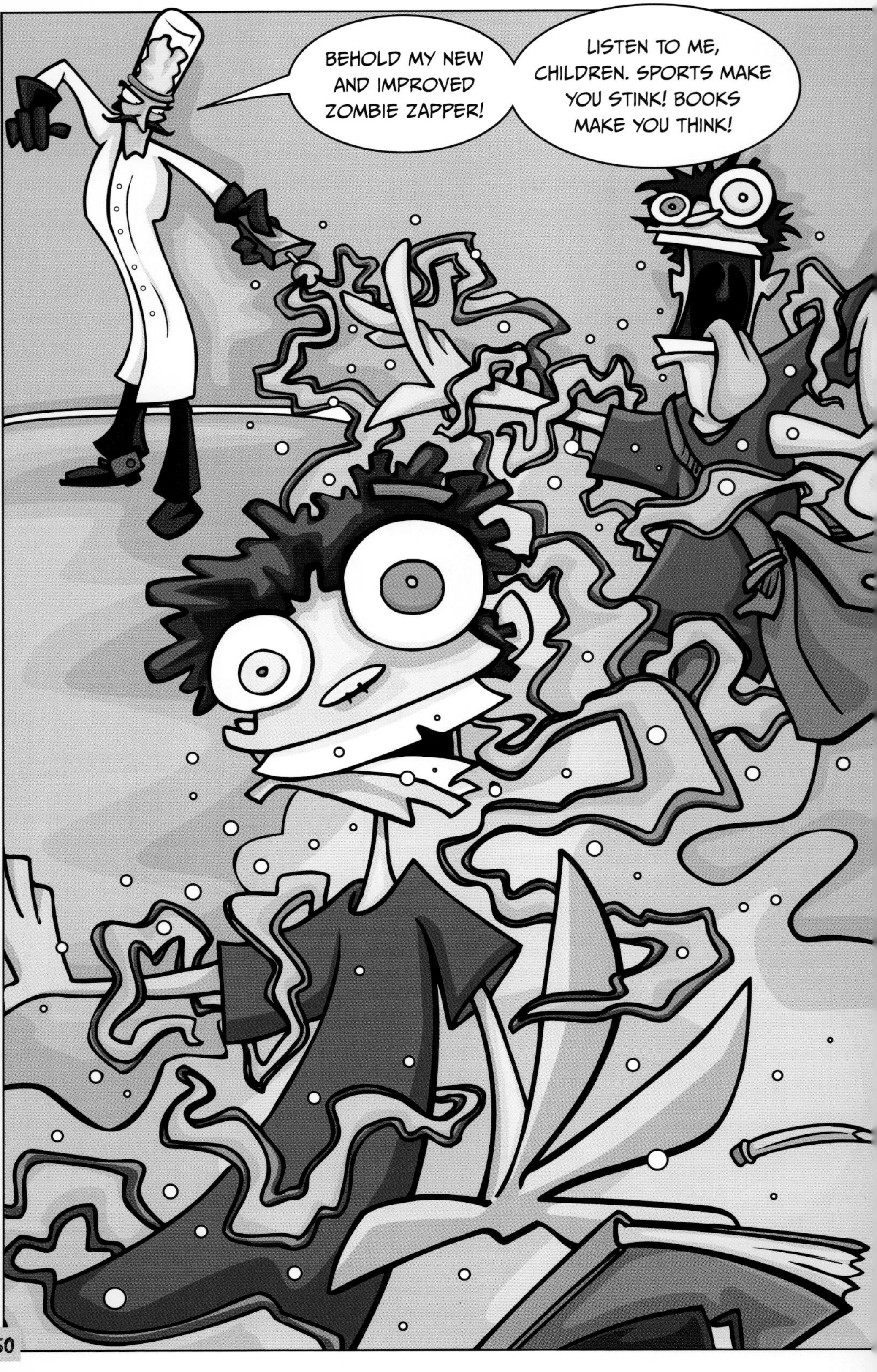
BEHOLD MY NEW AND IMPROVED ZOMBIE ZAPPER!
LISTEN TO ME, CHILDREN. SPORTS MAKE YOU STINK! BOOKS MAKE YOU THINK!

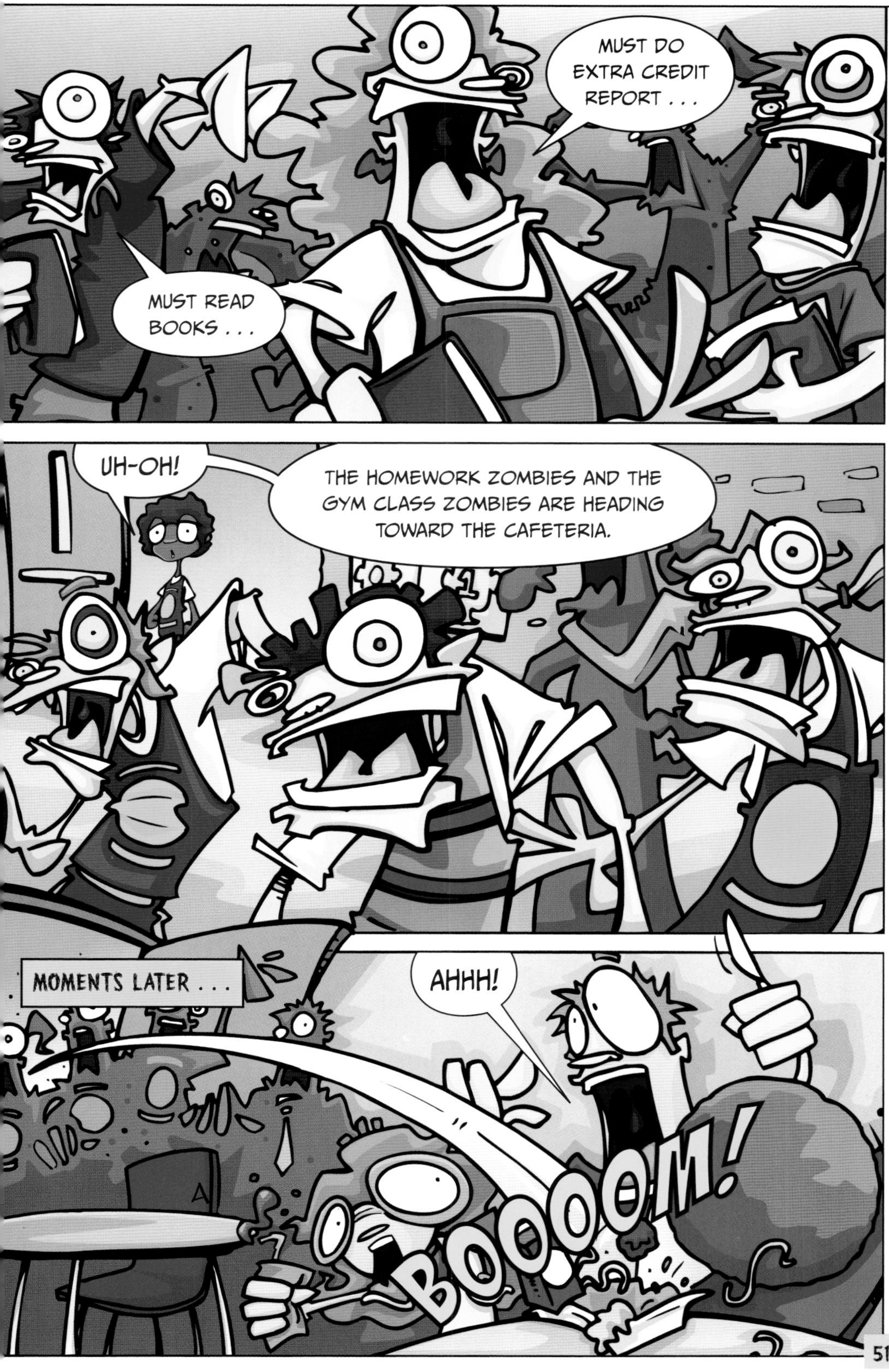
MUST DO EXTRA CREDIT REPORT . . .
MUST READ BOOKS . . .
UH-OH!
THE HOMEWORK ZOMBIES AND THE GYM CLASS ZOMBIES ARE HEADING TOWARD THE CAFETERIA.
MOMENTS LATER . . .
AHHH!
BOOOOOM!

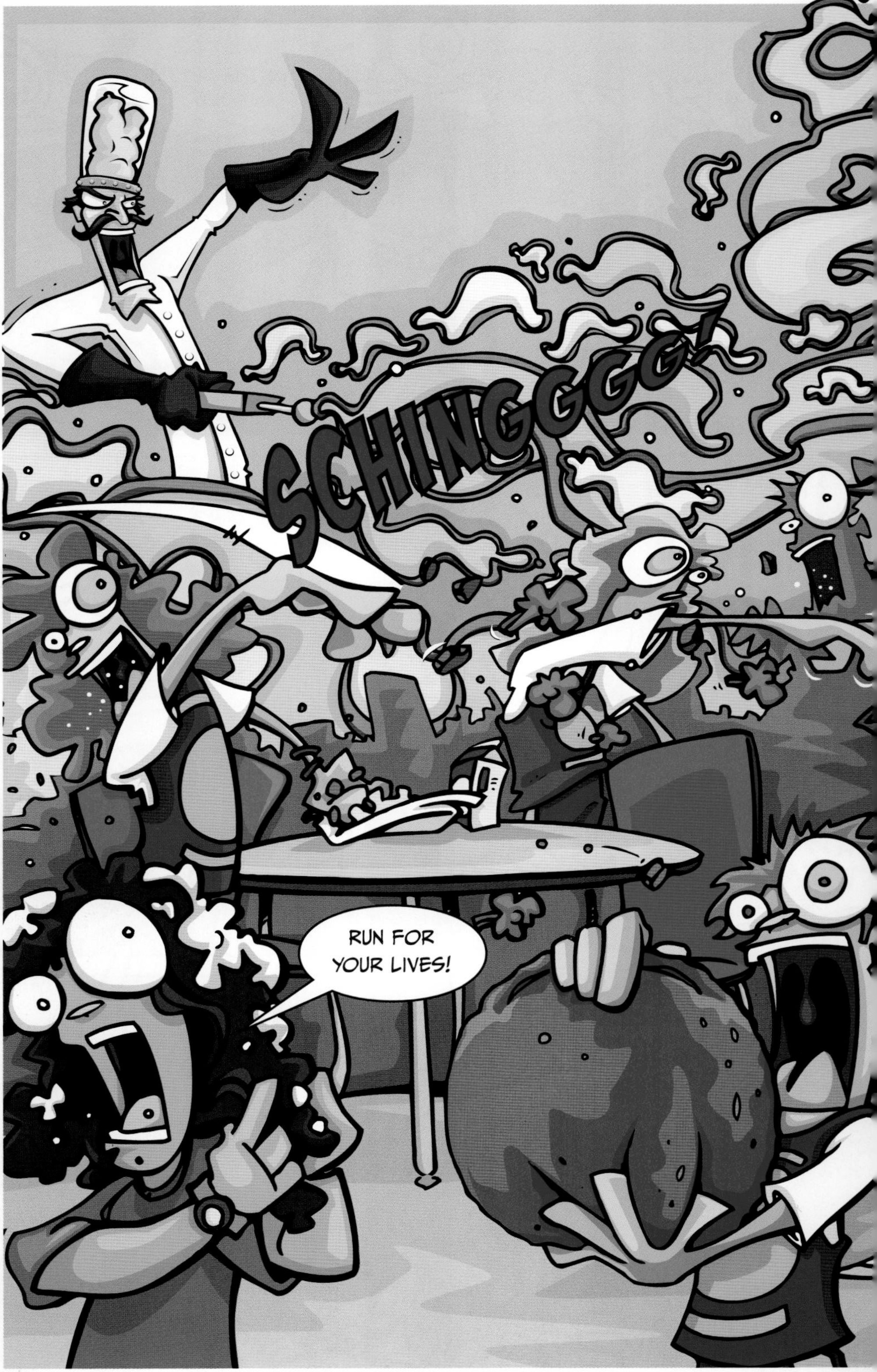
SCHINGGGGG!
RUN FOR YOUR LIVES!

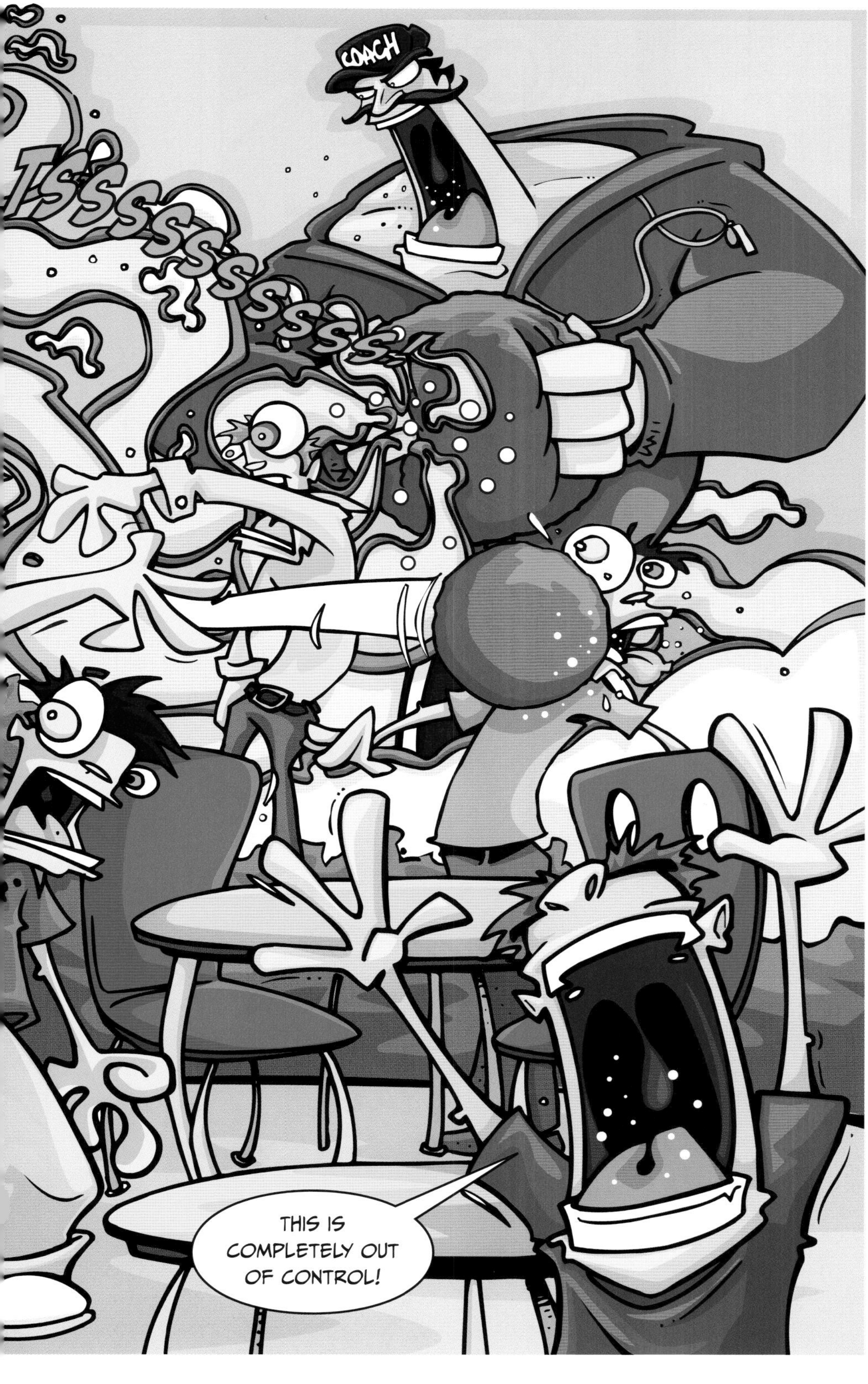
COACH
TSSSSSSSSSSS!
THIS IS COMPLETELY OUT OF CONTROL!

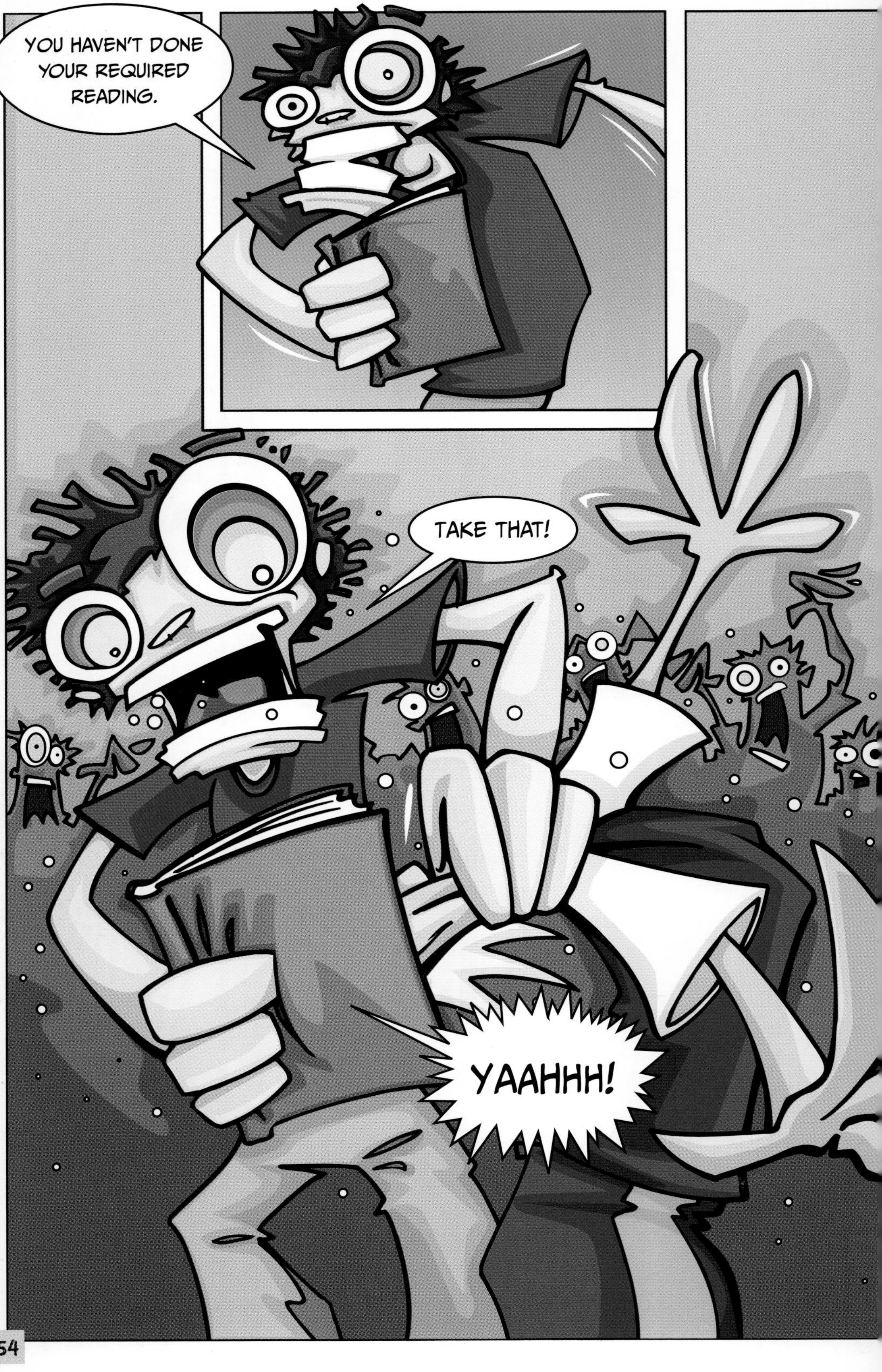
YOU HAVEN'T DONE YOUR REQUIRED READING.
TAKE THAT!
YAAHHH!

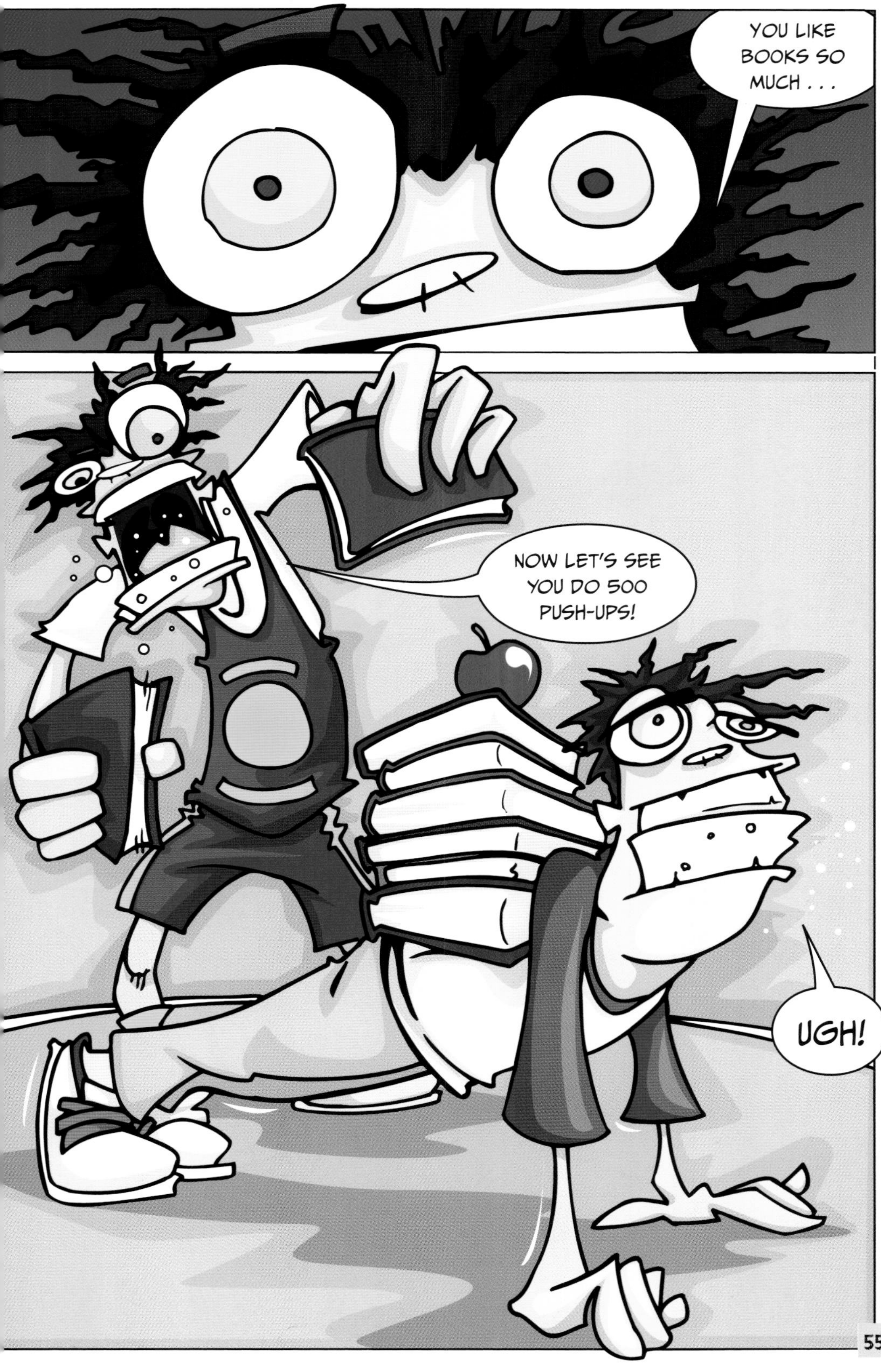
YOU LIKE BOOKS SO MUCH . . .
NOW LET'S SEE YOU DO 500 PUSH-UPS!
UGH!

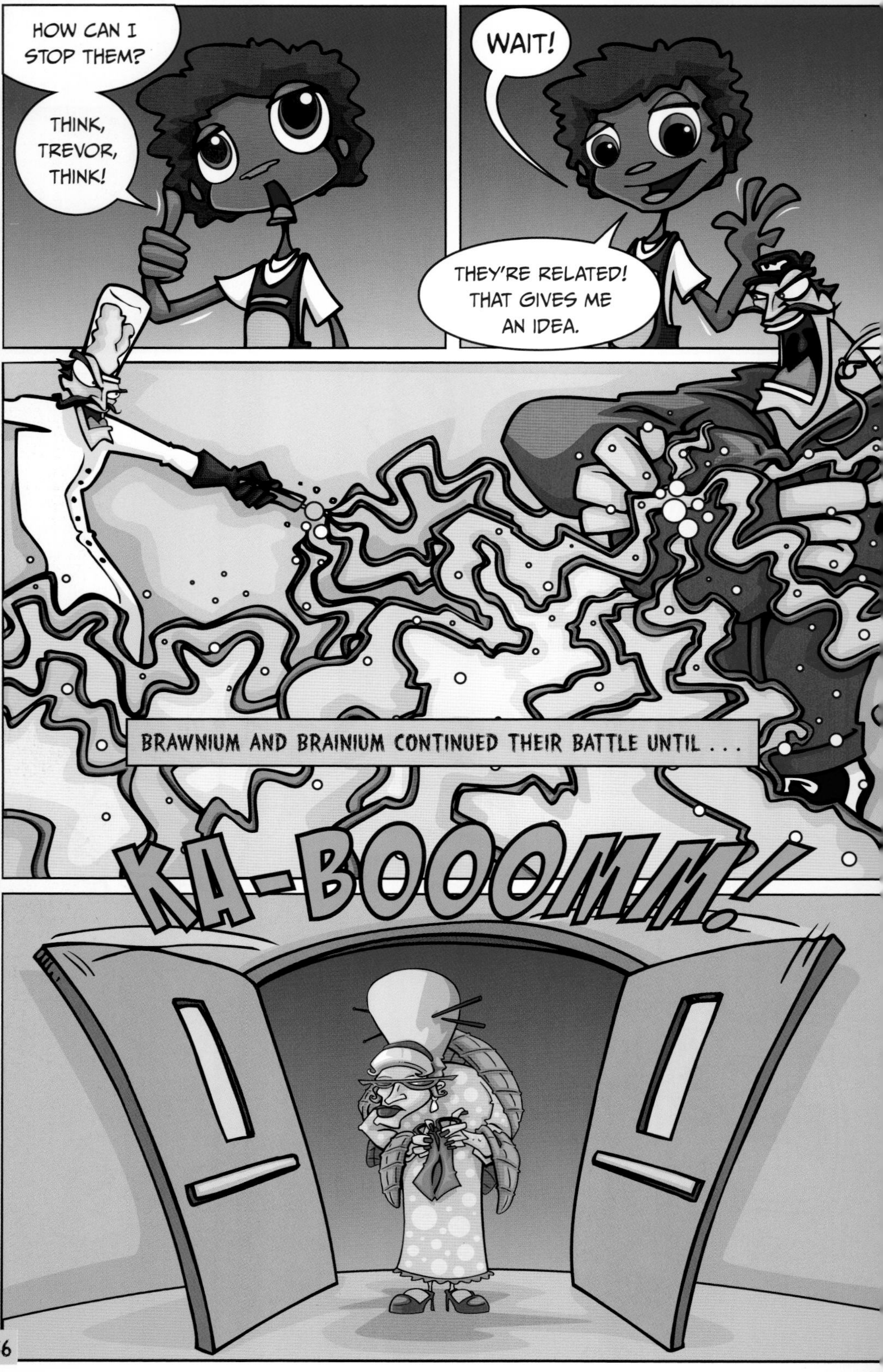
HOW CAN I STOP THEM?
THINK, TREVOR, THINK!
WAIT!
THEY'RE RELATED! THAT GIVES ME AN IDEA.
BRAWNIUM AND BRAINIUM CONTINUED THEIR BATTLE UNTIL . . .
KA-BOOOMM!

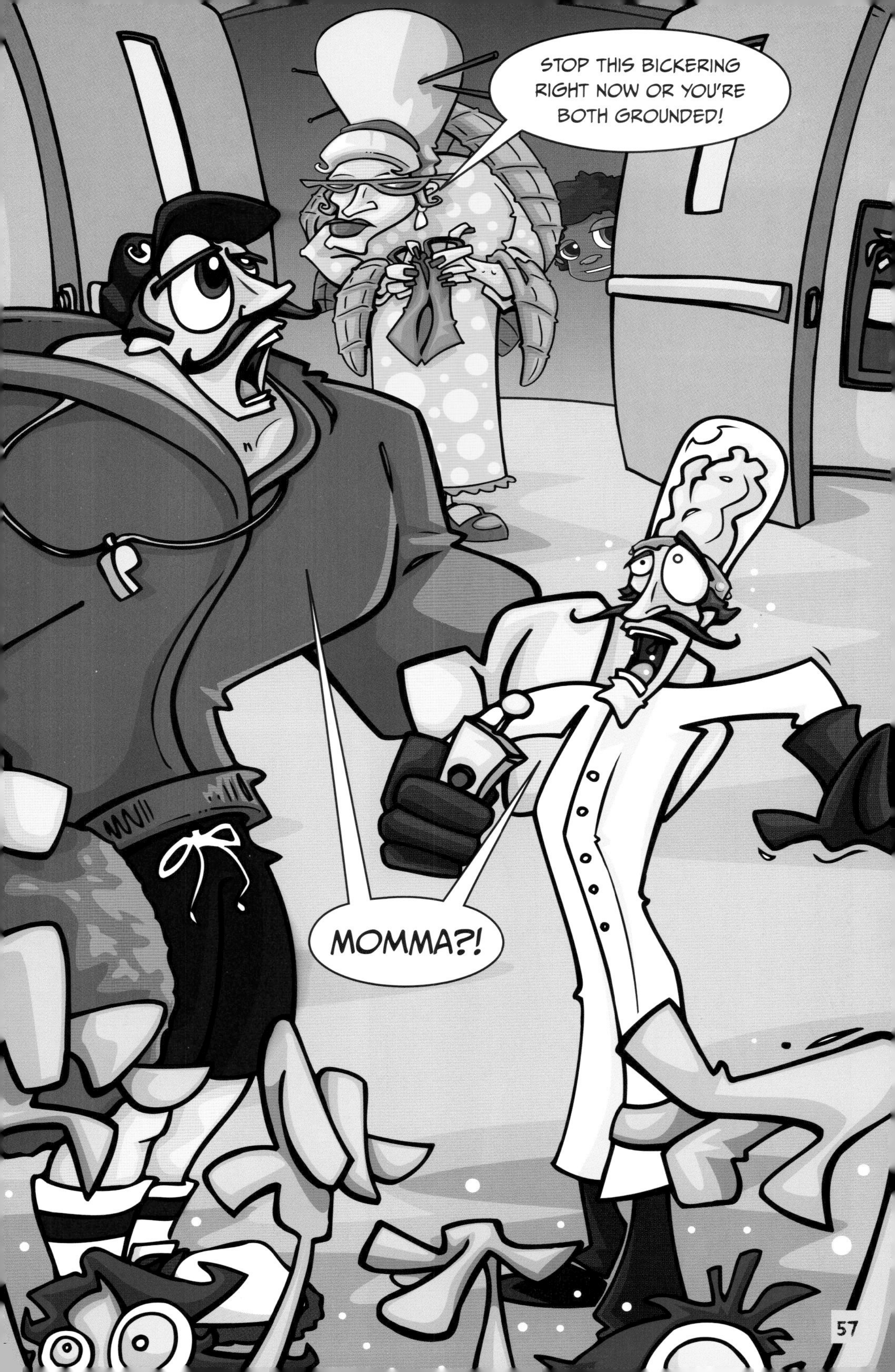
STOP THIS BICKERING RIGHT NOW OR YOU'RE BOTH GROUNDED!
MOMMA?!

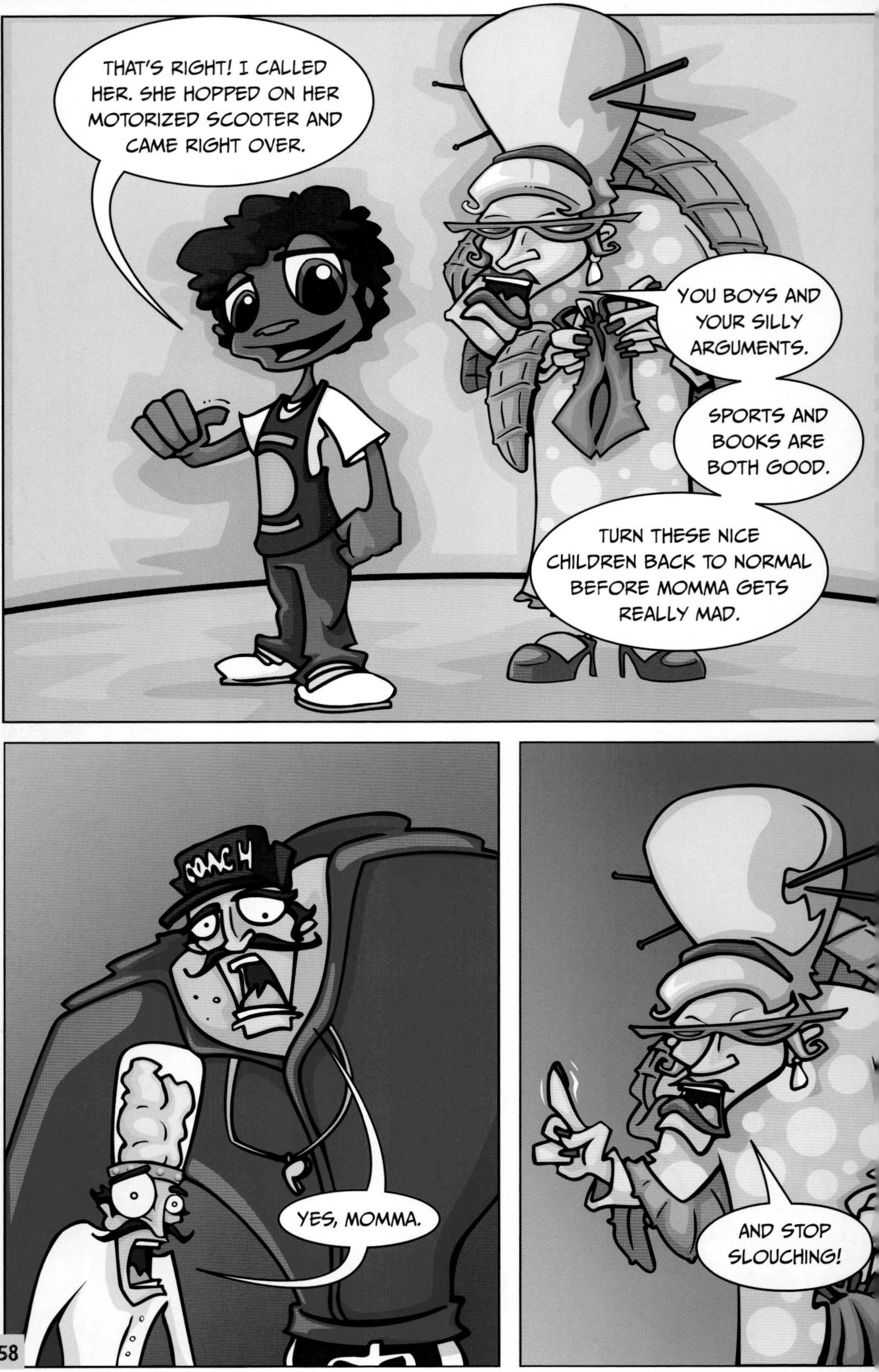
THAT'S RIGHT! I CALLED HER. SHE HOPPED ON HER MOTORIZED SCOOTER AND CAME RIGHT OVER.
YOU BOYS AND YOUR SILLY ARGUMENTS.
SPORTS AND BOOKS ARE BOTH GOOD.
TURN THESE NICE CHILDREN BACK TO NORMAL BEFORE MOMMA GETS REALLY MAD.
COACH
YES, MOMMA.
AND STOP SLOUCHING!

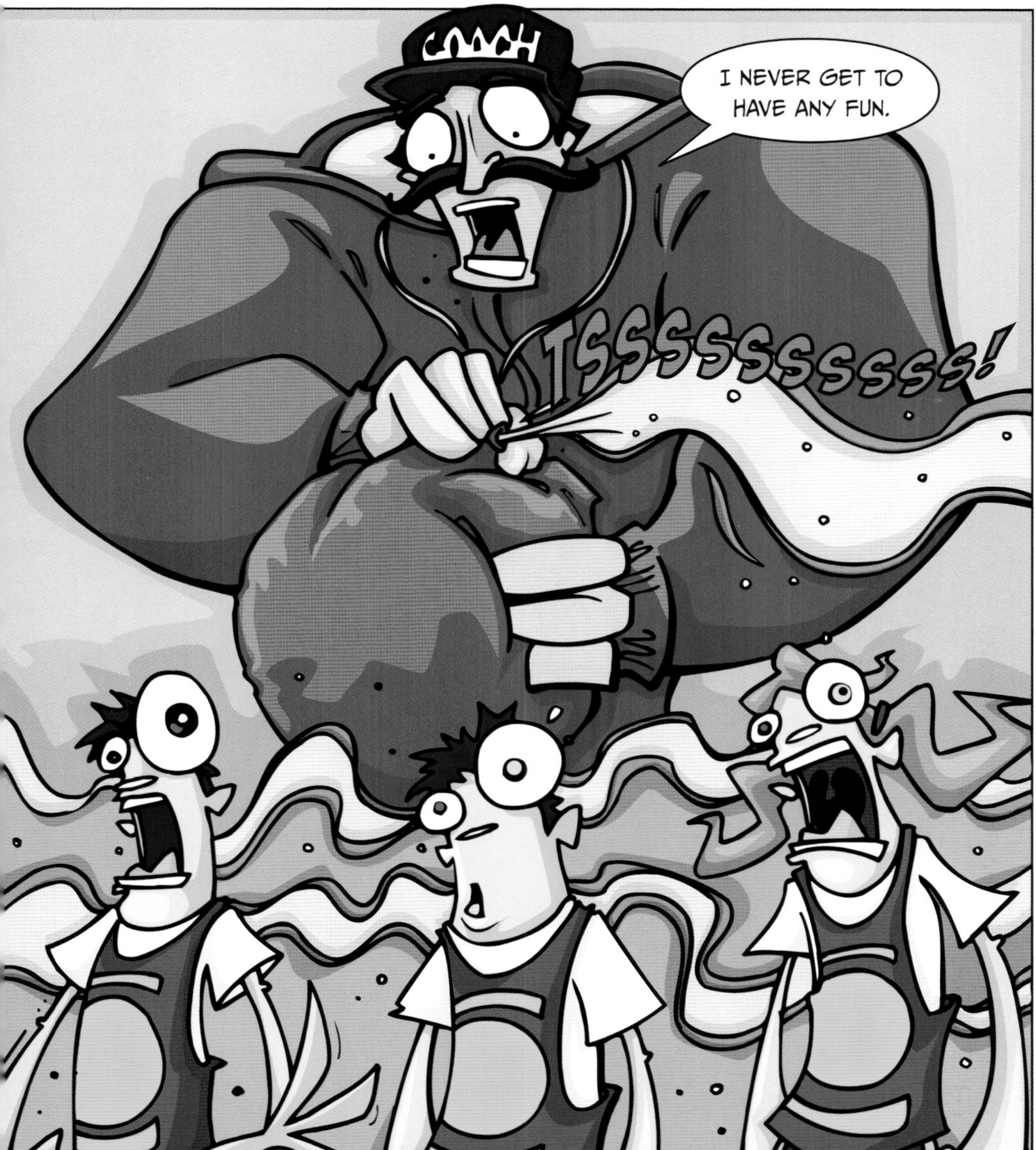
COACH
I NEVER GET TO HAVE ANY FUN.
TSSSSSSSSSSS!

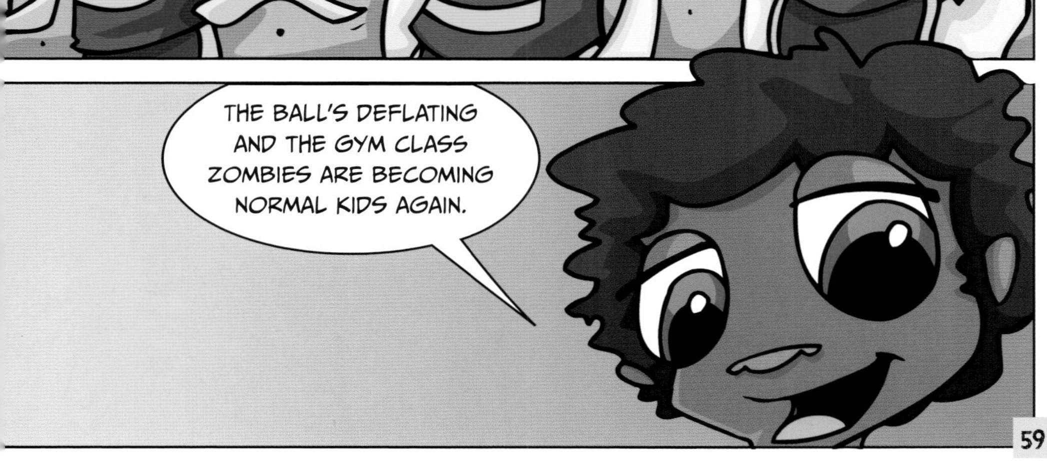
THE BALL'S DEFLATING AND THE GYM CLASS ZOMBIES ARE BECOMING NORMAL KIDS AGAIN.

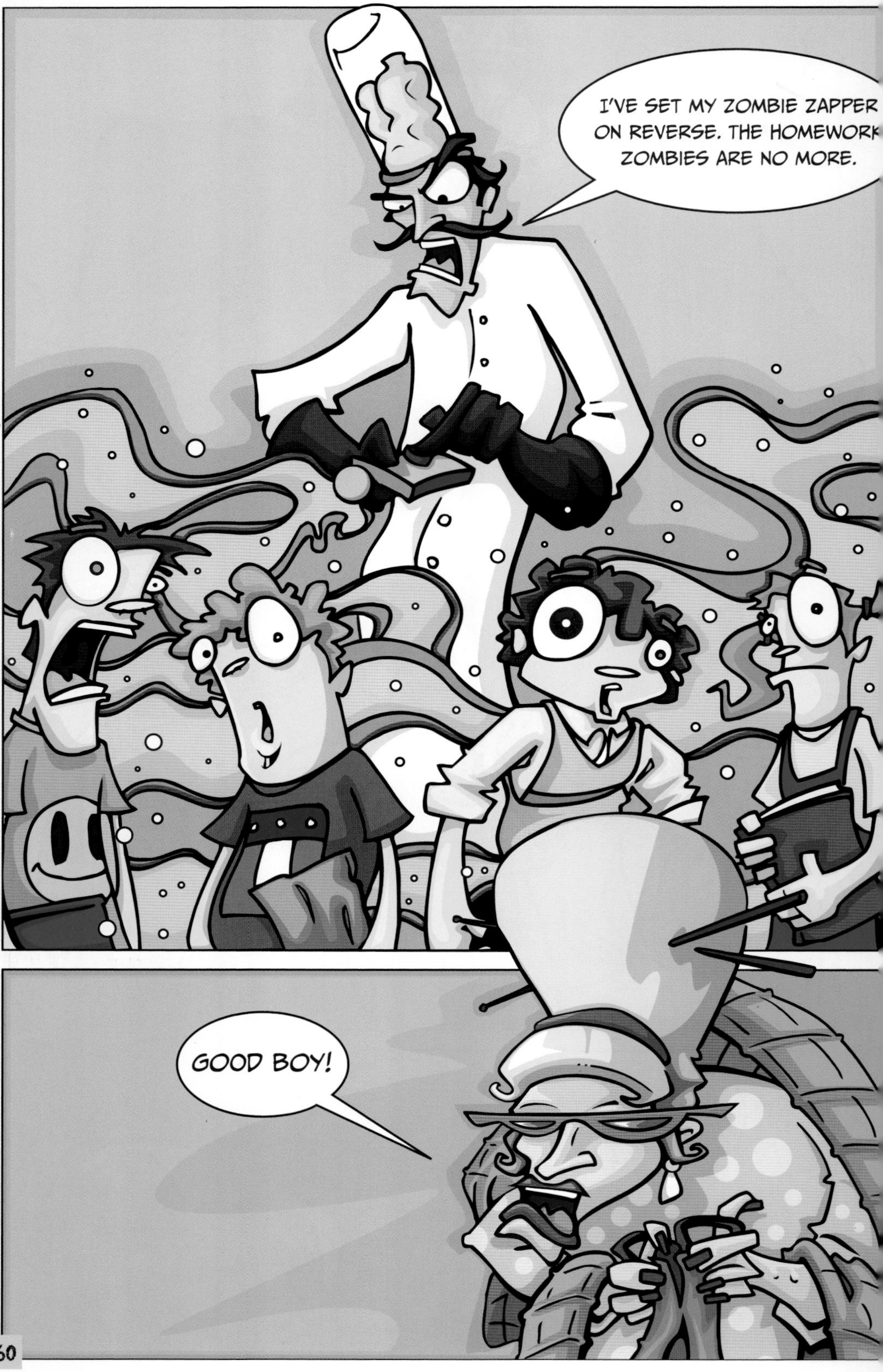
I'VE SET MY ZOMBIE ZAPPER ON REVERSE. THE HOMEWORK ZOMBIES ARE NO MORE.
GOOD BOY!

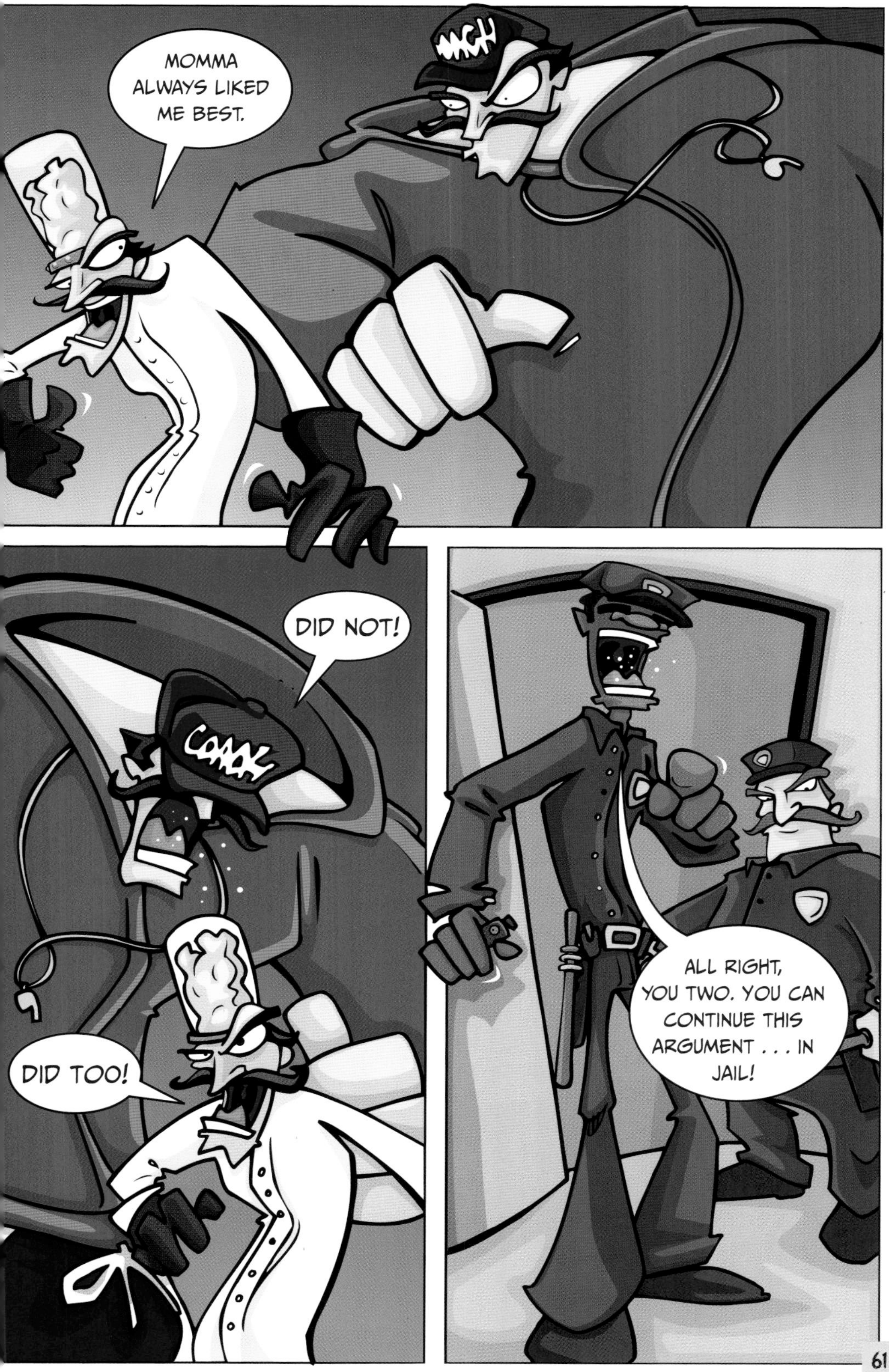
MOMMA ALWAYS LIKED ME BEST.
DID NOT!
DID TOO!
ALL RIGHT, YOU TWO. YOU CAN CONTINUE THIS ARGUMENT . . . IN JAIL!

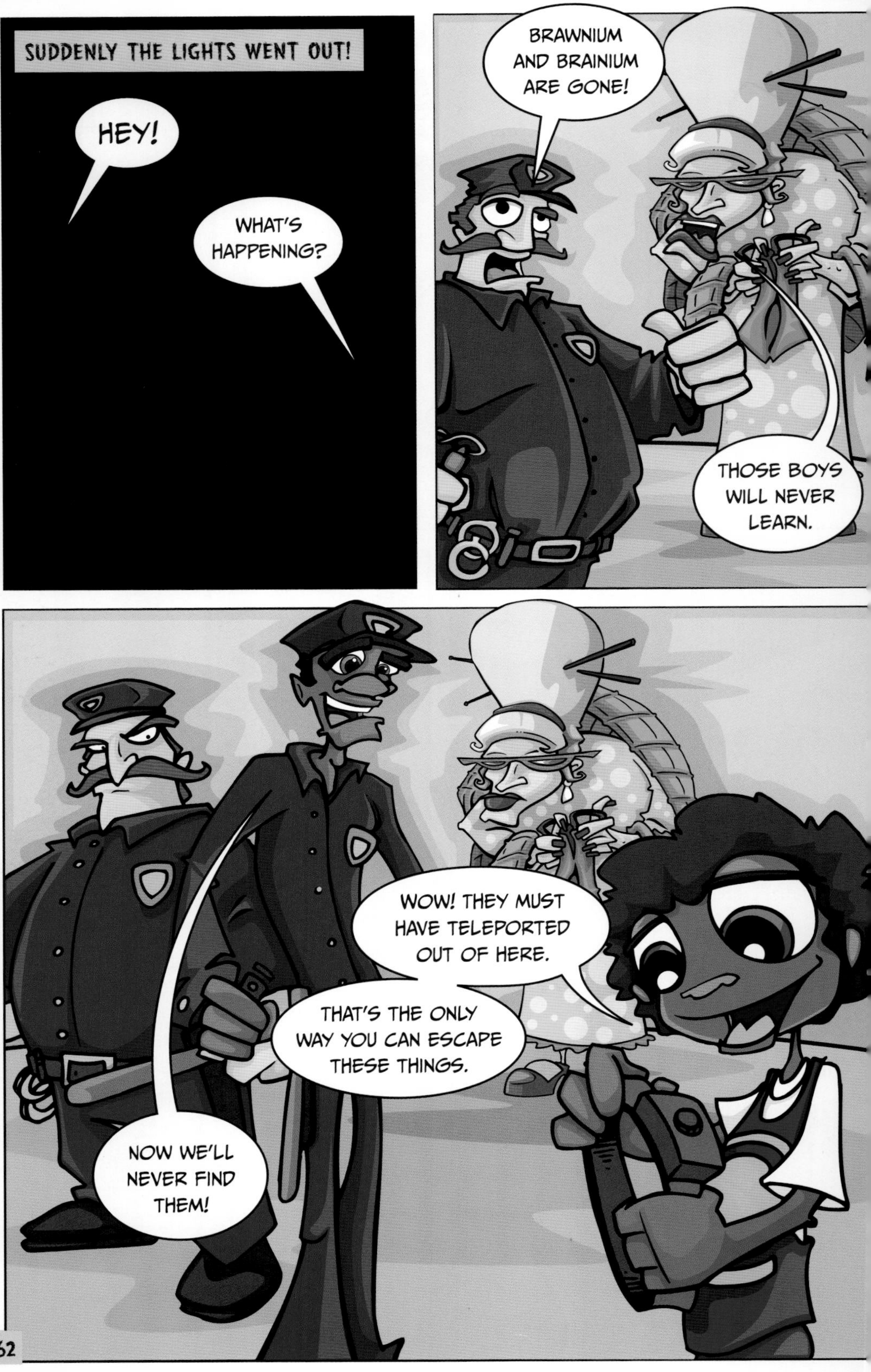
SUDDENLY THE LIGHTS WENT OUT!
HEY!
WHAT'S HAPPENING?
BRAWNIUM AND BRAINIUM ARE GONE!
THOSE BOYS WILL NEVER LEARN.
NOW WE'LL NEVER FIND THEM!
WOW! THEY MUST HAVE TELEPORTED OUT OF HERE.
THAT'S THE ONLY WAY YOU CAN ESCAPE THESE THINGS.

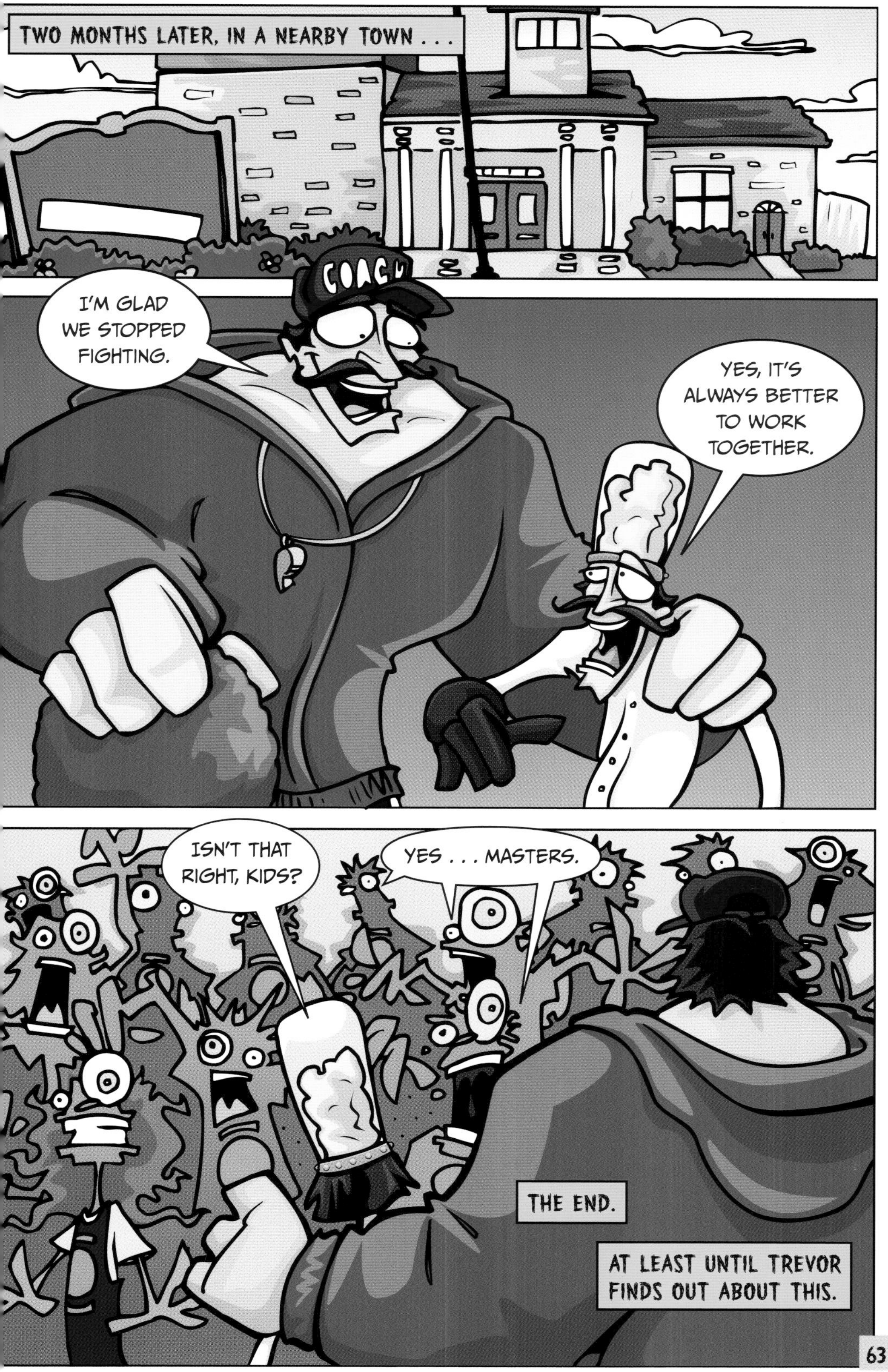
TWO MONTHS LATER, IN A NEARBY TOWN . . .
I'M GLAD WE STOPPED FIGHTING.
YES, IT'S ALWAYS BETTER TO WORK TOGETHER.
ISN'T THAT RIGHT, KIDS?
YES . . . MASTERS.
THE END.
AT LEAST UNTIL TREVOR FINDS OUT ABOUT THIS.

DAY OF THE FIELD TRIP ZOMBIES

BY SCOTT NICKEL
ILLUSTRATED BY CEDRIC HOHNSTADT

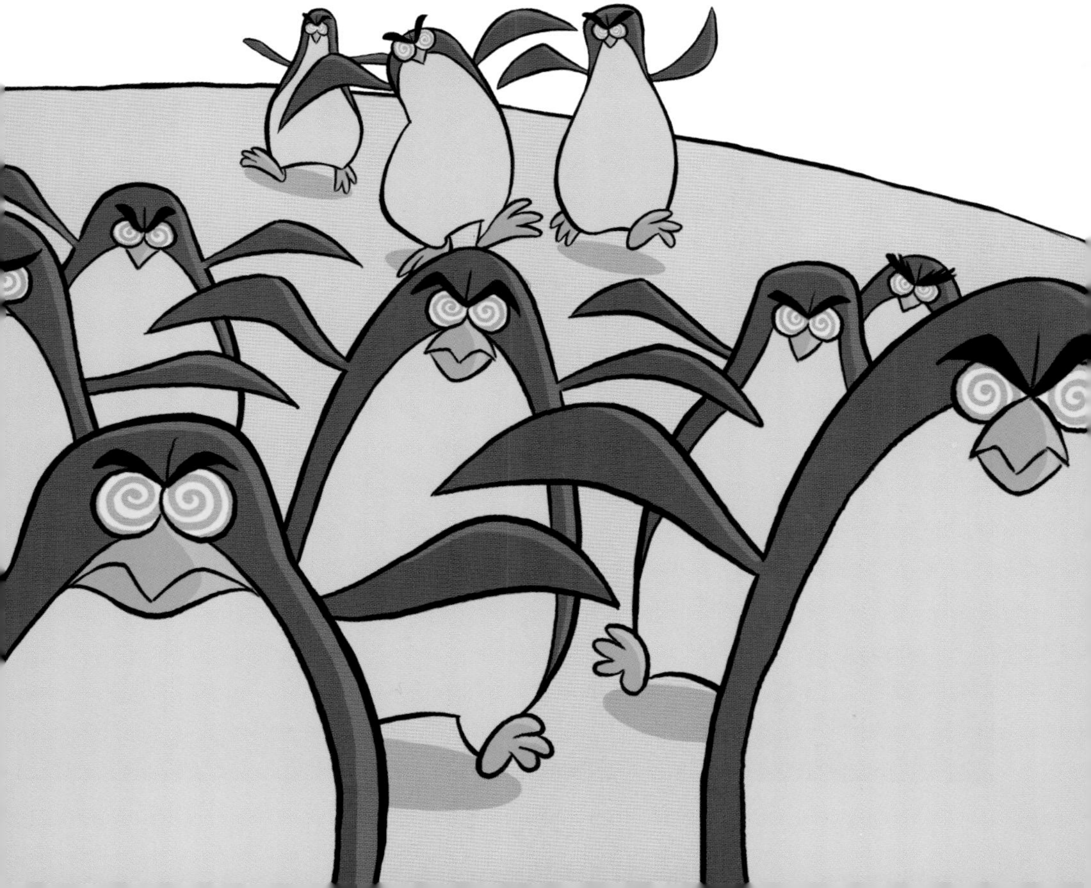

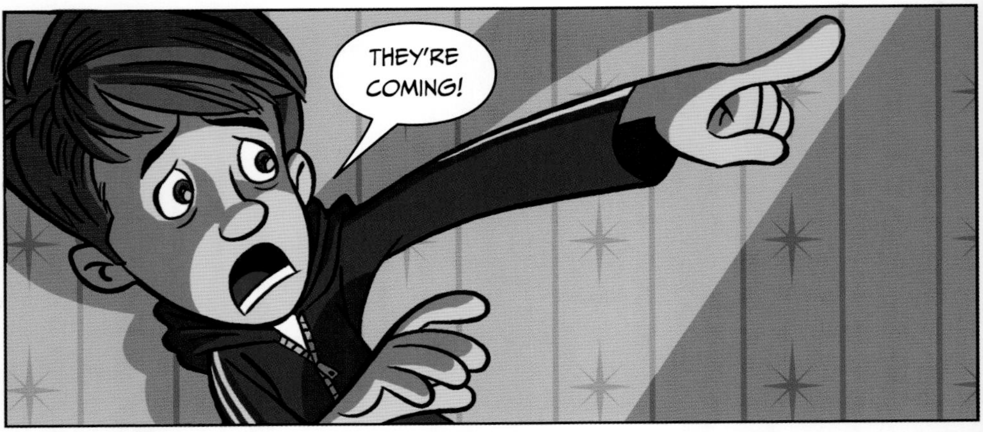
THEY'RE COMING!

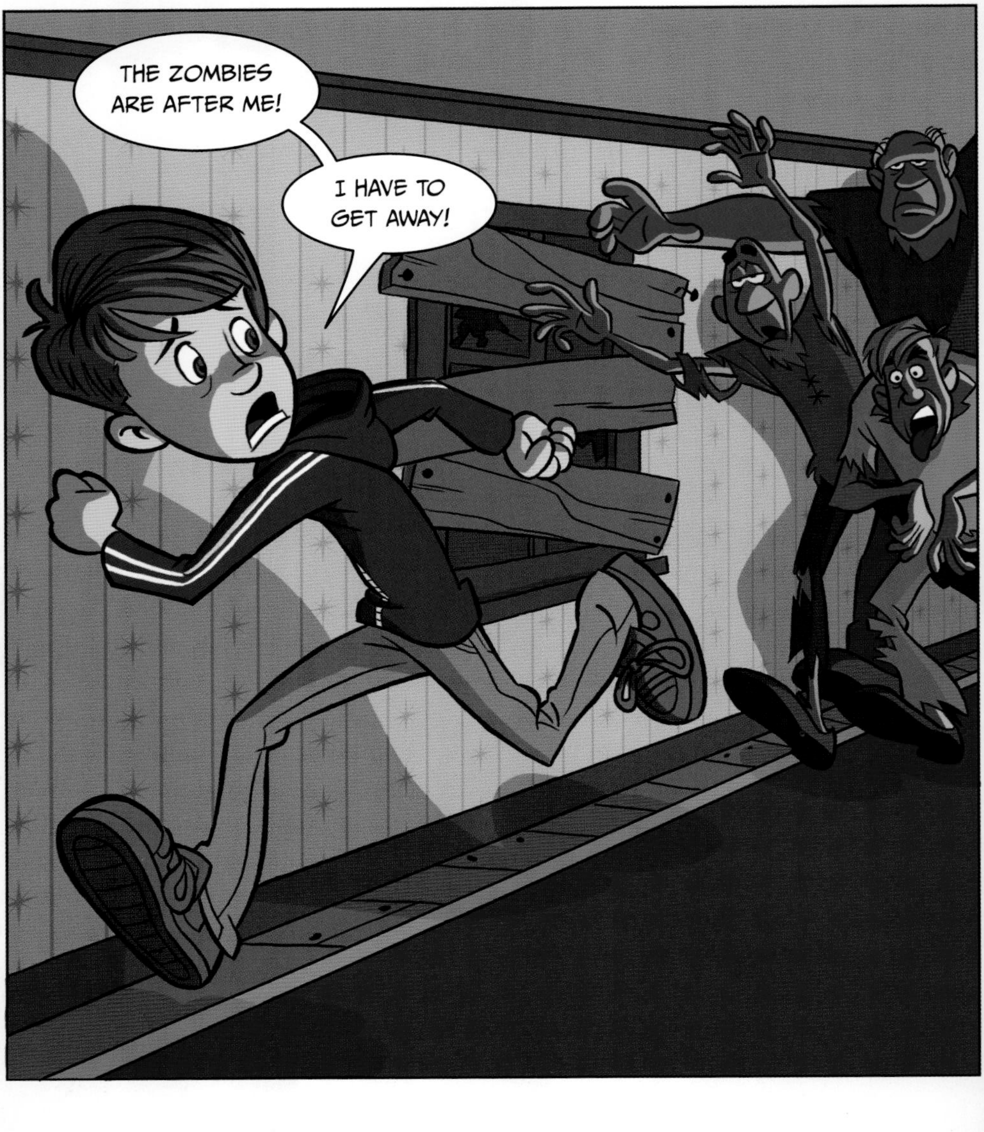
THE ZOMBIES ARE AFTER ME!
I HAVE TO GET AWAY!

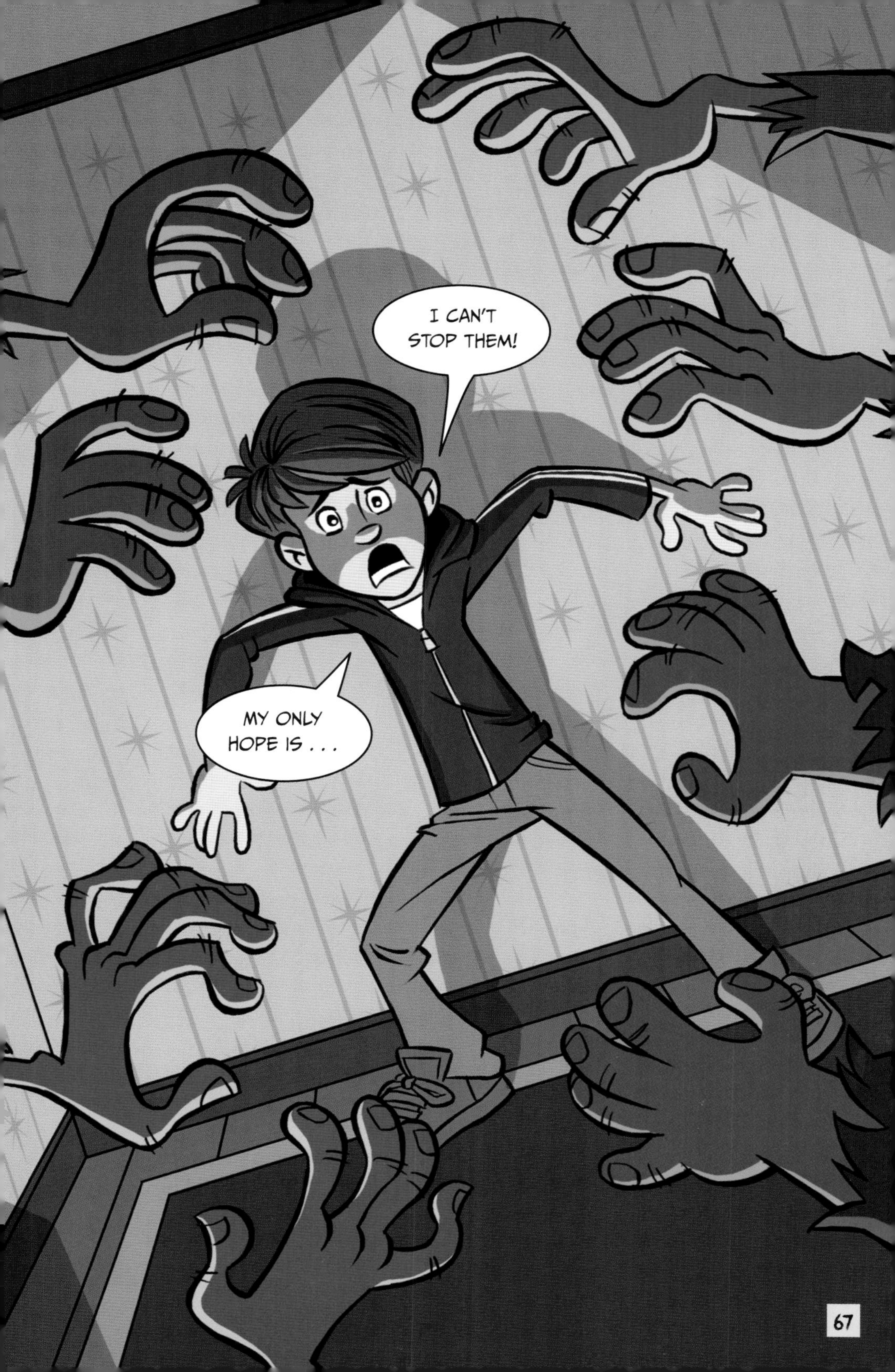
I CAN'T STOP THEM!
MY ONLY HOPE IS . . .

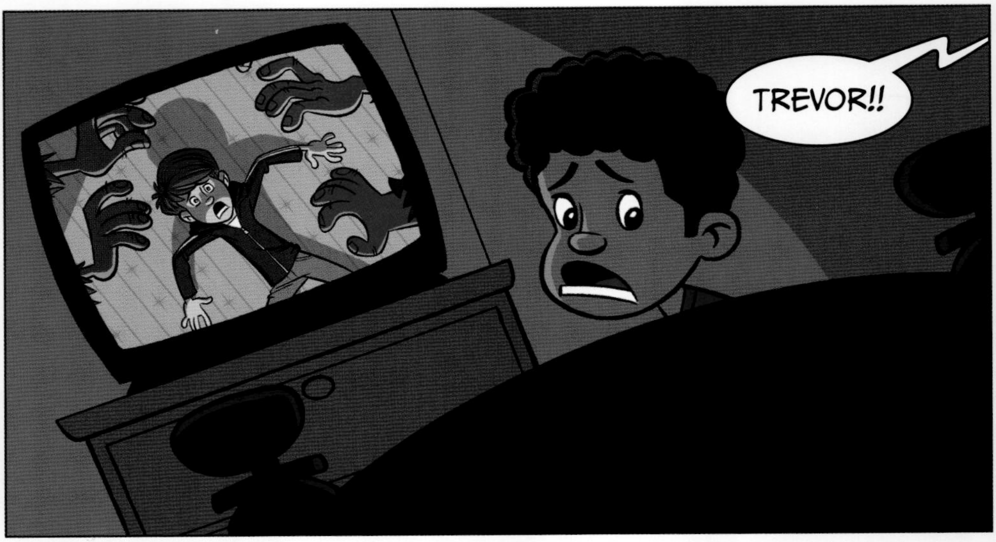
TREVOR!!

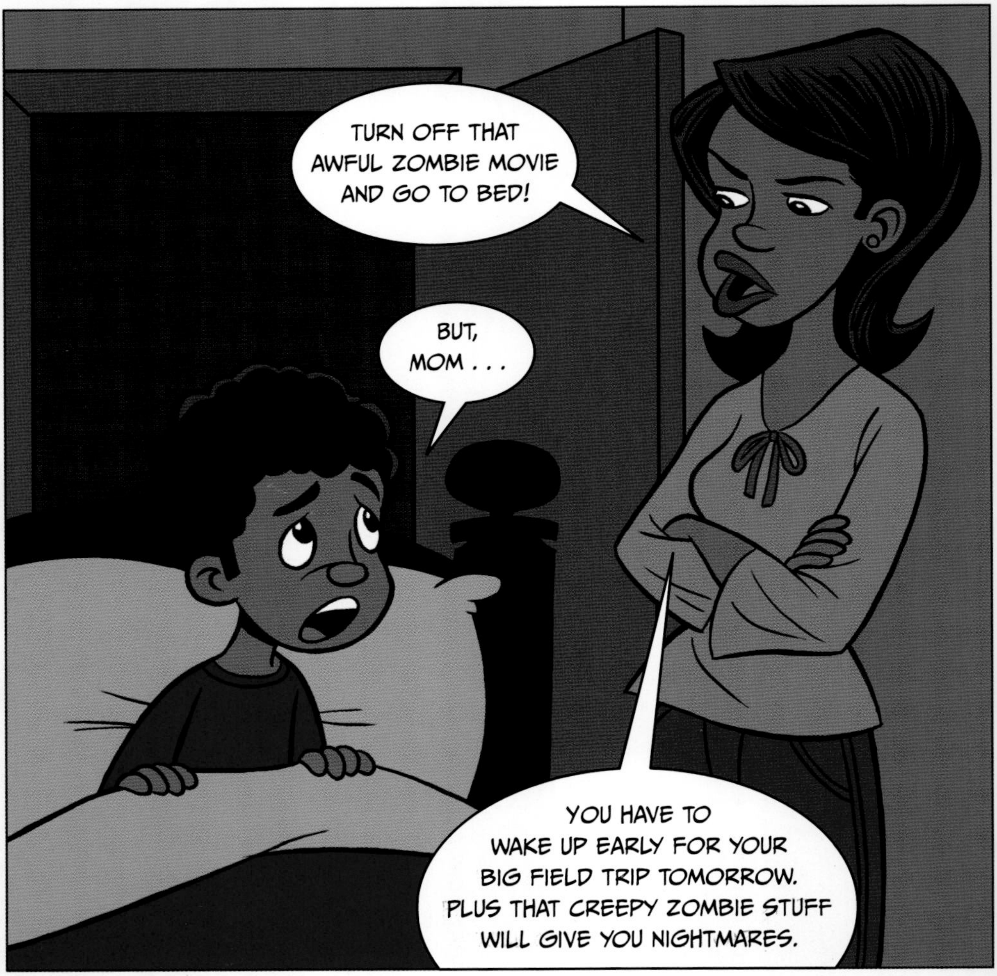
TURN OFF THAT AWFUL ZOMBIE MOVIE AND GO TO BED!
BUT, MOM . . .
YOU HAVE TO WAKE UP EARLY FOR YOUR BIG FIELD TRIP TOMORROW. PLUS THAT CREEPY ZOMBIE STUFF WILL GIVE YOU NIGHTMARES.

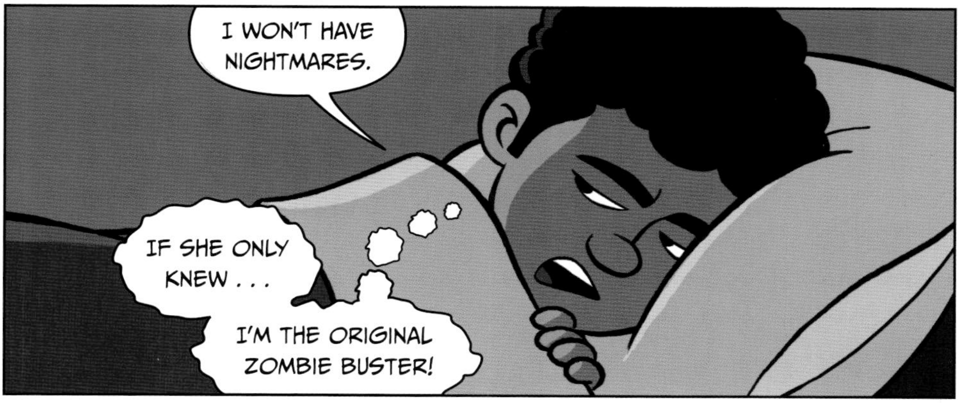
I WON'T HAVE NIGHTMARES.
IF SHE ONLY KNEW . . .
I'M THE ORIGINAL ZOMBIE BUSTER!

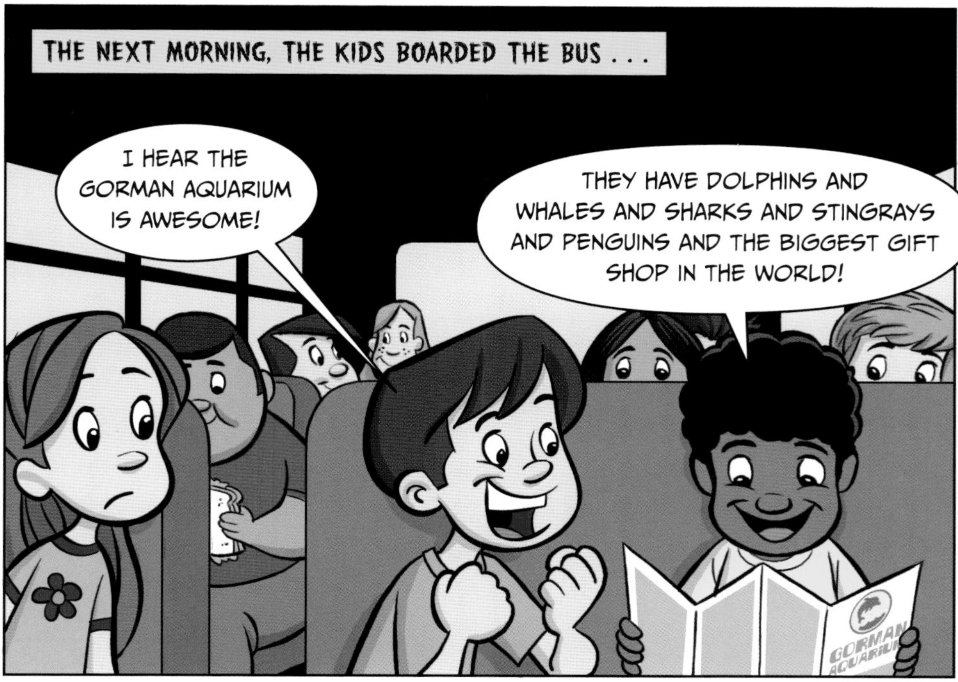
THE NEXT MORNING, THE KIDS BOARDED THE BUS . . .
I HEAR THE GORMAN AQUARIUM IS AWESOME!
THEY HAVE DOLPHINS AND WHALES AND SHARKS AND STINGRAYS AND PENGUINS AND THE BIGGEST GIFT SHOP IN THE WORLD!
GORMAN AQUARIUM

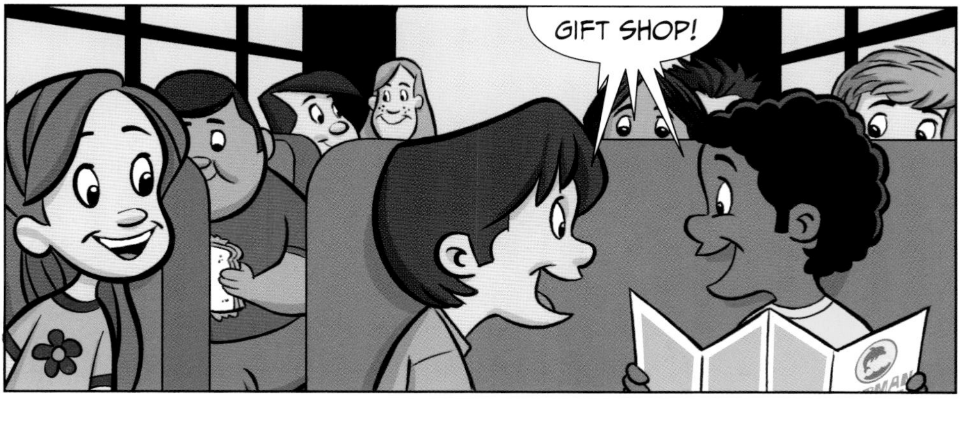
GIFT SHOP!

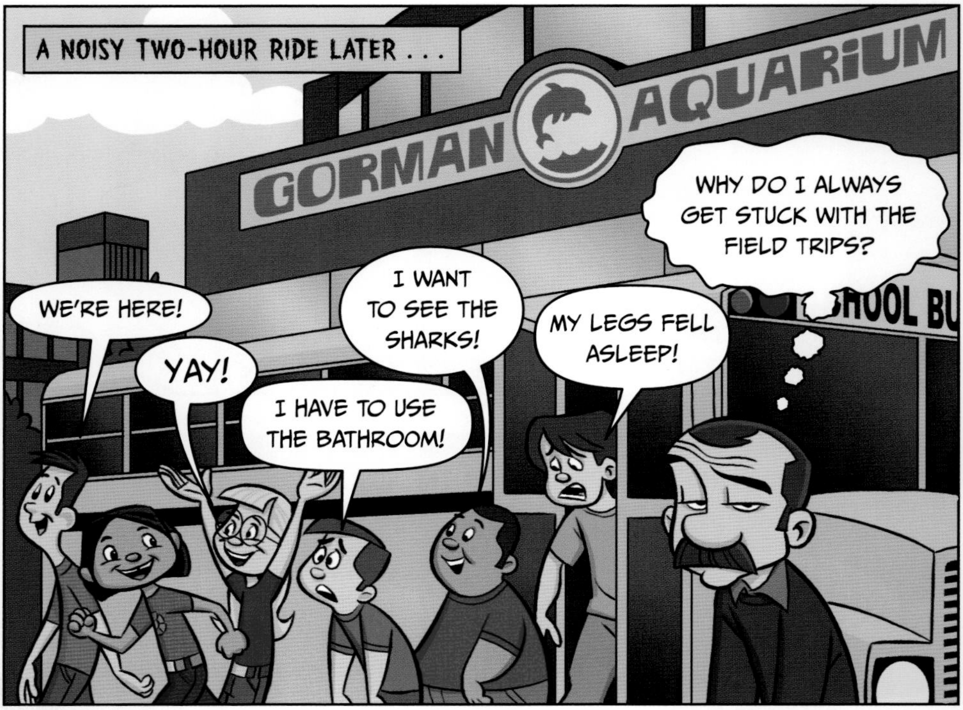
A NOISY TWO-HOUR RIDE LATER . . .
GORMAN AQUARIUM
WHY DO I ALWAYS GET STUCK WITH THE FIELD TRIPS?
WE'RE HERE!
YAY!
I WANT TO SEE THE SHARKS!
I HAVE TO USE THE BATHROOM!
MY LEGS FELL ASLEEP!

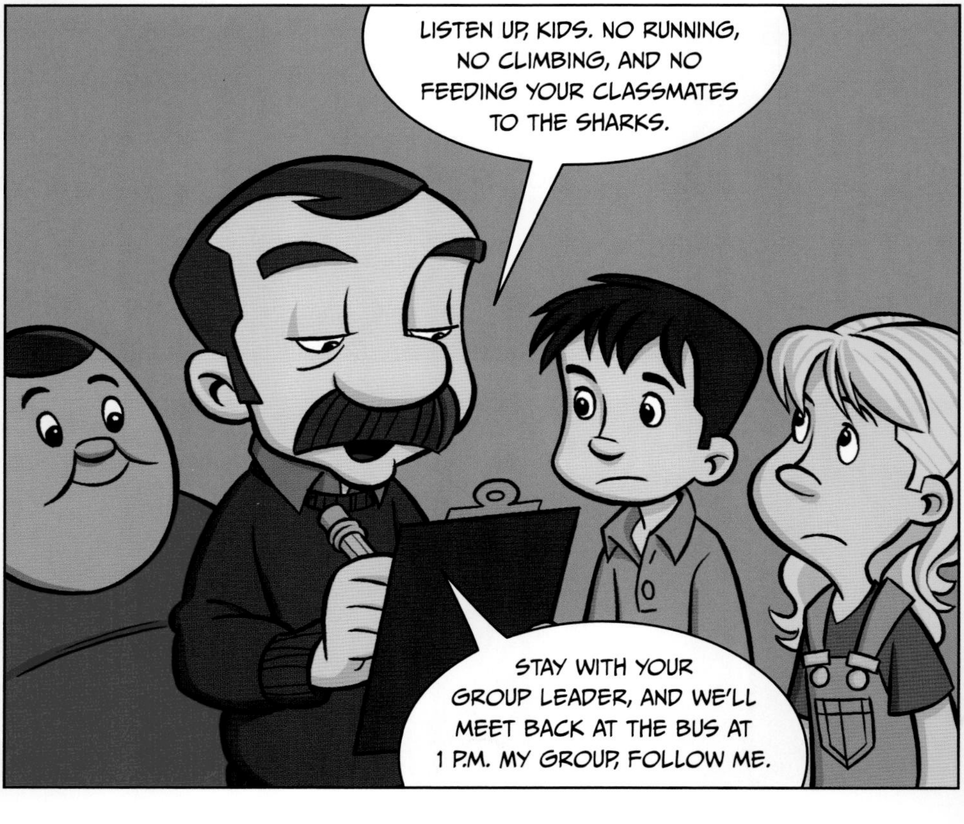
LISTEN UP, KIDS. NO RUNNING, NO CLIMBING, AND NO FEEDING YOUR CLASSMATES TO THE SHARKS.
STAY WITH YOUR GROUP LEADER, AND WE'LL MEET BACK AT THE BUS AT 1 P.M. MY GROUP, FOLLOW ME.

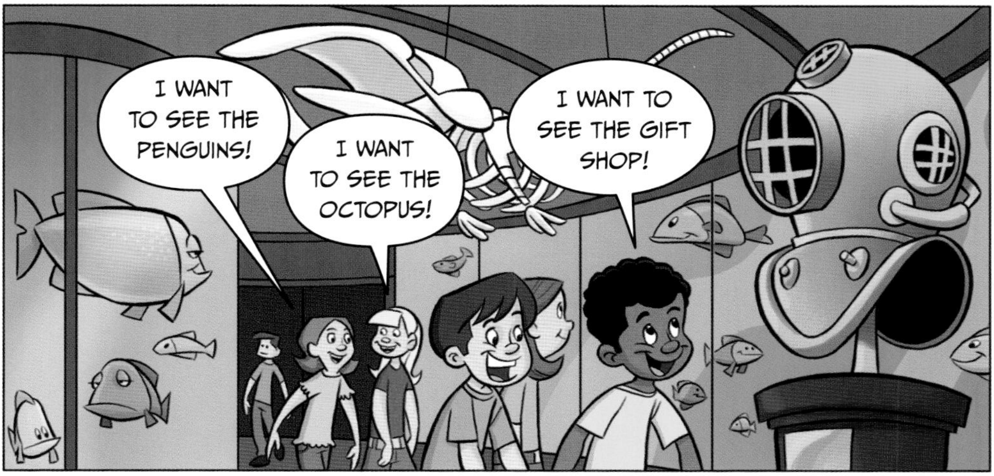
I WANT TO SEE THE PENGUINS!
I WANT TO SEE THE OCTOPUS!
I WANT TO SEE THE GIFT SHOP!

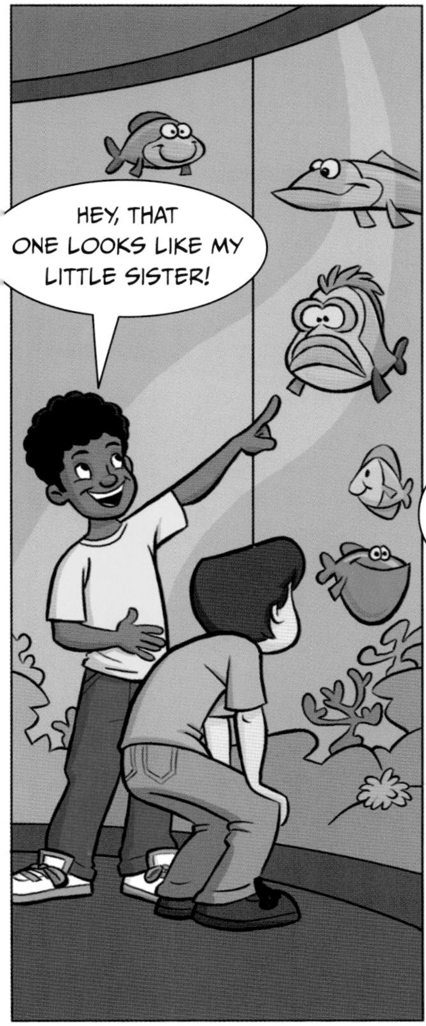
HEY, THAT ONE LOOKS LIKE MY LITTLE SISTER!

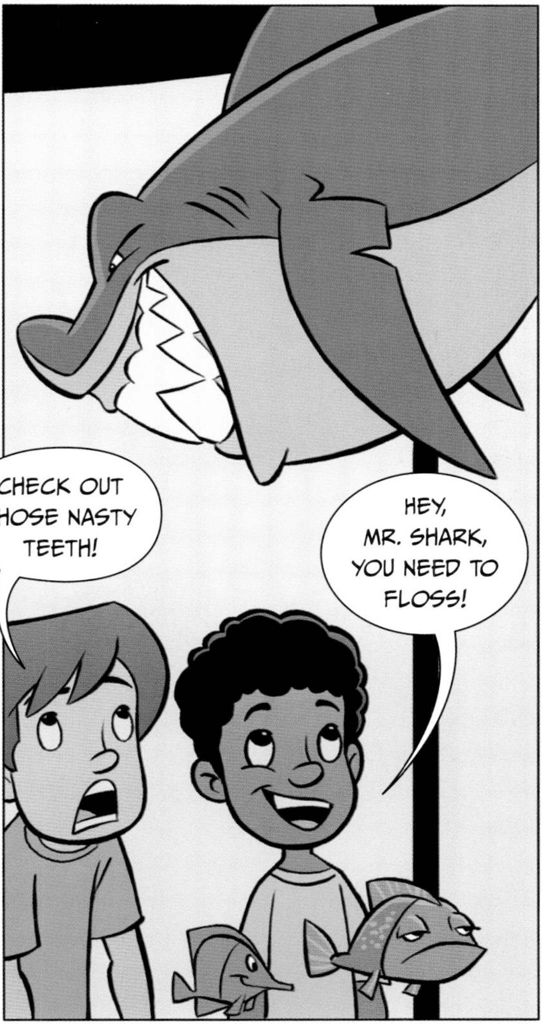
CHECK OUT THOSE NASTY TEETH!
HEY, MR. SHARK, YOU NEED TO FLOSS!

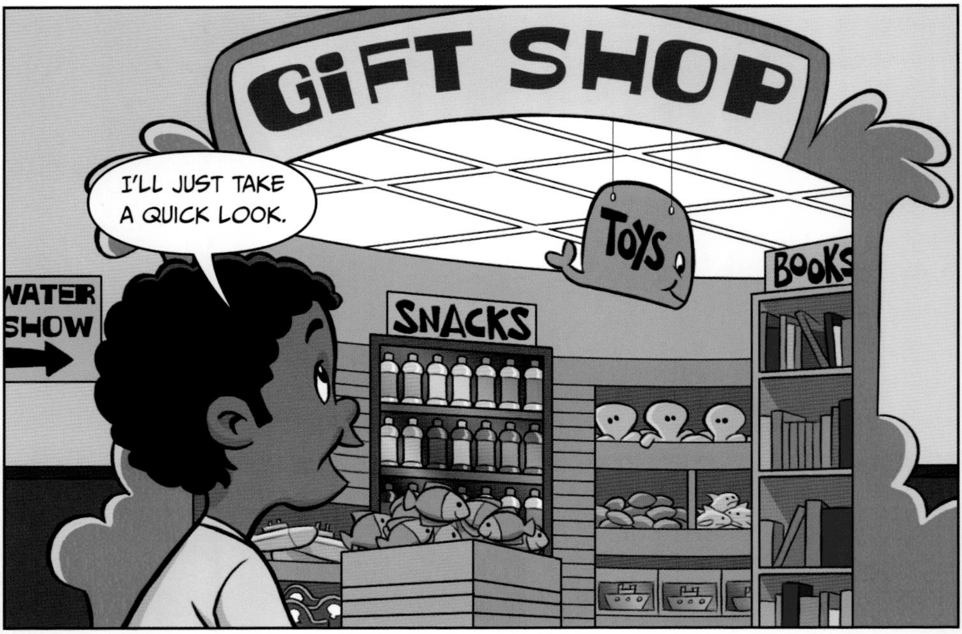
GIFT SHOP
I'LL JUST TAKE A QUICK LOOK.
WATER SHOW
TOYS
BOOKS
SNACKS

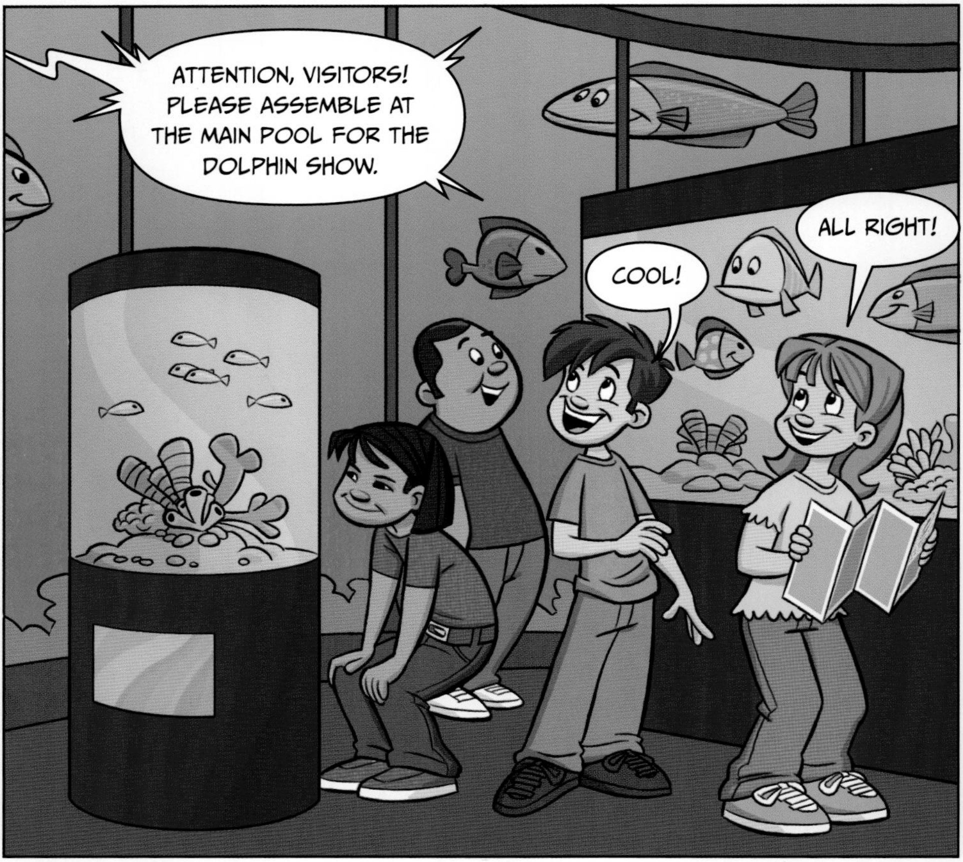
ATTENTION, VISITORS! PLEASE ASSEMBLE AT THE MAIN POOL FOR THE DOLPHIN SHOW.
COOL!
ALL RIGHT!

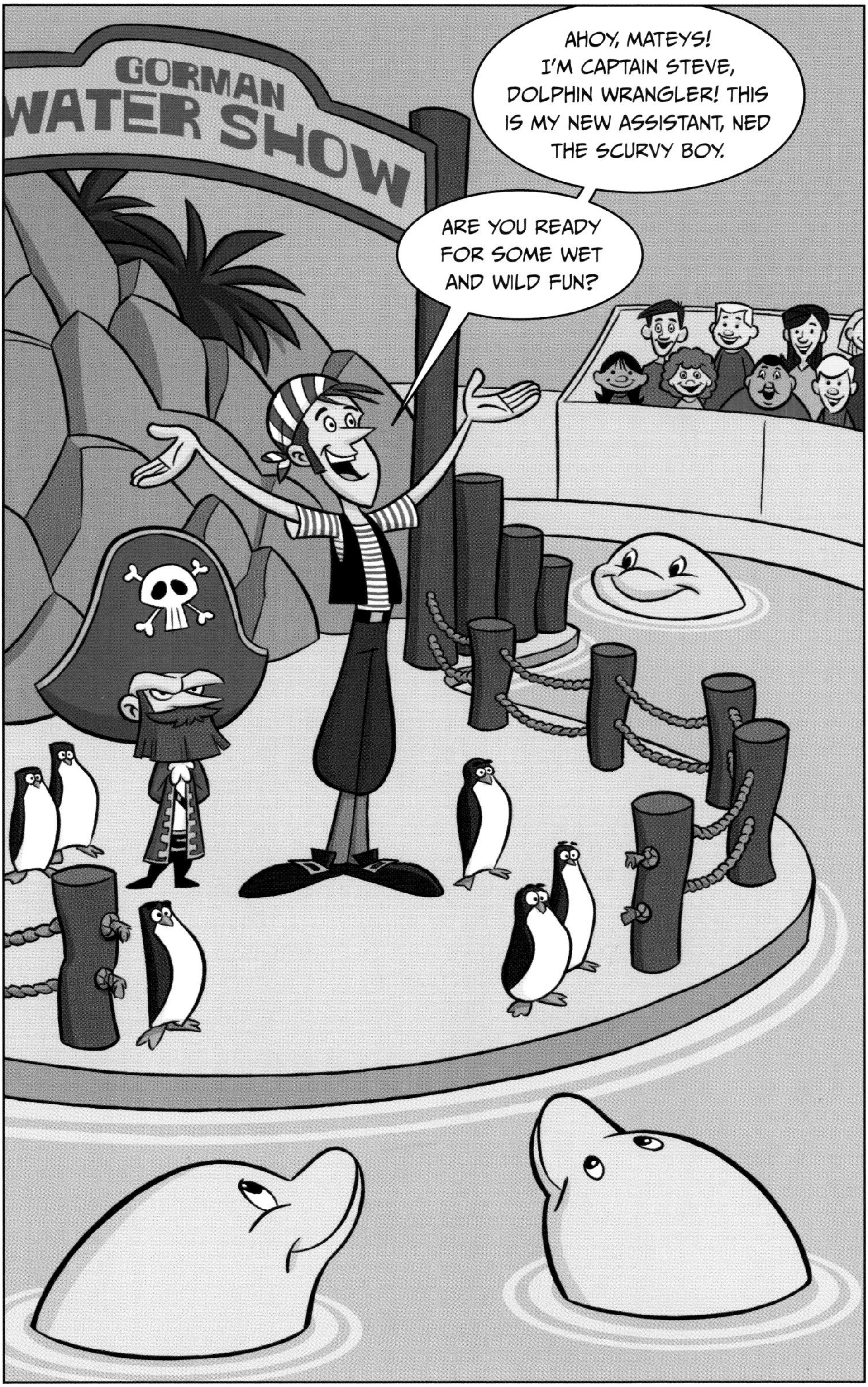
GORMAN WATER SHOW
AHOY, MATEYS! I'M CAPTAIN STEVE, DOLPHIN WRANGLER! THIS IS MY NEW ASSISTANT, NED THE SCURVY BOY.
ARE YOU READY FOR SOME WET AND WILD FUN?

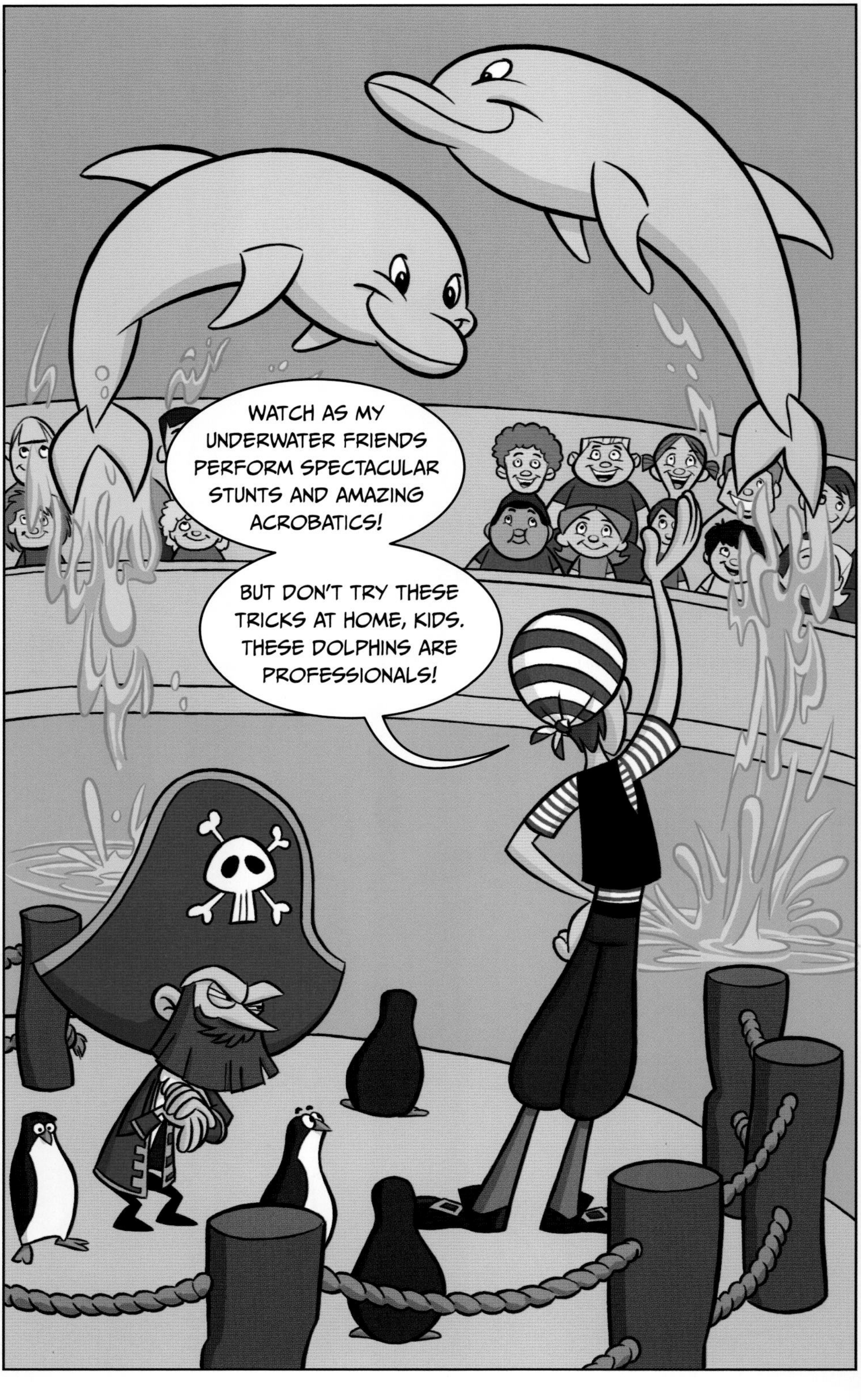
WATCH AS MY UNDERWATER FRIENDS PERFORM SPECTACULAR STUNTS AND AMAZING ACROBATICS!
BUT DON'T TRY THESE TRICKS AT HOME, KIDS. THESE DOLPHINS ARE PROFESSIONALS!

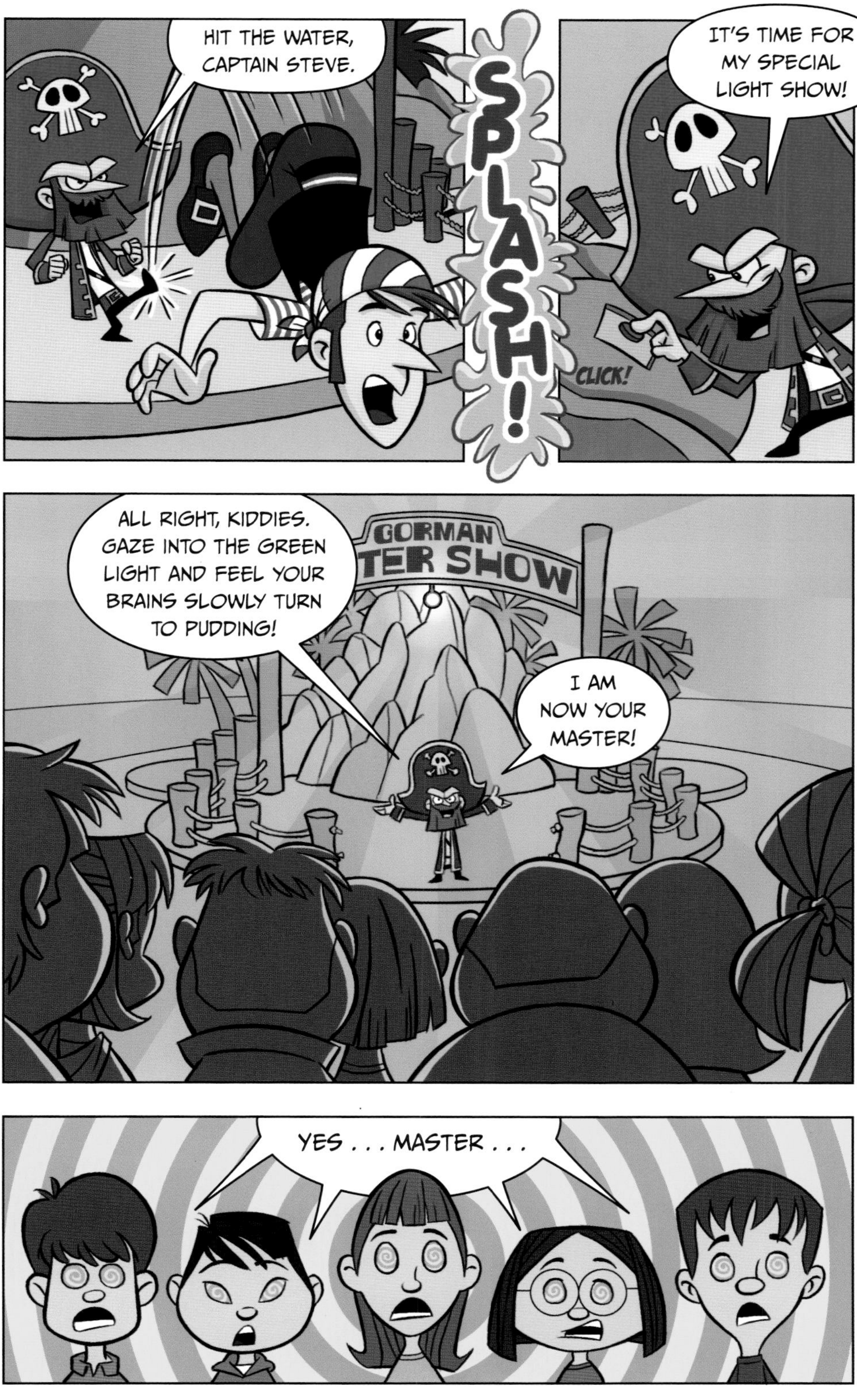
HIT THE WATER, CAPTAIN STEVE.
SPLASH!
IT'S TIME FOR MY SPECIAL LIGHT SHOW!
CLICK!
ALL RIGHT, KIDDIES. GAZE INTO THE GREEN LIGHT AND FEEL YOUR BRAINS SLOWLY TURN TO PUDDING!
GORMAN
TER SHOW
I AM NOW YOUR MASTER!
YES . . . MASTER . . .

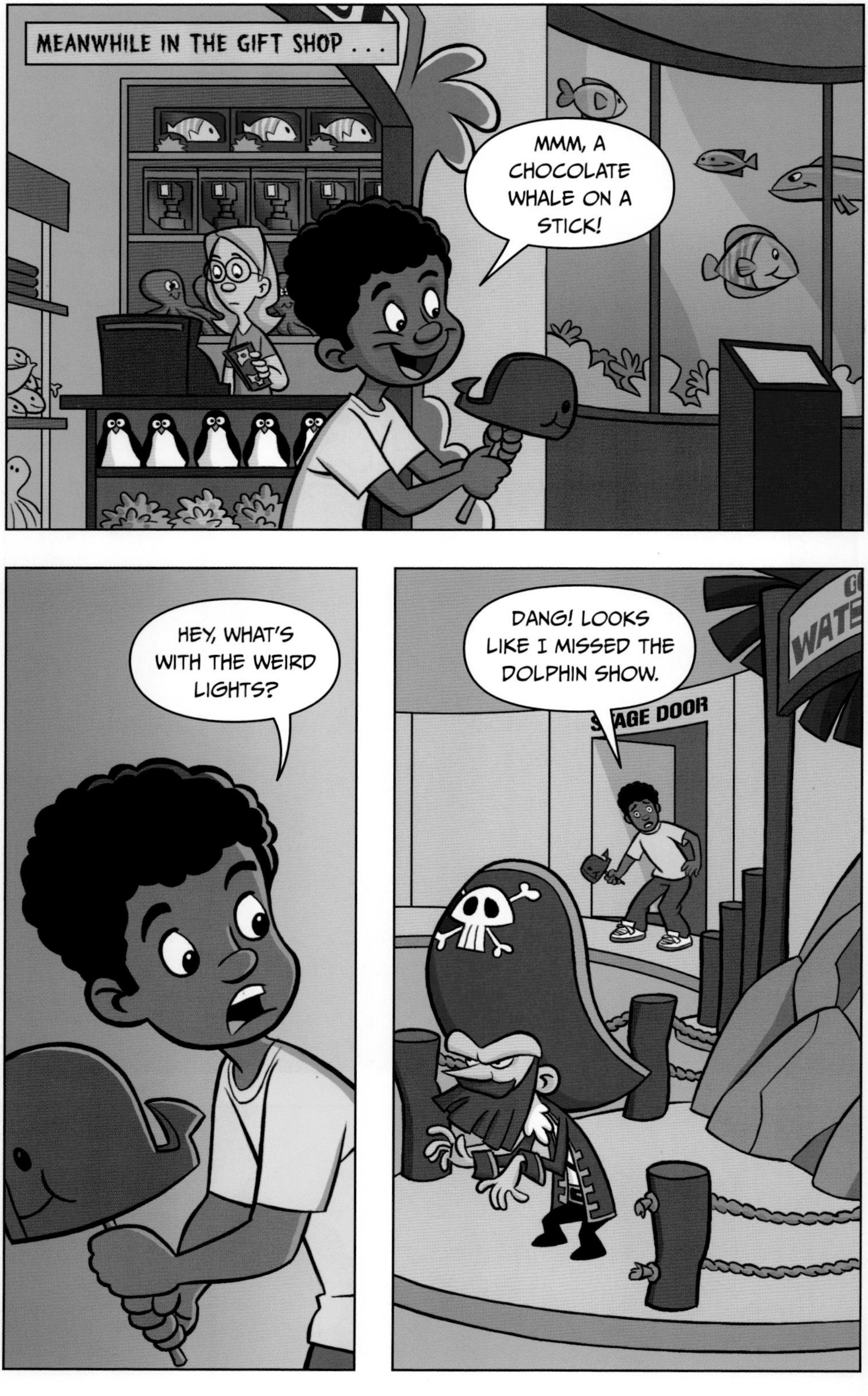
MEANWHILE IN THE GIFT SHOP . . .
MMM, A CHOCOLATE WHALE ON A STICK!
HEY, WHAT'S WITH THE WEIRD LIGHTS?
DANG! LOOKS LIKE I MISSED THE DOLPHIN SHOW.

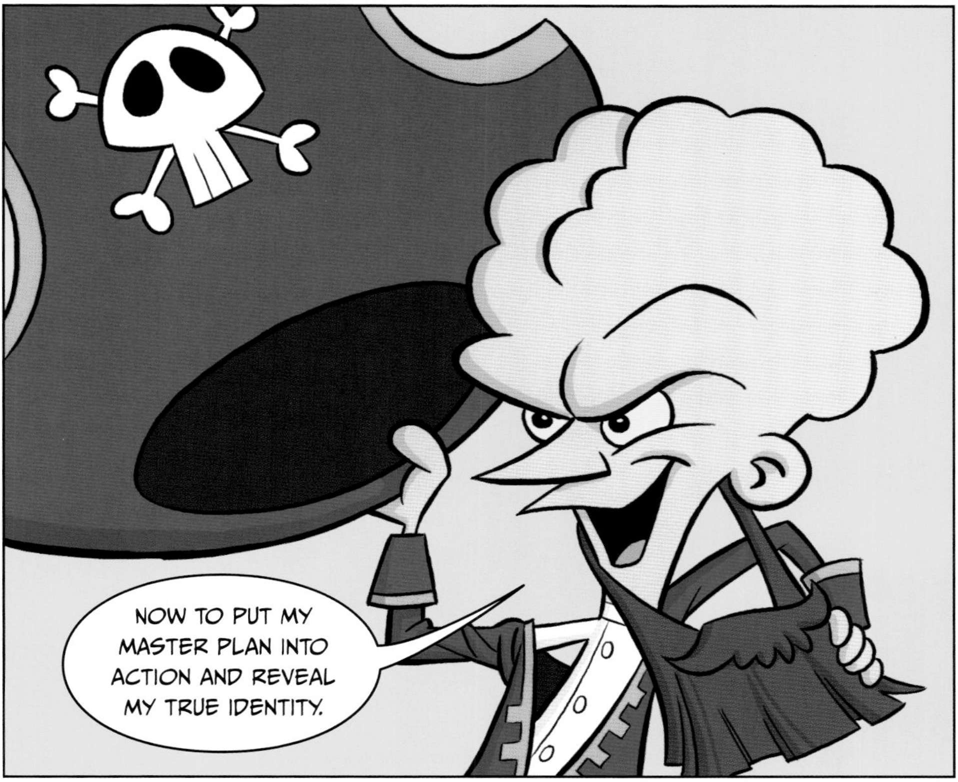
NOW TO PUT MY MASTER PLAN INTO ACTION AND REVEAL MY TRUE IDENTITY.

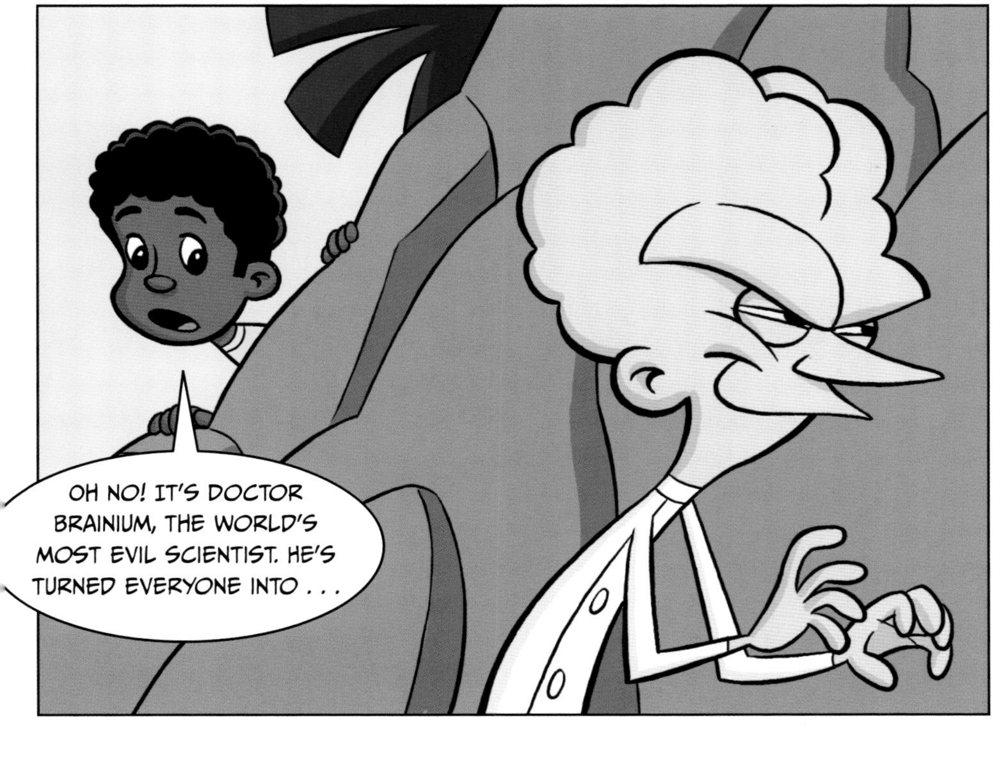
OH NO! IT'S DOCTOR BRAINIUM, THE WORLD'S MOST EVIL SCIENTIST. HE'S TURNED EVERYONE INTO . . .

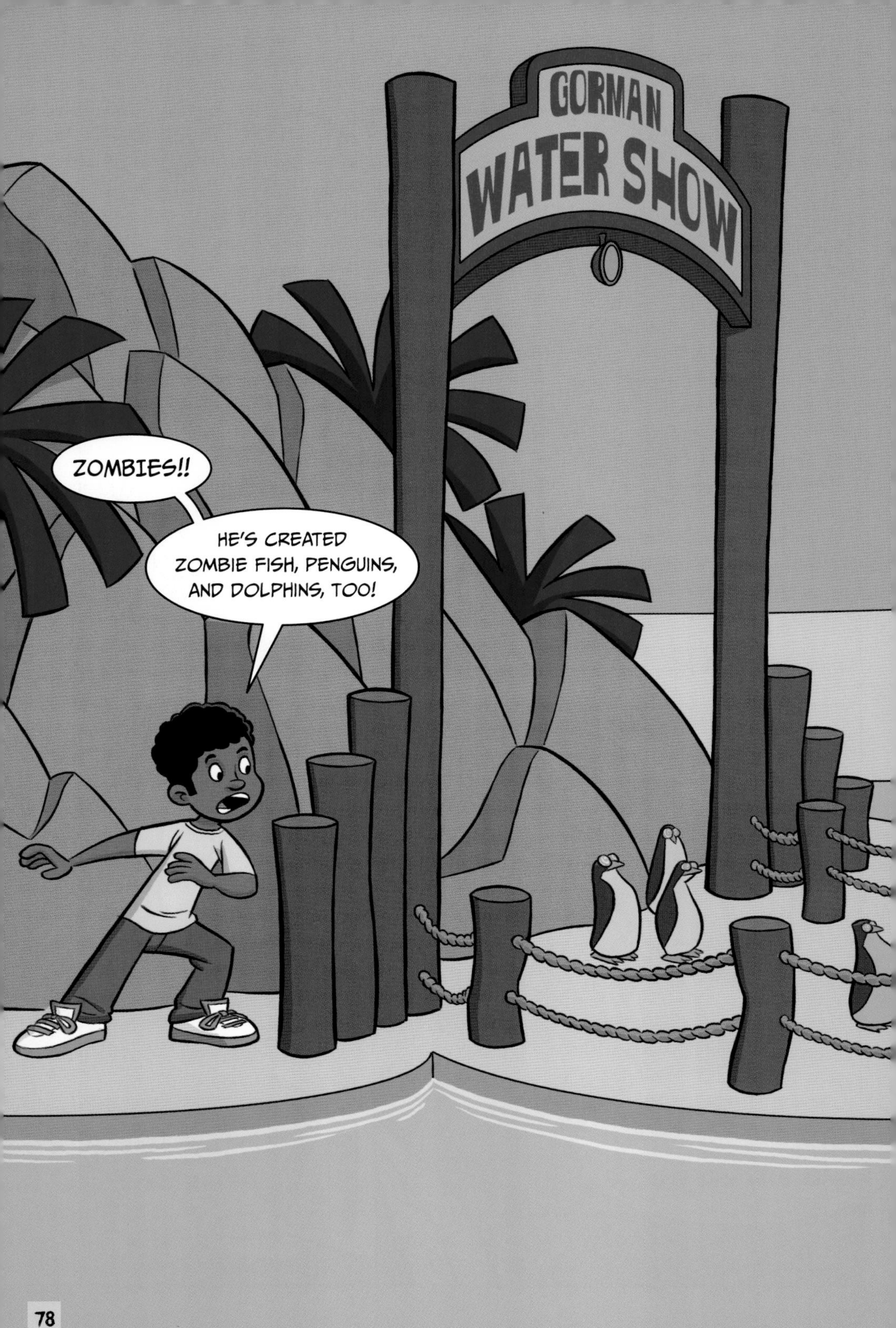
GORMAN
WATER SHOW
ZOMBIES!!
HE'S CREATED ZOMBIE FISH, PENGUINS, AND DOLPHINS, TOO!

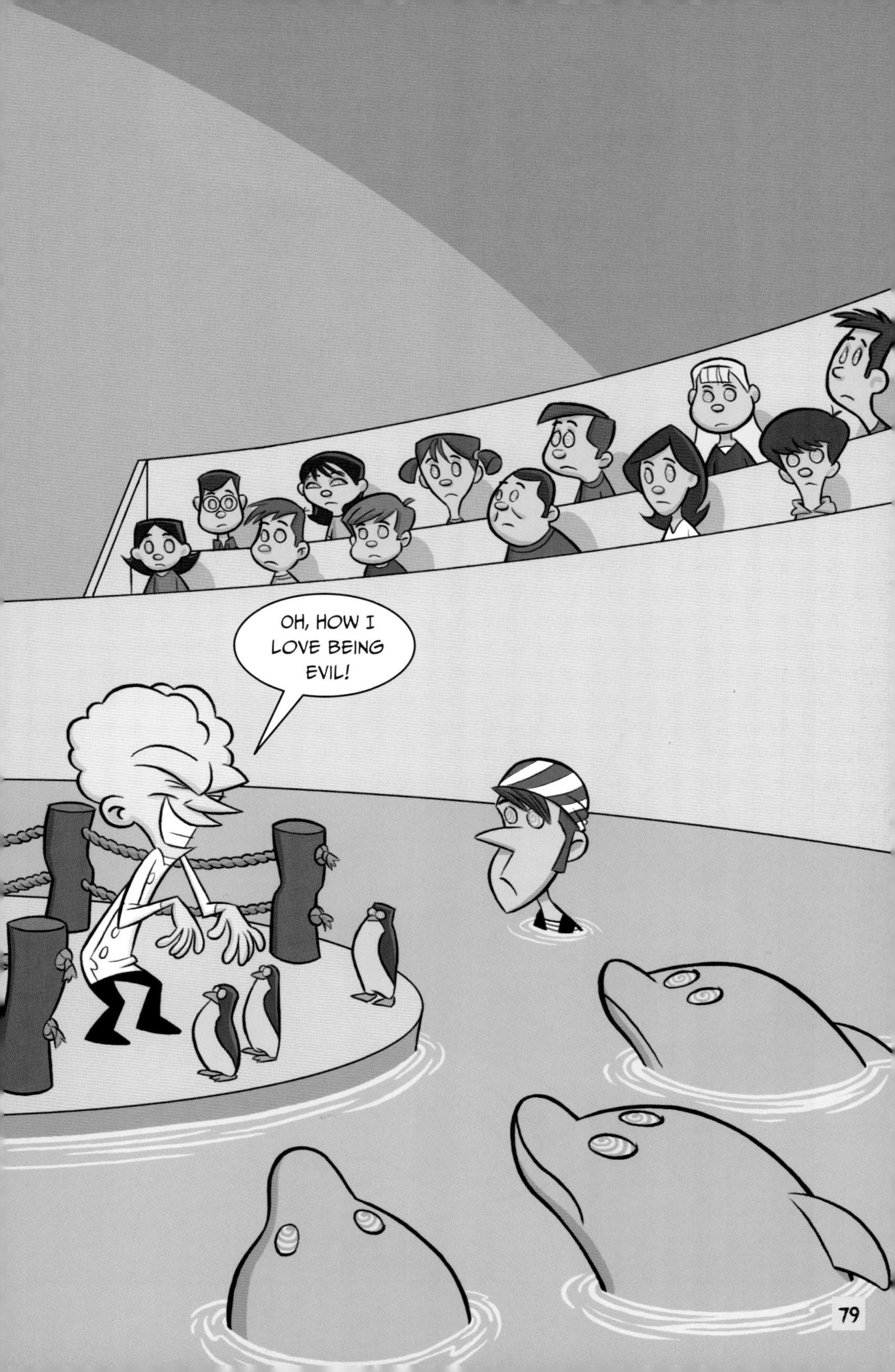
OH, HOW I LOVE BEING EVIL!

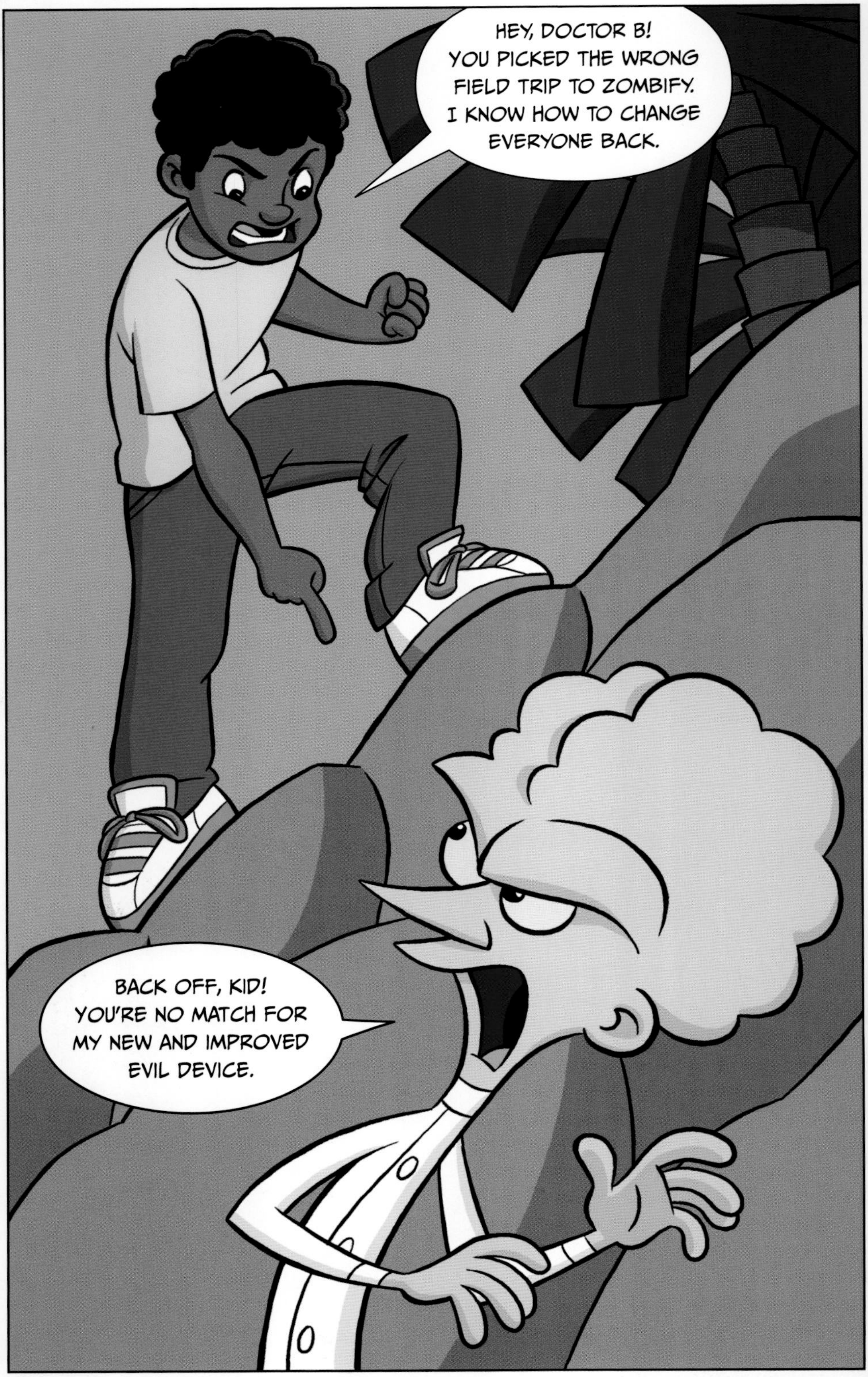
HEY, DOCTOR B! YOU PICKED THE WRONG FIELD TRIP TO ZOMBIFY. I KNOW HOW TO CHANGE EVERYONE BACK.
BACK OFF, KID! YOU'RE NO MATCH FOR MY NEW AND IMPROVED EVIL DEVICE.

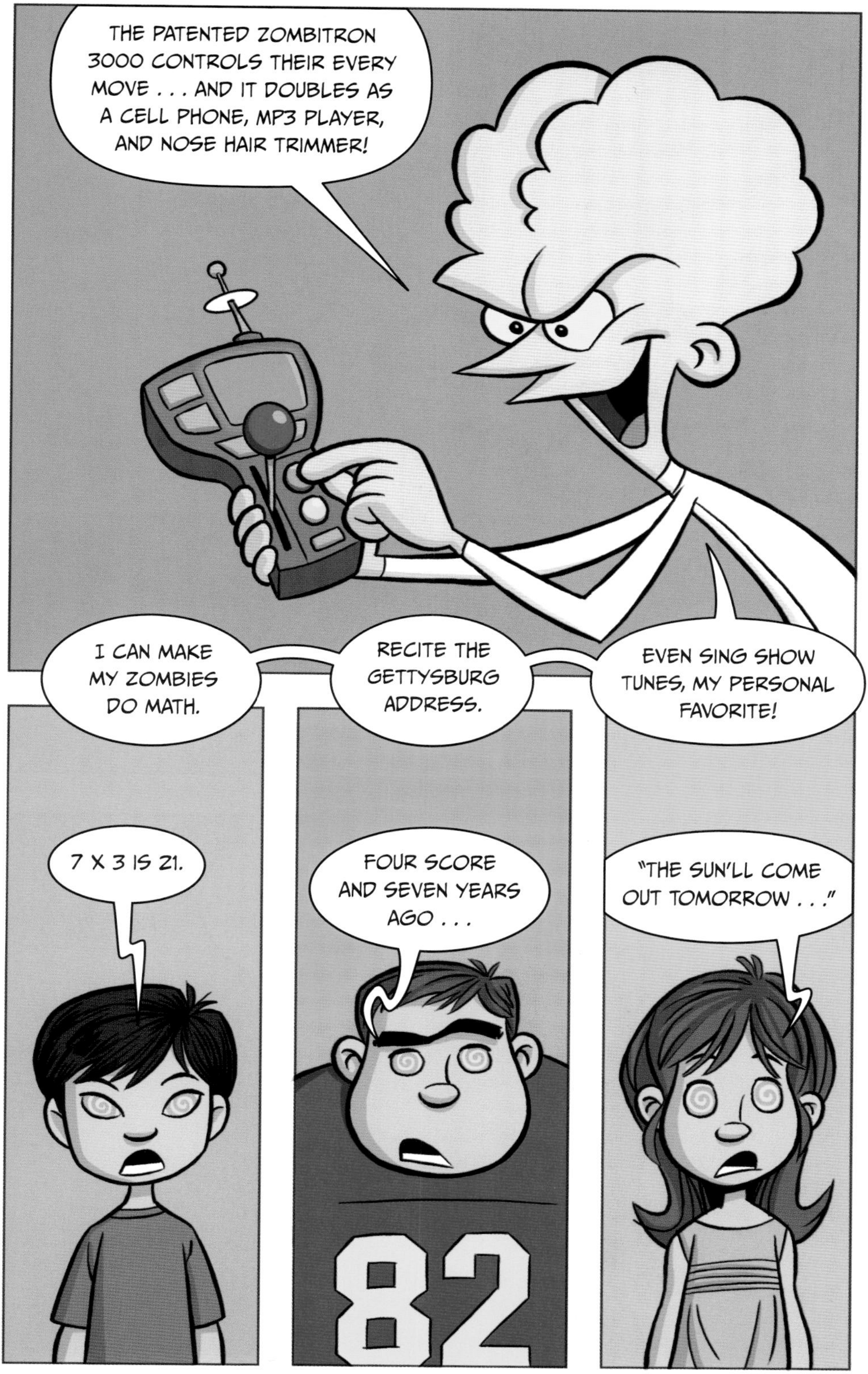
THE PATENTED ZOMBITRON 3000 CONTROLS THEIR EVERY MOVE . . . AND IT DOUBLES AS A CELL PHONE, MP3 PLAYER, AND NOSE HAIR TRIMMER!
I CAN MAKE MY ZOMBIES DO MATH.
RECITE THE GETTYSBURG ADDRESS.
EVEN SING SHOW TUNES, MY PERSONAL FAVORITE!
7 X 3 IS 21.
FOUR SCORE AND SEVEN YEARS AGO . . .
"THE SUN'LL COME OUT TOMORROW . . ."
82

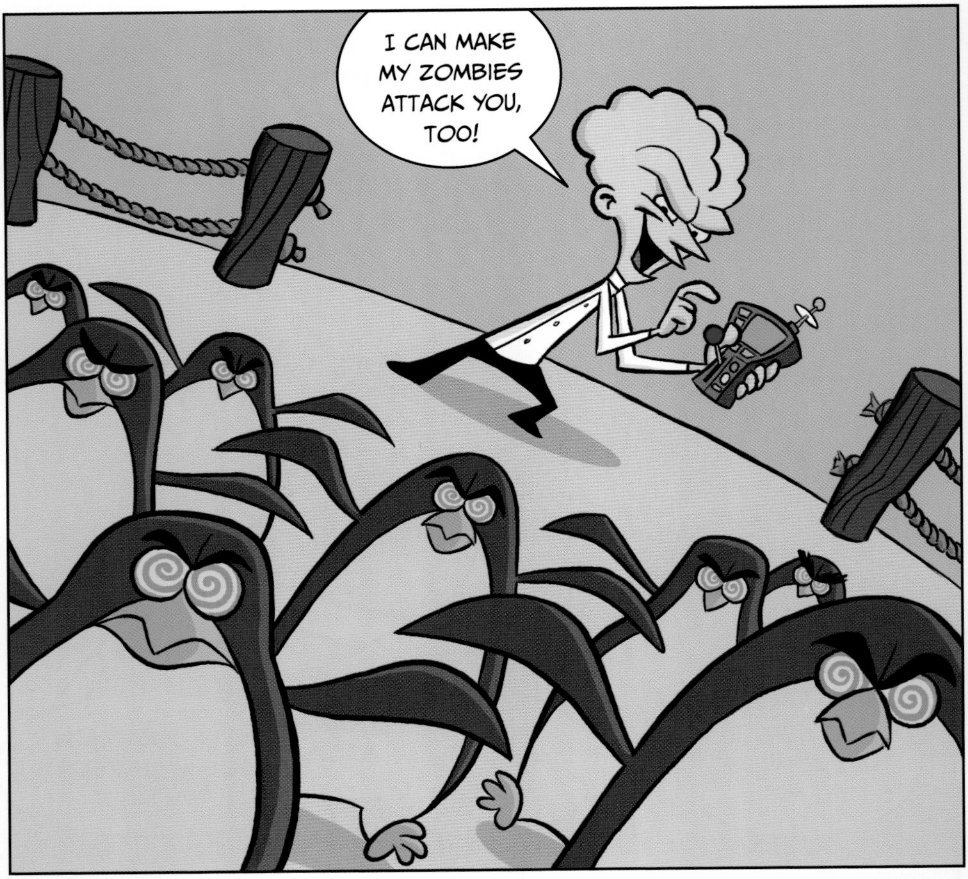
I CAN MAKE MY ZOMBIES ATTACK YOU, TOO!

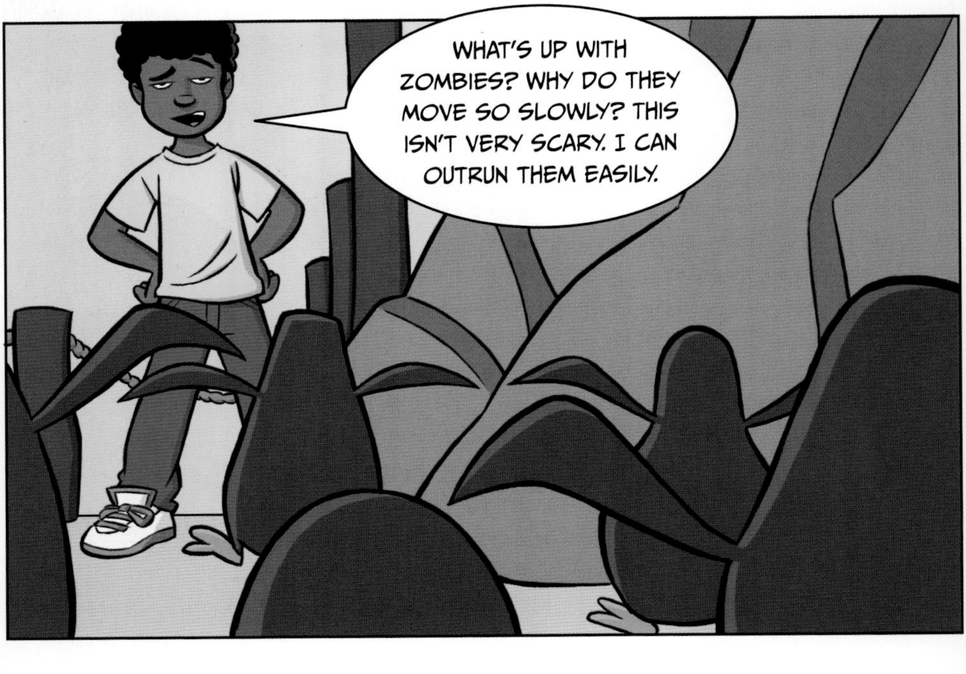
WHAT'S UP WITH ZOMBIES? WHY DO THEY MOVE SO SLOWLY? THIS ISN'T VERY SCARY. I CAN OUTRUN THEM EASILY.

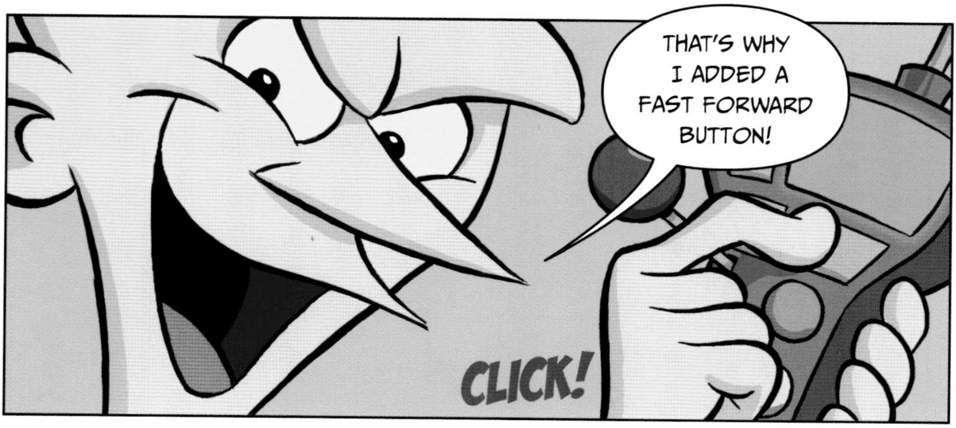
THAT'S WHY I ADDED A FAST FORWARD BUTTON!
CLICK!

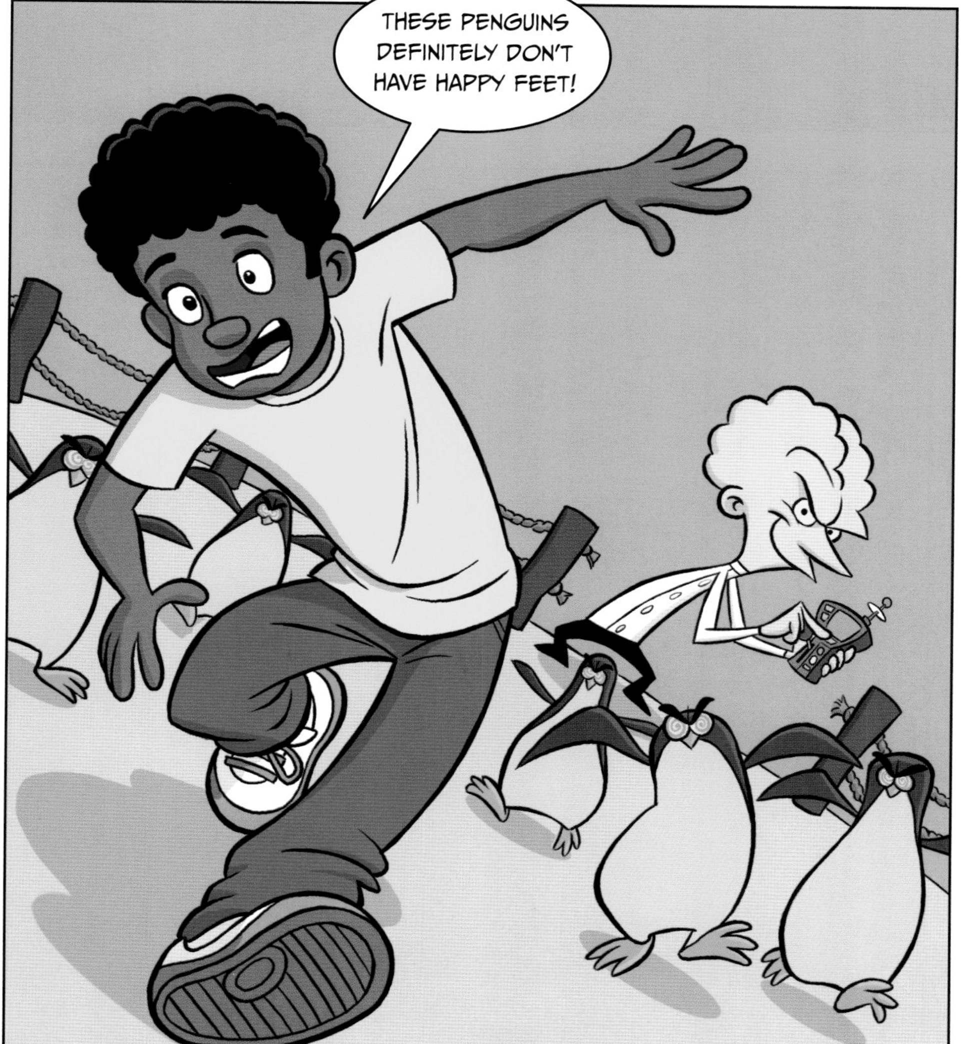
THESE PENGUINS DEFINITELY DON'T HAVE HAPPY FEET!

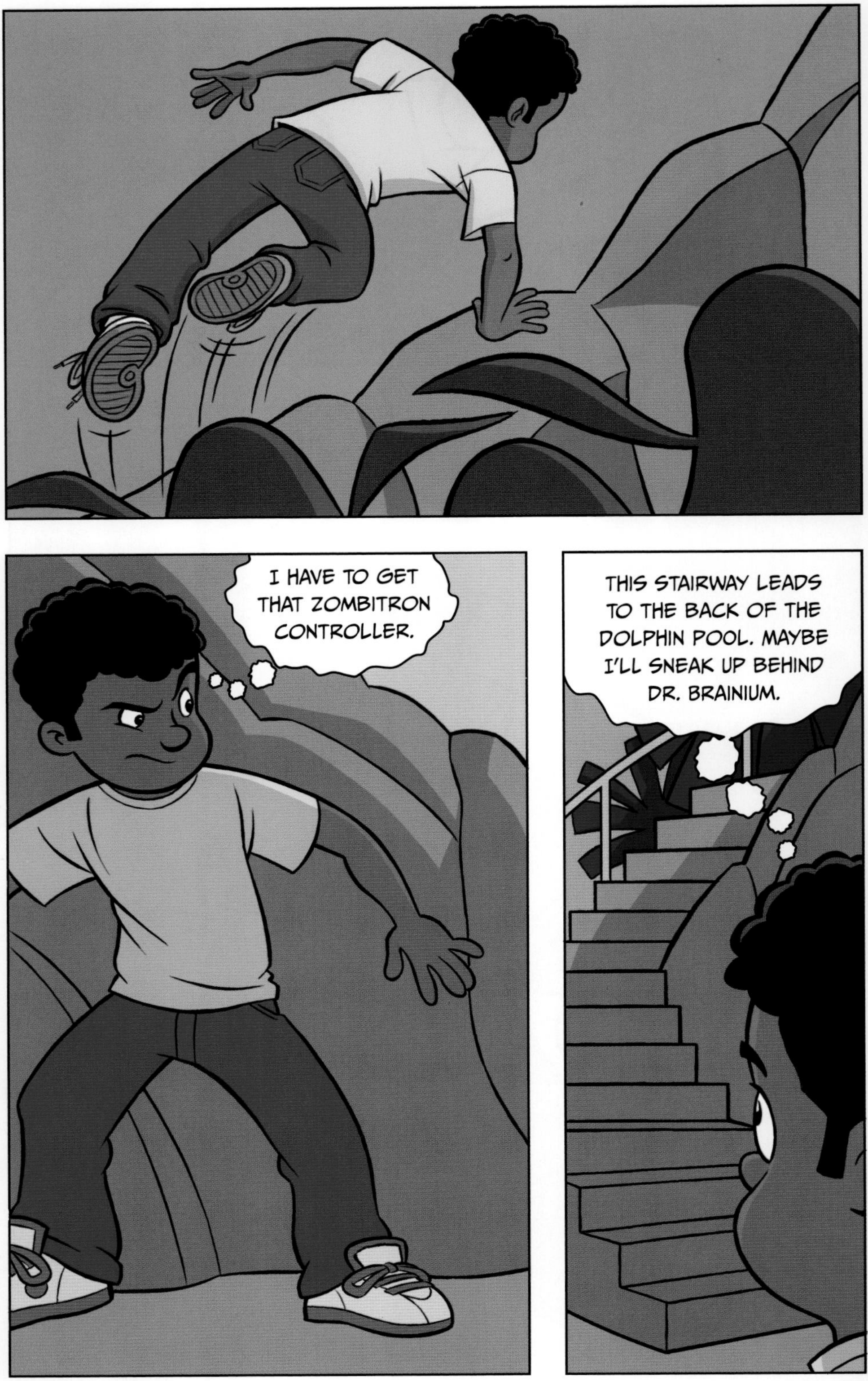
I HAVE TO GET THAT ZOMBITRON CONTROLLER.
THIS STAIRWAY LEADS TO THE BACK OF THE DOLPHIN POOL. MAYBE I'LL SNEAK UP BEHIND DR. BRAINIUM.

QUIT HOGGING THE REMOTE!

WHAP!

OOF!

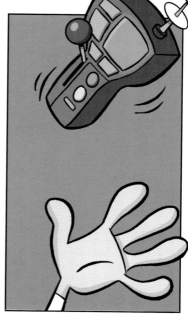

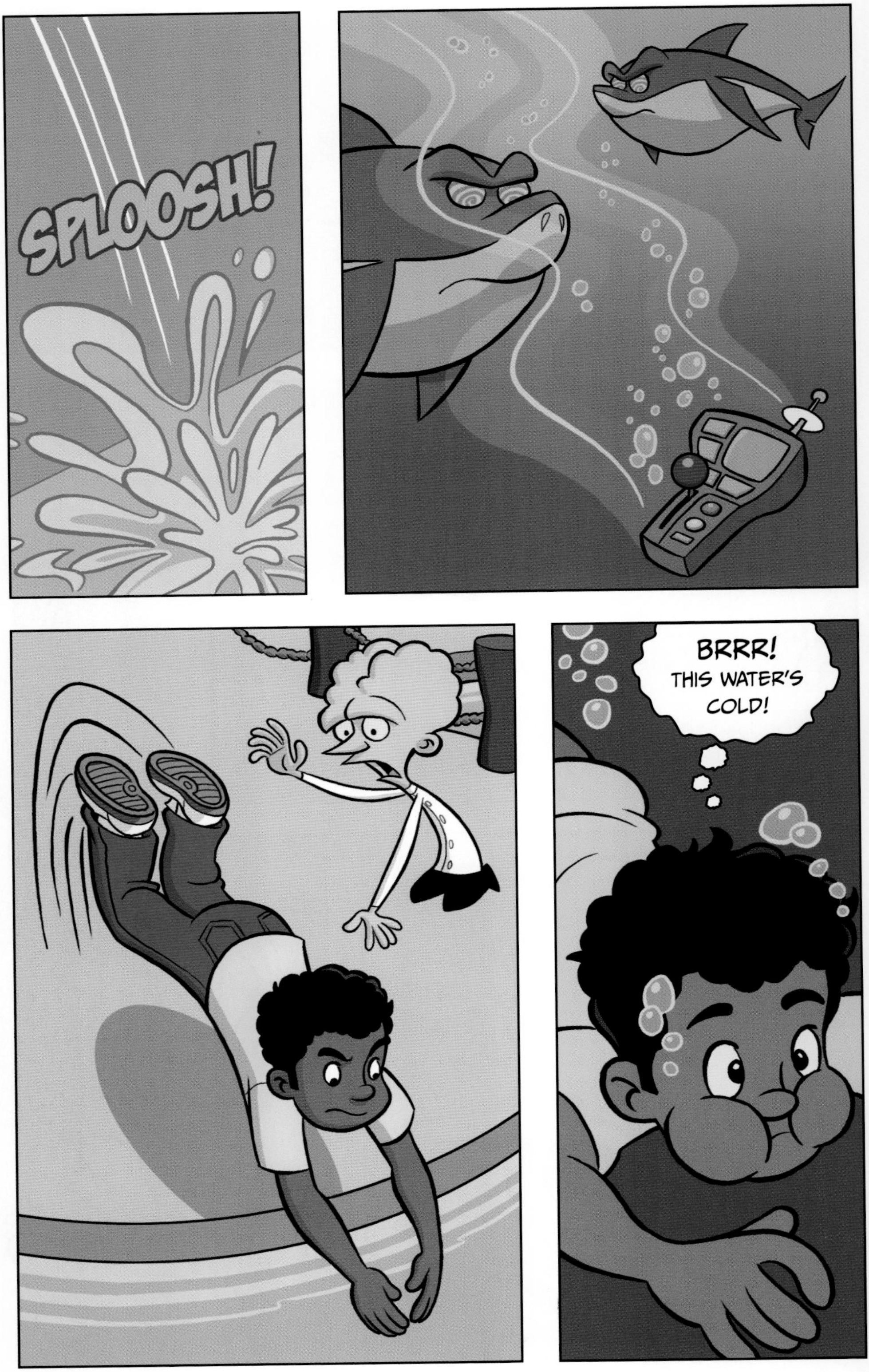
SPLOOSH!
BRRR! THIS WATER'S COLD!

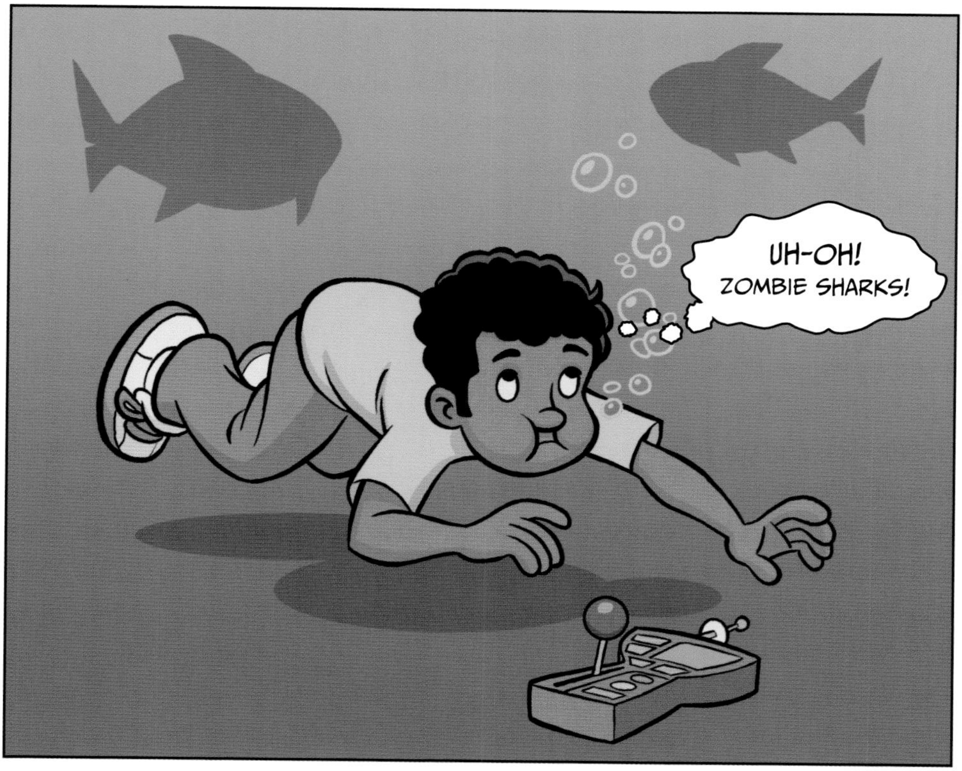
UH-OH!
ZOMBIE SHARKS!

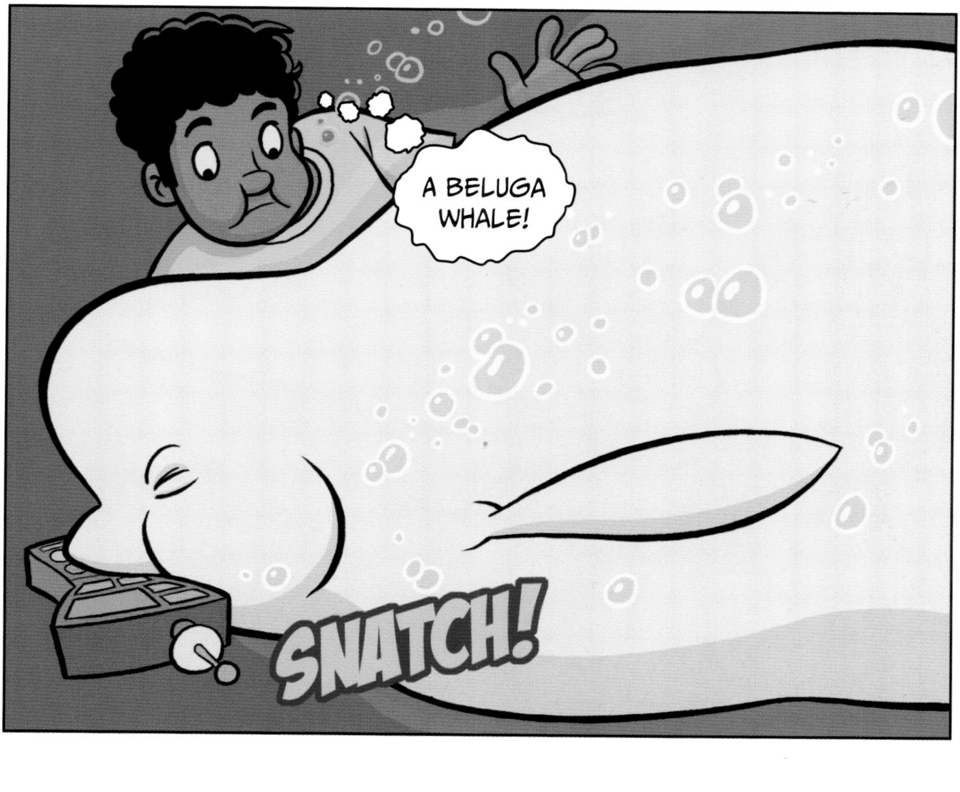
A BELUGA WHALE!
SNATCH!

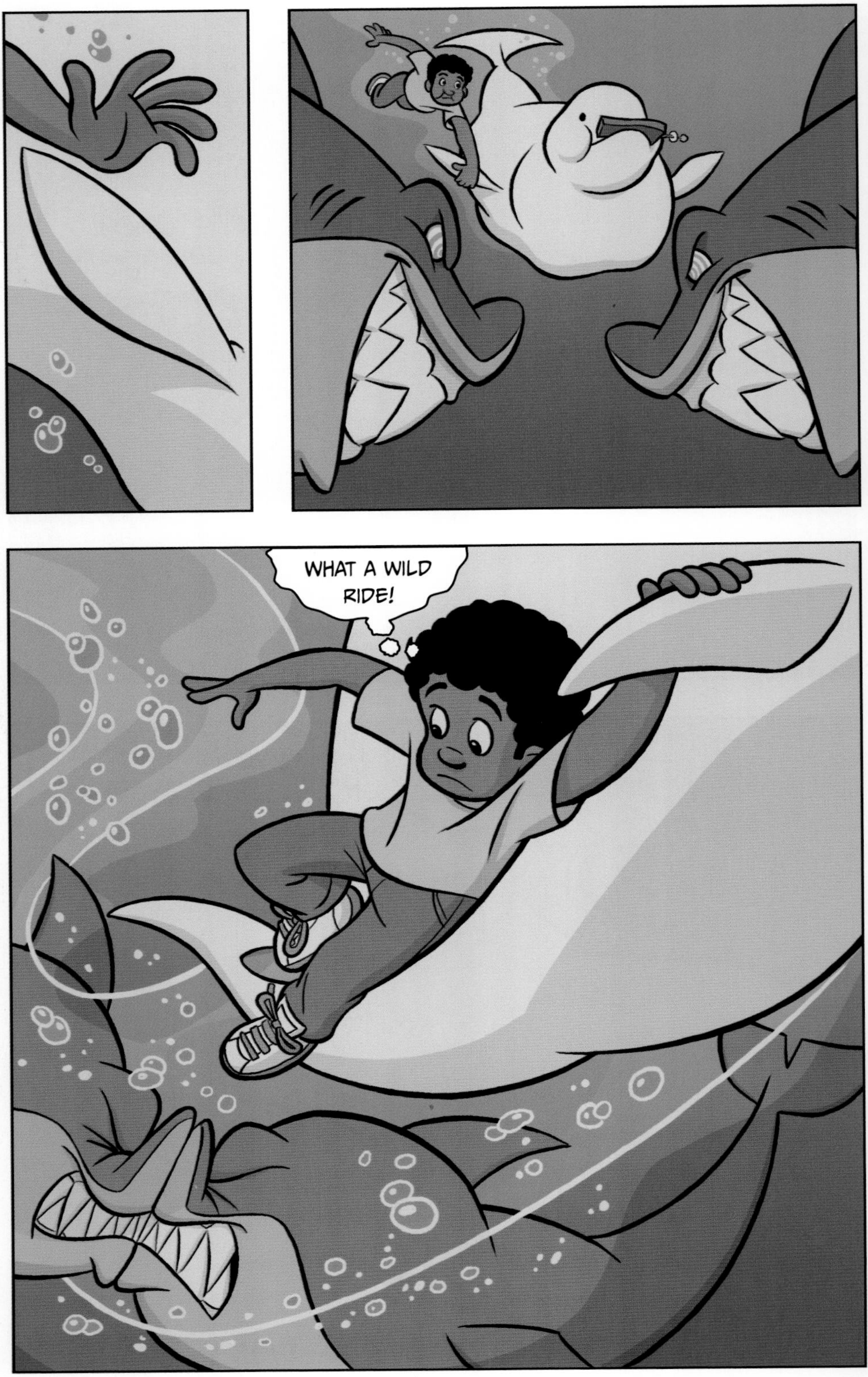
WHAT A WILD RIDE!

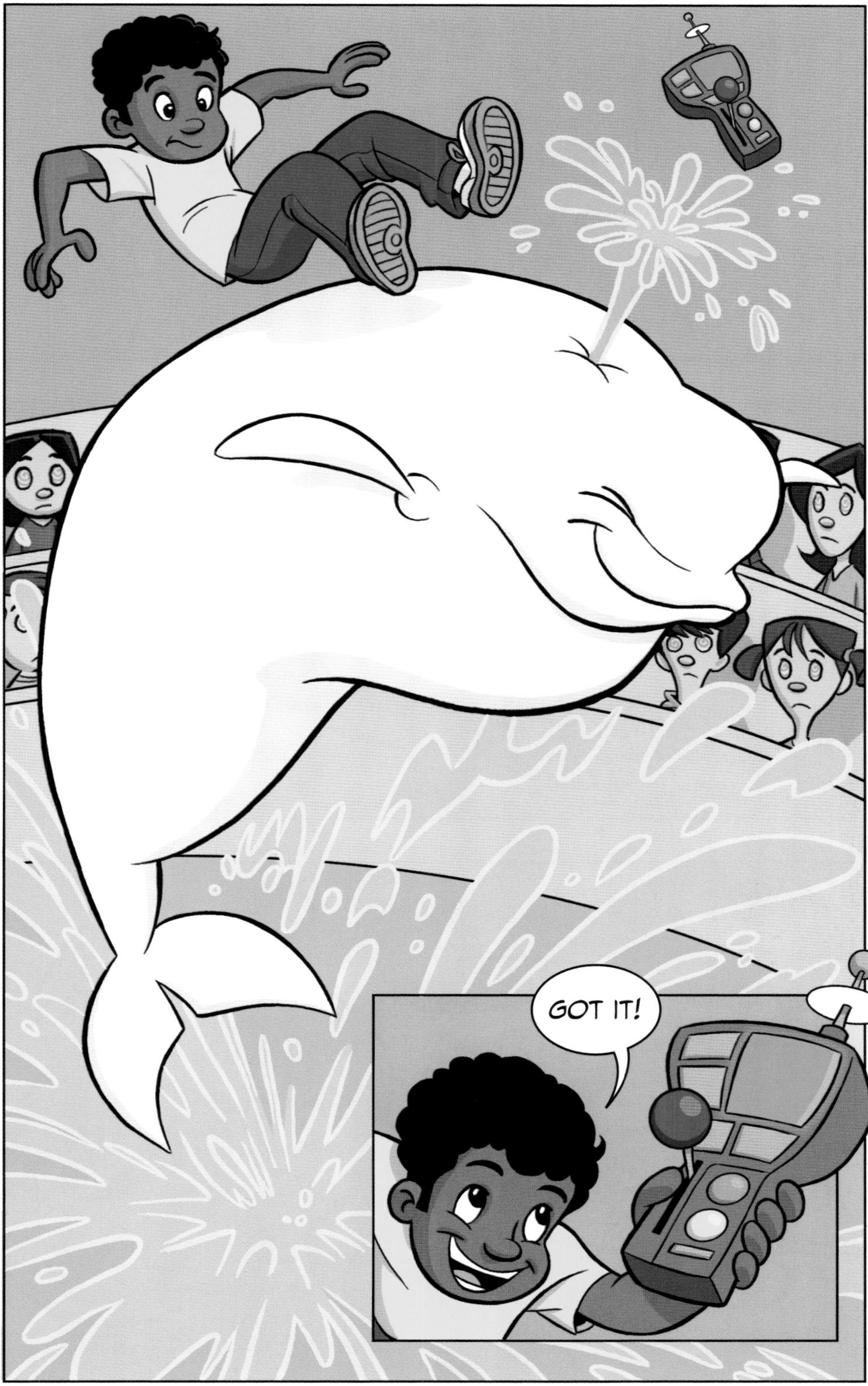
GOT IT!

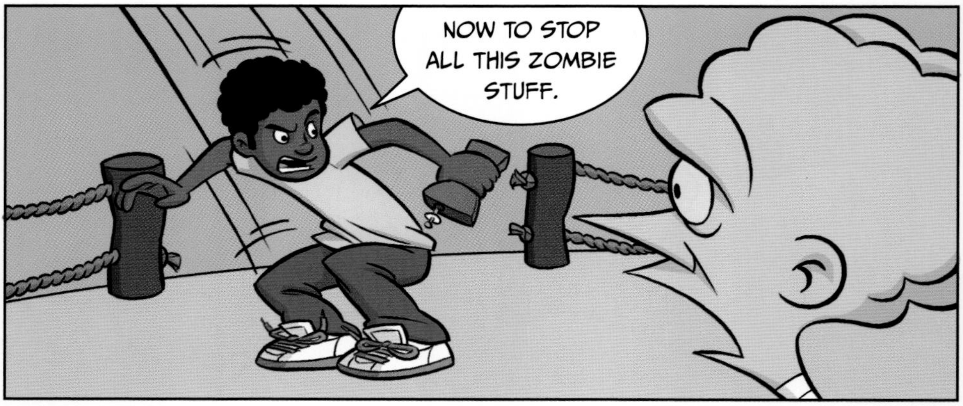
NOW TO STOP ALL THIS ZOMBIE STUFF.

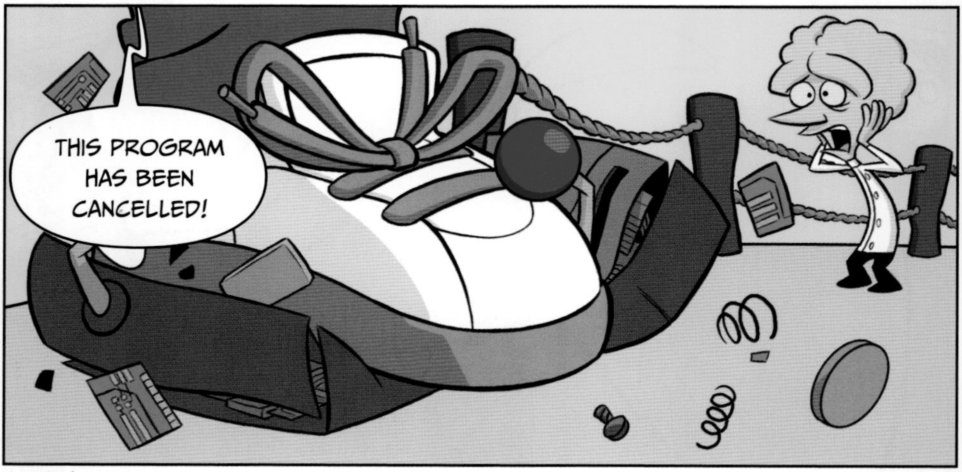
THIS PROGRAM HAS BEEN CANCELLED!

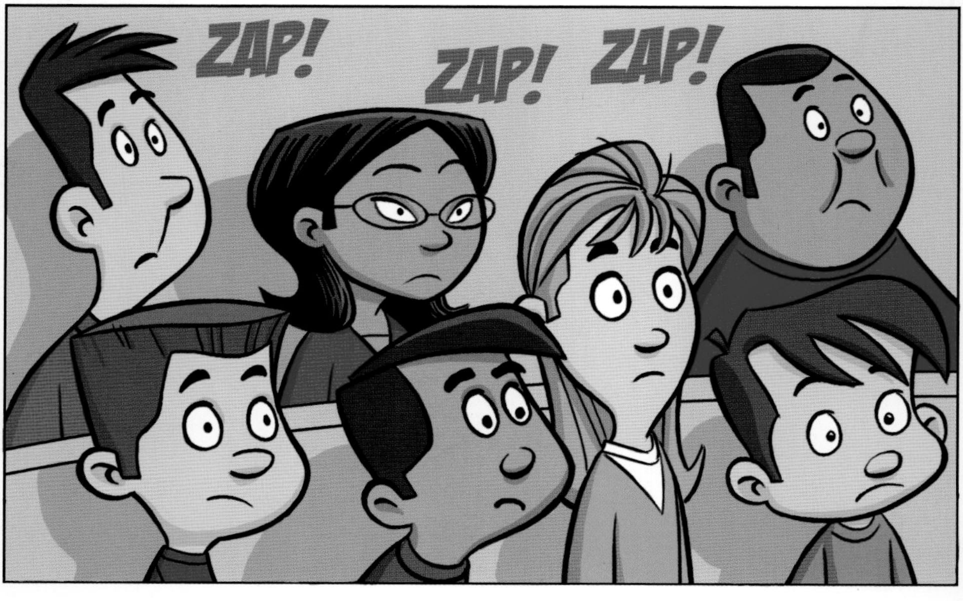
ZAP!
ZAP!
ZAP!

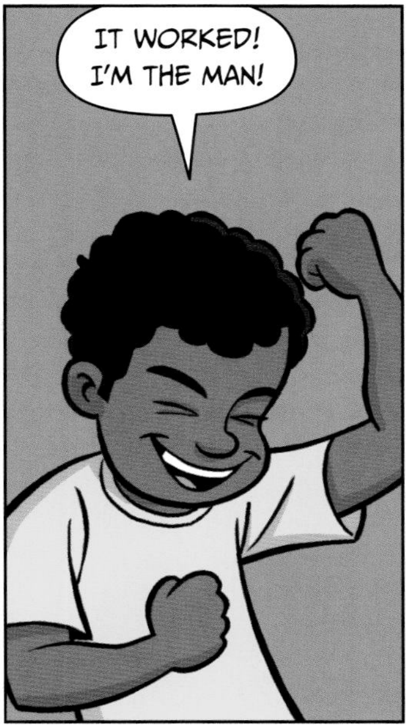
IT WORKED! I'M THE MAN!

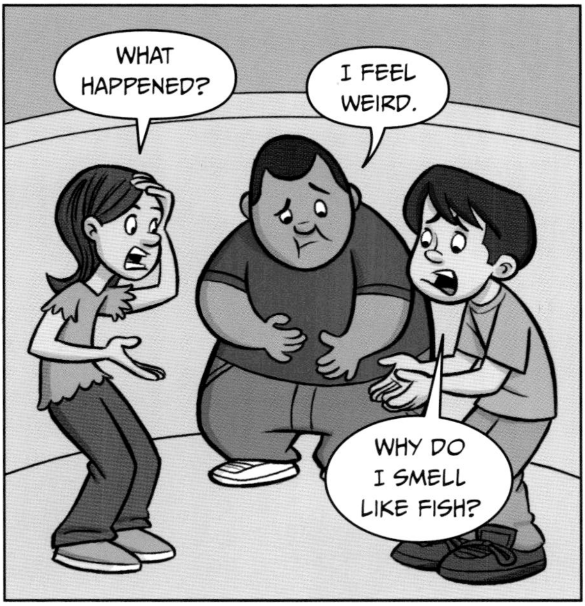
WHAT HAPPENED?
I FEEL WEIRD.
WHY DO I SMELL LIKE FISH?

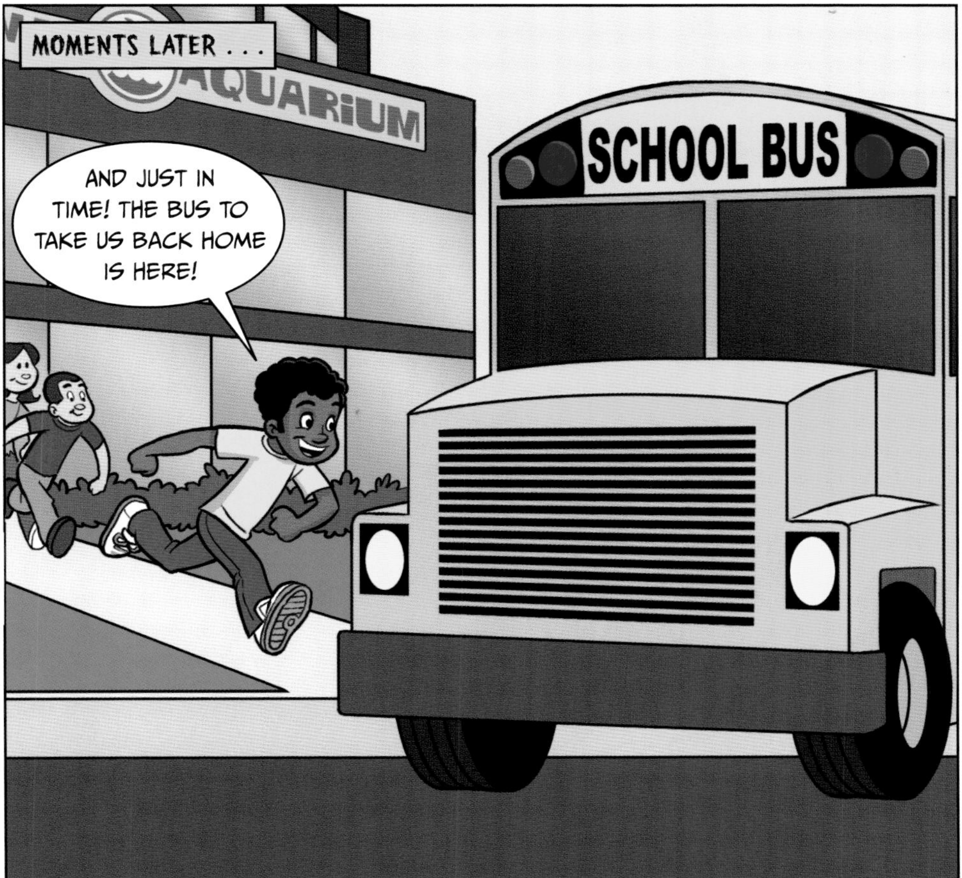
MOMENTS LATER . . .
AQUARIUM
SCHOOL BUS
AND JUST IN TIME! THE BUS TO TAKE US BACK HOME IS HERE!

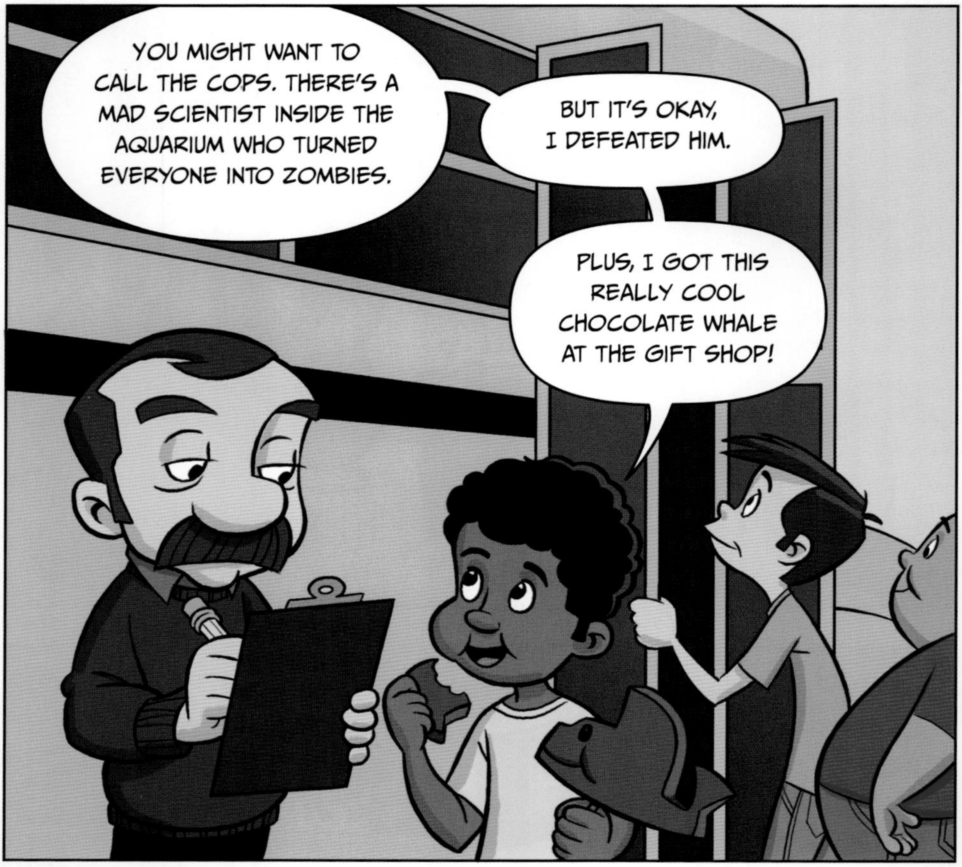
YOU MIGHT WANT TO CALL THE COPS. THERE'S A MAD SCIENTIST INSIDE THE AQUARIUM WHO TURNED EVERYONE INTO ZOMBIES.
BUT IT'S OKAY, I DEFEATED HIM.
PLUS, I GOT THIS REALLY COOL CHOCOLATE WHALE AT THE GIFT SHOP!

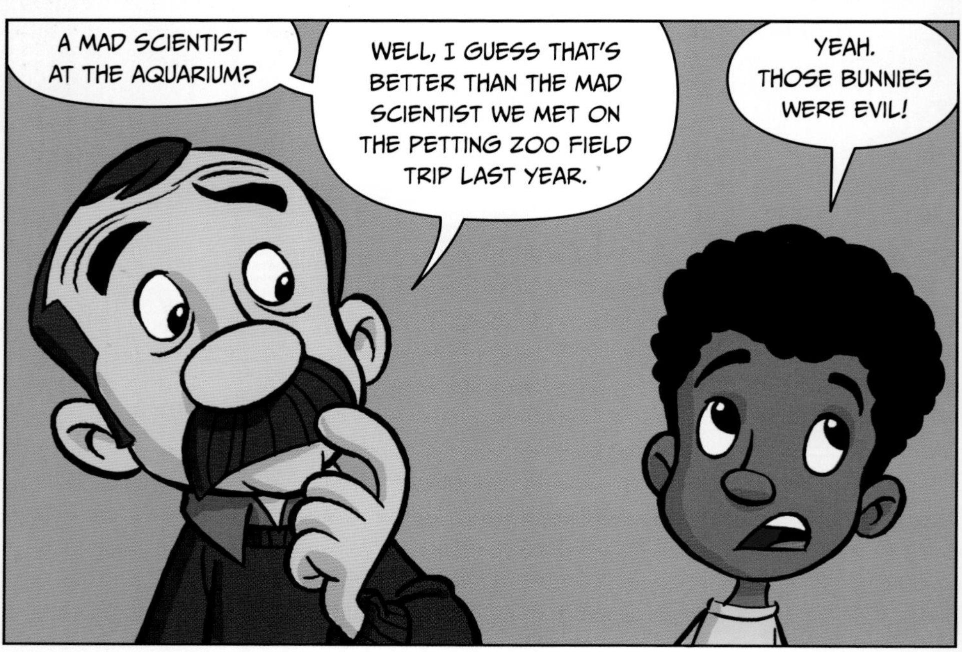
A MAD SCIENTIST AT THE AQUARIUM?
WELL, I GUESS THAT'S BETTER THAN THE MAD SCIENTIST WE MET ON THE PETTING ZOO FIELD TRIP LAST YEAR.
YEAH. THOSE BUNNIES WERE EVIL!

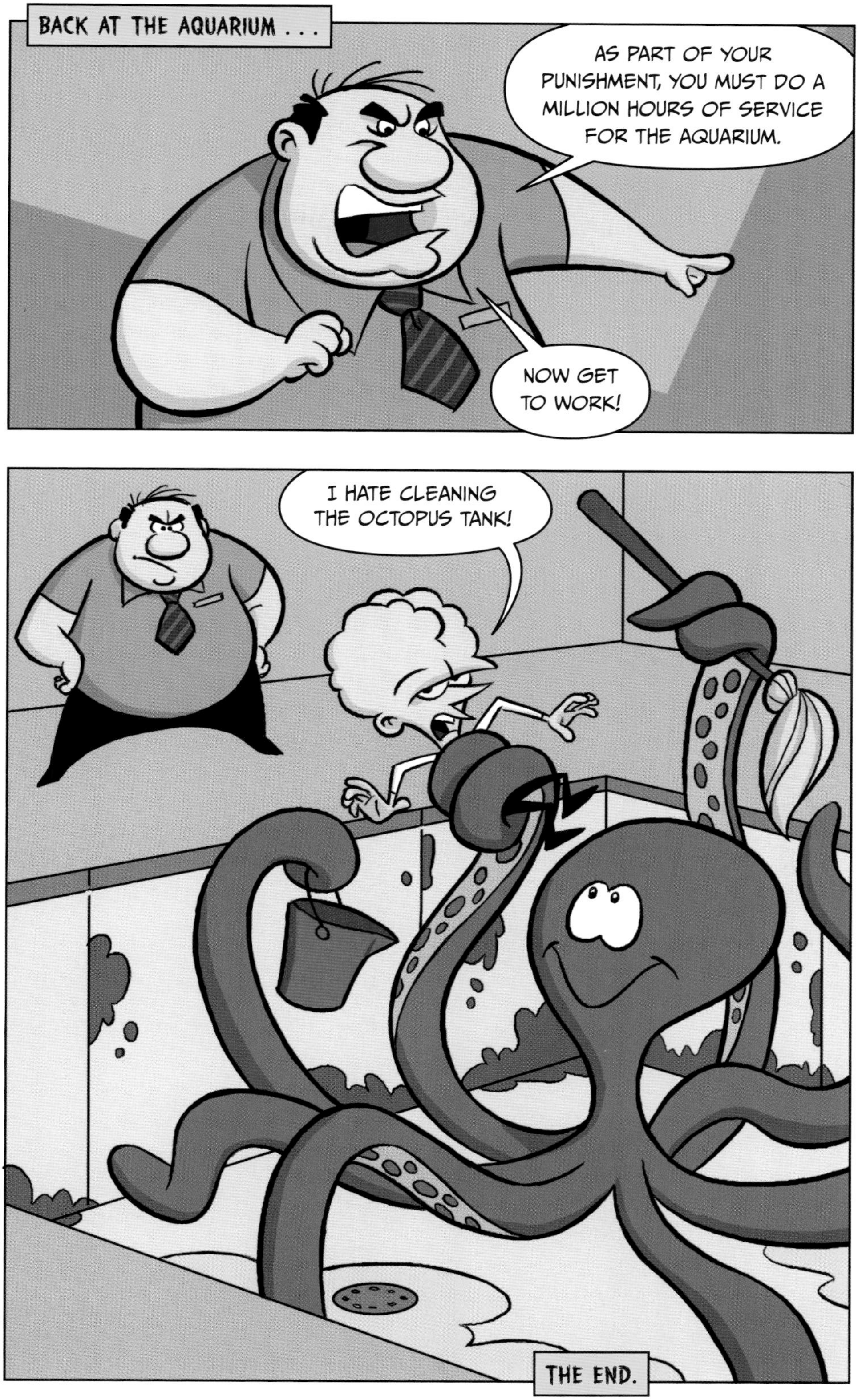
BACK AT THE AQUARIUM . . .
AS PART OF YOUR PUNISHMENT, YOU MUST DO A MILLION HOURS OF SERVICE FOR THE AQUARIUM.
NOW GET TO WORK!
I HATE CLEANING THE OCTOPUS TANK!
THE END.

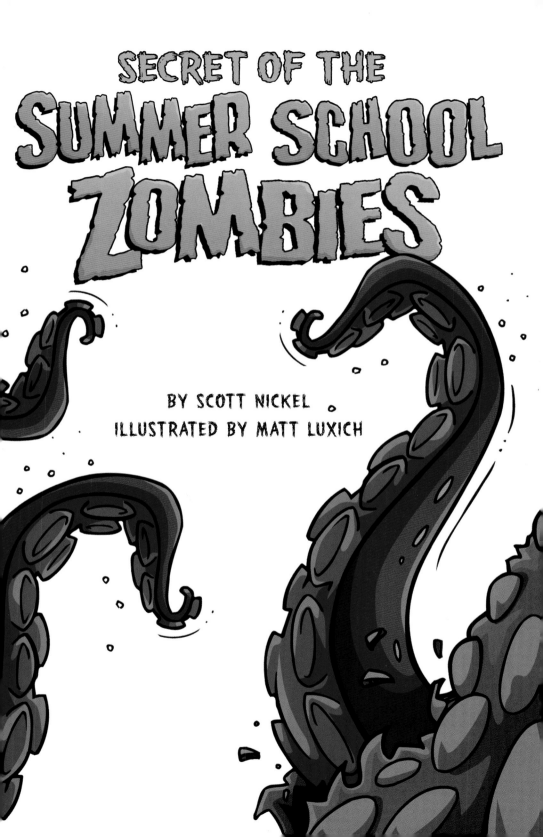

SECRET OF THE SUMMER SCHOOL ZOMBIES

BY SCOTT NICKEL
ILLUSTRATED BY MATT LUXICH

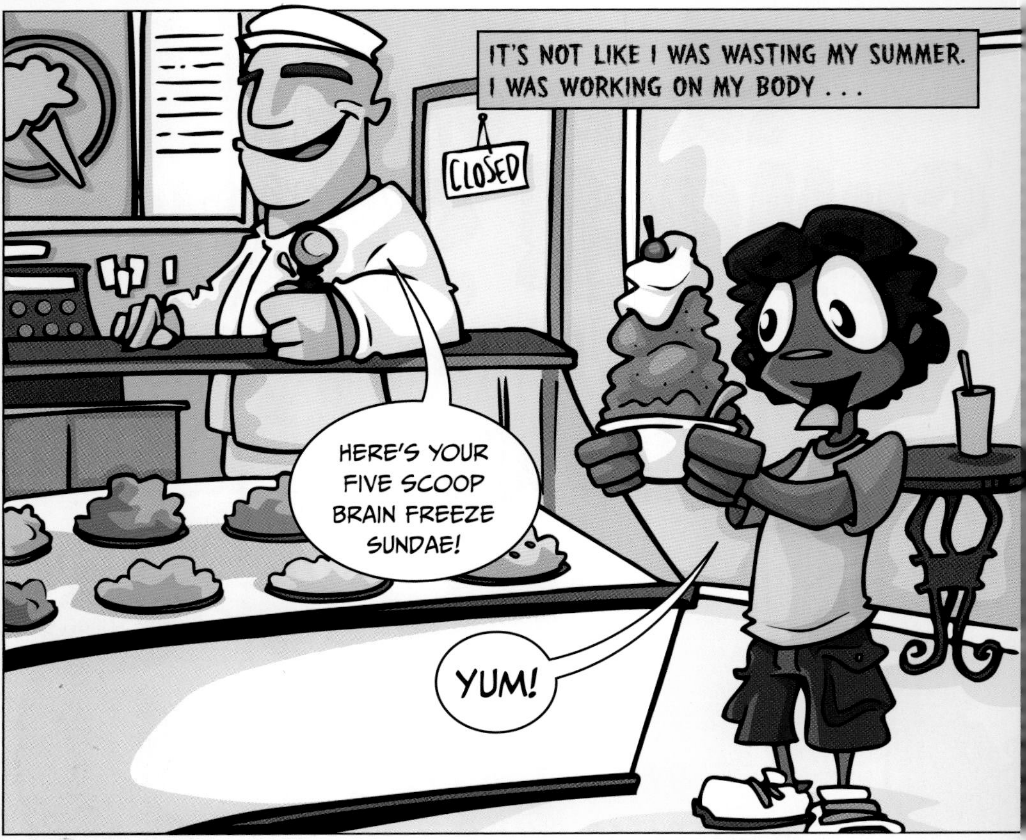
IT'S NOT LIKE I WAS WASTING MY SUMMER. I WAS WORKING ON MY BODY . . .
CLOSED
HERE'S YOUR FIVE SCOOP BRAIN FREEZE SUNDAE!
YUM!

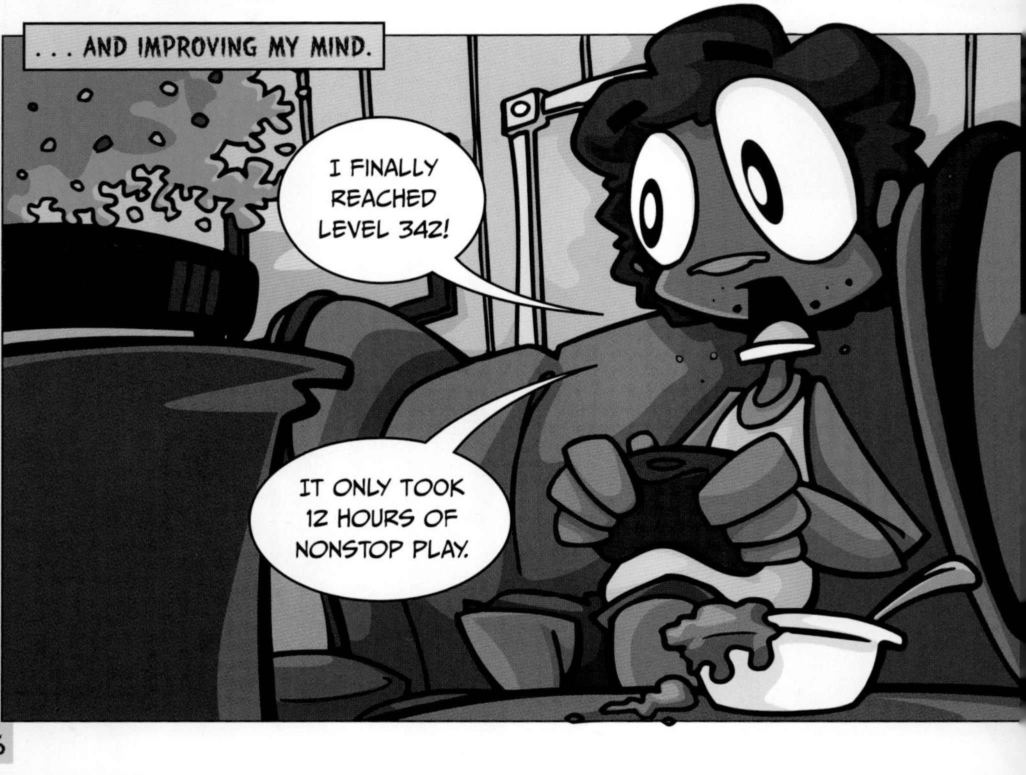
. . . AND IMPROVING MY MIND.
I FINALLY REACHED LEVEL 342!
IT ONLY TOOK 12 HOURS OF NONSTOP PLAY.

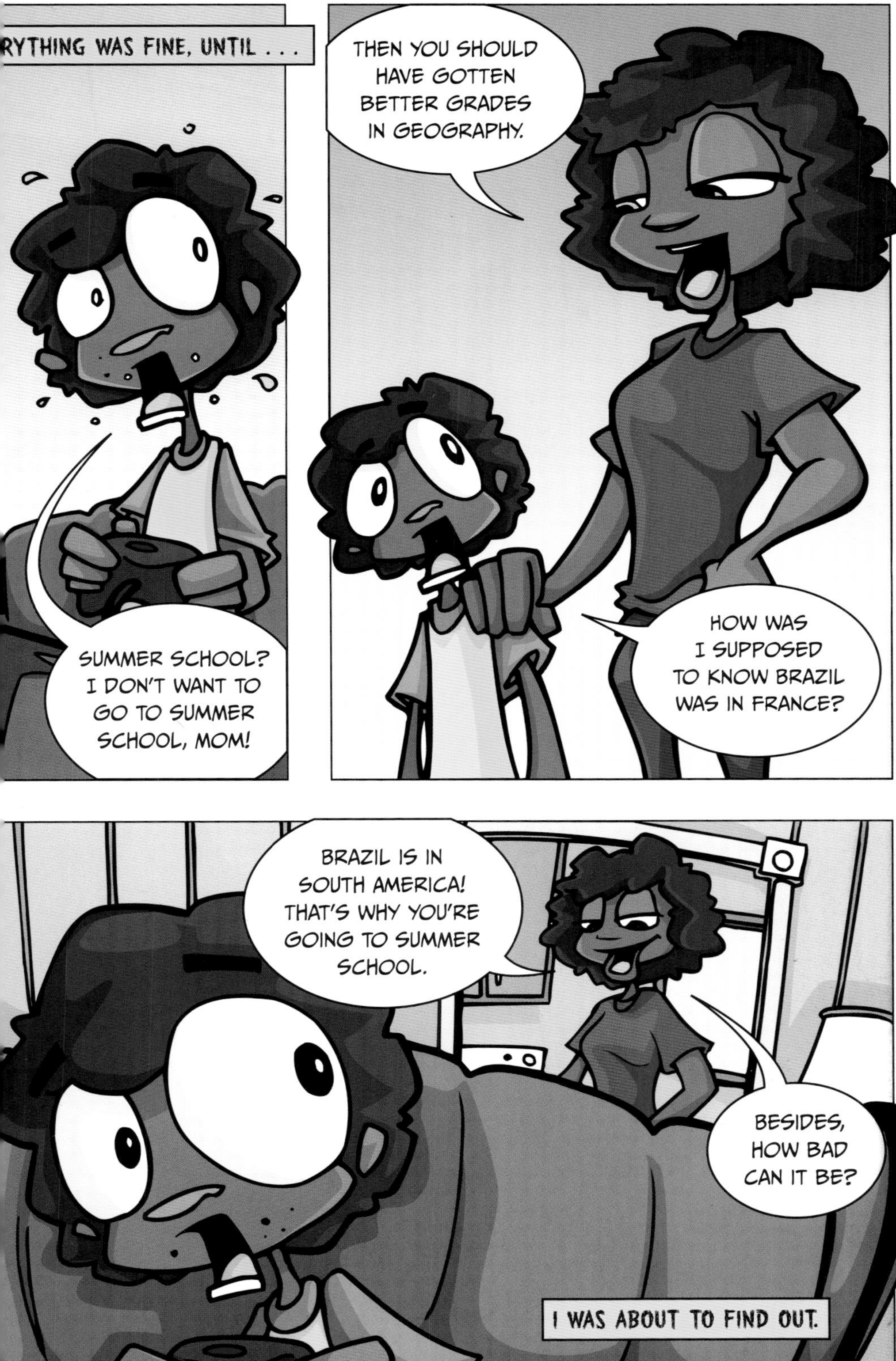
RYTHING WAS FINE, UNTIL . . .
SUMMER SCHOOL? I DON'T WANT TO GO TO SUMMER SCHOOL, MOM!
THEN YOU SHOULD HAVE GOTTEN BETTER GRADES IN GEOGRAPHY.
HOW WAS I SUPPOSED TO KNOW BRAZIL WAS IN FRANCE?
BRAZIL IS IN SOUTH AMERICA! THAT'S WHY YOU'RE GOING TO SUMMER SCHOOL.
BESIDES, HOW BAD CAN IT BE?
I WAS ABOUT TO FIND OUT.

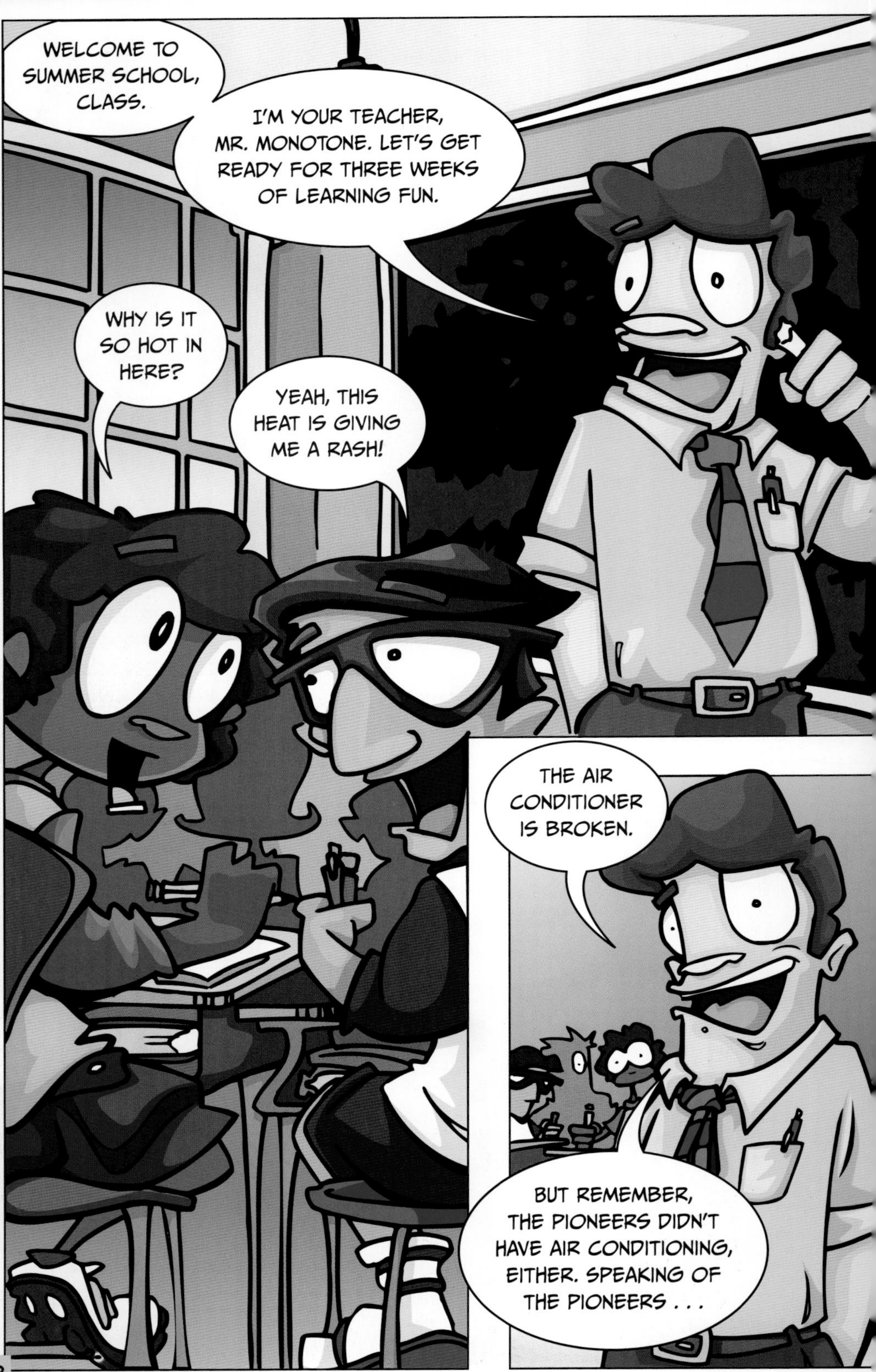
WELCOME TO SUMMER SCHOOL, CLASS.
I'M YOUR TEACHER, MR. MONOTONE. LET'S GET READY FOR THREE WEEKS OF LEARNING FUN.
WHY IS IT SO HOT IN HERE?
YEAH, THIS HEAT IS GIVING ME A RASH!
THE AIR CONDITIONER IS BROKEN.
BUT REMEMBER, THE PIONEERS DIDN'T HAVE AIR CONDITIONING, EITHER. SPEAKING OF THE PIONEERS . . .

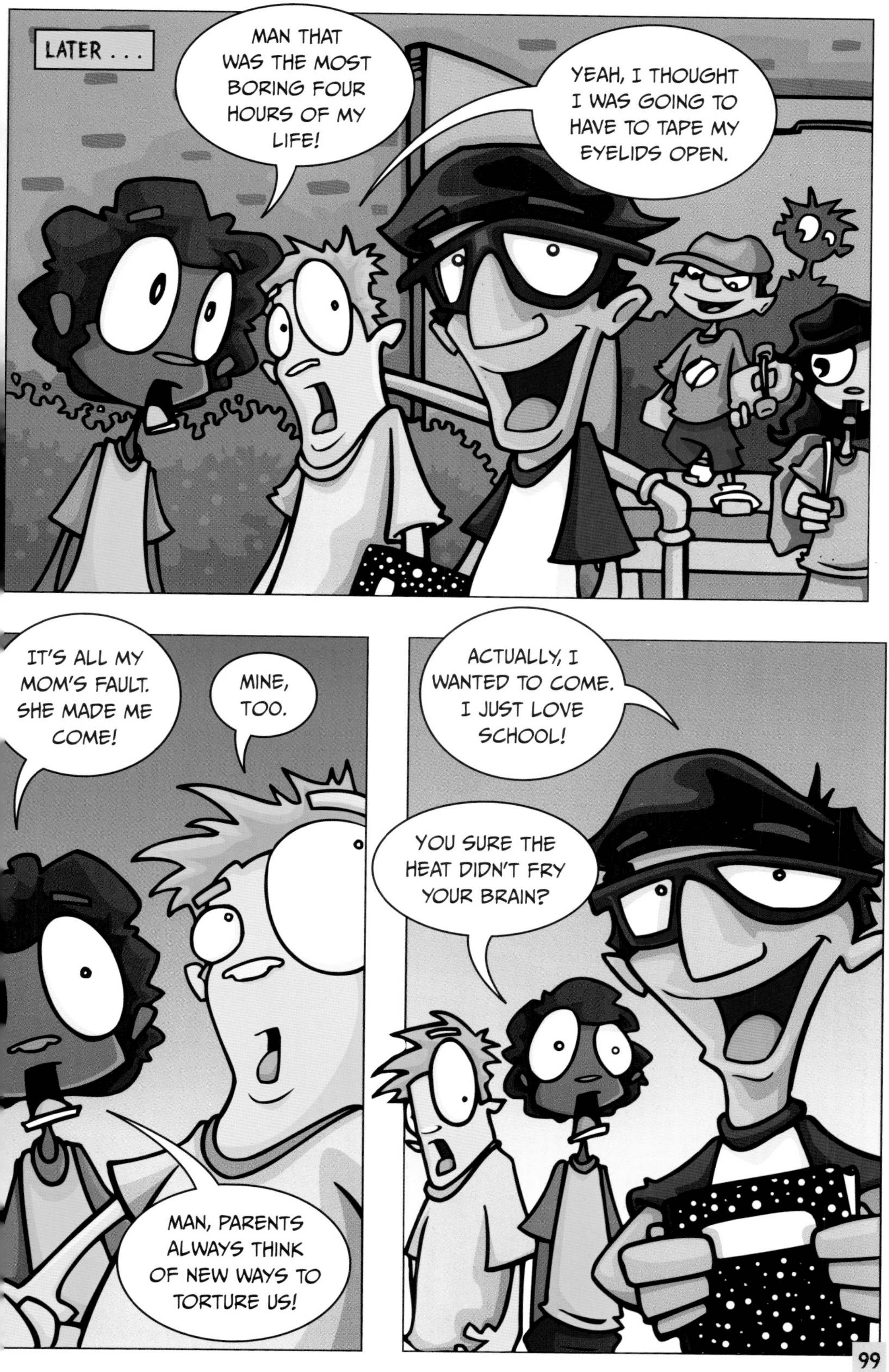
LATER . . .
MAN THAT WAS THE MOST BORING FOUR HOURS OF MY LIFE!
YEAH, I THOUGHT I WAS GOING TO HAVE TO TAPE MY EYELIDS OPEN.
IT'S ALL MY MOM'S FAULT. SHE MADE ME COME!
MINE, TOO.
MAN, PARENTS ALWAYS THINK OF NEW WAYS TO TORTURE US!
ACTUALLY, I WANTED TO COME. I JUST LOVE SCHOOL!
YOU SURE THE HEAT DIDN'T FRY YOUR BRAIN?

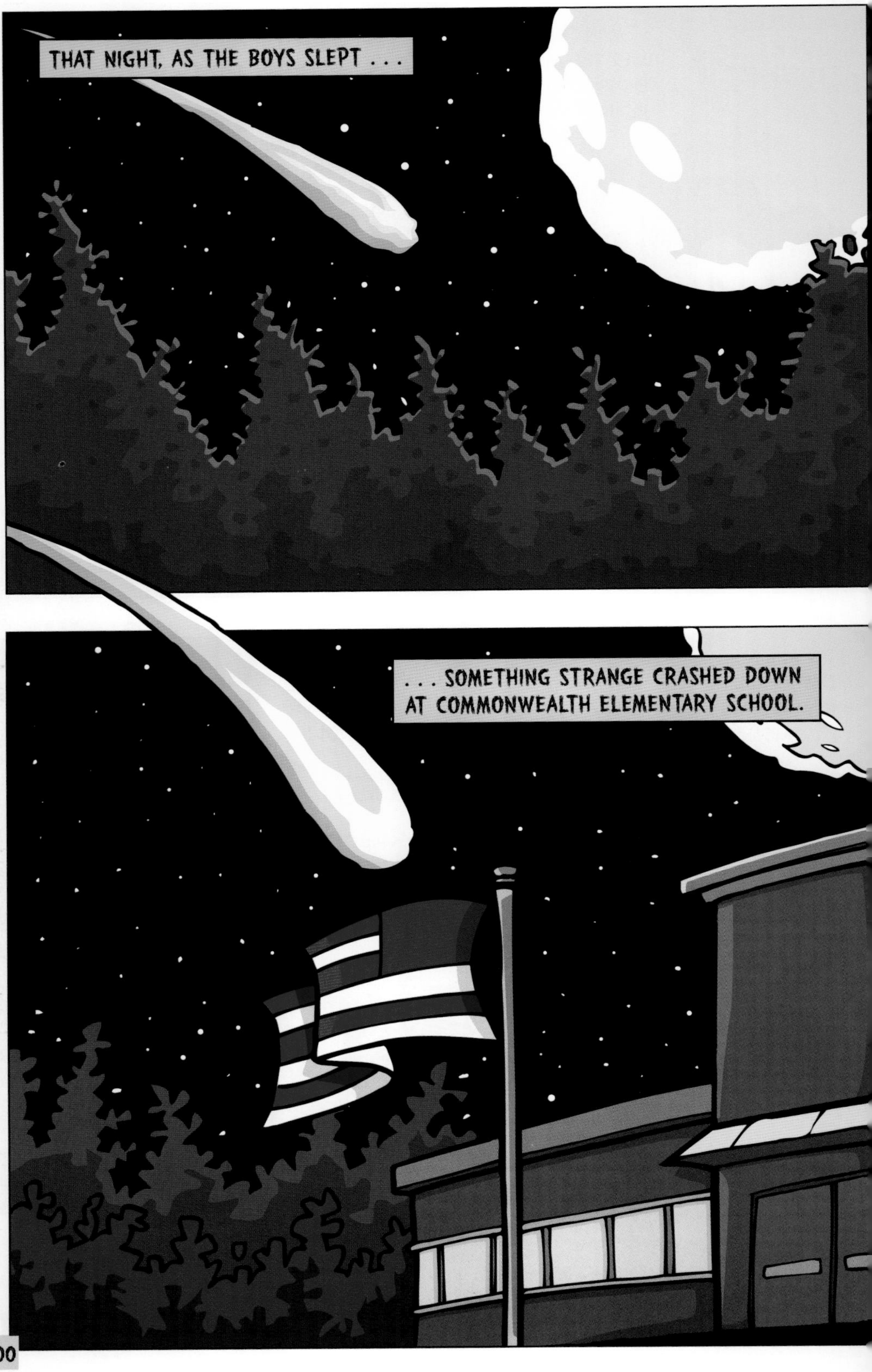
THAT NIGHT, AS THE BOYS SLEPT . . .
. . . SOMETHING STRANGE CRASHED DOWN AT COMMONWEALTH ELEMENTARY SCHOOL.

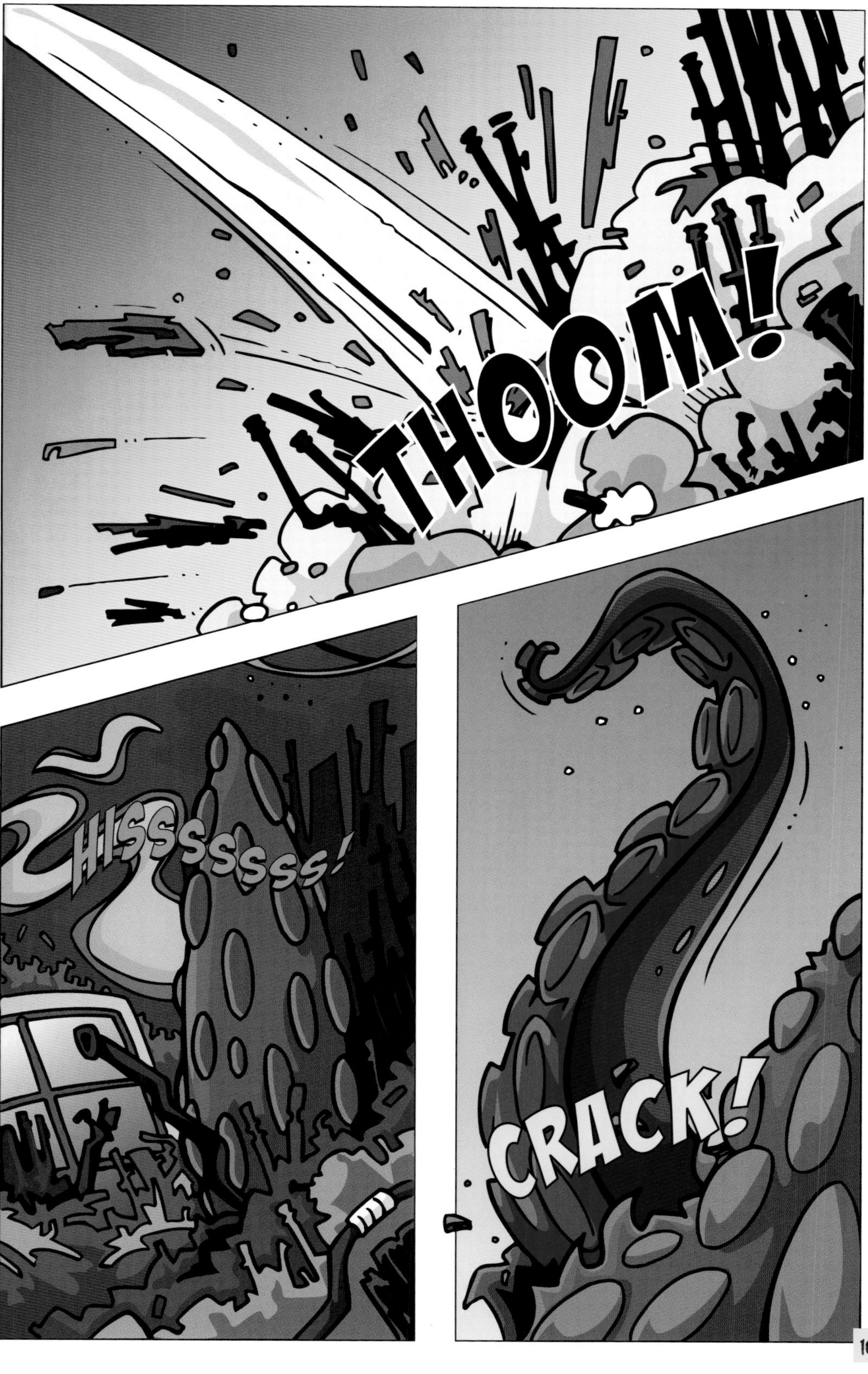
THOOM!
HISSSSSSSS!
CRACK!

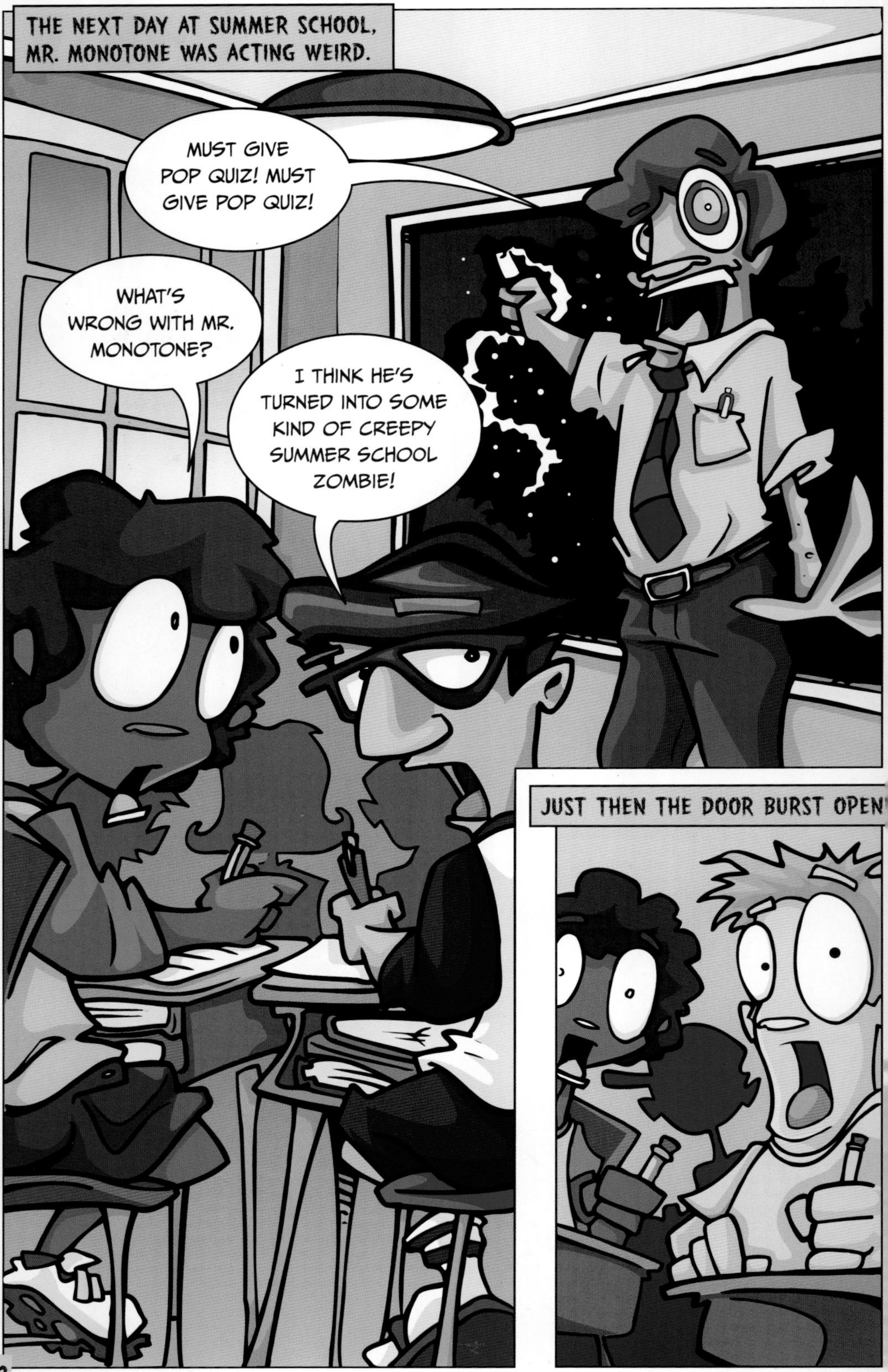
THE NEXT DAY AT SUMMER SCHOOL, MR. MONOTONE WAS ACTING WEIRD.
MUST GIVE POP QUIZ! MUST GIVE POP QUIZ!
WHAT'S WRONG WITH MR. MONOTONE?
I THINK HE'S TURNED INTO SOME KIND OF CREEPY SUMMER SCHOOL ZOMBIE!
JUST THEN THE DOOR BURST OPEN

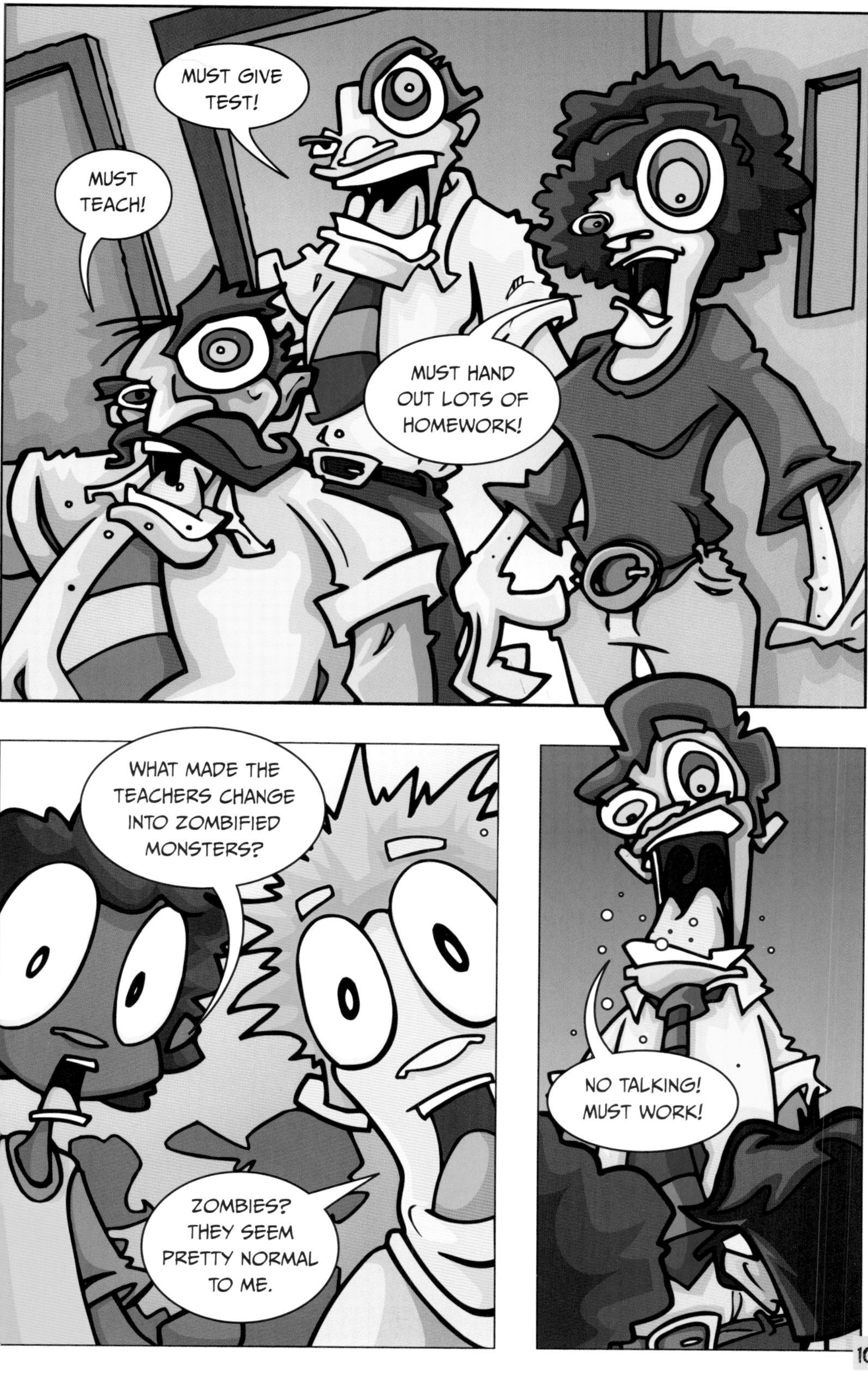
MUST TEACH!
MUST GIVE TEST!
MUST HAND OUT LOTS OF HOMEWORK!
WHAT MADE THE TEACHERS CHANGE INTO ZOMBIFIED MONSTERS?
ZOMBIES? THEY SEEM PRETTY NORMAL TO ME.
NO TALKING! MUST WORK!

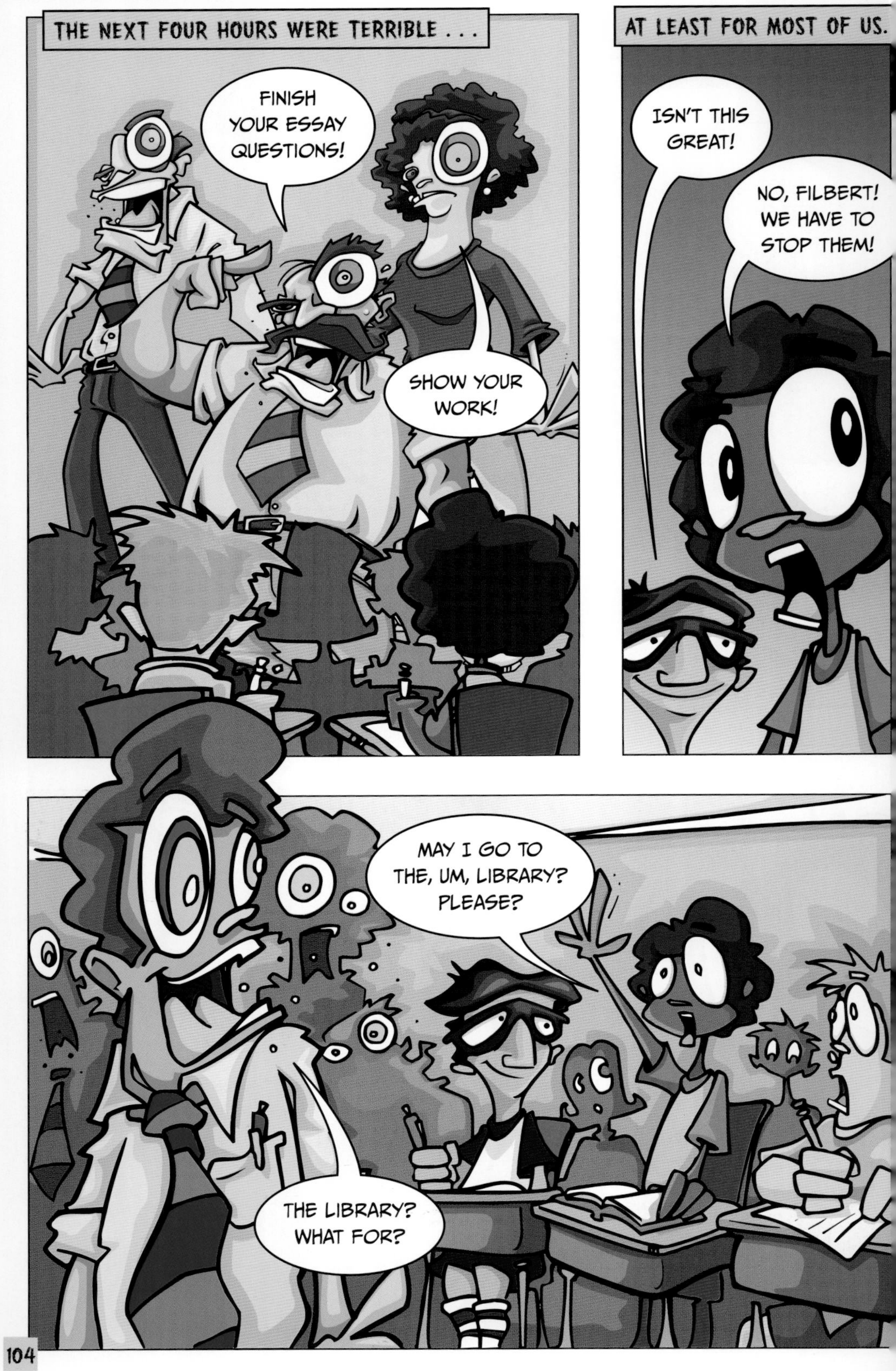
THE NEXT FOUR HOURS WERE TERRIBLE . . .
FINISH YOUR ESSAY QUESTIONS!
SHOW YOUR WORK!
AT LEAST FOR MOST OF US.
ISN'T THIS GREAT!
NO, FILBERT! WE HAVE TO STOP THEM!
MAY I GO TO THE, UM, LIBRARY? PLEASE?
THE LIBRARY? WHAT FOR?

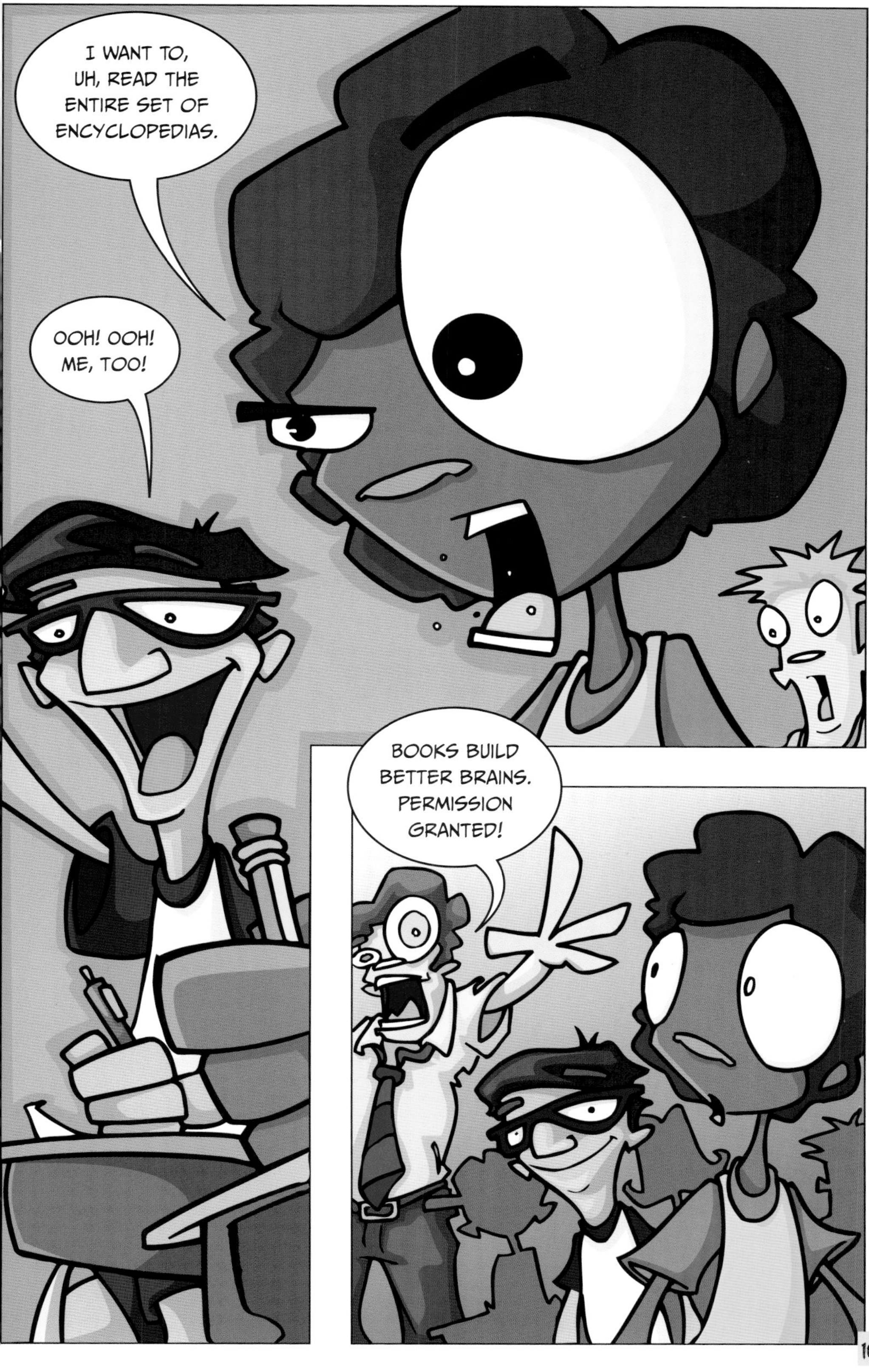
I WANT TO, UH, READ THE ENTIRE SET OF ENCYCLOPEDIAS.
OOH! OOH! ME, TOO!
BOOKS BUILD BETTER BRAINS. PERMISSION GRANTED!

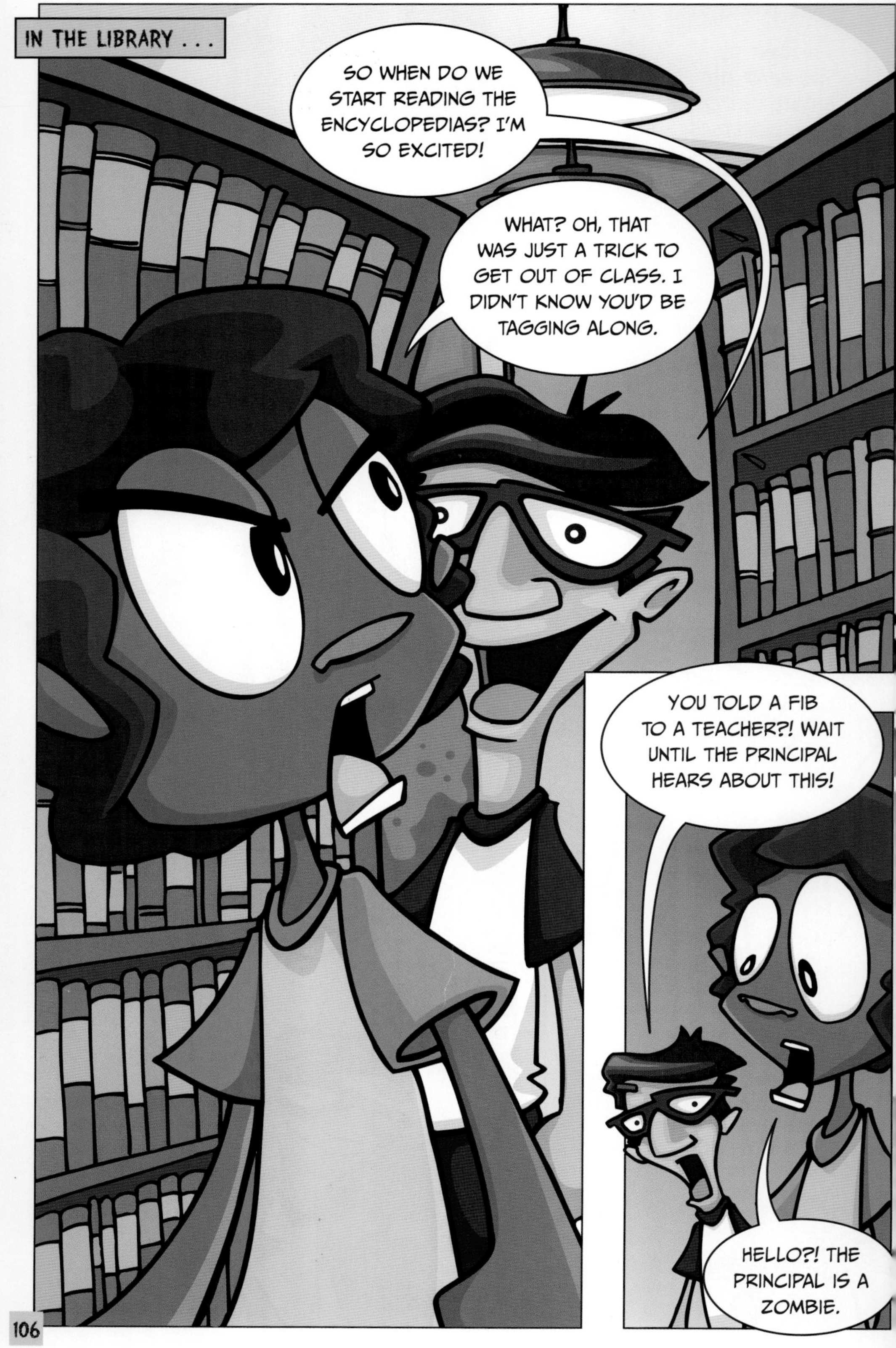
IN THE LIBRARY . . .
SO WHEN DO WE START READING THE ENCYCLOPEDIAS? I'M SO EXCITED!
WHAT? OH, THAT WAS JUST A TRICK TO GET OUT OF CLASS. I DIDN'T KNOW YOU'D BE TAGGING ALONG.
YOU TOLD A FIB TO A TEACHER?! WAIT UNTIL THE PRINCIPAL HEARS ABOUT THIS!
HELLO?! THE PRINCIPAL IS A ZOMBIE.

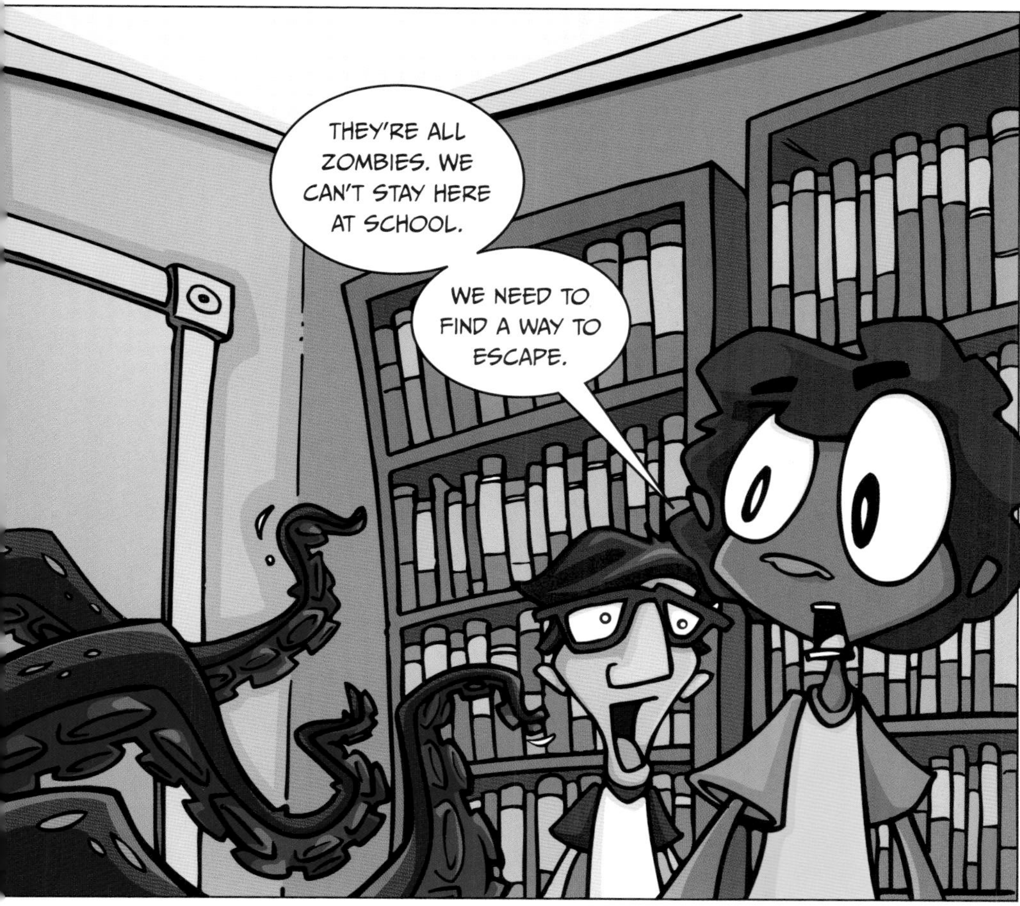
THEY'RE ALL ZOMBIES. WE CAN'T STAY HERE AT SCHOOL.
WE NEED TO FIND A WAY TO ESCAPE.

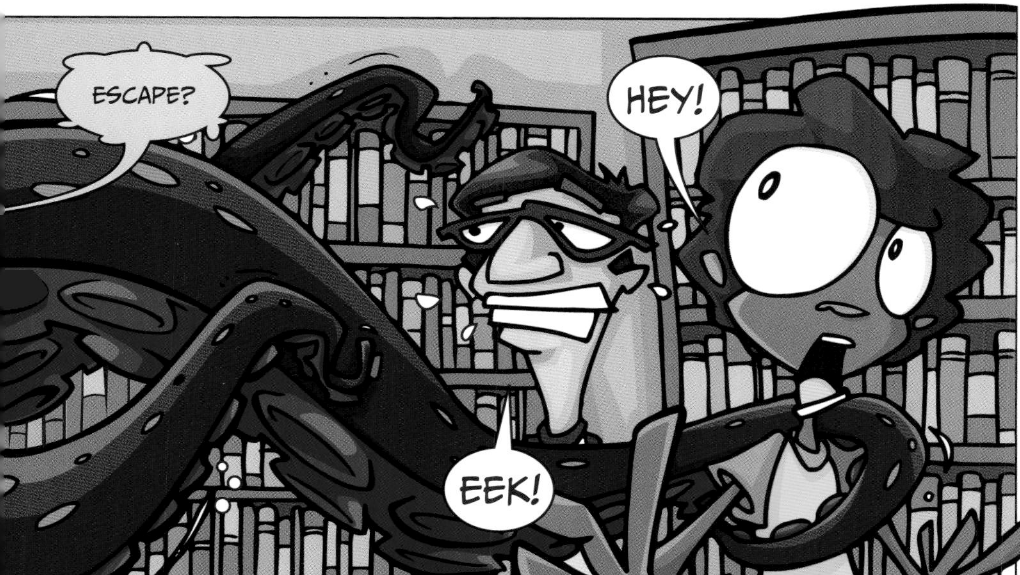
ESCAPE?
HEY!
EEK!

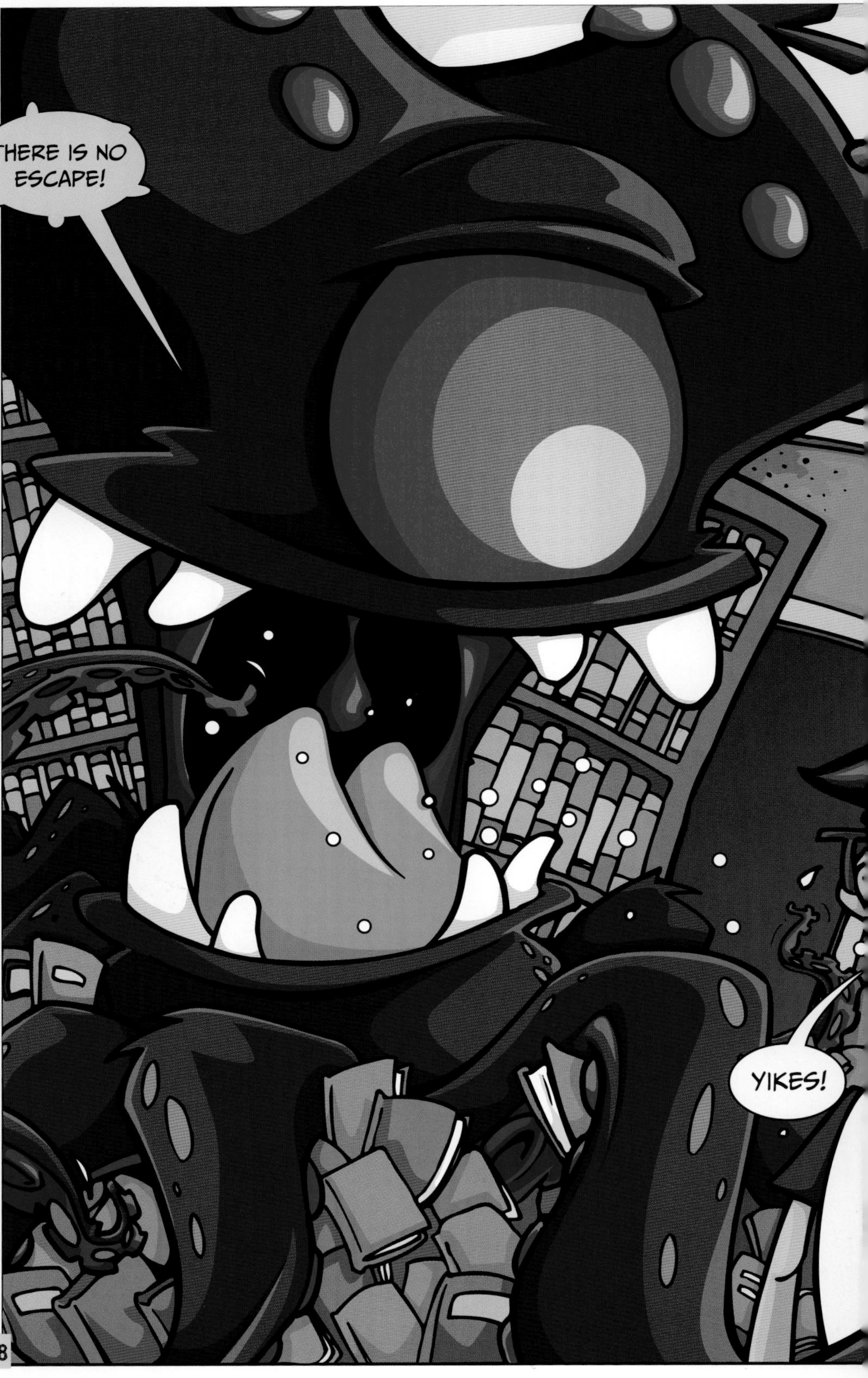
THERE IS NO ESCAPE!
YIKES!

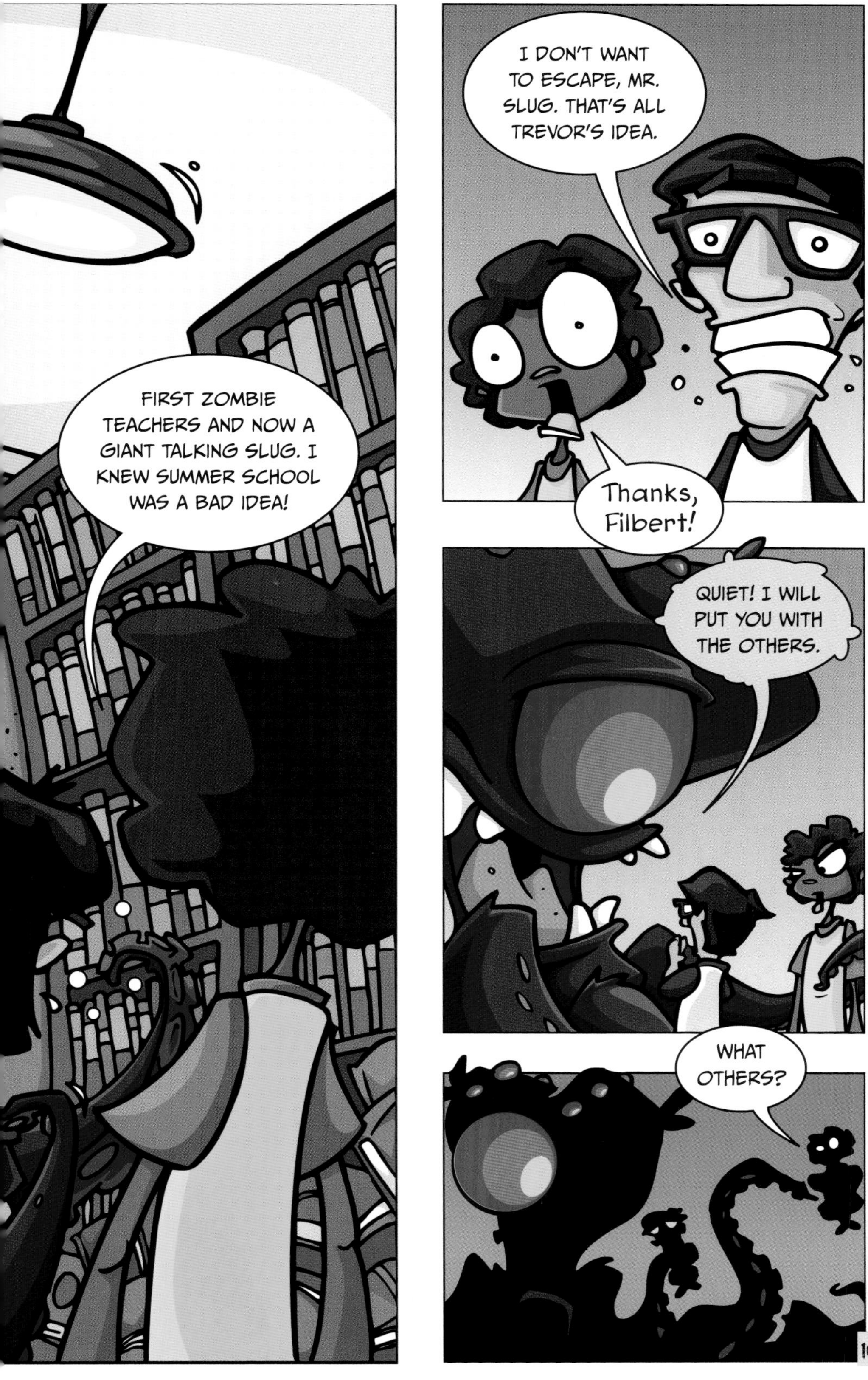
FIRST ZOMBIE TEACHERS AND NOW A GIANT TALKING SLUG. I KNEW SUMMER SCHOOL WAS A BAD IDEA!
I DON'T WANT TO ESCAPE, MR. SLUG. THAT'S ALL TREVOR'S IDEA.
Thanks, Filbert!
QUIET! I WILL PUT YOU WITH THE OTHERS.
WHAT OTHERS?

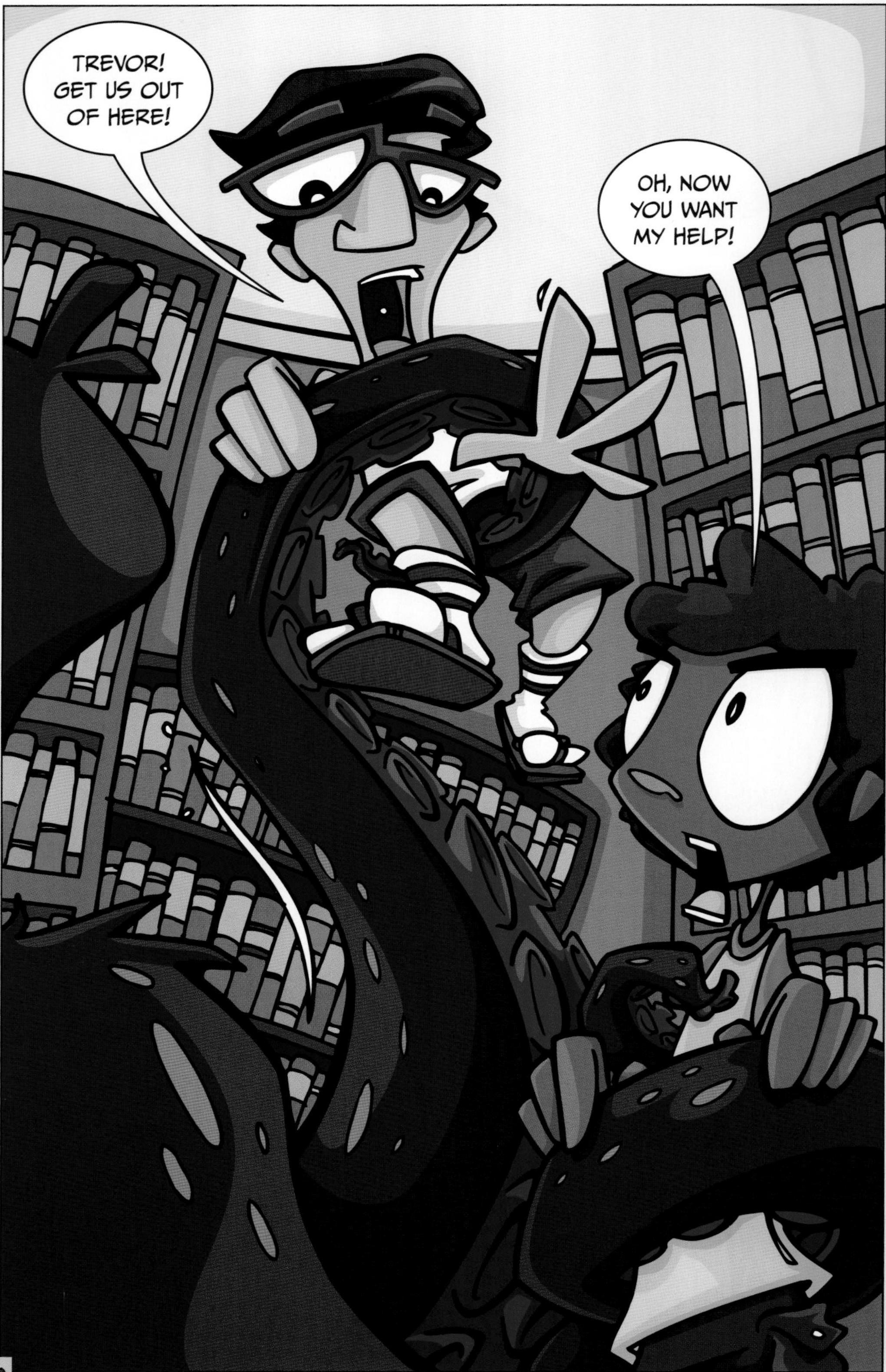
TREVOR! GET US OUT OF HERE!
OH, NOW YOU WANT MY HELP!

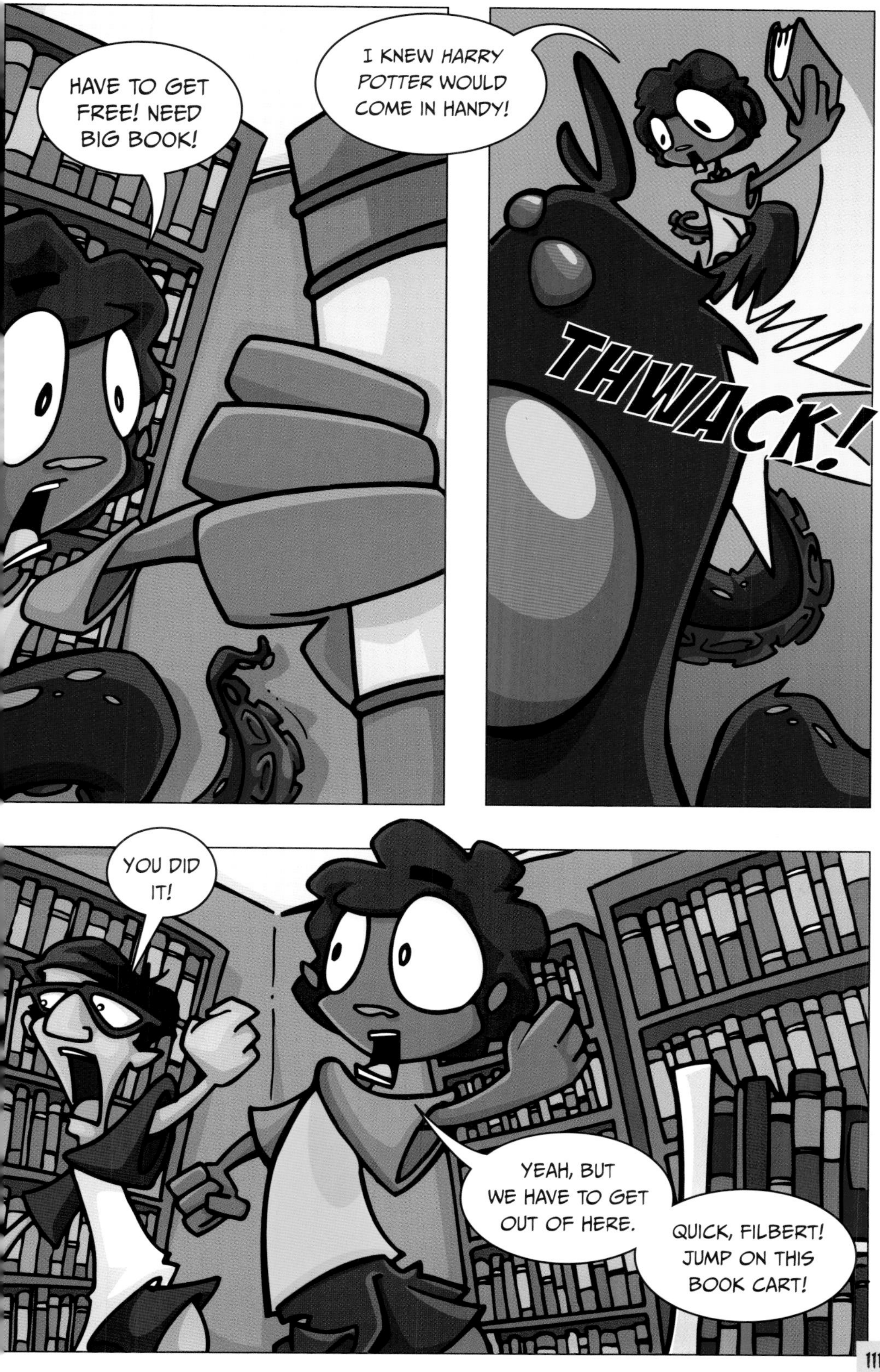
HAVE TO GET FREE! NEED BIG BOOK!
I KNEW HARRY POTTER WOULD COME IN HANDY!
THWACK!
YOU DID IT!
YEAH, BUT WE HAVE TO GET OUT OF HERE.
QUICK, FILBERT! JUMP ON THIS BOOK CART!

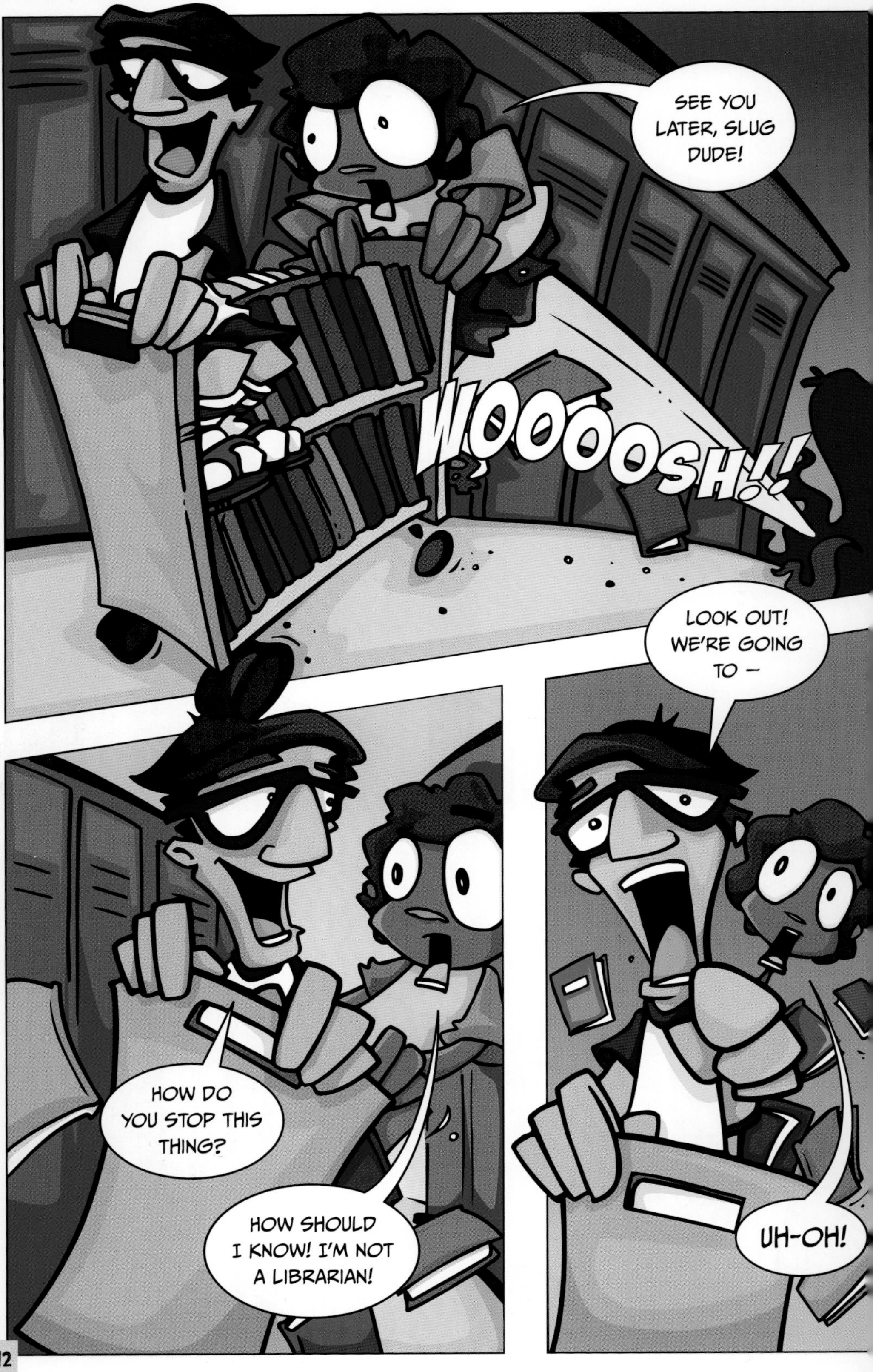
SEE YOU LATER, SLUG DUDE!
WOOOOSH!!
LOOK OUT! WE'RE GOING TO —
HOW DO YOU STOP THIS THING?
HOW SHOULD I KNOW! I'M NOT A LIBRARIAN!
UH-OH!

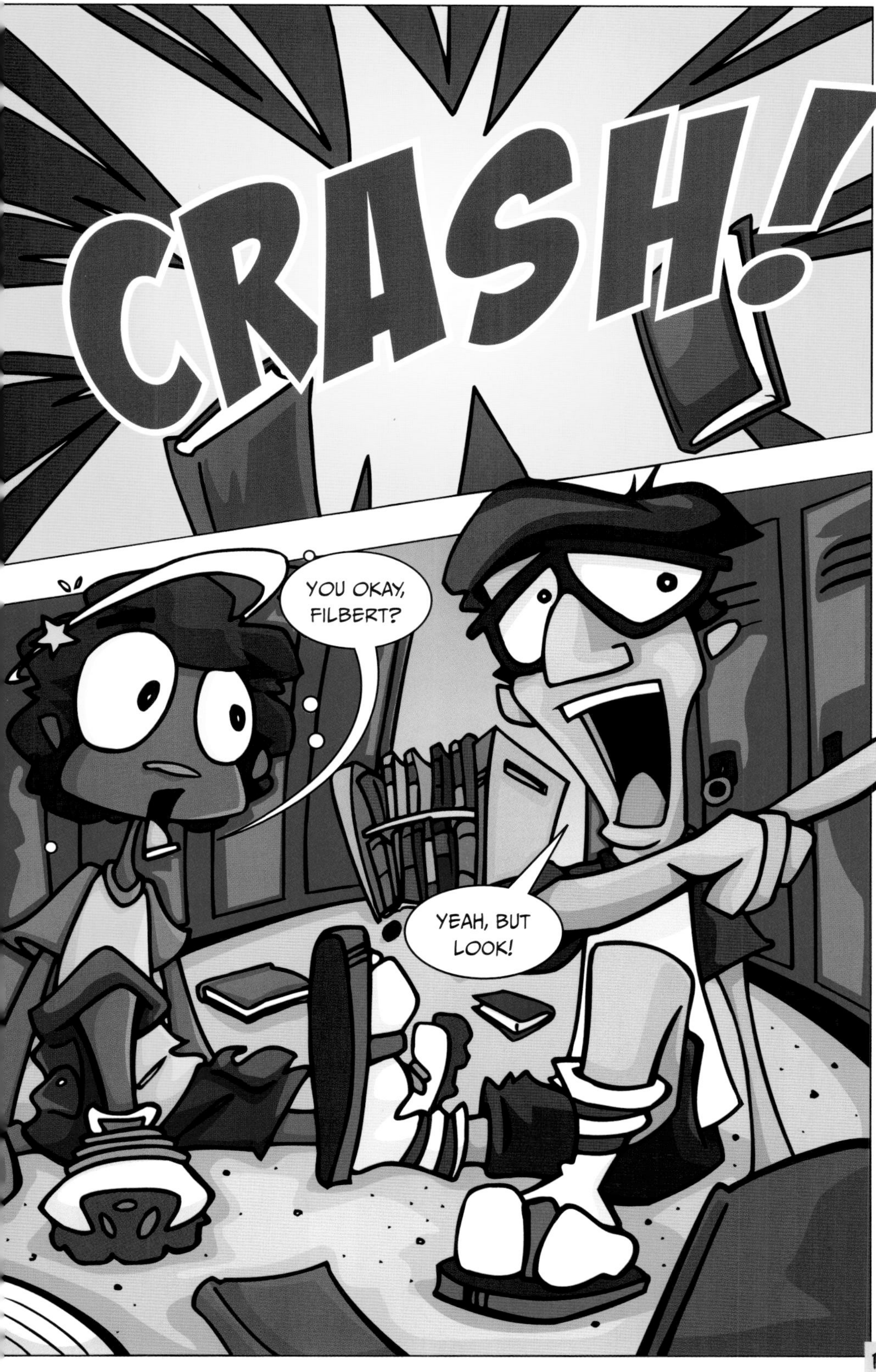
CRASH!
YOU OKAY, FILBERT?
YEAH, BUT LOOK!

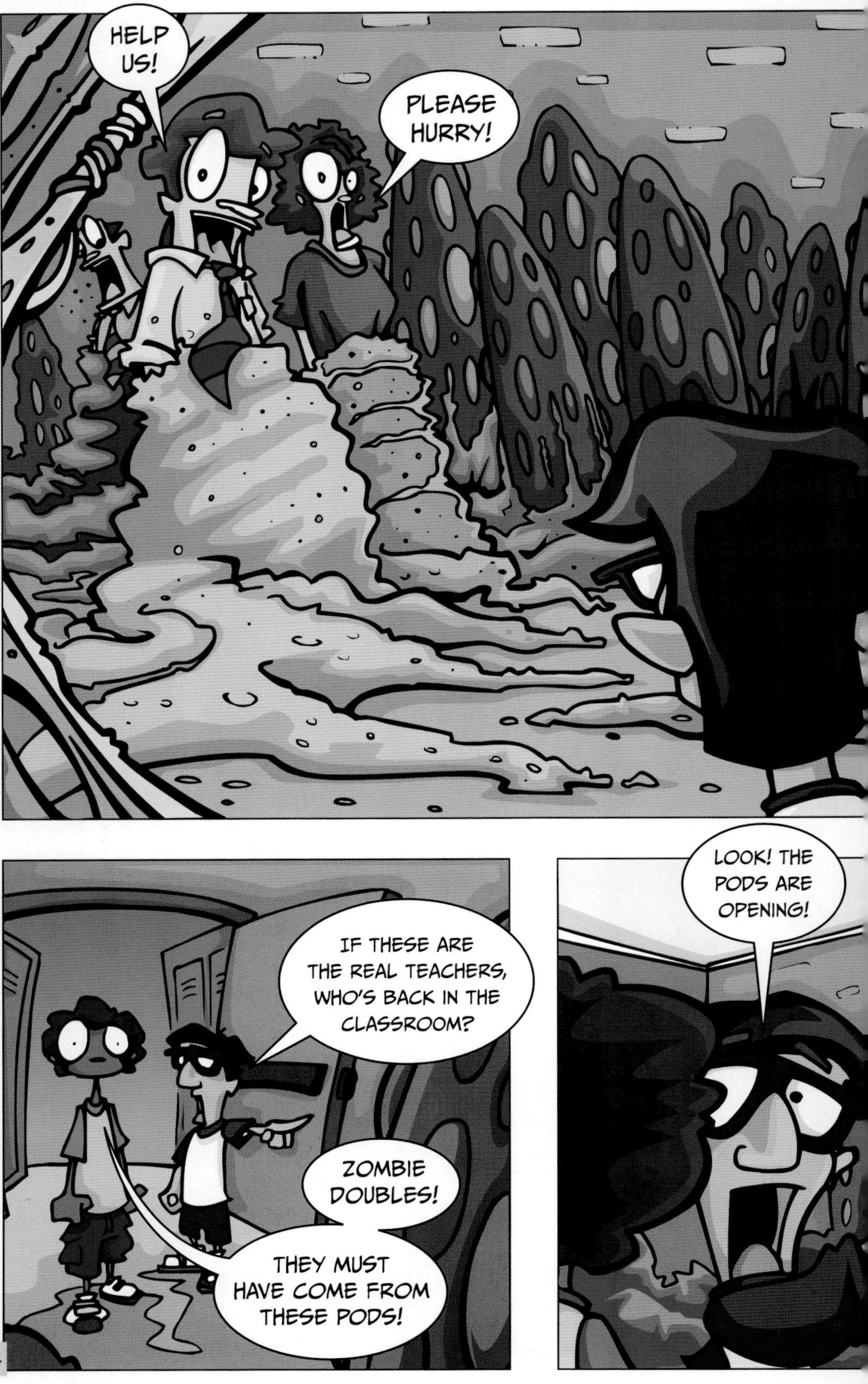
HELP US!
PLEASE HURRY!
IF THESE ARE THE REAL TEACHERS, WHO'S BACK IN THE CLASSROOM?
ZOMBIE DOUBLES!
THEY MUST HAVE COME FROM THESE PODS!
LOOK! THE PODS ARE OPENING!

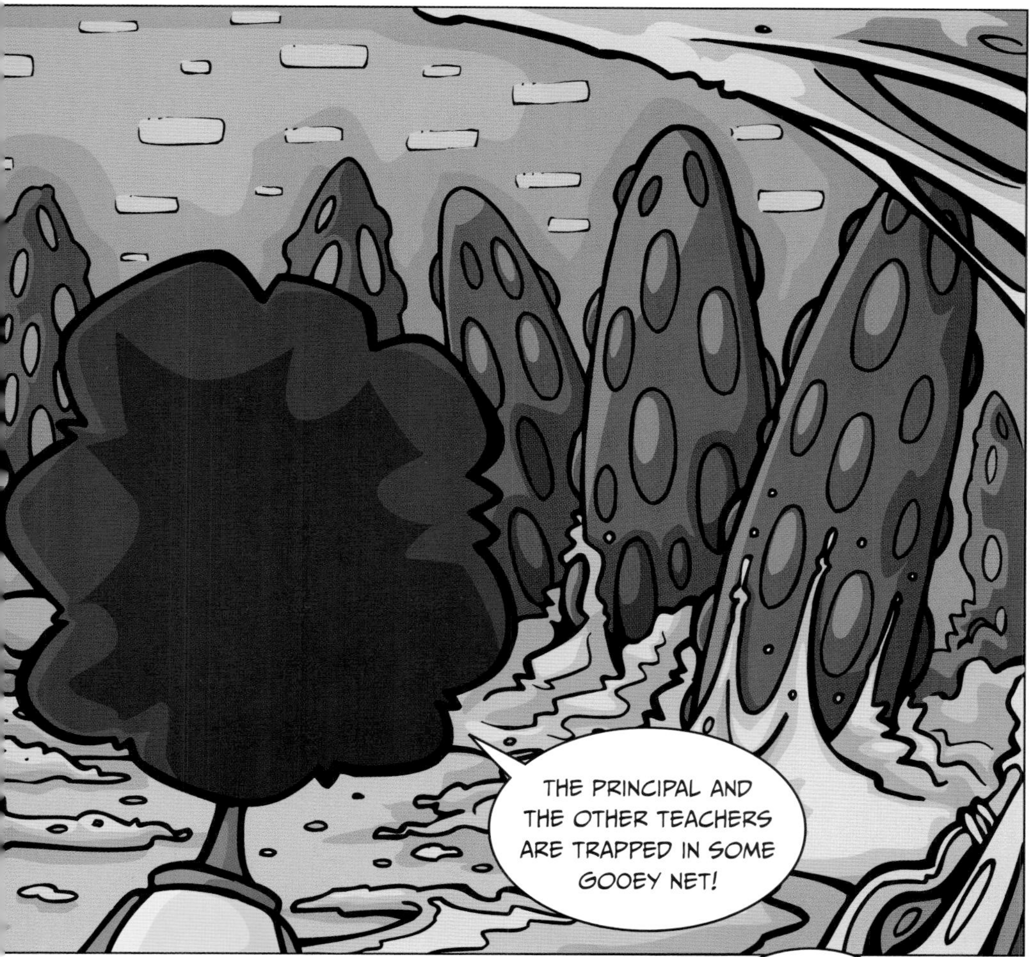
THE PRINCIPAL AND THE OTHER TEACHERS ARE TRAPPED IN SOME GOOEY NET!
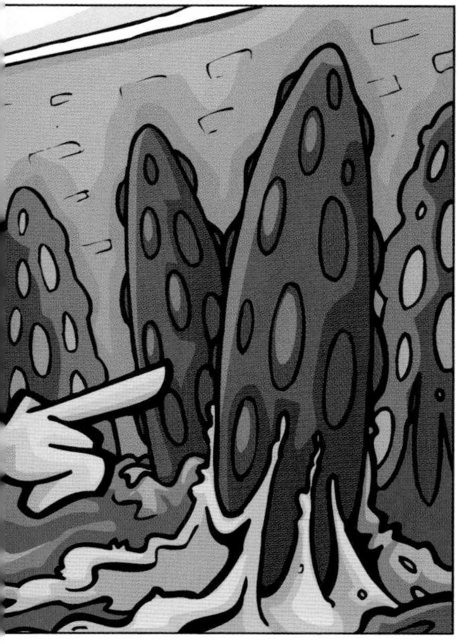
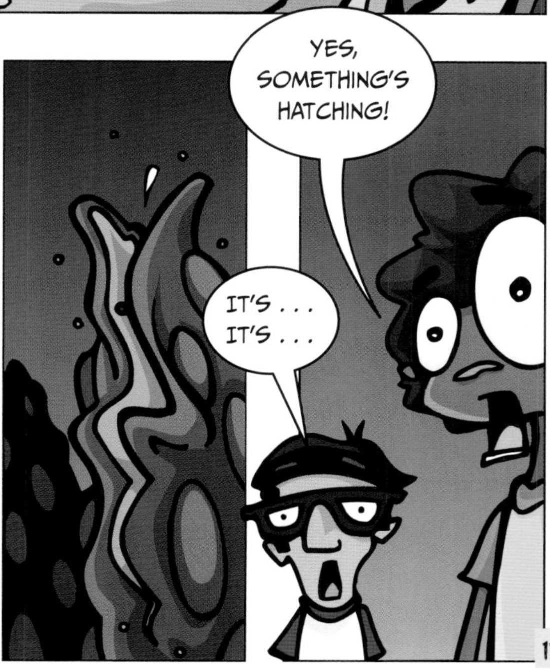
YES, SOMETHING'S HATCHING!
IT'S . . . IT'S . . .

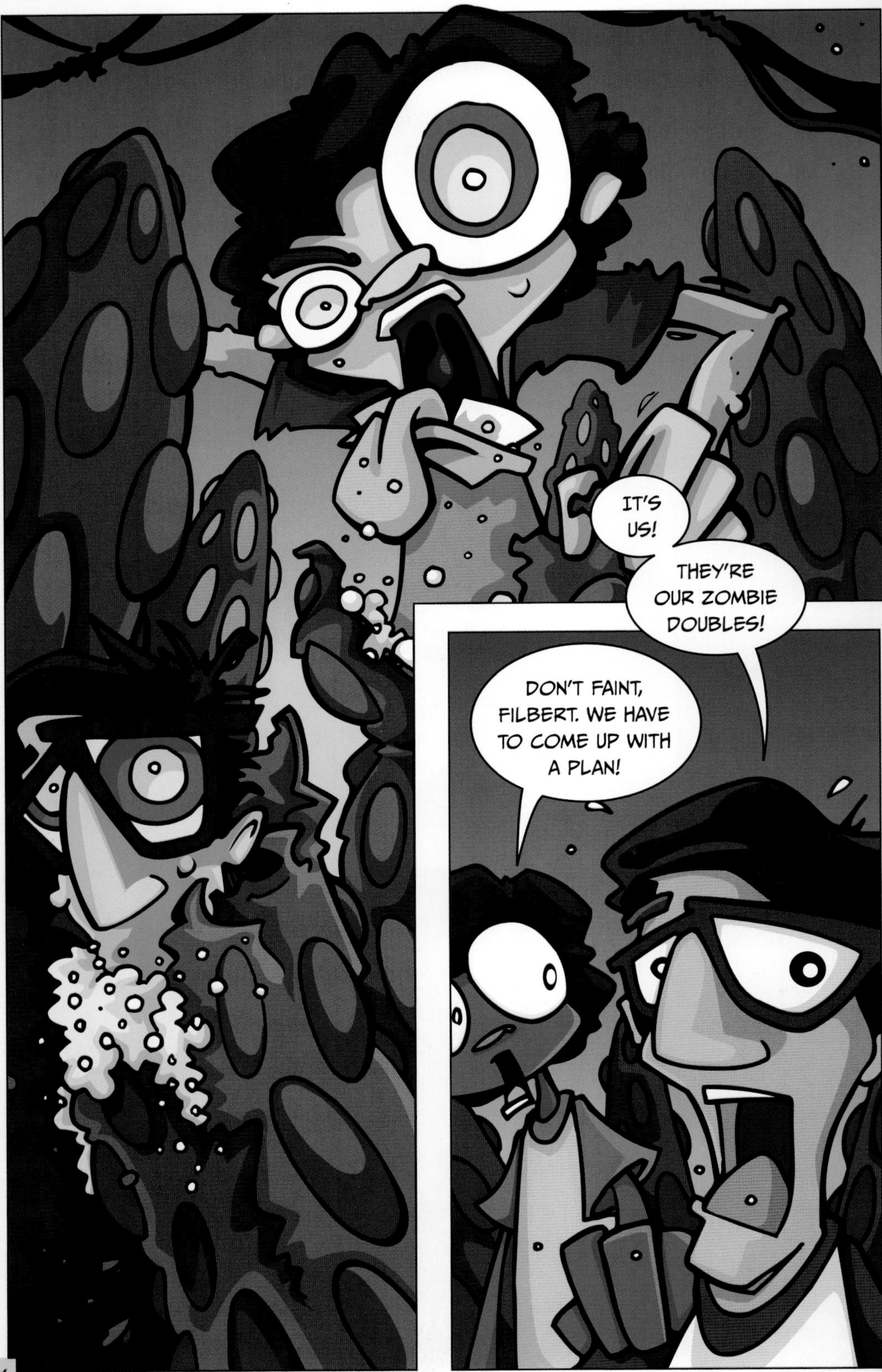
IT'S US!
THEY'RE OUR ZOMBIE DOUBLES!
DON'T FAINT, FILBERT. WE HAVE TO COME UP WITH A PLAN!

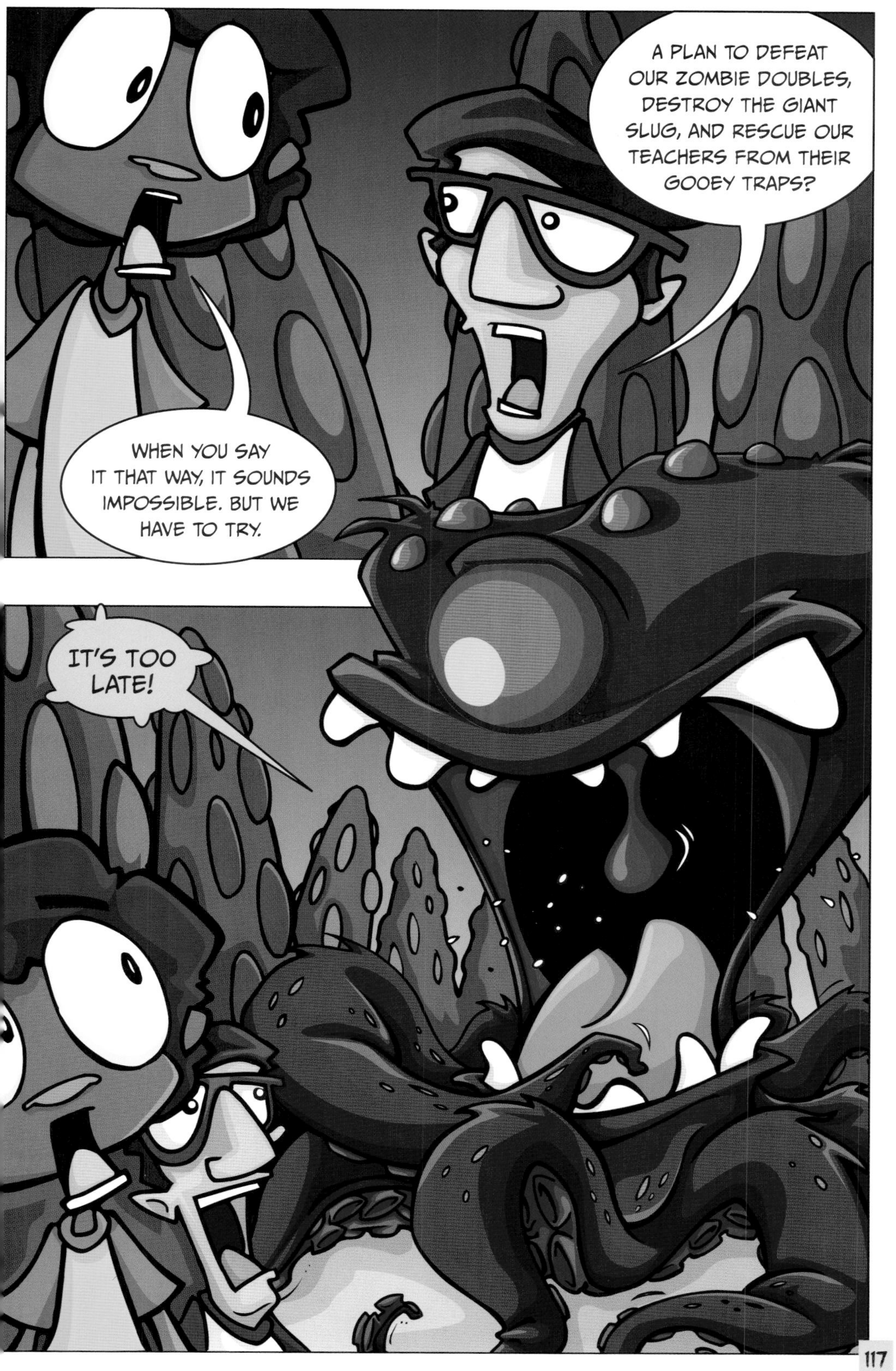
A PLAN TO DEFEAT OUR ZOMBIE DOUBLES, DESTROY THE GIANT SLUG, AND RESCUE OUR TEACHERS FROM THEIR GOOEY TRAPS?
WHEN YOU SAY IT THAT WAY, IT SOUNDS IMPOSSIBLE. BUT WE HAVE TO TRY.
IT'S TOO LATE!

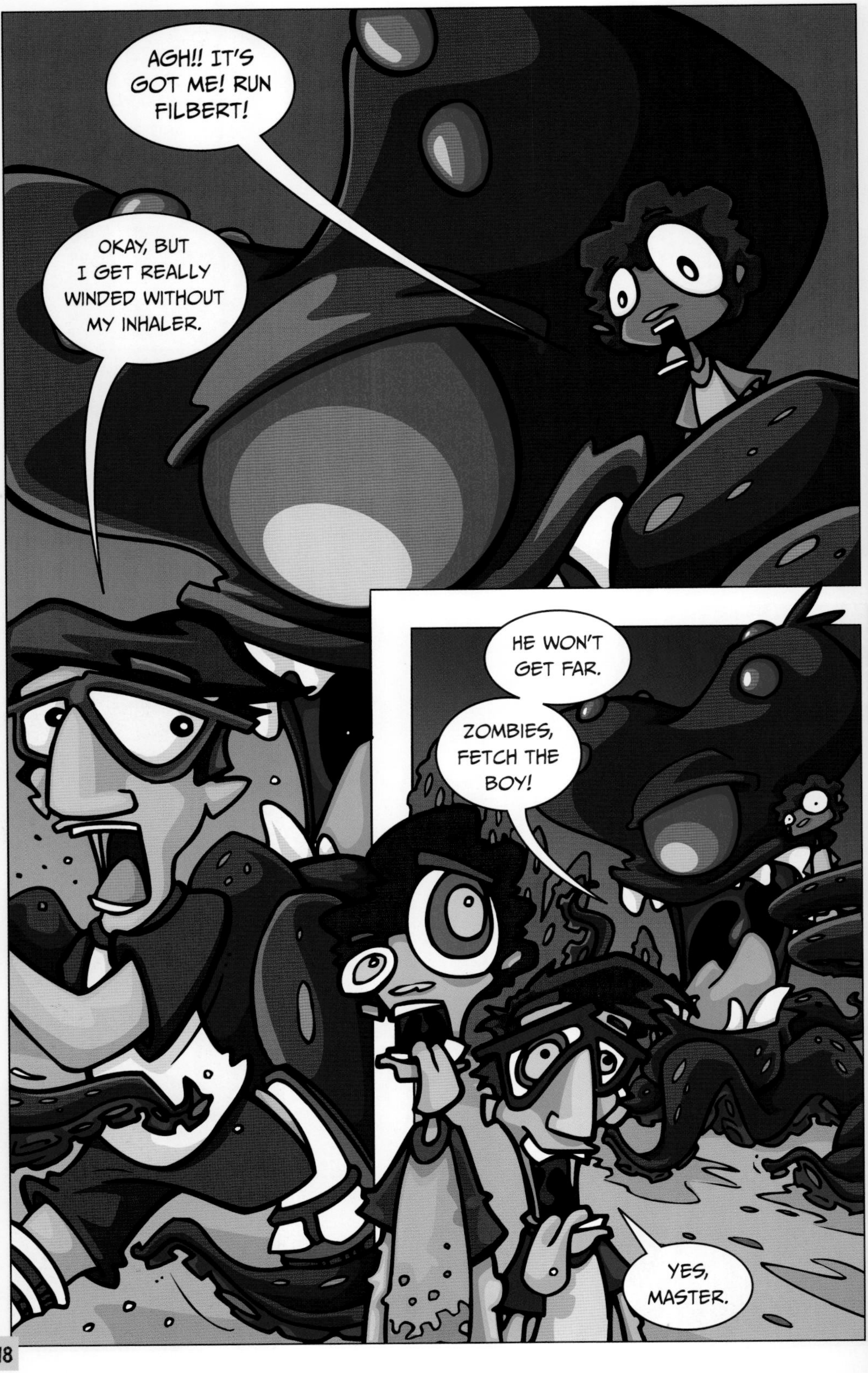
AGH!! IT'S GOT ME! RUN FILBERT!
OKAY, BUT I GET REALLY WINDED WITHOUT MY INHALER.
HE WON'T GET FAR.
ZOMBIES, FETCH THE BOY!
YES, MASTER.

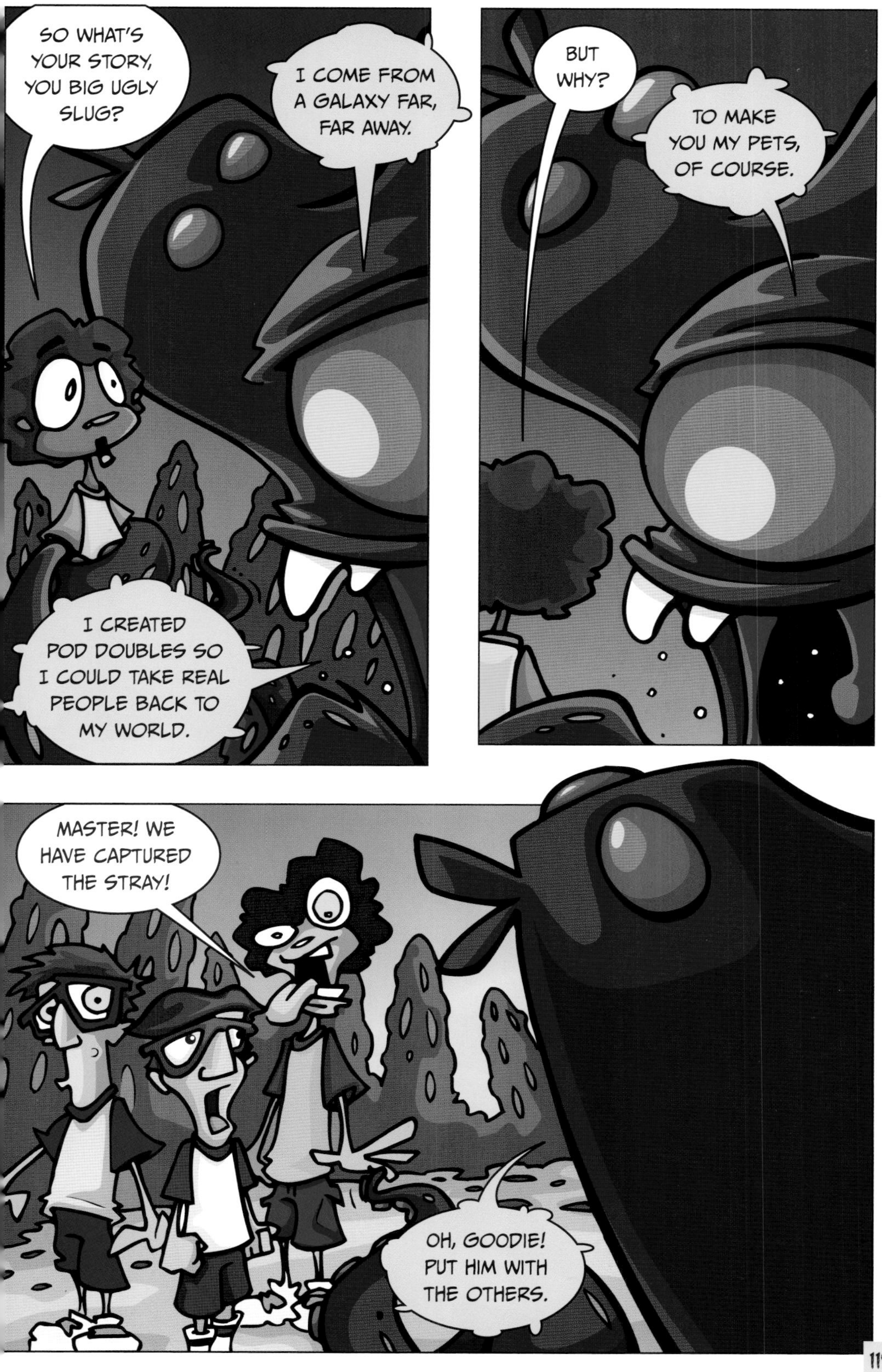
SO WHAT'S YOUR STORY, YOU BIG UGLY SLUG?
I COME FROM A GALAXY FAR, FAR AWAY.
I CREATED POD DOUBLES SO I COULD TAKE REAL PEOPLE BACK TO MY WORLD.
BUT WHY?
TO MAKE YOU MY PETS, OF COURSE.
MASTER! WE HAVE CAPTURED THE STRAY!
OH, GOODIE! PUT HIM WITH THE OTHERS.

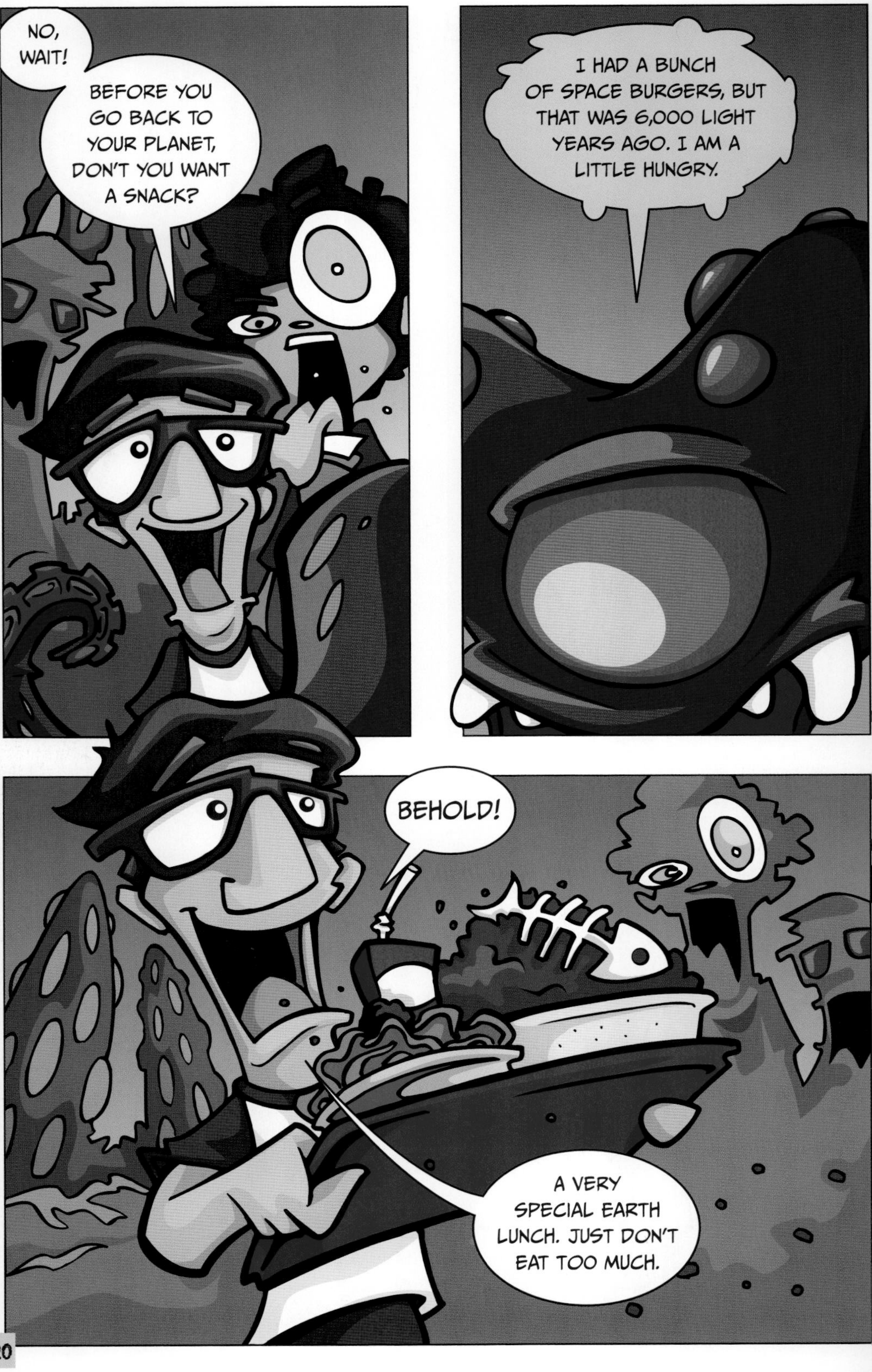

NO, WAIT!
BEFORE YOU GO BACK TO YOUR PLANET, DON'T YOU WANT A SNACK?
I HAD A BUNCH OF SPACE BURGERS, BUT THAT WAS 6,000 LIGHT YEARS AGO. I AM A LITTLE HUNGRY.
BEHOLD!
A VERY SPECIAL EARTH LUNCH. JUST DON'T EAT TOO MUCH.

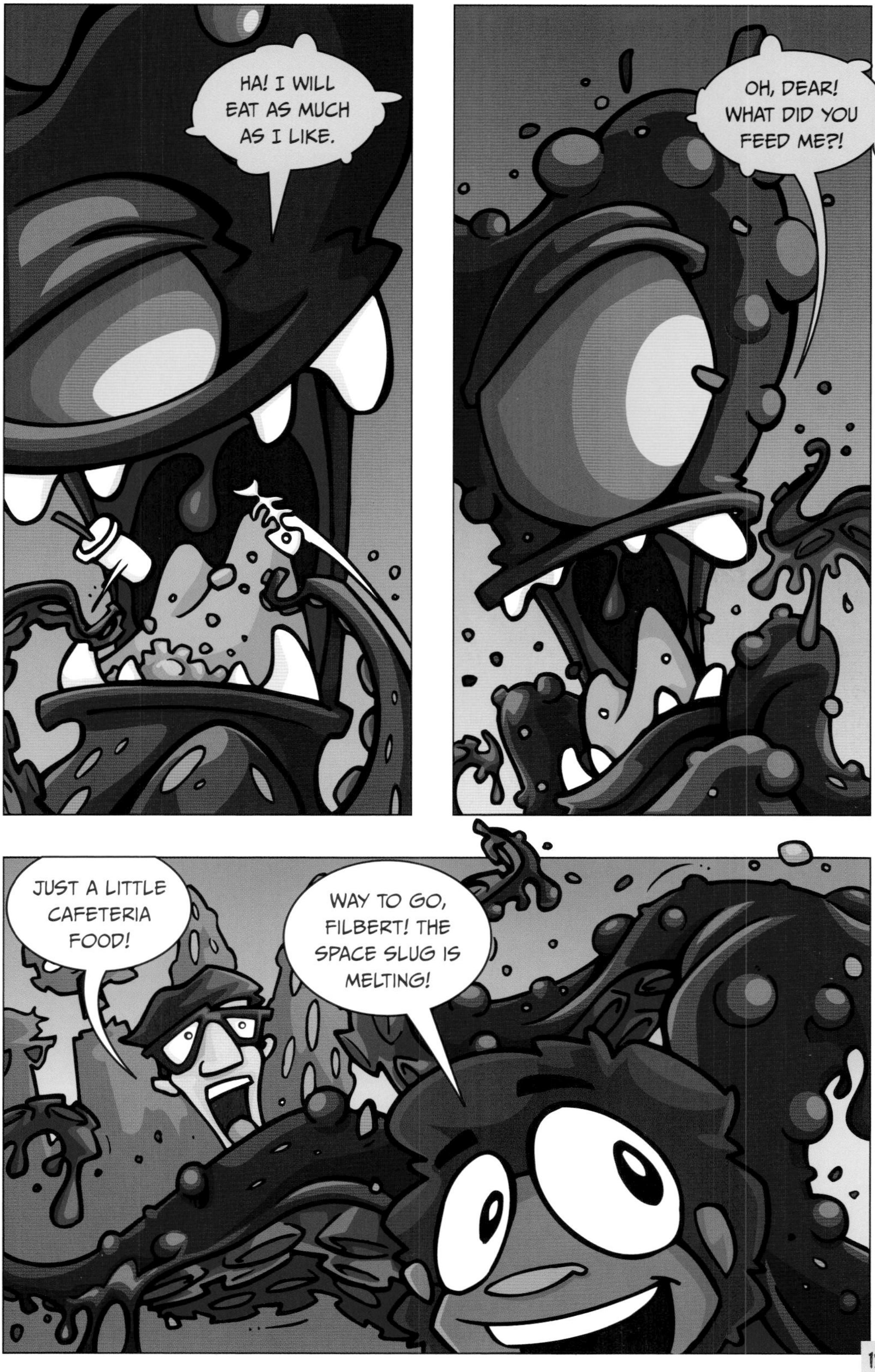
HA! I WILL EAT AS MUCH AS I LIKE.
OH, DEAR! WHAT DID YOU FEED ME?!
JUST A LITTLE CAFETERIA FOOD!
WAY TO GO, FILBERT! THE SPACE SLUG IS MELTING!

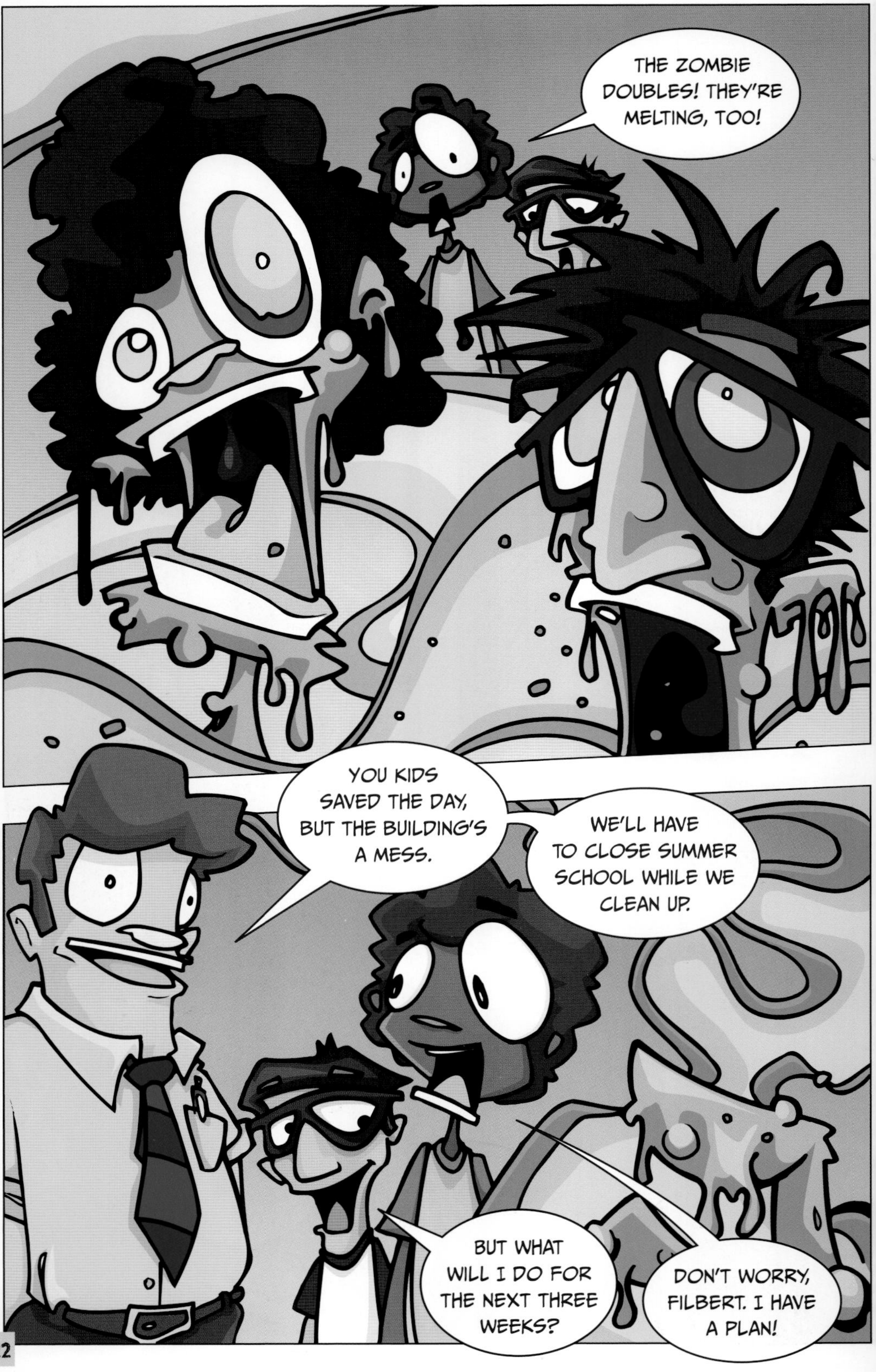
THE ZOMBIE DOUBLES! THEY'RE MELTING, TOO!
YOU KIDS SAVED THE DAY, BUT THE BUILDING'S A MESS.
WE'LL HAVE TO CLOSE SUMMER SCHOOL WHILE WE CLEAN UP.
BUT WHAT WILL I DO FOR THE NEXT THREE WEEKS?
DON'T WORRY, FILBERT. I HAVE A PLAN!

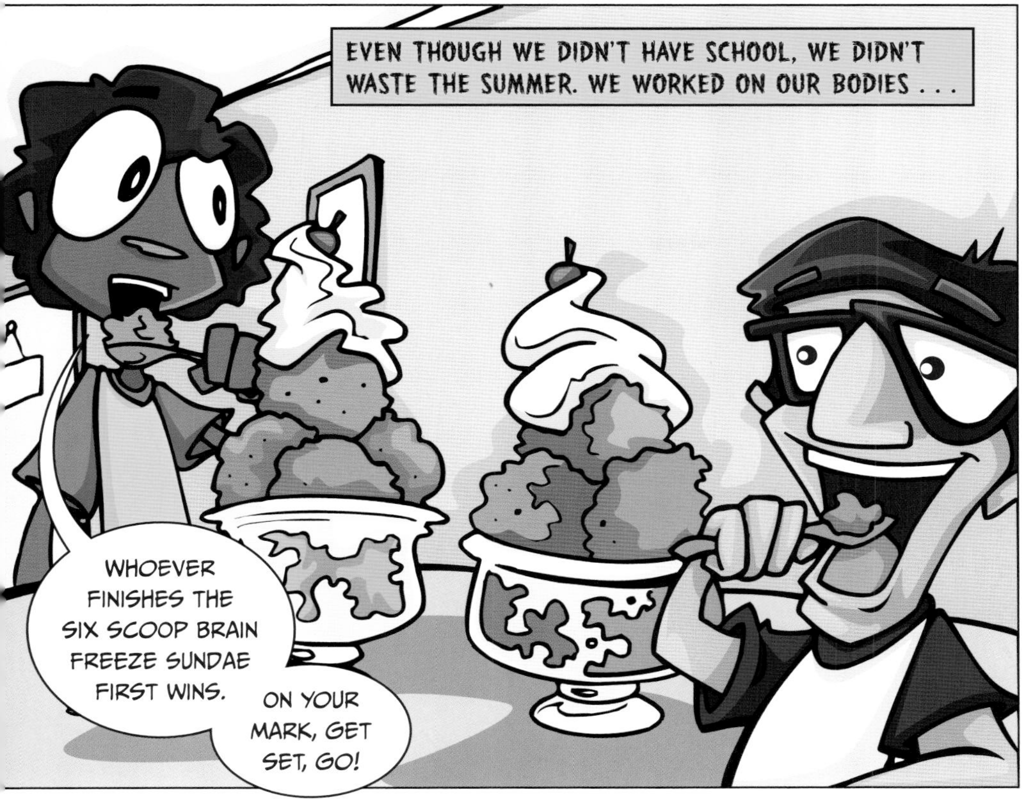
EVEN THOUGH WE DIDN'T HAVE SCHOOL, WE DIDN'T WASTE THE SUMMER. WE WORKED ON OUR BODIES . . .
WHOEVER FINISHES THE SIX SCOOP BRAIN FREEZE SUNDAE FIRST WINS.
ON YOUR MARK, GET SET, GO!

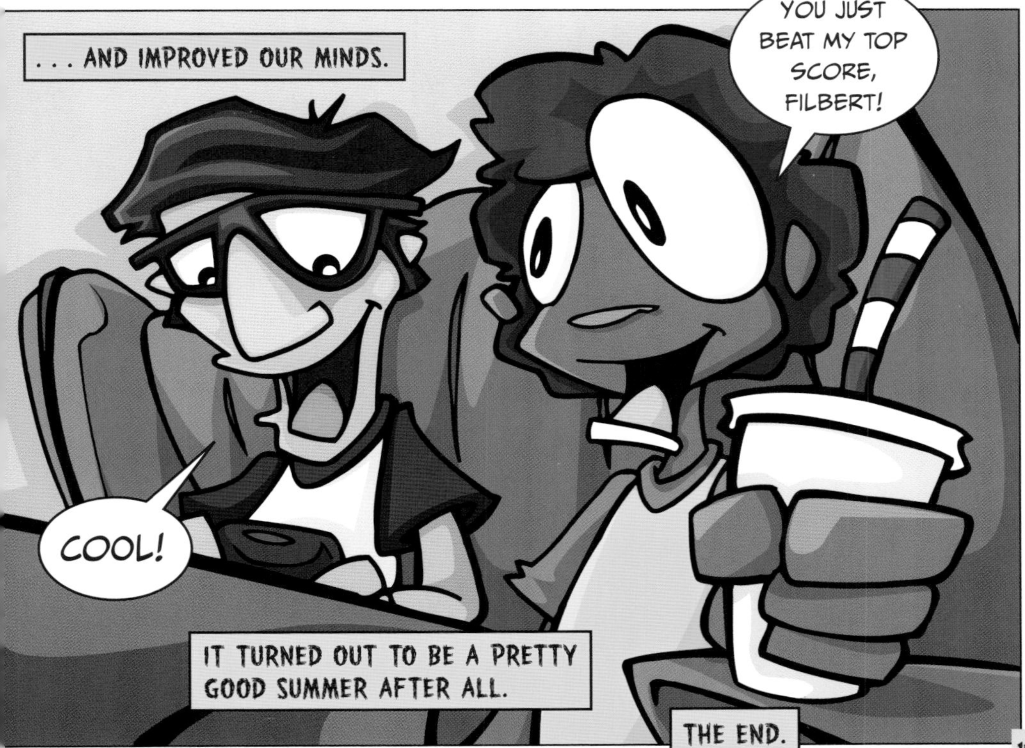
. . . AND IMPROVED OUR MINDS.
YOU JUST BEAT MY TOP SCORE, FILBERT!
COOL!
IT TURNED OUT TO BE A PRETTY GOOD SUMMER AFTER ALL.
THE END.

THE END?

MORE ABOUT ZOMBIES

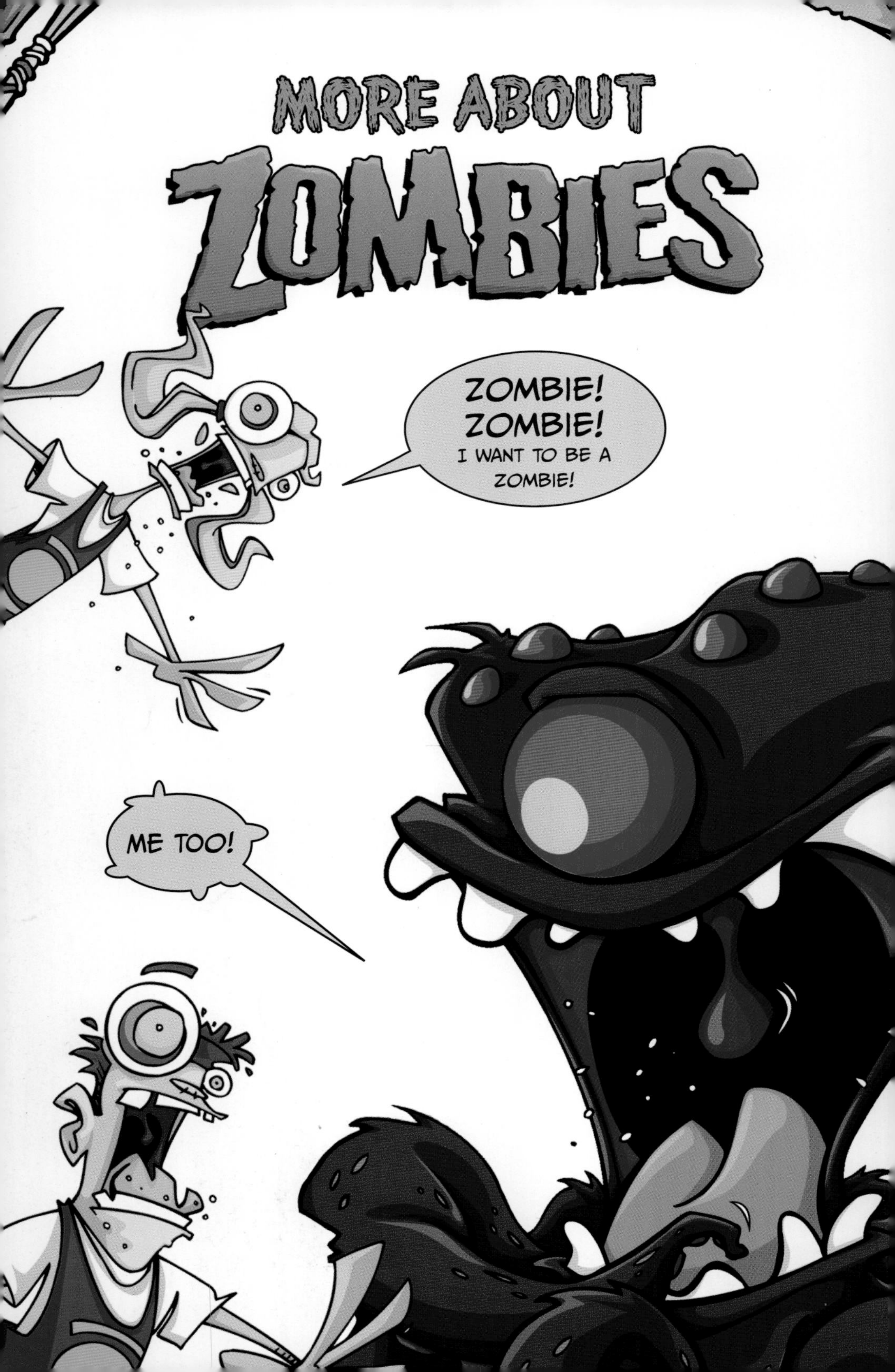
ZOMBIE! ZOMBIE! I WANT TO BE A ZOMBIE!
ME TOO!

ARE ZOMBIES REAL?

SOME PEOPLE THINK SO. ON THE ISLANDS OF THE CARIBBEAN, SOME PEOPLE PRACTICE A RELIGION KNOWN AS VOUDON, OR VOODOO. VOODOO BELIEFS SAY THAT A DEAD BODY CAN COME BACK TO LIFE. A SPIRIT, CALLED A ZOMBI, ENTERS THE DEAD BODY AND GIVES IT THE POWER TO MOVE.

WHAT DOES A ZOMBIE LOOK LIKE?

ZOMBIES DO NOT EAT OR DRINK. THEY MOVE STIFFLY, HAVE BLANK FACES, AND CANNOT SPEAK. REAL PEOPLE WHO ACT LIKE THIS, MAYBE GROWN-UPS AFTER A HARD DAY AT THE OFFICE, ARE SOMETIMES CALLED ZOMBIES.

ACCORDING TO VOODOO, ZOMBIES ARE UNDER THE CONTROL OF THE PERSON WHO BROUGHT THEM BACK TO LIFE. SOME SCIENTISTS THINK THAT PEOPLE GIVEN POWERFUL DRUGS CAN BEHAVE LIKE ZOMBIES. THE DRUGS WEAKEN THEIR MINDS SO THAT THEY WILL EASILY OBEY ANOTHER PERSON.

COMPUTERS CAN ALSO BE ZOMBIES. A ZOMBIE COMPUTER IS ONE THAT IS REMOTELY CONTROLLED BY ANOTHER PERSON IN SECRET.

THE FAMOUS WRITER ZORA NEALE HURSTON MET PEOPLE ON THE ISLAND OF HAITI WHO CLAIMED TO HAVE SEEN A REAL ZOMBIE. A WOMAN WHO HAD BEEN BURIED 30 YEARS EARLIER WAS WALKING THE STREETS OF A VILLAGE. LATER, HURSTON FOUND OUT THAT THIS WAS JUST A RUMOR.